Marion Lennox is a countr[...] dairy farm. She moved on-[...] just weren't interested in he[...] special doctor', Marion writes Medical™ Romances as well as Mills & Boon® Romance (she used a different name for each category for a while—if you're looking for her past Mills & Boon Romances, search for author Trisha David as well). She's now had over 75 romance novels accepted for publication.

In her non-writing life Marion cares for kids, cats, dogs, chooks and goldfish. She travels, she fights her rampant garden (she's losing) and her house dust (she's lost).

Having spun in circles for the first part of her life, she's now stepped back from her 'other' career, which was teaching statistics at her local university. Finally she's reprioritised her life, figured what's important and discovered the joys of deep baths, romance and chocolate.

Preferably all at the same time!

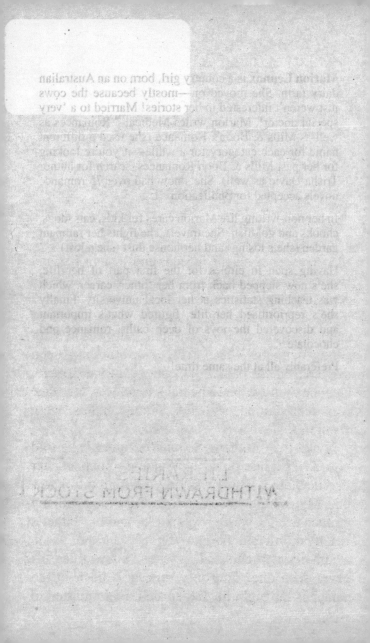

father.

PROLOGUE

'RAMÓN spends his life in jeans and ancient T-shirts.
He has money and he has freedom. Why would he
want the Crown?'

Señor Rodriguez, legal advisor to the Crown of
Cepheus, regarded the woman before him with
some sympathy. The Princess Sofía had been
evicted from the palace of Cepheus sixty years ago,
and she didn't wish to be back here now. Her face
was tear-stained and her plump hands were
wringing.

'I had two brothers, Señor Rodriguez,' she told
him, as if explaining her story could somehow alter
the inevitable. 'But I was only permitted to know
one. My younger brother and I were exiled with my
mother when I was ten years old, and my father's
cruelty didn't end there. And now… I haven't seen
a tiara in sixty years and, as far as I know, Ramón's
never seen one. The only time he's been in the
palace is the night his father died. I've returned to

the palace because my mother raised me with a sense of duty, but how can we demand that from Ramón? To return to the place that killed his father…'

'The Prince Ramón has no choice,' the lawyer said flatly. 'And of course he'll want the Crown.'

'There's no "of course" about it,' Sofía snapped. 'Ramón spends half of every year building houses for some charity in Bangladesh, and the rest of his life on his beautiful yacht. Why should he give that up?'

'He'll be Crown Prince.'

'You think royalty's everything?' Sofía gave up hand wringing and stabbed at her knitting as if she'd like it to be the late, unlamented Crown Prince. 'My nephew's a lovely young man and he wants nothing to do with the throne. The palace gives him nightmares, as it gives us all.'

'He must come,' Señor Rodriguez said stiffly.

'So how will you find him?' Sofía muttered. 'When he's working in Bangladesh Ramón checks his mail, but for the rest of his life he's around the world in that yacht of his, who knows where? Since his mother and sister died he lets the wind take him where it will. And, even if you do find him, how do you think he'll react to being told he has to fix this mess?'

'There won't be a mess if he comes home. He'll come, as you have come. He must see there's no choice.'

'And what of the little boy?'

'Philippe will go into foster care. There's no choice there, either. The child is nothing to do with Prince Ramón.'

'Another child of no use to the Crown,' Sofía whispered, and she dropped two stiches without noticing. 'But Ramón has a heart. Oh, Ramón, if I were you I'd keep on sailing.'

CHAPTER ONE

'JENNY, lose your muffins. Get a life!'

Gianetta Bertin, known to the Seaport locals as Jenny, gave her best friend a withering look and kept right on spooning double choc chip muffin mixture into pans. Seaport Coffee 'n' Cakes had been crowded all morning, and her muffin tray was almost bare.

'I don't have time for lectures,' she told her friend severely. 'I'm busy.'

'You need to have time for lectures. Honest, Jen.' Cathy hitched herself up onto Jenny's prep bench and grew earnest. 'You can't stay stuck in this hole for ever.'

'There's worse holes to be stuck in, and get off my bench. If Charlie comes in he'll sack me, and I won't have a hole at all.'

'He won't,' Cathy declared. 'You're the best cook in Seaport. You hold this place up. Charlie's treating you like dirt, Jen, just because you don't have the energy to do anything about it. I know you owe him, but you could get a job and repay him some other way.'

'Like how?' Jenny shoved the tray into the oven, straightened and tucked an unruly curl behind her ear. Her cap was supposed to hold back her mass of dark curls, but they kept escaping. She knew she'd now have a streak of flour across her ear but did it matter what she looked like?

And, as if in echo, Cathy continued. 'Look at you,' she declared. 'You're gorgeous. Twenty-nine, figure to die for, cute as a button, a woman ripe and ready for the world, and here you are, hidden in a shapeless white pinafore with flour on your nose— yes, flour on your nose, Jen—no don't wipe it, you've made it worse.'

'It doesn't matter,' Jenny said. 'Who's looking? Can I get on? There's customers out there.'

'There are,' Cathy said warmly, peering out through the hatch but refusing to let go of her theme. 'You have twenty people out there, all coming here for one of your yummy muffins and then heading off again for life. You should be out there with them. Look at that guy out there, for instance. Gorgeous or what? That's what you're missing out on, Jen, stuck in here every day.'

Jenny peered out the hatch as well, and it didn't take more than a glance to see who Cathy was referring to.

The guy looked to be in his mid-thirties. He was a yachtie—she could tell that by his gear—and he was seriously good-looking. It had been raining this morning. He was wearing battered jeans, salt-stained boating shoes and a faded black T-shirt, stretched tight over a chest that looked truly impressive. He'd shrugged a battered sou'wester onto the back of his chair.

Professional, she thought.

After years of working in Coffee 'n' Cakes she could pick the classes of boaty. Holding the place up were the hard-core fishermen. Then there were the battered old salts who ran small boats on the smell of an oily rag, often living on them. Next there was the cool set, arriving at weekends, wearing gear that came out of the designer section of the *Nautical Monthly* catalogue, and leaving when they realized Coffee 'n' Cakes didn't sell Chardonnay.

And finally there were the serious yachties. Seaport was a deep water harbour just south of Sydney, and it attracted yachts doing amazing journeys. Seaport had a great dry dock where repairs could be carried out expertly and fast, so there were often one or two of these classy yachts in port.

This guy looked as if he was from one of these. His coat looked battered but she knew the brand, even from this distance. It was the best. Like the man. The guy himself also looked a bit battered, but in a good way. Worn by the sea. His tan was deep and real, his eyes were crinkled as if he spent his life in the sun, and his black hair was only really black at the roots. The tips were sun-bleached to almost fair.

He was definitely a professional sailor, she thought, giving herself a full minute to assess him. And why not? He was well worth assessing.

She knew the yachting hierarchy. The owners of the big sea-going yachts tended to be middle-aged or older. They spent short bursts of time on their boats but left serious seafaring to paid staff. This guy looked younger, tougher, leaner than a boat-owner. He looked seriously competent. He'd be being paid to take a yacht to where its owner wanted it to be.

And for a moment—just for a moment—Jenny let herself be consumed by a wave of envy. Just to go where the wind took you… To walk away from Seaport…

No. That'd take effort and planning and hope—all the things she no longer cared about. And there was also debt, an obligation like a huge anchor chained around her waist, hauling her down.

But her friend was thinking none of these things. Cathy was prodding her, grinning, rolling her eyes at the sheer good looks of this guy, and Jenny smiled and gazed a little bit more. Cathy was right—this guy was definite eye-candy. What was more, he was munching on one of her muffins— lemon and pistachio. Her favourite, she thought in approval.

And then he looked up and saw her watching. He grinned and raised his muffin in silent toast, then chuckled as she blushed deep crimson and pushed the hatch closed.

Cathy laughed her delight. 'There,' she said in satisfaction. 'You see what's out there? He's gorgeous, Jen. Why don't you head on out and ask him if he'd like another muffin?'

'As if,' she muttered, thoroughly disconcerted. She shoved her mixing bowl into the sink. 'Serving's Susie's job. I'm just the cook. Go away, Cathy. You're messing with my serenity.'

'Stuff your serenity,' Cathy said crudely. 'Come on, Jen. It's been two years…' Then, as she saw the pain wash across Jenny's face, she swung herself off the bench and came and hugged her. 'I know. Moving on can't ever happen completely, but you can't keep hiding.'

'Dr Matheson says I'm doing well,' Jenny said stubbornly.

'Yeah, he's prescribing serenity,' Cathy said dourly. 'Honey, you've had enough peace. You want life. Even sailing… You love the water, but now you don't go near the sea. There's so many people who'd like a weekend crew. Like the guy out there, for instance. If he offered me a sail I'd be off for more than a weekend.'

'I don't want…'

'Anything but to be left alone,' Cathy finished for her. 'Oh, enough. I won't let you keep on saying it.' And, before Jenny could stop her, she opened the hatch again. She lifted the bell Jenny used to tell Susie an order was ready and rang it like there was a shipwreck in the harbour. Jenny made a grab for it but Cathy swung away so her body protected the bell. Then, when everyone was watching…

'Attention, please,' she called to the room in general, in the booming voice she used for running the Seaport Ladies' Yoga Sessions. 'Ladies and gentlemen, I know this is unusual but I'd like to announce a fantastic offer. Back here in the kitchen is the world's best cook and the world's best sailor. Jenny's available as crew for anyone offering her excitement, adventure and a way out of this town. All she needs is a fantastic wage and a boss who appreciates her. Anyone interested, apply right here, right now.'

'Cathy!' Jenny stared at her friend in horror. She made a grab for the hatch doors and tugged them shut as Cathy collapsed into laughter. 'Are you out of your mind?'

'I love you, sweetheart,' Cathy said, still chuckling. 'I'm just trying to help.'

'Getting me sacked won't help.'

'Susie won't tell Charlie,' Cathy said. 'She agrees

with me. Don't you, Susie?' she demanded as the middle-aged waitress pushed her way through the doors. 'Do we have a queue out there, Suse, all wanting to employ our Jen?'

'You shouldn't have done it,' Susie said severely, looking at Jenny in concern. 'You've embarrassed her to death.'

'There's no harm done,' Cathy said. 'They're all too busy eating muffins to care. But honest, Jen, put an ad in the paper, or at least start reading the Situations Vacant. Susie has a husband, four kids, two dogs and a farm. This place is a tiny part of her life. But for you… This place has become your life. You can't let it stay that way.'

'It's all I want,' Jenny said stubbornly. 'Serenity.'

'That's nonsense,' Susie declared.

'Of course it's nonsense,' Cathy said, jumping off the bench and heading for the door. 'Okay, Stage One of my quest is completed. If it doesn't have an effect then I'll move to Stage Two, and that could be really scary.'

Coffee 'n' Cakes was a daytime café. Charlie was supposed to lock up at five, but Charlie's life was increasingly spent in the pub, so at five Jenny locked up, as she was starting to do most nights.

At least Charlie hadn't heard of what had happened that morning. Just as well, Jenny thought as she turned towards home. For all Cathy's assurances that she wouldn't be sacked, she wasn't so sure. Charlie's temper was unpredictable and she had debts to pay. Big debts.

Once upon a time Charlie had been a decent boss. Then his wife died, and now…

Loss did ghastly things to people. It had to her. Was living in a grey fog of depression worse than spending life in an alcoholic haze? How could she blame Charlie when she wasn't much better herself?

She sighed and dug her hands deep into her jacket pockets. The rain from this morning had disappeared. It was warm enough, but she wanted the comfort of her coat. Cathy's behaviour had unsettled her.

She would've liked to take a walk along the harbour before she went home, only in this mood it might unsettle her even more.

All those boats, going somewhere.

She had debts to pay. She was going nowhere.

'Excuse me?'

The voice came from behind her. She swung around and it was him. The guy with the body, and with the smile.

Okay, that was a dumb thing to think, but she couldn't help herself. The combination of ridiculously good-looking body and a smile to die for meant it was taking everything she had not to drop her jaw.

It had been too long, she thought. No one since…
No. Don't even think about going there.

'Can I talk to you? Are you Jenny?'

He had an accent—Spanish maybe, she thought, and seriously sexy. Uh oh. Body of a god, killer smile and a voice that was deep and lilting and gorgeous. Her knees felt wobbly. Any minute now he'd have her clutching the nearest fence for support.

Hey! She was a grown woman, she reminded herself sharply. Where was a bucket of ice when she needed one? Making do as best she could, she tilted her chin, met his gaze square on and fought for composure.

'I'm Jenny.' Infuriatingly, her words came out a squeak. She turned them into a cough and tried again. 'I…sure.'

'The lady in the café said you were interested in a job,' he said. 'I'm looking for help. Can we talk about it?'

He was here to offer her a job?

His eyes were doing this assessing thing while he talked. She was wearing old jeans and an ancient duffel, built for service rather than style. Was he working out where she fitted in the social scale? Was he working out whether she cared what she wore?

Suddenly she found herself wishing she had something else on. Something with a bit of…glamour?

Now that was crazy. She was heading home to put her feet up, watch the telly and go to bed. What would she do with glamour?

He was asking her about a job. Yeah, they all needed deckhands, she thought, trying to ground herself. Lots of big yachts came into harbour here. There'd be one guy in charge—someone like this. There'd also be a couple of deckies, but the guy in charge would be the only one paid reasonable wages by the owners. Deckies were to be found in most ports—kids looking for adventure, willing to work for cheap travel. They'd get to their destination and disappear to more adventure, to be replaced by others.

Did this man seriously think she might be interested in such a job?

'My friend was having fun at my expense,' she said, settling now she knew what he wanted. Still trying to firm up her knees, though. 'Sorry, but I'm a bit old to drop everything and head off into the unknown.'

'Are you ever too old to do that?'

'Yes,' she snapped before she could stop herself—and then caught herself. 'Sorry. Look, I need to get on.'

'So you're not interested.'

'There's a noticeboard down at the yacht club,' she told him. 'There's always a list of kids looking for work. I already have a job.'

'You do have a job.' His smile had faded. He'd ditched his coat, leaving only his jeans and T-shirt. They were faded and old and…nice. He was tall and broad-shouldered. He looked loose-limbed, casually at ease with himself and quietly confident. His eyes were blue as the sea, though they seemed to darken when he smiled, and the crinkles round his eyes said smiling was what he normally did. But suddenly he was serious.

'If you made the muffins I ate this morning you're very, very good at your job,' he told her. 'If you're available as crew, a man'd be crazy not to take you on.'

'Well, I'm not.' He had her rattled and she'd snapped again. Why? He was a nice guy offering her a job. 'Sorry,' she said. 'But no.'

'Do you have a passport?'

'Yes, but…'

'I'm sailing for Europe just as soon as I can find some company. It's not safe to do a solo where I'm going.'

'Round the Horn?' Despite herself, she was interested.

'Round the Horn,' he agreed. 'It's fastest.'

That'd be right. The boaties in charge of the expensive yachts were usually at the call of owners. She'd met enough of them to know that. An owner fancied a sailing holiday in Australia? He'd pay a guy like this to bring his boat here and have it ready for him. Maybe he'd join the boat on the interesting bits, flying in and out at will. Now the owner would be back in Europe and it'd be up to the employed skipper—this guy?—to get the boat back there as soon as he could.

With crew. But not with her.

'Well, good luck,' she said, and started to walk away, but he wasn't letting her leave. He walked with her.

'It's a serious offer.'

'It's a serious rejection.'

'I don't take rejection kindly.'

'That's too bad,' she told him. 'The days of carting your crew on board drugged to the eyeballs is over. Press gangs are illegal.'

'They'd make my life easier,' he said morosely.

'You know I'm very sure they wouldn't.' His presence as he fell into step beside her was making her thoroughly disconcerted. 'Having a press-ganged crew waking up with hangovers a day out to sea surely wouldn't make for serene sailing.'

'I don't look for serenity,' he said, and it was so much an echo of her day's thoughts that she stopped dead.

But this was ridiculous. The idea was ridiculous. 'Serenity's important,' she managed, forcing her feet into moving again. 'So thank you, but I've said no. Is there anything else you want?'

'I pay well.'

'I know what deckies earn.'

'You don't know what I pay. Why don't you ask?'

'I'm not interested.'

'Do you really sail?' he asked curiously.

He wasn't going away. She was quickening her steps but he was keeping up with ease. She had the feeling if she broke into a run he'd keep striding beside her, effortlessly. 'Once upon a time, I sailed,' she said. 'Before life got serious.'

'Your life got serious? How?' Suddenly his eyes were creasing in concern. He paused and, before she could stop him, he lifted her left hand. She knew what he was looking for.

No ring.

'You have a partner?' he demanded.

'It's none of your business.'

'Yes, but I want to know,' he said in that gorgeous accent, excellent English but with that fabulous lilt—and there was that smile again, the smile she knew could get him anything he wanted if he tried hard enough. With these looks and that smile and that voice… Whew.

No. He couldn't get anything from her. She was impervious.

She had to be impervious.

But he was waiting for an answer. Maybe it wouldn't hurt to tell him enough to get him off her back. 'I'm happily single,' she said.

'Ah, but if you're saying life's serious then you're

not so happily single. Maybe sailing away on the next tide could be just what you want.'

'Look,' she said, tugging her hand away, exasperated. 'I'm not a teenager looking for adventure. I have obligations here. So you're offering me a trip to Europe? Where would that leave me? I'd get on your boat, I'd work my butt off for passage—I know you guys get your money's worth from the kids you employ—and then I'd end up wherever it is you're going. That's it. I know how it works. I wouldn't even have the fare home. I'm not a backpacker, Mr Whoever-You-Are, and I live here. I don't know you, I don't trust you and I'm not interested in your job.'

'My name's Ramón Cavellero,' he said, sounding not in the least perturbed by her outburst. 'I'm very trustworthy.' And he smiled in a way that told her he wasn't trustworthy in the least. 'I'm sailing on the *Marquita*. You've seen her?'

Had she seen her? Every person in Seaport had seen the *Marquita*. The big yacht's photograph had been on the front of their local paper when she'd come into port four days ago. With good reason. Quite simply she was the most beautiful boat Jenny had ever seen.

And probably the most expensive.

If this guy was captaining the *Marquita* then maybe he had the funds to pay a reasonable wage. That was an insidious little whisper in her head, but she stomped on it before it had a chance to grow. There was no way she could walk away from this place. Not for years.

She had to be sensible.

'Look, Mr Cavellero, this has gone far enough,' she said, and she turned back to face him directly. 'You have the most beautiful boat in the harbour. You can have your pick of any deckie in the market—I know a dozen kids at least who would kill to be on that boat. But, as for me… My friend was making a joke but that's all it was. Thank you and goodbye.'

She reached out and took his hand, to give it a good firm handshake, as if she was a woman who knew how to transact business, as if she should be taken seriously. He took it, she shook, but, instead of pulling away after one brief shake, she found he was holding on.

Or maybe it was that she hadn't pulled back as she'd intended.

His hand was strong and warm and his grip as decisive as hers. Or more. Two strong wills, she thought fleetingly, but more…

But then, before she could think any further, she was aware of a car sliding to a halt beside them. She glanced sideways and almost groaned.

Charlie.

She could sense his drunkenness from here. One of these days he'd be caught for drink-driving, she thought, and half of her hoped it'd be soon, but the other half knew that'd put her boss into an even more foul mood than he normally was. Once upon a time he'd been a nice guy—but that was when he was sober, and she could barely remember when he'd been sober. So she winced and braced herself for an explosion as Charlie emerged from the car and headed towards them.

Ramón kept on holding her hand. She tugged it back and he released her but he shifted in closer. Charlie's body language was aggressive. He was a big man; he'd become an alcoholic bully, and it showed.

But, whatever else Ramón might be, it was clear he knew how to protect his own. His own? That was a dumb thing to think. Even so, she was suddenly glad that he was here right now.

'Hey, I want to speak to you, you stupid cow. Lose your friend,' Charlie spat at her.

Jenny flinched. Uh oh. This could mean only one thing—that one of the patrons of the café had told Charlie of Cathy's outburst. This was too small a town for such a joke to go unreported. Charlie had become universally disliked and the idea that one of his staff was advertising for another job would be used against him.

At her expense.

And Ramón's presence here would make it worse. Protective or not, Charlie was right; she needed to lose him.

'See you later,' she said to Ramón, stepping deliberately away and turning her back on him. Expecting him to leave. 'Hello, Charlie.'

But Charlie wasn't into greetings. 'What the hell do you think you're doing, making personal announcements in my café, in my time?' He was close to yelling, shoving right into her personal space so she was forced to step backward. 'And getting another job? You walk away from me and I foreclose before the day's end. You know what you owe me, girl. You work for me for the next three years or I'll have you bankrupt and your friend with you. I could toss you out now. Your friend'll lose her house. Great mess that'd leave her in. You'll work the next four weekends with no pay to make up for this or you're out on your ear. What do you say to that?'

She closed her eyes. Charlie was quite capable of carrying out his threats. This man was capable of anything.

Why had she ever borrowed money from him?

Because she'd been desperate, that was why. It had been right at the end of Matty's illness. She'd sold everything, but there was this treatment… There'd been a chance. It was slim, she'd known, but she'd do anything.

She'd been sobbing, late at night, in the back room of the café. She'd been working four hours a day to pay her rent. The rest of the time she'd spent with Matty. Cathy had found her there, and Charlie came in and found them both.

He'd loan her the money, he said, and the offer was so extraordinary both women had been rendered almost speechless.

Jenny could repay it over five years, he'd told them, by working for half wages at the café. Only he needed security. 'In case you decide to do a runner.'

'She'd never do a runner,' Cathy had said, incensed. 'When Matty's well she'll settle down and live happily ever after.'

'I don't believe in happy ever after,' Charlie had said. 'I need security.'

'I'll pledge my apartment that she'll repay you,' Cathy had said hotly. 'I trust her, even if you don't.'

What a disaster. They'd been so emotional they hadn't thought it through. All Jenny had wanted was to get back to the hospital, to get back to Matty, and she didn't care how. Cathy's generosity was all she could see.

So she'd hugged her and accepted and didn't see the ties. Only ties there were. Matty died a month later and she was faced with five years bonded servitude.

Cathy's apartment had been left to her by her mother. It was pretty and neat and looked out over the harbour. Cathy was an artist. She lived hand to mouth and her apartment was all she had.

Even Cathy hadn't realised how real the danger of foreclosure was, Jenny thought dully. Cathy had barely glanced at the loan documents. She had total faith in her friend to repay her loan. Of course she had.

So now there was no choice. Jenny dug her hands deep into her pockets, she bit back angry words, as she'd bitten them back many times before, and she nodded.

'Okay. I'm sorry, Charlie. Of course I'll do the weekends.'

'Hey!' From behind them came Ramón's voice, laced with surprise and the beginnings of anger. 'What is this? Four weekends to pay for two minutes of amusement?'

'It's none of your business,' Charlie said shortly. 'Get lost.'

'If you're talking about what happened at the café, I was there. It was a joke.'

'I don't do jokes. Butt out. And she'll do the weekends. She has no choice.'

And then he smiled, a drunken smile that made her shiver. 'So there's the joke,' he jeered. 'On you, woman, not me.'

And that was that. He stared defiance at Ramón, but Ramón, it seemed, was not interested in a fight. He gazed blankly back at him, and then watched wordlessly as Charlie swung himself unsteadily back into his car and weaved off into the distance.

Leaving silence.

How to explain what had just happened? Jenny thought, and decided she couldn't. She took a few tentative steps away, hoping Ramón would leave her to her misery.

He didn't. Instead, he looked thoughtfully at the receding car, then flipped open his cellphone and spoke a few sharp words. He snapped it shut and walked after Jenny, catching up and once again falling into step beside her.

'How much do you owe him?' he asked bluntly.

She looked across at him, startled. 'Sorry?'

'You heard. How much?'

'I don't believe that it's…'

'Any of my business,' he finished for her. 'Your boss just told me that. But, as your future employer, I can make it my business.'

'You're not my future employer.'

'Just tell me, Jenny,' he said, and his voice was suddenly so concerned, so warm, so laced with caring that, to her astonishment, she found herself telling him. Just blurting out the figure, almost as if it didn't matter.

He thought about it for a moment as they kept walking. 'That's not so much,' he said cautiously.

'To you, maybe,' she retorted. 'But to me… My best friend signed over her apartment as security. If I don't pay, then she loses her home.'

'You could get another job. You don't have to be

beholden to this swine-bag. You could transfer the whole loan to the bank.'

'I don't think you realise just how broke I am,' she snapped and then she shook her head, still astounded at how she was reacting to him. 'Sorry. There's no need for me to be angry with you when you're being nice. I'm tired and I'm upset and I've got myself into a financial mess. The truth is that I don't even have enough funds to miss a week's work while I look for something else, and no bank will take me on. Or Cathy either, for that matter—she's a struggling painter and has nothing but her apartment. So there you go. That's why I work for Charlie. It's also why I can't drop everything and sail away with you. If you knew how much I'd love to…'

'Would you love to?' He was studying her intently. The concern was still there but there was something more. It was as if he was trying to make her out. His brow was furrowed in concentration. 'Would you really? How good a sailor are you?'

That was a weird question but it was better than talking about her debts. So she told him that, too. Why not? 'I was born and bred on the water,' she told him. 'My dad built a yacht and we sailed it together until he died. In the last few years of his life we lived on board. My legs are more at home at sea than on land.'

'Yet you're a cook.'

'There's nothing like spending your life in a cramped galley to make you lust after proper cooking.' She gave a wry smile, temporarily distracted from her bleakness. 'My mum died early so she couldn't teach me, but I longed to cook. When I was seventeen I got an apprenticeship with the local baker. I had to force Dad to keep the boat in port during my shifts.'

'And your boat? What was she?'

'A twenty-five footer, fibreglass, called *Wind Trader*. Flamingo, if you know that class. She wasn't anything special but we loved her.'

'Sold now to pay debts?' he asked bluntly.

'How did you know?' she said, crashing back to earth. 'And, before you ask, I have a gambling problem.'

'Now why don't I believe that?'

'Why would you believe anything I tell you?' She took a deep breath. 'Look, this is dumb. I'm wrecked and I need to go home. Can we forget we had this conversation? It was crazy to tell you my troubles and I surely don't expect you to do anything about them. But thank you for letting me talk.'

She hesitated then. For some reason, it was really hard to walk away from this man, but she had no choice. 'Goodbye, Mr Cavellero,' she managed. 'Thank you for thinking of me as a potential deckhand. It was very nice of you, and you know what? If I didn't have this debt I'd be half tempted to take it on.'

Once more she turned away. She walked about ten steps, but then his voice called her back.

'Jenny?'

She should have just kept on walking, but there was something in his voice that stopped her. It was the concern again. He sounded as if he really cared.

That was crazy, but the sensation was insidious, like a siren song forcing her to turn around.

'Yes?'

He was standing where she'd left him. Just standing. Behind him, down the end of the street, she could see the harbour. That was where he belonged, she thought. He was a man of the sea. He looked a man from the sea. Whereas she…

'Jenny, I'll pay your debts,' he said.

She didn't move. She didn't say anything.

She didn't know what to say.

'This isn't charity,' he said quickly as she felt her colour rise. 'It's a proposition.'

'I don't understand.'

'It's a very sketchy proposition,' he told her. 'I've not had time to work out the details so we may have to smooth it off round the edges. But, essentially, I'll pay your boss out if you promise to come and work with me for a year. You'll be two deckies instead of one—crew when I need it and cook for the rest of the time. Sometimes you'll be run off your feet but mostly not. I'll also add a living allowance,' he said and he mentioned a sum that made her feel winded.

'You'll be living on the boat so that should be sufficient,' he told her, seemingly ignoring her amazement. 'Then, at the end of the year, I'll organise you a flight home, from wherever *Marquita* ends up. So how about it, Jenny?' And there was that smile again, flashing out to warm parts of her she hadn't known had been cold. 'Will you stay here as Charlie's unpaid slave, or will you come with me, cook your cakes on my boat and see the world? What do you say? *Marquita*'s waiting, Jenny. Come sail away.'

'It's three years' debt,' she gasped finally. Was he mad?

'Not to me. It's one year's salary for a competent cook and sailor, and it's what I'm offering.'

'Your owner could never give the authority to pay those kind of wages.'

He hesitated for a moment—for just a moment—but then he smiled. 'My owner doesn't interfere with how I run my boat,' he told her. 'My owner knows if I…if he pays peanuts, he gets monkeys. I want good and loyal crew and with you I believe I'd be getting it.'

'You don't even know me. And you're out of your mind. Do you know how many deckies you could get with that money?'

'I don't want deckies. I want you.' And then, as she kept right on staring, he amended what had been a really forceful statement. 'If you can cook the muffins I had this morning you'll make my life—and everyone else who comes onto the boat—a lot more pleasant.'

'Who does the cooking now?' She was still fighting for breath. What an offer!

'Me or a deckie,' he said ruefully. 'Not a lot of class.'

'I'd…I'd be expected to cook for the owner?'

'Yes.'

'Dinner parties?'

'There's not a lot of dinner parties on board the *Marquita*,' he said, sounding a bit more rueful. 'The owner's pretty much like me. A retiring soul.'

'You don't look like a retiring soul,' she retorted, caught by the sudden flash of laughter in those blue eyes.

'Retiring or not, I still need a cook.'

Whoa… To be a cook on a boat… With this man…

Then she caught herself. For a moment she'd allowed herself to be sucked in. To think *what if*.

What if she sailed away?

Only she'd jumped like this once before, and where had it got her? Matty, and all the heartbreak that went with him.

Her thoughts must have shown on her face. 'What is it?' Ramón asked, and his smile suddenly faded. 'Hey, Jenny, don't look like that. There's no strings attached to this offer. I swear you won't find yourself the seventeenth member of my harem, chained up for my convenience in the hold. I can even give you character references if you want. I'm extremely honourable.'

He was trying to make her smile. She did smile, but it was a wavery smile. 'I'm sure you're honourable,' she said—despite the laughter lurking behind his amazing eyes suggesting he was nothing of the kind—'but, references or not, I still don't know you.' Deep breath. *Be sensible.* 'Sorry,' she managed. 'It's an amazing offer, but I took a loan from Charlie when I wasn't thinking straight, and look where that got me. And there have been…other times…when I haven't thought straight either, and trouble's followed. So I don't act on impulse any more. I've learned to be sensible. Thank you for your offer, Mr Cavellero…'

'Ramón.'

'Mr Cavellero,' she said stubbornly. 'With the wages you're offering, I know you'll find just the crew you're looking for, no problem at all. So thank you again and goodnight.'

Then, before she could let her treacherous heart do any more impulse urging—before she could be as stupid as she'd been in the past—she turned resolutely away.

She walked straight ahead and she didn't look back.

CHAPTER TWO

HER heart told her she was stupid all the way home. Her head told her she was right.

Her head addressed her heart with severity. This was a totally ridiculous proposition. She didn't know this man.

She'd be jumping from the frying pan into the fire, she told herself. To be indebted to a stranger, then sail away into the unknown… He *could* be a white slave trader!

She knew he wasn't. Take a risk, her heart was commanding her, but then her heart had let her down before. She wasn't going down that road again.

So, somehow, she summoned the dignity to keep on walking.

'Think about it,' Ramón called after her and she almost hesitated, she almost turned back, only she was a sensible woman now, not some dumb teenager who'd jump on the nearest boat and head off to sea.

So she walked on. Round the next corner, and the next, past where Charlie lived.

A police car was pulled up beside Charlie's front door, and Charlie hadn't made it inside. Her boss was being breathalysed. He'd be way over the alcohol limit. He'd lose his licence for sure.

She thought back and remembered Ramón lifting his cellphone. Had he…

Whoa. She scuttled past, feeling like a guilty rabbit.

Ramón had done it, not her.

Charlie would guess. Charlie would never forgive her.

Uh oh, uh oh, uh oh.

By the time she got home she felt as if she'd forgotten to breathe. She raced up the steps into her little rented apartment and she slammed the door behind her.

What had Ramón done? Charlie, without his driving licence? Charlie, thinking it was her fault?

But suddenly she wasn't thinking about Charlie. She was thinking about Ramón. Numbly, she crossed to the curtains and drew them aside. Just checking. Just in case he'd followed. He hadn't and she was aware of a weird stab of disappointment.

Well, what did you expect? she told herself. I told him press gangs don't work.

What if they did? What if he came up here in the dead of night, drugged her and carted her off to sea?

What if she woke on his beautiful yacht, far away from this place?

I'd be chained to the sink down in the galley, she told herself with an attempt at humour. Nursing a hangover from the drugs he used to get me there.

But oh, to be on that boat…

He'd offered to pay all her bills. Get her away from Charlie…

What was she about, even beginning to think about such a crazy offer? If he was giving her so much money, then he'd be expecting something other than the work a deckie did.

But a man like Ramón wouldn't have to pay, she thought, her mind flashing to the nubile young backpackers she knew would jump at the chance to be crew to Ramón. They'd probably jump at the chance to be anything else. So why did he want her?

Did he have a thing for older women?

She stared into the mirror and what she saw there almost made her smile. It'd be a kinky man who'd desire her like she was. Her hair was still flour-streaked from the day. She'd been working in a hot kitchen and she'd been washing up over steaming sinks. She didn't have a spot of make-up on, and her nose was shiny. *Very* shiny.

Her clothes were ancient and nondescript and her eyes were shadowed from lack of sleep. Oh, she had plenty of time for sleep, but where was sleep when you needed it? She'd stopped taking the pills her doctor prescribed. She was trying desperately to move on, but how?

'What better way than to take a chance?' she whispered to her image. 'Charlie's going to be unbearable to work with now. And Ramón's gorgeous and he seems really nice. His boat's fabulous. He's not going to chain me to the galley, I'm sure of it.' She even managed a smile at that. 'If he does, I won't be able to help him with the sails. He'd have to unchain me a couple of times a day at least. And I'd be at sea. At sea!'

So maybe…maybe…

Her heart and head were doing battle but her heart was suddenly in the ascendancy. It was trying to convince her it could be sensible as well.

Wait, she told herself severely. She ran a bath and wallowed and let her mind drift. Pros and cons. Pros and cons.

If it didn't work, she could get off the boat at New Zealand.

He'd demand his money back.

So? She'd then owe money to Ramón instead of to Charlie, and there'd be no threat to Cathy's apartment. The debt would be hers and hers alone.

That felt okay. Sensible, even. She felt a prickle of pure excitement as she closed her eyes and sank as deep as she could into the warm water. To sail away with Ramón…

Her eyes flew open. She'd been stupid once. One gorgeous sailor, and…Matty.

So I'm not that stupid, she told herself. I can take precautions before I go.

Before she went? This wasn't turning out to be a relaxing bath. She sat bolt upright in the bath and thought, *what am I thinking?*

She was definitely thinking of going.

'You told him where to go to find deckies,' she said out loud. 'He'll have asked someone else by now.'

No!

'So get up, get dressed and go down to that boat. Right now, before you chicken out and change your mind.

'You're nuts.

'So what can happen that's worse than being stuck here?' she told herself and got out of the bath and saw her very pink body in the mirror. Pink? The sight was somehow a surprise.

For the last two years she'd been feeling grey. She'd been concentrating on simply putting one foot after another, and sometimes even that was an effort.

And now…suddenly she felt pink.

'So go down to the docks, knock on the hatch of Ramón's wonderful boat and say—yes, please, I want to come with you, even if you are a white slave trader, even if I may be doing the stupidest thing of my life. Jumping from the frying pan into the fire? Maybe, but, crazy or not, I want to jump,' she told the mirror.

And she would.

'You're a fool,' she told her reflection, and her reflection agreed.

'Yes, but you're not a grey fool. Just do it.'

What crazy impulse had him offering a woman passage on his boat? A needy woman. A woman who looked as if she might cling.

She was right, he needed a couple of deckies, kids who'd enjoy the voyage and head off into the unknown as soon as he reached the next port. Then he could find more.

But he was tired of kids. He'd been starting to think he'd prefer to sail alone, only *Marquita* wasn't a yacht to sail by himself. She was big and old-fashioned and her sails were heavy and complicated. In good weather one man might manage her, but Ramón didn't head into good weather. He didn't look for storms but he didn't shy away from them either.

The trip back around the Horn would be long and tough, and he'd hardly make it before he was due to return to Bangladesh. He'd been looking forward to the challenge, but at the same time not looking forward to the complications crew could bring.

The episode in the café this morning had made him act on impulse. The woman—Jenny—looked light years from the kids he generally employed. She looked warm and homely and mature. She also looked as if she might have a sense of humour and, what was more, she could cook.

He could make a rather stodgy form of paella. He could cook a steak. Often the kids he employed couldn't even do that.

He was ever so slightly over paella.

Which was why the taste of Jenny's muffins, the cosiness of her café, the look of her with a smudge of flour over her left ear, had him throwing caution to the winds and offering her a job. And then, when he'd realised just where that bully of a boss had her, he'd thrown in paying off her loan for good measure.

Sensible? No. She'd looked at him as if she suspected him of buying her for his harem, and he didn't blame her.

It was just as well she hadn't accepted, he told himself. Move on.

It was time to eat. Maybe he could go out to one of the dockside hotels.

He didn't feel like it. His encounter with Jenny had left him feeling strangely flat—as if he'd seen something he wanted but he couldn't have it.

That made him sound like his Uncle Iván, he thought ruefully. Iván, Crown Prince of Cepheus, arrogance personified.

Why was he thinking of Iván now? He was really off balance.

He gave himself a fast mental shake and forced himself to go back to considering dinner. Even if he didn't go out to eat he should eat fresh food while in port. He retrieved steak, a tomato and lettuce from the refrigerator. A representation of the height of his culinary skill.

Dinner. Then bed?

Or he could wander up to the yacht club and check the noticeboard for deckies. The sooner he found a crew, the sooner he could leave, and suddenly he was eager to leave.

Why had the woman disturbed him? She had nothing to do with him. He didn't need to regard Jenny's refusal as a loss.

'Hello?'

For a moment he thought he was imagining things, but his black mood lifted, just like that, as he abandoned his steak and made his way swiftly up to the deck.

He wasn't imagining things. Jenny was on the jetty, looking almost as he'd last seen her but cleaner. She was still in her battered coat and jeans, but the flour was gone and her curls were damp from washing.

She looked nervous.

'Jenny,' he said and he couldn't disguise the pleasure in his voice. Nor did he want to. Something inside him was very pleased to see her again. *Extremely* pleased.

'I just… I just came out for a walk,' she said.

'Great,' he said.

'Charlie was arrested for drink-driving.'

'Really?'

'That wouldn't have anything to do with you?'

'Who, me?' he demanded, innocence personified. 'Would you like to come on board?'

'I…yes,' she said, and stepped quickly onto the deck as if she was afraid he might rescind his invitation. And suddenly her nerves seemed to be gone. She gazed around in unmistakable awe. 'Wow!'

'Wow' was right. Ramón had no trouble agreeing with Jenny there. *Marquita* was a gracious old lady of the sea, built sixty years ago, a wooden schooner crafted by boat builders who knew their trade and loved what they were doing.

Her hull and cabins were painted white but the timbers of her deck and her trimmings were left unpainted, oiled to a warm honey sheen. Brass fittings glittered in the evening light and, above their heads, *Marquita*'s vast oak masts swayed majestically, matching the faint swell of the incoming tide.

Marquita was a hundred feet of tradition and pure unashamed luxury. Ramón had fallen in love with her the moment he'd seen her, and he watched Jenny's face now and saw exactly the same response.

'What a restoration,' she breathed. 'She's exquisite.'

Now that was different. Almost everyone who

saw this boat looked at Ramón and said: 'She must have cost a fortune.'

Jenny wasn't thinking money. She was thinking beauty.

Beauty… There was a word worth lingering on. He watched the delight in Jenny's eyes as she gazed around the deck, taking in every detail, and he thought it wasn't only his boat that was beautiful.

Jenny was almost as golden-skinned as he was; indeed, she could be mistaken for having the same Mediterranean heritage. She was small and compact. Neat, he thought and then thought, no, make that cute. Exceedingly cute. And smart. Her green eyes were bright with intelligence and interest. He thought he was right about the humour as well. She looked like a woman who could smile.

But she wasn't smiling now. She was too awed.

'Can I see below?' she breathed.

'Of course,' he said, and he'd hardly got the words out before she was heading down. He smiled and followed. A man could get jealous. This was one beautiful woman, taking not the slightest interest in him. She was totally entranced by his boat.

He followed her down into the main salon, but was brought up short. She'd stopped on the bottom step, drawing breath, seemingly awed into silence.

He didn't say anything; just waited.

This was the moment for people to gush. In truth,

there was much to gush about. The rich oak wainscoting, the burnished timber, the soft worn leather of the deep settees. The wonderful colours and fabrics of the furnishing, the silks and velvets of the cushions and curtains, deep crimsons and dark blues, splashed with touches of bright sunlit gold.

When Ramón had bought this boat, just after the accident that had claimed his mother and sister, she'd been little more than a hull. He'd spent time, care and love on her renovation and his Aunt Sofía had helped as well. In truth, maybe Sofía's additions were a little over the top, but he loved Sofía and he wasn't about to reject her offerings. The result was pure comfort, pure luxury. He loved the *Marquita*—and right now he loved Jenny's reaction.

She was totally entranced, moving slowly around the salon, taking in every detail. This was the main room. The bedrooms were beyond. If she was interested, he'd show her those too, but she wasn't finished here yet.

She prowled, like a small cat inspecting each tiny part of a new territory. Her fingers brushed the burnished timber, lightly, almost reverently. She crossed to the galley and examined the taps, the sink, the stove, the attachments used to hold things steady in a storm. She bent to examine the additional safety features on the stove. Gas stoves on boats could be lethal. Not his. She opened the cupboard below the sink and proceeded to check out the plumbing.

He found he was smiling, enjoying her awe. Enjoying her eye for detail. She glanced up from where she was inspecting the valves below the sink and caught him smiling. And flushed.

'I'm sorry, but it's just so interesting. Is it okay to look?'

'It's more than okay,' he assured her. 'I've never had someone gasp at my plumbing before.'

She didn't return his smile. 'This pump,' she breathed. 'I've seen one in a catalogue. You've got them all through the boat?'

'There are three bathrooms,' he told her, trying not to sound smug. 'All pumped on the same system.'

'You have three bathrooms?' She almost choked. 'My father didn't hold with plumbing. He said real sailors used buckets. I gather your owner isn't a bucket man.'

'No,' he agreed gravely. 'My owner definitely isn't a bucket man.'

She did smile then, but she was still on the prowl. She crossed to the navigation desk, examining charts, checking the navigation instruments, looking at the radio. Still seeming awed.

Then… 'You leave your radio off?'

'I only use it for outgoing calls.'

'Your owner doesn't mind? With a boat like this, I'd imagine he'd be checking on you daily.'

Your owner…

Now was the time to say he was the owner; this was his boat. But Jenny was starting to relax, becoming companionable, friendly. Ramón had seen enough of other women's reactions when they realised the level of his wealth. For some reason, he didn't want that reaction from Jenny.

Not yet. Not now.

'My owner and I are in accord,' he said gravely. 'We keep in contact when we need to.'

'How lucky,' she said softly. 'To have a boss who doesn't spend his life breathing down your neck.' And then she went right on prowling.

He watched, growing more fascinated by the moment. He'd had boat fanatics on board before— of course he had—and most of them had checked out his equipment with care. Others had commented with envy on the luxury of his fittings and furnishings. But Jenny was seeing the whole thing. She was assessing the boat, and he knew a part of her was also assessing him. In her role as possible hired hand? *Yes*, he thought, starting to feel optimistic. She was now under the impression that his owner trusted him absolutely, and such a reference was obviously doing him no harm.

If he wanted her trust, such a reference was a great way to start.

Finally, she turned back to him, and her awe had been replaced by a level of satisfaction. As if she'd seen a work of art that had touched a chord deep within. 'I guess now's the time to say, *Isn't she gorgeous*?' she said, and she smiled again. 'Only it's not a question. She just is.'

'I know she is,' he said. He liked her smile. It was just what it should be, lighting her face from within.

She didn't smile enough, he thought.

He thought suddenly of the women he worked with in Bangladesh. Jenny was light years away from their desperate situations, but there was still that shadow behind her smile. As if she'd learned the hard way that she couldn't trust the world.

'Would you like to see the rest of her?' he asked, suddenly unsure where to take this. A tiny niggle was starting in the back of his head. Take this further and there would be trouble…

It was too late. He'd asked. 'Yes, please. Though…it seems an intrusion.'

'It's a pleasure,' he said and he meant it. Then he thought, hey, he'd made his bed this morning. There was a bonus. His cabin practically looked neat.

He took her to the second bedroom first. The cabin where Sofía had really had her way. He'd restored *Marquita* in the months after his mother's and sister's death, and Sofía had poured all her concern into furnishings. 'You spend half your life living on the floor in mud huts in the middle of nowhere,' she'd scolded. 'Your grandmother's money means we're both rich beyond our dreams so there's no reason why you should sleep on the floor here.'

There was certainly no need now for him, or anyone else on this boat, to sleep on the floor. He'd kept a rein on his own room but in this, the second cabin, he'd let Sofía have her way. He opened the door and Jenny stared in stunned amazement—and then burst out laughing.

'It's a boudoir,' she stammered. 'It's harem country.'

'Hey,' he said, struggling to sound serious, even offended, but he found he was smiling as well. Sofía had indeed gone over the top. She'd made a special trip to Marrakesh, and she'd furnished the cabin like a sheikh's boudoir. Boudoir? Who knew? Whatever it was that sheikhs had.

The bed was massive, eight feet round, curtained with burgundy drapes and piled with quilts and pillows of purple and gold. The carpet was thick as grass, a muted pink that fitted beautifully with the furnishings of the bed. Sofía had tied in crisp, pure white linen, and matched the whites with silk hangings of sea scenes on the walls. The glass windows were open while the *Marquita* was in port and the curtains blew softly in the breeze. The room was luxurious, yet totally inviting and utterly, utterly gorgeous.

'This is where you'd sleep,' Ramón told Jenny and she turned and stared at him as if he had two heads.

'Me. The deckie!'

'There are bunkrooms below,' he said. 'But I don't see why we shouldn't be comfortable.'

'This *is* harem country.'

'You don't like it?'

'I love it,' she confessed, eyes huge. 'What's not to love? But, as for sleeping in it… The owner doesn't mind?'

'No.'

'Where do you sleep?' she demanded. 'You can't give me the best cabin.'

'This isn't the best cabin.'

'You're kidding me, right?'

He smiled and led the way back down the companionway. Opened another door. Ushered her in.

He'd decorated this room. Sofía had added a couple of touches—actually, Sofía had spoken to his plumber so the bathroom was a touch…well, a touch embarrassing—but the rest was his.

It was bigger than the stateroom he'd offered Jenny. The bed here was huge but he didn't have hangings. It was more masculine, done in muted tones of the colours through the rest of the boat. The sunlit yellows and golds of the salon had been extended here, with only faint touches of the crimson and blues. The carpet here was blue as well, but short and functional.

There were two amazing paintings on the wall. Recognizable paintings. Jenny gasped with shock. 'Please tell me they're not real.'

Okay. 'They're not real.' They were. 'You want

to see the bathroom?' he asked, unable to resist, and he led her through. Then he stood back and grinned as her jaw almost hit the carpet.

While the *Marquita* was being refitted, he'd had to return to Bangladesh before the plumbing was done, and Sofía had decided to put her oar in here as well. And Sofía's oar was not known as sparse and clinical. Plus she had this vision of him in sackcloth and ashes in Bangladesh and she was determined to make the rest of his life what she termed 'comfortable'.

Plus she read romance novels.

He therefore had a massive golden bath in the shape of a Botticelli shell. It stood like a great marble carving in the middle of the room, with carved steps up on either side. Sofía had made concessions to the unsteadiness of bathing at sea by putting what appeared to be vines all around. In reality, they were hand rails but the end result looked like a tableau from the Amazon rainforest. There were gold taps, gold hand rails, splashes of crimson and blue again. *There was trompe l'oeil—* a massive painting that looked like reality—on the wall, making it appear as if the sea came right inside. She'd even added towels with the monogram of the royal family his grandmother had belonged to.

When he'd returned from Bangladesh he'd come in here and nearly had a stroke. His first reaction had been horror, but Sofía had been beside him, so anxious she was quivering.

'I so wanted to give you something special,' she'd said, and Sofía was all the family he had and there was no way he'd hurt her.

He'd hugged her and told her he loved it—and that night he'd even had a bath in the thing. She wasn't to know he usually used the shower down the way.

'You…you sleep in here?' Jenny said, her bottom lip quivering.

'Not in the bath,' he said and grinned.

'But where does the owner sleep?' she demanded, ignoring his attempt at levity. She was gazing around in stupefaction. 'There's not room on his boat for another cabin like this.'

'I… At need I use the bunkroom.' And that was a lie, but suddenly he was starting to really, really want to employ this woman. Okay, he was on morally dubious ground, but did it matter if she thought he was a hired hand? He watched as the strain eased from her face and turned to laughter, and he thought surely this woman deserved a chance at a different life. If one small lie could give it to her…

Would it make a difference if she knew the truth? If he told her he was so rich the offer to pay her debts meant nothing to him… How would she react?

With fear. He'd seen her face when he'd offered

her the job. There'd been an intuitive fear that he wanted her for more than her sailing and her cooking. How much worse would it be if she knew he could buy and sell her a thousand times over?

'The owner doesn't mind?' she demanded.

He gave up and went along with it. 'The owner likes his boat to be used and enjoyed.'

'Wow,' she breathed and looked again at the bath. 'Wow!'

'I use the shower in the shared bathroom,' he confessed and she chuckled.

'What a waste.'

'You'd be welcome to use this.'

'In your dreams,' she muttered. 'This place is Harems-R-Us.'

'It's great,' he said. 'But it's still a working boat. I promise you, Jenny, there's not a hint of harem about her.'

'You swear?' she demanded and she fixed him with a look that said she was asking for a guarantee. And he knew what that guarantee was.

'I swear,' he said softly. 'I skipper this boat and she's workmanlike.'

She looked at him for a long, long moment and what she saw finally seemed to satisfy her. She gave a tiny satisfied nod and moved on. 'You have to get her back to Europe fast?'

'Three months, at the latest.' That, at least, was true. His team started work in Bangladesh then and he intended to travel with them. 'So do you want to come?'

'You're still offering?'

'I am.' He ushered her back out of the cabin and closed the door. The sight of that bath didn't make for businesslike discussions on any level.

'You're not employing anyone else?'

'Not if I have you.'

'You don't even know if I can sail,' she said, astounded all over again.

He looked at her appraisingly. The corridor here was narrow and they were too close. He'd like to be able to step back a bit, to see her face. He couldn't.

She was still nervous, he thought, like a deer caught in headlights. But caught she was. His offer seemed to have touched something in her that longed to respond, and even the sight of that crazy bath hadn't made her back off. She was just like he was, he thought, raised with a love of the sea. Aching to be out there.

So…she was caught. All he had to do was reel her in.

'So show me that you can sail,' he said. 'Show me now. The wind's getting up enough to make it interesting. Let's take her out.'

'What, tonight?'

'Tonight. Now. Dare you.'

'I can't,' she said, sounding panicked.

'Why not?'

She stared up at him as if he were a species she'd never seen.

'You just go. Whenever you feel like it.'

'The only thing holding us back is a couple of lines tied to bollards on the wharf,' he said and then, as her look of panic deepened, he grinned. 'But we will bring her back tonight, if that's what's worrying you. It's seven now. We can be back in harbour by midnight.'

'You seriously expect me to sail with you? Now?'

'There's a great moon,' he said. 'The night is ours. Why not?'

So, half an hour later, they were sailing out through the heads, heading for Europe.

Or that was what it felt like to Jenny. Ramón was at the wheel. She'd gone up to the bow to tighten a stay, to see if they could get a bit more tension in the jib. The wind was behind them, the moon was rising from the east, moonlight was shimmering on the water and she was free.

The night was warm enough for her to take off her coat, to put her bare arms out to catch a moonbeam. She could let her hair stream behind her and become a bow-sprite, she thought. An omen of good luck to sailors.

An omen of good luck to Ramón?

She turned and looked back at him. He was a dark shadow in the rear of the boat but she knew he was watching her from behind the wheel. She was being judged?

So what? The boat was as tightly tuned as she could make her. Ramón had asked her to set the sails herself. She'd needed help in this unfamiliar environment but he'd followed her instructions rather than the other way round.

This boat was far bigger than anything she'd sailed on, but she'd spent her life in a sea port, talking to sailors, watching the boats come in. She'd seen yachts like this; she'd watched them and she'd ached to be on one.

She'd brought Matty down to the harbour and she'd promised him his own boat.

'When you're big. When you're strong.'

And suddenly she was blinking back tears. That was stupid. She didn't cry for Matty any more. It was no use; he was never coming back.

'Are you okay?'

Had he seen? The moonlight wasn't that strong. She swiped her fist angrily across her cheeks, ridding herself of the evidence of her distress, and made her way slowly aft. She had a lifeline clipped to her and she had to clip it and unclip it along the way. She was as sure-footed as a cat at sea, but it didn't hurt to show him she was safety conscious— and, besides, it gave her time to get her face in order.

'I'm fine,' she told him as she reached him.

'Take over the wheel, then,' he told her. 'I need to cook dinner.'

Was this a test, too? she wondered. Did she really have sea legs? Cooking below deck on a heavy swell was something no one with a weak stomach could do.

'I'll do it.' She could.

'You really don't get seasick?'

'I really don't get seasick.'

'A woman in a million,' he murmured and then he grinned. 'But no, it's not fair to ask you to cook. This is your night at sea and, after the day you've had, you deserve it. Take the wheel. Have you eaten?'

'Hours ago.'

'There's steak to spare.' He smiled at her and wham, there it was again, his smile that had her heart saying, *Beware, Beware, Beware*.

'I really am fine,' she said and sat and reached for the wheel and when her hand brushed his—she could swear it was accidental—the *Beware* grew so loud it was a positive roar.

But, seemingly unaware of any roaring on deck, he left her and dropped down into the galley. In minutes the smell of steak wafted up. Nothing else. Just steak.

Not my choice for a lovely night at sea, she thought, but she wasn't complaining. The rolling swell was coming in from the east. She nosed the boat into the swell and the boat steadied on course.

She was the most beautiful boat.

Could she really be crew? She was starting to feel as if, when Ramón had made the offer, she should have signed a contract on the spot. Then, as he emerged from the galley bearing two plates and smiling, she knew why she hadn't. That smile gave her so many misgivings.

'I cooked some for you, too,' he said, looking dubiously down at his plates. 'If you really aren't seasick…'

'I have to eat something to prove it?'

'It's a true test of grit,' he said. 'You eat my cooking, then I know you have a cast iron stomach.' He sat down beside her and handed her a plate.

She looked down at it. Supermarket steak, she thought, and not a good cut.

She poked it with a fork and it didn't give.

'You have to be polite,' he said. 'Otherwise my feelings will be hurt.'

'Get ready for your feelings to be hurt.'

'Taste it at least.'

She released the wheel, fought the steak for a bit and then said, 'Can we put her on automatic pilot? This is going to take some work.'

'Hey, I'm your host,' he said, sounding offended.

'And I'm a cook. How long did you fry this?'

'I don't know. Twenty minutes, maybe? I needed

to check the charts to remind myself of the lights for harbour re-entry.'

'So your steak cooked away on its own while you concentrated on other things.'

'What's wrong with that?'

'I'd tell you,' she said darkly, stabbing at her steak and finally managing to saw off a piece. Manfully chewing and then swallowing. 'Only you're right; you're my host.'

'I'd like to be your employer. Will you be cook on the *Marquita*?'

Whoa. So much for concentrating on steak. This, then, was when she had to commit. To craziness or not.

To life—or not.

'You mean…you really were serious with your offer?'

'I'm always serious. It was a serious offer. It *is* a serious offer.'

'You'd only have to pay me a year's salary. I could maybe organise something…' But she knew she couldn't, and he knew it, too. His response was immediate.

'The offer is to settle your debts and sail away with you, debt free. That or nothing.'

'That sounds like something out of a romance novel. Hero on white charger, rescuing heroine from villain. I'm no wimpy heroine.'

He grinned. 'You sound just like my Aunt Sofía.

She reads them, too. But no, I never said you were wimpy. I never thought you were wimpy.'

'I'd repay…'

'No,' he said strongly and took her plate away from her and set it down. He took her hands then, strong hands gripping hers so she felt the strength of him, the sureness and the authority. Authority? This was a man used to getting his own way, she thought, suddenly breathless, and once more came the fleeting thought, *I should run*.

There was nowhere to run. If she said yes there'd be nowhere to run for a year.

'You will not repay,' he growled. 'A deal's a deal, Jenny. You will be my crew. You will be my cook. I'll ask nothing more.'

This was serious. Too serious. She didn't want to think about the implications behind those words.

And maybe she didn't want that promise. *I'll ask nothing more…*

He'd said her debt was insignificant. Maybe it was to him. To her it was an insurmountable burden. She had her pride, but maybe it was time to swallow it, stand aside and let him play hero.

'Thank you,' she said, trying to sound meek.

'Jenny?'

'Yes.'

'I'm captain,' he said. 'But I will not tolerate subordination.'

'Subordination?'

'It's my English,' he apologised, sounding suddenly very Spanish. 'As in captains say to their crew, "*I will not tolerate insubordination!*" just before they give them a hundred lashes and toss them in the brink.'

'What's the brink?'

'I have no idea,' he confessed. 'I'm sure the *Marquita* doesn't have one, which is what I'm telling you. Whereas most captains won't tolerate insubordination, I am the opposite. If you'd like to argue all the way around the Horn, it's fine by me.'

'You want me to argue?' She was too close to him, she thought, and he was still holding her hands. The sensation was worrying.

Worryingly good, though. Not worryingly bad. Arguing with this guy all the way round the Horn…

'Yes. I will also expect muffins,' he said and she almost groaned.

'Really?'

'Take it or leave it,' he said. 'Muffins and insubordination. Yes or no?'

She stared up at him in the moonlight. He stared straight back at her and she felt her heart do this strange surge, as if her fuel-lines had just been doubled.

What am I getting into, she demanded of herself, but suddenly she didn't care. The night was warm, the boat was lovely and this man was holding her hands, looking down at her in the moonlight and his hands were imparting strength and sureness and promise.

Promise? What was he promising? She was being fanciful.

But she had to be careful, she told herself fiercely. She must.

It was too late.

'Yes,' she said before she could change her mind—and she was committed.

She was heading to the other side of the world with a man she'd met less than a day ago.

Was she out of her mind?

What had he done? What was he getting himself into?

He'd be spending three months at sea with a woman called Jenny.

Jenny what? Jenny who? He knew nothing about her other than she sailed and she cooked.

He spent more time on background checks for the deckies he employed. He always ran a fast check on the kids he employed, to ensure there weren't skeletons in the closet that would come bursting out the minute he was out of sight of land.

And he didn't employ them for a year. The deal was always that they'd work for him until the next port and then make a mutual decision as to whether they wanted to go on.

He'd employed Jenny for a year.

He wasn't going to be on the boat for a year. Had he thought that through? No, so he'd better think it through now. Be honest? Should he say, *Jenny, I made the offer because I felt sorry for you, and there was no way you'd have accepted my offer of a loan if you knew I'm only offering three months' work?*

He wasn't going to say that, because it wasn't true. He'd made the offer for far more complicated reasons than sympathy, and that was what was messing with his head now.

In three months he'd be in Bangladesh.

Did he need to go to Bangladesh?

In truth, he didn't need to go anywhere. His family inheritance had been massive, he'd invested it with care and if he wished he could spend the rest of his life in idle luxury.

Only…his family had never been like that. Excluded from the royal family, Ramón's grandmother had set about making herself useful. The royal family of Cepheus was known for indolence, mindless indulgence, even cruelty. His grandmother had left the royal palace in fear, for good reason. But then she'd started making herself a life—giving life to others. So she and her children, Ramón's father and aunt, had set up a charity in Bangladesh. They built homes in the low lying delta regions, houses that could be raised as flood levels rose, homes that could keep a community safe and dry.

Ramón had been introduced to it early and found the concept fascinating.

His father's death had made him even more determined to stay away from royalty; to make a useful life for himself, so at seventeen he'd apprenticed himself to one of Cepheus's top builders. He'd learned skills from the ground up. Now it wasn't just money he was throwing at this project—it was his hands as well as his heart.

During the wet season he couldn't build. During these months he used to stay on the island he still called home, spending time with his mother and sister. He'd also spent it planning investments so the work they were doing could go on for ever.

But then his mother and his sister died. One drunken driver and his family was wiped out. Suddenly he couldn't bear to go home. He employed a team of top people to take over his family's financial empire, and he'd bought the *Marquita*.

He still worked in Bangladesh—hands-on was great, hard manual work which drove away the demons. But for the rest of the year he pitted himself against the sea and felt better for it.

But there was a gaping hole where his family had been; a hole he could never fill. Nor did he want to, he decided after a year or so. If it hurt so much to lose…to get close to someone again seemed stupid.

So why ask Jenny onto his boat? He knew instinctively that closeness was a very real risk with this woman. But it was as if another part of him, a part he didn't know existed, had emerged and done the asking.

He'd have to explain Bangladesh to her. Or would he? When he got to Cepheus he could simply say there was no need for the boat, the owner wanted her in dry dock for six months. Jenny was free to fly back to Australia—he'd pay her fare— and she could fill the rest of her contract six months later.

That'd mean he had crew not only for now but for the future as well.

A crew of one woman.

This was danger territory. The Ramón he knew well, the Ramón he trusted, was screaming a warning.

No. He could be sensible. This was a big enough boat for him to keep his own counsel. He'd learned to do that from years of sailing with deckies. The kids found him aloof, he knew, but aloof was good. Aloof meant you didn't open yourself to gut-wrenching pain.

Aloof meant you didn't invite a woman like Jenny to sail around the world with you.

A shame that he just had.

'The *Marquita*'s reported as having left Fiji two weeks ago. We think Ramón's in Australia.'

'For heaven's sake!' Sofía pushed herself up on

her cushions and stared at the lawyer, perplexed. 'What's he doing in Australia?'

'Who would know?' the lawyer said with asperity. 'He's left no travel plans.'

'He could hardly expect this awfulness,' Sofía retorted. 'There's never been a thought that Ramón could inherit.'

'Well, it makes life difficult for us,' the lawyer snapped. 'He doesn't even answer incoming radio calls.'

'Ramón's been a loner since his mother and sister died,' Sofía said, and she sighed. 'It affected me deeply, so who knows how it affected him? If he wants to be alone, who are we to stop him?'

'He can't be alone any longer,' the lawyer said. 'I'm flying out.'

'To Australia?'

'Yes.'

'Isn't Australia rather big?' Sofía said cautiously. 'I mean… I don't want to discourage you, but if you flew to Perth and he ended up at Darwin… I've read about Australia and it does sound a little larger than Cepheus.'

'I believe the smallest of its states is bigger than Cepheus,' the lawyer agreed. 'But if he's coming from Fiji he'll be heading for the east coast. We have people looking out for him at every major port. If I wait in Sydney I can be with him in hours rather than days.'

'You don't think we could wait until he makes contact?' Sofía said. 'He does email me. Eventually.'

'He needs to take the throne by the end of the month or Carlos inherits.'

'Carlos?' Sofía said, and her face crumpled in distress. 'Oh, dear.'

'So you see the hurry,' the lawyer said. 'If I'm in Australia, as soon as we locate his boat I can be there. He has to come home. Now.'

'I wish we could find him before I make a decision about Philippe,' she said. 'Oh, dear.'

'I thought you'd found foster parents for him.'

'Yes, but…it seems wrong to send him away from the palace. What would Ramón do, do you think?'

'I hardly think Prince Ramón will wish to be bothered with a child.'

'No,' Sofía said sadly. 'Maybe you're right. There are so many things Ramón will be bothered with now—how can he want a say in the future of a child he doesn't know?'

'He won't. Send the child to foster parents.'

'Yes,' Sofía said sadly. 'I don't know how to raise a child myself. He's had enough of hired nannies. I think it's best for everyone.'

CHAPTER THREE

THIS was really, really foolish. She was allowing an unknown Spaniard to pay her debts and sweep her off in his fabulous yacht to the other side of the world. She was so appalled at herself she couldn't stop grinning.

Watching Cathy's face had been a highlight. 'I can't let you do it,' she'd said in horror. 'I know I joked about it but I never dreamed you'd take me seriously. You know nothing about him. This is awful.'

And Jenny had nodded solemn agreement.

'It is awful. If I turn up in some Arabic harem on the other side of the world it's all your fault,' she told her friend. 'You pointed him out to me.'

'No. Jenny, I never would have… No!'

She'd chuckled and relented. 'Okay, I won't make you come and rescue me. I know this is a risk, my love, but honestly, he seems nice. I don't think there's a harem but even if there is…I'm a big girl and I take responsibility for my own decision. I know it's playing with fire, but honestly, Cathy, you were right. I'm out of here any way I can.'

And what a way! Sailing out of the harbour on board the *Marquita* with Ramón at the helm was like something out of a fairy tale.

Fairy tales didn't include scrubbing decks, though, she conceded ruefully. There was enough of reality to keep her grounded—or as grounded as one could be at sea. Six days later, Jenny was on her knees swishing a scrubbing brush like a true deck-hand. They'd been visited by a flock of terns at dawn—possibly the last they'd see until they neared land again. She certainly hoped so. The deck was a mess.

But making her feel a whole lot better about scrubbing was the fact that Ramón was on his knees scrubbing as well. That didn't fit the fairy tale either. Knight on white charger scrubbing bird droppings? She glanced over and found he was watching her. He caught her grin and he grinned back.

'Not exactly the romantic ideal of sailing into the sunset,' he said, and it was so much what she'd been thinking that she laughed. She sat back on her heels, put her face up to the sun and soaked it in. The *Marquita* was on autopilot, safe enough in weather like this. There was a light breeze—enough to make *Marquita* slip gracefully through the water like a skier on a downhill run. On land it would be hot, but out here on the ocean it was just plain fabulous. Jenny was wearing shorts and T-shirt and nothing else. Her feet were bare, her hair was scrunched up in a ponytail to keep it out of her eyes, her nose was white with sunscreen—and she was perfectly, gloriously happy.

'You're supposed to complain,' Ramón said, watching her. 'Any deckie I've ever employed would be complaining by now.'

'What on earth would I be complaining about?'

'Scrubbing, maybe?'

'I'd scrub from here to China if I could stay on this boat,' she said happily and then saw his expression and hastily changed her mind. 'No. I didn't mean that. You keep right on thinking I'm working hard for my money. But, honestly, you have the best job in the world, Ramón Cavellero, and I have the second best.'

'I do, don't I?' he said, but his smile faded, and something about him said he had shadows too. Did she want to ask?

Maybe not.

She'd known Ramón for over a week now, and she'd learned a lot in that time. She'd learned he was a wonderful sailor, intuitive, clever and careful. He took no unnecessary risks, yet on the second night out there'd been a storm. A nervous sailor might have reefed in everything and sat it out. Ramón, however, had looked at the charts, altered his course and let the jib stay at full stretch. The *Marquita* had flown across the water with a speed Jenny found unbelievable, and when the dawn came and the storm abated they were maybe three hundred miles further towards New Zealand than they'd otherwise have been.

She'd taken a turn at the wheel that night but she knew Ramón hadn't slept. She'd been conscious of his shadowy presence below, aware of what the boat was doing, aware of how she was handling her. It wasn't that he didn't trust her, but she was new crew and to sleep in such a storm while she had such responsibility might have been dangerous.

His competence pleased her, as did the fact that he hadn't told her he was checking on her. Lots of things about him pleased her, she admitted—but Ramón kept himself to himself. Any thoughts she may have had of being an addition to his harem were quickly squashed. Once they were at sea, he was reserved to the point of being aloof.

'How long have you skippered this boat?' she asked suddenly, getting back to scrubbing, not looking up. She was learning that he responded better that way, talking easily as they worked together. Once work stopped he retreated again into silence.

'Ten years,' he said.

'Wow. You must have been at kindergarten when you were first employed.'

'I got lucky,' he said brusquely, and she thought,

don't go there. She'd asked a couple of things about the owner, and she'd learned quickly that was the way to stop a conversation dead.

'So how many crews would you have employed in that time?' she asked. And then she frowned down at what she was scrubbing. How on earth had the birds managed to soil under the rim of the forward hatch? She tried to imagine, and couldn't.

'How long's a piece of string?' Ramón said. 'I get new people at every port.'

'But you have me for a year.'

'That's right, I have,' he said and she glanced up and caught a flash of something that might be satisfaction. She smiled and went back to scrubbing, unaccountably pleased.

'That sounds like you liked my lunch time paella.'

'I loved your lunch time paella. Where did you learn to cook something so magnificently Spanish?'

'I'm part Spanish,' she said and he stopped scrubbing and stared.

'Spanish?'

'Well, truthfully, I'm all Australian,' she said, 'but my father was Spanish. He moved to Australia when he met my mother. My mother's mother was Spanish as well. Papà came as an adventuring young man. He contacted my grandmother as a family friend and the rest is history.

'So,' Ramón said slowly, sounding dazed. *'Habla usted español?* Can you speak Spanish?'

'*Sí*,' she said, and tried not to sound smug.

'I don't believe it.'

'There's no end to my talents,' she agreed and grinned, and then peered under the hatch. 'Speaking of talent… How did these birds do this? They must have lain on their sides and aimed.'

'It's a competition between them and me,' Ramón said darkly. 'They don't like my boat looking beautiful. All I can do is sail so far out to sea they can't reach me. But…you have a Spanish background? Why didn't you tell me?'

'You never asked,' she said, and then she hesitated. 'There's lots you didn't ask, and your offer seemed so amazing I saw no reason to mess it with detail. I could have told you I play a mean game of netball, I can climb trees, I have my bronze surf life-saving certificate and I can play *Waltzing Matilda* on a gum leaf. You didn't ask and how could I tell you? You might have thought I was skiting.'

'Skiting?'

'Making myself out to be Miss Wonderful.'

'I seem to have employed Miss Wonderful regardless,' he said. And then… 'Jenny?'

'Mmm?'

'No, I mean, what sort of Spanish parents call their daughter Jenny?'

'It's Gianetta.'

'Gianetta.' He said it with slow, lilting pleasure, and he said it the way it was supposed to sound. The way her parents had said it. She blinked and then she thought no. Actually, the way Ramón said it wasn't the way her parents had said it. He had the pronunciation right but it was much, much better. He rolled it, he almost growled it, and it sounded so sexy her toes started to curl.

'I would have found out when you signed your contract,' Ramón was saying while she attempted a bit of toe uncurling. Then he smiled. 'Speaking of which, maybe it's time you did sign up. I don't want to let anyone who can play *Waltzing Matilda* on a gum leaf get away.'

'It's a dying art,' she said, relieved to be on safer ground. In fact she'd been astounded that he hadn't yet got round to making her sign any agreement.

The day before they'd sailed he'd handed Charlie a cheque. 'How do you know you can trust me to fill my part of the bargain?' she'd asked him, stunned by what he was doing, and Ramón had looked down at her for a long moment, his face impassive, and he'd given a small decisive nod.

'I can,' he'd said, and that was that.

'Playing a gum leaf's a dying art?' he asked now, cautiously.

'It's something I need to teach my grandchildren,' she told him. And then she heard what she'd said. *Grandchildren*. The void, always threatening, was suddenly right under her. She hauled herself back with an effort.

'What is it?' Ramón said and he was looking at her with concern. The void disappeared. There went her toes again, curling, curling. Did he have any idea of what those eyes did to her? They helped, though. She was back again now, safe. She could move on. If she could focus on something other than those eyes.

'So I'm assuming you're Spanish, too?' she managed.

'No!'

'You're not Spanish?'

'Absolutely not.'

'You sound Spanish.' Then she hesitated. Here was another reason she hadn't told him about her heritage—she wasn't sure. There was something else in his accent besides Spain. France? It was a sexy mix that she couldn't quite place.

'I come from Cepheus,' he said, and all was explained.

Cepheus. She knew it. A tiny principality on the Mediterranean, fiercely independent and fiercely proud.

'My father told me about Cepheus,' she said, awed that here was an echo from her childhood. 'Papà was born not so far away from the border and he went there as a boy. He said it's the most beautiful country in the world—but he also said it belonged to Spain.'

'If he's Spanish then he would say that,' Ramón

growled. 'If he was French he'd say the same thing. They've been fighting over my country for generations, like eagles over a small bird. What they've come to realize, however, is that the small bird has claws and knows how to protect itself. For now they've dropped us—they've let us be. We are Cepheus. Nothing more.'

'But you speak Spanish?'

'The French and the Spanish have both taken part of our language and made it theirs,' he said, and she couldn't help herself. She chuckled.

'What's funny?' He was suddenly practically glowering.

'Your patriotism,' she said, refusing to be deflected. 'Like Australians saying the English speak Australian with a plum in their mouths.'

'It's not the same,' he said but then he was smiling again. She smiled back—and wham.

What was it with this man?

She knew exactly what it was. Quite simply he was the most gorgeous guy she'd ever met. Tall, dark and fabulous, a voice like a god, rugged, clever...and smiling. She took a deep breath and went back to really focused scrubbing. It was imperative that she scrub.

She was alone on a boat in the middle of the ocean with a man she was so attracted to her toes were practically ringlets. And she was crew. Nothing more. She was cook and deckhand. Remember it!

'So why the debt?' he asked gently, and she forgot about being cook and deckhand. He was asking as if he cared.

Should she tell him to mind his own business? Should she back away?

Why? He'd been extraordinarily kind and if he wanted to ask… He didn't feel like her boss, and at this moment she didn't feel like a deckie.

Maybe he even had the right to know.

'I lost my baby,' she said flatly, trying to make it sound as if it was history. Only of course she couldn't. Two years on, it still pierced something inside her to say it. 'Matty was born with a congenital heart condition. He had a series of operations, each riskier than the last. Finally, there was only one procedure left to try—a procedure so new it cost the earth. It was his last chance and I had to take it, but of course I'd run out of what money I had. I was working for Charlie for four hours a day over the lunch time rush—Matty was in hospital and I hated leaving him but I had to pay the rent, so when things hit rock bottom Charlie knew. So Charlie loaned me what I needed on the basis that I keep working on for him.'

She scrubbed fiercely at a piece of deck that had already been scrubbed. Ramón didn't say anything. She scrubbed a bit more. Thought about not saying more and then decided—why not say it all?

'You need to understand…I'd been cooking on the

docks since I was seventeen and people knew my food. Charlie's café was struggling and he needed my help to keep it afloat. But the operation didn't work. Matty died when he was two years, three months and five days old. I buried him and I went back to Charlie's café and I've been there ever since.'

'I am so sorry.' Ramón was sitting back on his heels and watching her. She didn't look up—she couldn't. She kept right on scrubbing.

The boat rocked gently on the swell. The sun shone down on the back of her neck and she was acutely aware of his gaze. So aware of his silence.

'Charlie demanded that you leave your baby, for those hours in the last days of his life?' he said at last, and she swallowed at that, fighting back regret that could never fade.

'It was our deal.' She hesitated. 'You've seen the worst of Charlie. Time was when he was a decent human being. Before the drink took over. When he offered me a way out—I only saw the money. I guess I just trusted. And after I borrowed the money there was no way out.'

'So where,' he asked, in his soft, lilting accent that seemed to have warmth and sincerity built into it, 'was Matty's father?'

'On the other side of the world, as far as I know,' she said, and she blinked back self-pity and found herself smiling. 'My Kieran. Or, rather, no one's Kieran.'

'You're smiling?' He sounded incredulous, as well he might.

'Yes, that's stupid. And yes, I was really stupid.' Enough with the scrubbing—any more and she'd start taking off wood. She tossed her brush into the bucket and stood up, leaning against the rail and letting the sun comfort her. How to explain Kieran? 'My father had just died, and I was bleak and miserable. Kieran came into port and he was just… alive. I met him on the wharf one night, we went dancing and I fell in love. Only even then I knew I wasn't in love with Kieran. Not with the person. I was in love with what he represented. Happiness. Laughter. Life. At the end of a wonderful week he sailed away and two weeks later I discovered our precautions hadn't worked. I emailed him to tell him. He sent me a dozen roses and a cheque for a termination. The next time I emailed, to tell him I was keeping our baby, there was no reply. There's been no reply since.'

'Do you mind?' he said gently.

'I mind that Kieran didn't have a chance to meet his son,' she said. 'It was his loss. Matty was wonderful.' She pulled herself together and managed to smile again. 'But I'd imagine all mothers say that about their babies. Any minute now I'll be tugging photographs out of my purse.'

'It would be my privilege to see them.'

'You don't mean that.'

'Why would I not?'

Her smile faded. She searched his face and saw only truth.

'It's okay,' she said, disconcerted. She was struggling to understand this man. She'd accepted this job suspecting he was another similar to Kieran, sailing the world to escape responsibility, only the more she saw of him the more she realized there were depths she couldn't fathom.

She had armour now to protect herself against the likes of Kieran. She knew she did—that was why she'd taken the job. But this man's gentle sympathy and practical help were something new. She tried to imagine Kieran scrubbing a deck when he didn't have to, and she couldn't.

'So where's your family?' she asked, too abruptly, and she watched his face close. Which was what she was coming to expect. He'd done this before to her, simply shutting himself off from her questions. She thought it was a method he'd learned from years of employing casual labour, setting boundaries and staying firmly behind them.

Maybe that was reasonable, she conceded. Just because she'd stepped outside her personal boundaries, it didn't mean he must.

'Sorry. I'll put the buckets away,' she said, but he didn't move and neither did she.

'I don't like talking of my family.'

'That's okay. That's your right.'

'You didn't have to tell me about your son.'

'Yes, but I like talking about Matty,' she said. She thought about it. It wasn't absolutely true. Or was it?

She only talked about Matty to Cathy, to Susie, to those few people who'd known him. But still…

'Talking about him keeps him real,' she said, trying to figure it out as she spoke. 'Keeping silent locks him in my heart and I'm scared he'll shrivel. I want to be able to have him out there, to share him.' She shrugged. 'It makes no sense but there it is. Your family…you keep them where you need to have them. I'm sorry I intruded.'

'I don't believe you could ever intrude,' he said, so softly she could hardly hear him. 'But my story's not so peaceful. My father died when I was seven. He and my grandfather…well, let's just say they didn't get on. My grandfather was what might fairly be described as a wealthy thug. He mistreated my grandmother appallingly, and finally my father thought to put things right by instigating legal proceedings. Only when it looked like my father and grandmother might win, my grandfather's thugs bashed him—so badly he died.'

'Oh, Ramón,' she whispered, appalled.

'It's old history,' he said in a voice that told her it wasn't. It still had the power to hurt. 'Nothing could ever be proved, so we had to move on as best we could. But my grandmother never got over it. She died when I was ten, and then my mother and my sister were killed in a car accident when I was little more than a teenager. So that's my family. Or, rather, that was my family. I have an aunt I love, but that's all.'

'So you don't have a home,' she said softly.

'The sea makes a wonderful mistress.'

'She's not exactly cuddly,' Jenny retorted before she thought it through, and then she heard what she'd said and she could have kicked herself. But it seemed her tongue was determined to keep her in trouble. 'I mean… Well, the sea. A *mistress*? Wouldn't you rather have a real one?'

His lips twitched. 'You're asking why don't I have a woman?'

'I didn't mean that at all,' she said, astounded at herself. 'If you don't choose to…'

But she stopped herself there. She was getting into deeper water at every word and she was floundering.

'Would you rate yourself as cuddly?' he asked, a slight smile still playing round his mouth, and she felt herself colouring from the toes up. She'd walked straight into that one.

He thoroughly disconcerted her. It was as if there was some sort of connection between them, like an electric current that buzzed back and forth, no matter how she tried to subdue it.

She had to subdue it. Ramón was her boss. She had to maintain a working relationship with him for a year.

'No. No!' She shook her head so hard the tie came loose and her curls went flying every which way. 'Of course I'm not cuddly. I got myself in one horrible mess with Kieran, and I'm not going down that path again, thank you very much.'

'So maybe the sea is to be your partner in life, too?'

'I don't want a partner,' she said with asperity. 'I don't need one, thank you very much. You're very welcome to your sea, Mr Cavellero, but I'll stick to cooking, sailing and occasional scrubbing. What more could a woman want? It sounds like relationships, for both of us, are a thing of the past.' And then she paused. She stared out over Ramón's shoulder. 'Oh!' She put her hand up to shade her eyes. 'Oh, Ramón, look!'

Ramón wheeled to see what she was seeing, and he echoed her gasp.

They'd been too intent on each other to notice their surroundings—the sea was clear to the horizon so there was no threat, but suddenly there was a great black mound, floating closer and closer to the *Marquita*. On the far side of the mound was another, much smaller.

The smaller mound was gliding through the water, surfacing and diving, surfacing and diving. The big mound lay still, like a massive log, three-quarters submerged.

'Oh,' Jenny gasped, trying to take in what she was seeing. 'It's a whale and its calf. But why…'

Why was the larger whale so still?

They were both staring out to starboard now. Ramón narrowed his eyes, then swore and made his way swiftly aft. He retrieved a pair of field glasses, focused and swore again.

'She's wrapped in a net.' He flicked off the auto-pilot. 'Jenny, we're coming about.'

The boat was already swinging. Jenny dropped her buckets and moved like lightning, reefing in the main with desperate haste so the boom wouldn't slam across with the wind shift.

Even her father wouldn't have trusted her to move so fast, she thought, as she winched in the stays with a speed even she hadn't known was possible. Ramón expected the best of her and she gave it.

But Ramón wasn't focused on her. All his attention was on the whale. With the sails in place she could look again at what was in front of her. And what she saw… She drew in her breath in distress.

The massive whale—maybe fifty feet long or more—was almost completely wrapped in a damaged shark net. Jenny had seen these nets. They were set up across popular beaches to keep swimmers safe, but occasionally whales swam in too close to shore and became entangled, or swam into a net that had already been dislodged.

The net was enfolding her almost completely, with a rope as thick as Jenny's wrist tying her from head to tail, forcing her to bend. As the *Marquita* glided past, Jenny saw her massive pectoral fins were fastened uselessly to her sides. She was rolling helplessly in the swell.

Dead?

No. Just as she thought it, the creature gave a massive shudder. She was totally helpless, and by her side her calf swam free, but helpless as well in the shadow of her mother's entrapment.

'*Dios*,' she whispered. It was the age-old plea she'd learned from her mother, and she heard the echo of it from Ramón's lips.

'It's a humpback,' she said in distress. 'The net's wrapped so tight it's killing her. What can we do?'

But Ramón was already moving. 'We get the sails down and start the motor,' he said. 'The sails won't give us room to manoeuvre. Gianetta, I need your help. Fast.'

He had it. The sails were being reefed in almost before he finished speaking, as the motor hummed seamlessly into life.

He pushed it into low gear so the sound was a low hum. The last thing either of them wanted was to panic the whale. As it was, the calf was moving nervously away from them, so the mother was between it and the boat.

'If she panics there's nothing we can do,' Jenny said grimly. 'Can we get near enough to cut?'

They couldn't. Ramón edged the *Marquita* close,

the big whale rolled a little, the swell separated them and Jenny knew they could never simply reach out and cut.

'Can we call someone?' she said helplessly. 'There's whale rescue organisations. Maybe they could come out.'

'We're too far from land,' Ramón said. 'It's us or no one.'

No one, Jenny thought as they tried one more pass. It was hopeless. For them to cut the net the whale had to be right beside the boat. With the lurching of the swell there was no way they could steer the boat alongside and keep her there.

How else to help? To get into the water and swim, then cling and cut was far, far too risky. Jenny was a good swimmer but...

'It's open water, the job's too big, there's no way I could count on getting back into the boat,' Ramón said, and she knew he was thinking the same.

'You would do it if you could?' she asked, incredulous.

'If I knew it'd be effective. But do you think she's going to stay still while I cut? If she rolled, if I was pushed under and caught...'

As if on cue, the whale rolled again. Her massive pectoral fins were fastened hard against her, so a sideways roll was all she could do. She blew—a spray of water misted over Jenny's face, but Jenny's face was wet anyway.

'We can't leave her like this,' she whispered. 'We have to try.'

'We do,' Ramón said. 'Jenny, are you prepared to take a risk?'

There was no question. 'Of course.'

'Okay,' he said, reaching under the seat near the wheel and hauling out life jackets. 'Here's the plan. We put these on. We unfasten the life raft in case worst comes to worst and we let the authorities know what's happening. We radio in our position, we tell them what we intend to do and if they don't hear back from us then they'll know we're sitting in a life raft in the middle of the Pacific. We're wearing positional locators anyway. We should be fine.'

'What…what are we intending to do?' Jenny asked faintly.

'Pull the boat up beside the whale,' he said. 'If you're brave enough.'

She stared at him, almost speechless. How could he get so close? And, even if he did, if the whale rolled… 'You'd risk the boat?' she gasped.

'Yes.' Unequivocal.

'Could we be sure of rescue?'

'I'll set it up so we would be,' he said. 'I'm not risking our lives here. Only our boat and the cost of marine rescue.'

'Marine rescue… It'd cost a fortune.'

'Jenny, we're wasting time. Yes or no?'

She looked out at the whale. Left alone, she'd die,

dreadfully, agonisingly and, without her, her calf would slowly starve to death as well.

Ramón was asking her to risk all. She looked at him and he met her gaze, levelly and calmly.

'Gianetta, she's helpless,' he said. 'I believe at some subliminal level she'll understand we're trying to help and she won't roll towards us. But you know I can't guarantee that. There's a small chance we may end up sitting in a lifeboat for the next few hours waiting to be winched to safety. But I won't do it unless I have your agreement. It's not my risk, Gianetta. It's our risk.'

Our risk.

She thought about what he was asking—what he was doing. He'd have to explain to his owner that he'd lost his boat to save a whale. He'd lose his job at the very least. Maybe he'd be up for massive costs, for the boat and for rescue.

She looked at him and she saw it meant nothing.

He was free, she thought, with a sudden stab of something that could almost be jealousy. There was the whale to be saved. He'd do what needed to be done without thinking of the future.

Life… That was all that mattered, she thought suddenly, and with it came an unexpected lifting of the dreariness of the last couple of years. She'd fought long and hard for Matty. She'd lost but she'd had him and she'd loved him and she'd worried about the cost later.

She looked out at the whale and she knew there was only one answer to give.

'Of course,' she said. 'Just give me a couple of minutes to stick a ration pack in the life raft. If I'm going to float around for a day or so waiting for rescue flights then I want at least two bottles of champagne and some really good cheeses while I'm waiting.'

Jenny didn't have a clue what Ramón intended, but when she saw she was awed. With his safeguards in place, he stood on the highest point of the boat with a small anchor—one he presumably used in shallow waters when lowering the massive main anchor would potentially damage the sea bed.

This anchor was light enough for a man to hold. Or, rather, for Ramón to hold, Jenny corrected herself. It still looked heavy. But Ramón stood with the anchor attached by a long line and he held it as if it was no weight at all, while Jenny nosed the boat as close to the whale as she dared. Ramón swung the anchor round and round, in wider and wider circles, and then he heaved with every ounce of strength he had.

The whale was maybe fifteen feet from the boat. The anchor flew over the far side of her and slid down. As it slid, Ramón was already striding aft, a far more secure place to manoeuvre, and he was starting to tug the rope back in.

'Cut the motor,' he snapped. She did, and finally she realized what he was doing.

The anchor had fallen on the far side of the whale. As Ramón tugged, the anchor was being hauled up the whale's far side. Its hooks caught the ropes of the net and held, and suddenly Ramón was reeling in the anchor with whale attached. Or, rather, the *Marquita* was being reeled in against the whale, and the massive creature was simply submitting.

Jenny was by Ramón's side in an instant, pulling with him. Boat and whale moved closer. Closer still.

'Okay, hold her as close as you can,' Ramón said curtly as the whale's vast body came finally within an arm's length. 'If she pulls, you let go. No heroics, Gianetta, just do it. But keep tension on the rope so I'll know as soon as I have it free.'

Ramón had a lifeline clipped on. He was leaning over the side, with a massive gutting knife in his hand. Reaching so far Jenny was sure he'd fall.

The whale could roll this way, she thought wildly, and if she did he could be crushed. He was supporting himself on the whale itself, his legs still on the boat, but leaning so far over he was holding onto the netting. Slicing. Slicing. As if the danger was nothing.

She tugged on. If the whale pulled away, she'd have to release her. They'd lose the anchor. They had this one chance. Please…

But the whale didn't move, except for the steady rise and fall of the swell, where Jenny had to let out, reel in, let out, reel in, to try and keep Ramón's base steady against her.

He was slicing and slicing and slicing, swearing and slicing some more, until suddenly the tension on Jenny's rope was no longer there. The anchor lifted free, the net around the whale's midriff dislodged. Jenny, still pulling, was suddenly reeling in a mass of netting and an anchor.

And Ramón was back in the boat, pulling with her.

One of the whale's fins was free. The whale moved it a little, stretching, and she floated away. Not far. Twenty feet, no more.

The whale stilled again. One fin was not enough. She was still trapped.

On the far side of her, her calf nudged closer.

'Again,' Ramón said grimly as Jenny gunned the motor back into action and nosed close. He was already on top of the cabin, swinging the anchor rope once more. 'If she'll let us.'

'You'll hit the calf,' she said, almost to herself, and then bit her tongue. Of all the stupid objections. She knew what his answer must be.

'It's risk the calf having a headache, or both of them dying. No choice.'

But he didn't need to risk. As the arcs of the swinging anchor grew longer, the calf moved away again.

As if it knew.

And, once again, Ramón caught the net.

It took an hour, maybe longer, the times to catch the net getting longer as the amount of net left to cut off grew smaller. But they worked on, reeling her in, slicing, reeling her in, slicing, until the netting was a massive pile of rubbish on the deck.

Ramón was saving her, Jenny thought dazedly as she worked on. Every time he leaned out he was risking his life. She watched him work—and she fell in love.

She was magnificent. Ramón was working fever-ishly, slashing at the net while holding on to the rails and stretching as far as he could, but every moment he did he was aware of Jenny.

Gianetta.

She had total control of the anchor rope, somehow holding the massive whale against the side of the boat. But they both knew that to hold the boat in a fixed hold would almost certainly mean capsizing. What Jenny had to do was to work with the swells, holding the rope fast, then loosening it as the whale rose and the boat swayed, or the whale sank and the boat rose. Ramón had no room for anything but holding on to the boat and slashing but, thanks to Jenny, he had an almost stable platform to work with.

Tied together, boat and whale represented

tonnage he didn't want to think about, especially as he was risking slipping between the two.

He wouldn't slip. Jenny was playing her part, reading the sea, watching the swell, focused on the whale in case she suddenly decided to roll or pull away...

She didn't. Ramón could slash at will at the rope entrapment, knowing Jenny was keeping him safe.

He slipped once and he heard her gasp. He felt her hand grip his ankle.

He righted himself—it was okay—but the memory of her touch stayed.

Gianetta was watching out for him.

Gianetta. Where had she come from, this magical Gianetta?

It was working. Jenny was scarcely breathing. Please, please...

But somehow her prayers were being answered. Piece by piece the net was being cut away. Ramón was winning. They were both winning.

The last section to be removed was the netting and the ropes trapping and tying the massive tail, but catching this section was the hardest. Ramón threw and threw, but each time the anchor slipped uselessly behind the whale and into the sea.

To have come so far and not save her... Jenny felt sick.

But Ramón would not give up. His arm must be

dropping off, she thought, but just as she reached the point where despair took over, the whale rolled. She stretched and lifted her tail as far as she could within the confines of the net, and in doing so she made a channel to trap the anchor line as Ramón threw. And her massive body edged closer to the boat.

Ramón threw again, and this time the anchor held.

Once more Jenny reeled her in and once more Ramón sliced. Again. Again. One last slash—and the last piece of rope came loose into his hands.

Ramón staggered back onto the deck and Jenny was hauling the anchor in one last time. He helped her reel it in, then they stood together in the mass of tangled netting on the deck, silent, awed, stunned, as the whale finally floated free. Totally free. The net was gone.

But there were still questions. Were they too late? Had she been trapped too long?

Ramón's arm came round Jenny's waist and held, but Jenny was hardly aware of it. Or maybe she was, but it was all part of this moment. She was breathing a plea and she knew the plea was echoing in Ramón's heart as well as her own.

Please…

The whale was wallowing in the swell, rolling up and down, up and down. Her massive pectoral fins were free now. They moved stiffly outward, upward, over and over, while Jenny and Ramón held their breath and prayed.

The big tail swung lazily back and forth; she seemed to be stretching, feeling her freedom. Making sure the ropes were no longer there.

'She can't have been caught all that long,' Jenny whispered, breathless with wonder. 'Look at her tail. That rope was tied so tightly but there's hardly a cut.'

'She might have only just swum into it,' Ramón said and Jenny was aware that her awe was echoed in his voice. His arm had tightened around her and it seemed entirely natural. This was a prayer shared. 'If it was loosened from the shore by a storm it might have only hit her a day or so ago. The calf looks healthy enough.'

The calf was back at its mother's side now, nudging against her flank. Then it dived, straight down into the deep, and Jenny managed a faltering smile.

'He'll be feeding. She must still have milk. Oh, Ramón…'

'Gianetta,' Ramón murmured back, and she knew he was feeling exactly what she was feeling. Awe, hope, wonder. They might, they just might, have been incredibly, wondrously lucky.

And then the big whale moved. Her body seemed to ripple. Everything flexed at once, her tail, her fins… She rolled away, almost onto her back, as if to say to her calf: *No feeding, not yet, I need to figure if I'm okay.*

And figure she did. She swam forward in front of the boat, speeding up, speeding up. Faster, faster she swam, with her calf speeding after her.

And then, just as they thought they'd lost sight of her, she came sweeping back, a vast majestic mass of glossy black muscle and strength and bulk. Then, not a hundred yards from the boat, she rolled again, only higher, so her body was half out of the water, stretching, arching back, her pectoral fins outstretched, then falling backward with a massive splash that reached them on the boat and soaked them to the skin.

Neither of them noticed. Neither of them cared.

The whale was sinking now, deep, so deep that only a mass of still water on the surface showed her presence. Then she burst up one more time, arched back once more—and she dived once more and they saw her print on the water above as she adjusted course and headed for the horizon, her calf tearing after her.

Two wild creatures returned to the deep.

Tears were sliding uselessly down Jenny's face. She couldn't stop them, any more than she could stop smiling. And she looked up at Ramón and saw his smile echo hers.

'We did it,' she breathed. 'Ramón, we did it.'

'We did,' he said, and he tugged her hard against

him, then swung her round so he was looking into her tear-stained face. 'We did it, Gianetta, we saved our whale. And you were magnificent. Gianetta, you may be a Spanish-Australian woman in name but I believe you have your nationality wrong. A woman like you… I believe you're worthy of being a woman of Cepheus.'

And then, before she knew what he intended, before she could guess anything at all, he lifted her into his arms and he kissed her.

CHAPTER FOUR

ONE moment she was gazing out at the horizon, catching the last shimmer of the whale's wake on the translucence of the sea. The next she was being kissed as she'd never been kissed in her life.

His hands were lifting her, pulling her hard in against him so her feet barely touched the deck. His body felt rock-hard, the muscled strength he'd just displayed still at work, only now directed straight at her. Straight with her.

The emotions of the rescue were all around her. He was wet and wild and wonderful. She was soaking as well, and the dripping fabric of his shirt and hers meant their bodies seemed to cling and melt.

It felt right. It felt meant. It felt as if there was no room or sense to argue.

His mouth met hers again, his arms tightening around her so she was locked hard against him. He was so close she could feel the rapid beat of his heart. Her breasts were crushed against his chest, her face had tilted instinctively, her mouth was caught…

Caught? Merged, more like. Two parts of a whole finding their home.

He tugged her tighter, tighter still against him, moulding her lips against his. She was hard against him, closer, closer, feeling him, tasting him, wanting him…

To be a part of him seemed suddenly as natural, as right, as breathing. To be kissed by this man was an extension of what had just happened.

Or maybe it was more than that. Maybe it was an extension of the whole of the last week.

Maybe she'd wanted this from the moment she'd seen him.

Either way, she certainly wasn't objecting now. She heard herself give a tiny moan, almost a whimper, which was stupid because she didn't feel the least like whimpering. She felt like shouting, *Yes!*

His mouth was demanding, his tongue was searching for an entry, his arms holding her so tightly now he must surely bruise. But he couldn't hold her tight enough. She was holding him right back, desperate that she not be lowered, desperate that this miraculous contact not be lost.

He felt so good. He felt as if he was meant to be right here in her arms. That she'd been destined for this moment for ever and it had taken this long to find him.

He hadn't shaved this morning. She could feel the stubble on his jaw, she could almost taste it. There was salt on his face—of course there was, he'd been practically submerged, over and over. He smelled of salt and sea, and of pure testosterone.

He tasted of Ramón.

'Ramón.' She heard herself whisper his name, or maybe it was in her heart, for how could she possibly whisper when he was kissing as if he was a man starved for a woman, starved of *this* woman? She knew so clearly what was happening, and she accepted it with elation. This woman was who he wanted and he'd take her, he wanted her, she was his and he was claiming his own.

Like the whale rolling joyously in the sea, she thought, dazed and almost delirious, this was nature; it was right, it was meant.

She was in his arms and she wasn't letting go. Ramón.

'Gianetta…' His voice was ragged with heat and desire. Somehow he dragged himself back from her and held her at arm's length. 'Gianetta, *mia*…'

'If you're asking if I want you, then the answer's yes,' she said huskily, and almost laughed at the look of blazing heat that came straight back at her. His eyes were almost black, gleaming with tenderness and want and passion. But something else. He wouldn't take her yet. His eyes were searching.

'I'll take no woman against her will,' he growled.

'You think…you think this is against my will?' she whispered, as the blaze of desire became almost white-hot and she pressed herself against him, forcing him to see how much this was not the case.

'Gianetta,' he sighed, and there was laughter now as well as wonder and desire. Before she could respond he had her in his arms, held high, cradled against him, almost triumphant.

'You don't think maybe we should set the automatic pilot or something?' she murmured. 'We'll drift.'

'The radar will tell us if we're about to hit something big,' he said, his dark eyes gleaming. 'But it can't pick up things like jellyfish, so there's a risk. You want to risk death by jellyfish and come to my bed while we wait, my Gianetta?'

And what was a girl to say to an invitation like that?

'Yes, please,' she said simply and he kissed her and he held her tight and carried her down below.

To his bed. To his arms. To his pleasure.

'She left port six days ago, heading for New Zealand.'

The lawyer stared at the boat builder in consternation. 'You're sure? The *Marquita*?'

'That's the one. The guy skippering her—

Ramón, I think he said his name was—had her in dry dock here for a couple of days, checking the hull, but she sailed out on the morning tide on Monday. Took the best cook in the bay with him, too. Half the locals are after his blood. He'd better look after our Jenny.'

But the lawyer wasn't interested in Ramón's staff. He stood on the dock and stared out towards the harbour entrance as if he could see the *Marquita* sailing away.

'You're sure he was heading for Auckland?'

'I am. You're Spanish, right?'

'Cepheus country,' the lawyer said sharply. 'Not Spain. But no matter. How long would it take the *Marquita* to get to Auckland?'

'Coupla weeks,' the boat builder told him. 'Can't see him hurrying. I wouldn't hurry if I had a boat like the *Marquita* and Jenny aboard.'

'So if I go to Auckland…'

'I guess you'd meet him. If it's urgent.'

'It's urgent,' the lawyer said grimly. 'You have no idea how urgent.'

There was no urgency about the *Marquita*. If she took a year to reach Auckland it was too soon for Jenny.

Happiness was right now.

They could travel faster, but that would mean sitting by the wheel hour after hour, setting the sails to catch the slightest wind shift, being sailors.

Instead of being lovers.

She'd never felt like this. She'd melted against Ramón's body the morning of the whales and she felt as if she'd melted permanently. She'd shape shifted, from the Jenny she once knew to the Gianetta Ramón loved.

For that was what it felt like. Loved. For the first time in her life she felt truly beautiful, truly desirable—and it wasn't just for her body.

Yes, he made love to her, over and over, wonderful lovemaking that made her cry out in delight.

But more.

He wanted to know all about her.

He tugged blankets up on the deck. They lay in the sun and they solved the problems of the world. They watched dolphins surf in their wake. They fished. They compared toes to see whose little toe bent the most.

That might be ridiculous but there was serious stuff, too. Ramón now knew all about her parents, her life, her baby. She told him everything about Matty, she showed him pictures and he examined each of them with the air of a man being granted a privilege.

When Matty was smiling, Ramón smiled. She watched this big man respond to her baby's smile and she felt her heart twist in a way she'd never thought possible.

He let the boom net down off the rear deck, and

they surfed behind the boat, and when the wind came up it felt as if they were flying. They worked the sails as a team, setting them so finely that they caught up on time lost when they were below, lost in each other's bodies.

He touched her and her body reacted with fire.

Don't fall in love. Don't fall in love. It was a mantra she said over and over in her head, but she knew it was hopeless. She was hopelessly lost.

It wouldn't last. Like Kieran, this man was a nomad, a sailor of no fixed address, going where the wind took him.

He talked little about himself. She knew there'd been tragedy, the sister he'd loved, parents he'd lost, pain to make him shy from emotional entanglement.

Well, maybe she'd learned that lesson, too. So savour the moment, she told herself. For now it was wonderful. Each morning she woke in Ramón's arms and she thought: Ramón had employed her for a year! When they got back to Europe conceivably the owner would join them. She could go back to being crew. But Ramón would be crew as well, and the nights were long, and owners never stayed aboard their boats for ever.

'Tell me about the guy who owns this boat,' she said, two days out of Auckland and she watched a shadow cross Ramón's face. She was starting to know him so well—she watched him when he didn't know it—his strongly boned, aquiline face, his hooded eyes, the smile lines, the weather lines from years at sea.

What had suddenly caused the shadow?

'He's rich,' he said shortly. 'He trusts me. What else do you need to know?'

'Well, whether he likes muffins, for a start,' she said, with something approaching asperity, which was a bit difficult as she happened to be entwined in Ramón's arms as she spoke and asperity was a bit hard to manage. Breathless was more like it.

'He loves muffins,' Ramón said.

'He'll be used to richer food than I can cook. Do you usually employ someone with special training?'

'He eats my cooking.'

'Really?' She frowned and sat up in bed, tugging the sheet after her. She'd seen enough of Ramón's culinary skills to know what an extraordinary statement this was. 'He's rich and he eats your cooking?'

'As I said, he'll love your muffins.'

'So when will you next see him?'

'Back in Europe,' Ramón said, and sighed. 'He'll have to surface then, but not now. Not yet. There's three months before we have to face the world. Do you think we can be happy for three months, *cariño*?' And he tugged her back down to him.

'If you keep calling me *cariño*,' she whispered. 'Are we really being paid for this?'

He chuckled but then his smile faded once more. 'You know it can't last, my love. I will need to move on.'

'Of course you will,' she whispered, but she only said it because it was the sensible, dignified thing to say. A girl had some pride.

Move on?

She never wanted to move on. If her world could stay on this boat, with this man, for ever, she wasn't arguing at all.

She slept and Ramón held her in his arms and tried to think of the future.

He didn't have to think. Not yet. It was three months before he was due to leave the boat and return to Bangladesh.

Three months before he needed to tell Jenny the truth.

She could stay with the boat, he thought, if she wanted to. He always employed someone to stay on board while he was away. She could take that role.

Only that meant Jenny would be in Cepheus while he was in Bangladesh.

He'd told her he needed to move on. It was the truth. Maybe she could come with him.

The idea hit and stayed. His team always had volunteers to act as manual labour. Would Jenny enjoy the physical demands of construction, of helping make life bearable for those who had nothing?

Maybe she would.

What was he thinking? He'd never considered taking a woman to Bangladesh. He'd never considered that leaving a woman behind seemed unthinkable.

Gianetta…

His arms tightened their hold and she curved closer in sleep. He smiled and kissed the top of her head. Her curls were so soft.

Maybe he could sound her out about Bangladesh.

Give it time, he told himself, startled by the direction his thoughts were taking him. You've known her for less than two weeks.

Was it long enough?

There was plenty of time after Auckland. It was pretty much perfect right now, he thought. Let's not mess with perfection. He'd just hold this woman and hope that somehow the love he'd always told himself was an illusion might miraculously become real.

Anything was possible.

'How do you know he'll sail straight to Auckland?'

In the royal palace of Cepheus, Sofía was holding the telephone and staring into the middle distance, seeing not the magnificent suits of armour in the grand entrance but a vision of an elderly lawyer pacing anxiously on an unknown dock half a world away. She could understand his anxiety. Things in the palace were reaching crisis point.

The little boy had gone into foster care yesterday. Philippe needed love, Sofía thought bleakly. His neglect here—all his physical needs met, but no love, little affection, just a series of disinterested nannies—seemed tantamount to child abuse, and the country knew of it. She'd found him lovely foster parents, but his leaving the palace was sending the wrong message to the population—as if Ramón himself didn't care for the child.

Did Ramón even know about him?

'I don't know for sure where the Prince will sail,' the lawyer snapped. 'But I can hope. He'll want to restock fast to get around the Horn. It makes sense for him to come here.'

'So you'll wait.'

'Of course I'll wait. What else can I do?'

'But there's less than two weeks to go,' Sofía wailed. 'What if he's delayed?'

'Then we have catastrophe,' the lawyer said heavily. 'He has to get here. Then he has to get back to Cepheus and accept his new life.'

'And the child?'

'It doesn't matter about the child.'

Yes, it does, Sofía thought. Oh, Ramón, what are you facing?

They sailed into Auckland Harbour just after dawn. Jenny stood in the bow, ready to jump across to shore with the lines, ready to help in any way she could with berthing the *Marquita*. Ramón was at the wheel. She glanced back at him and had a pang of misgivings.

They hadn't been near land for two weeks. Why did it feel as if the world was waiting to crowd in?

How could it? Their plan was to restock and be gone again. Their idyll could continue.

But they'd booked a berth with the harbour master. Ramón had spoken to the authorities an hour ago, and after that he'd looked worried.

'Problem?' she'd asked.

'Someone's looking for me.'

'Debt collectors?' she'd teased, but he hadn't smiled.

'I don't have debts.'

'Then who…?'

'I don't know,' he said, and his worry sounded as if it was increasing. 'No one knows where I am.'

'Conceivably the owner knows.'

'What…?' He caught himself. 'I…yes. But he won't be here. I can't think…'

That was all he'd said but she could see worry building.

She turned and looked towards the dock. She'd looked at the plan the harbour master had faxed through and from here she could see the berth that had been allocated to them.

There was someone standing on the dock, at the berth, as if waiting. A man in a suit.

It must be the owner, she thought.

She glanced back at Ramón and saw him flinch.

'Rodriguez,' he muttered, and in the calm of the early morning she heard him swear. 'Trouble.'

'Is he the boat's owner?'

'No,' he said shortly. 'He's legal counsel to the Crown of Cepheus. I've met him once or twice when he had business with my grandmother. If he's here… I hate to imagine what he wants of me.'

Señor Rodriguez was beside himself. He had ten days to save a country. He glanced at his watch as the *Marquita* sailed slowly towards her berth, fretting as if every second left was vital.

What useless display of skill was this, to sail into harbour when motoring would be faster? And why was the woman in the bow, rather than Ramón himself? He needed to talk to Ramón, now!

The boat edged nearer. 'Can you catch my line?' the woman called, and he flinched and moved backward. He knew nothing about boats.

But it seemed she could manage without him. She jumped lightly over a gap he thought was far too wide, landing neatly on the dock, then hauled the boat into position and made her fast as Ramón tugged down the last sail.

'Good morning,' the woman said politely, casting him a curious glance. And maybe she was justified in her curiosity. He was in his customary suit, which he acknowledged looked out of place here. The woman was in the uniform of the sea—faded shorts, a T-shirt and nothing else. She looked windblown and free. Momentarily, he was caught by how good she looked, but only for an instant. His attention returned to Ramón.

'Señor Rodriguez,' Ramón called to him, cautious and wary.

'You remember me?'

'Yes,' Ramón said shortly. 'What's wrong?'

'Nothing's wrong,' the lawyer said, speaking in the mix of French and Spanish that formed the Cepheus language. 'As long as you come home.'

'My home's on the *Marquita*. You know that.'

'Not any more it's not,' the lawyer said. 'Your uncle and your cousin are dead. As of four weeks ago, you're the Crown Prince of Cepheus.'

There was silence. Jenny went on making all secure while Ramón stared at the man on the dock as if he'd spoken a foreign language.

Which he had, but Jenny had been raised speaking Spanish like a native, and she'd picked up French at school. There were so many similarities in form she'd slipped into it effortlessly. Now... She'd missed the odd word but she understood what the lawyer had said.

Or she thought she understood what he'd said.

Crown Prince of Cepheus. Ramón.

It might make linguistic sense. It didn't make any other sort of sense.

'My uncle's dead?' Ramón said at last, his voice without inflexion.

'In a light plane crash four weeks ago. Your uncle, your cousin and your cousin's wife, all killed. Only there's worse. It seems your cousin wasn't really married—he brought the woman he called his wife home and shocked his father and the country by declaring he was married, but now we've searched for proof, we've found none. So the child, Philippe, who stood to be heir, is illegitimate. You stand next in line. But if you're not home in ten days then Carlos inherits.'

'Carlos!' The look of flat shock left Ramón's face, replaced by anger, pure and savage. 'You're saying Carlos will inherit the throne?'

'Not if you come home. You must see that's the only way.'

'No!'

'Think about it.'

'I've thought.'

'Leave the woman to tend the boat and come with me,' Señor Rodriguez said urgently. 'We need to speak privately.'

'The woman's name is Gianetta.' Ramón's anger seemed to be building. 'I won't leave her.'

The man cast an uninterested glance at Jenny, as

if she was of no import. Which, obviously, was the case. 'Regardless, you must come.'

'I can look after the boat,' Jenny said, trying really hard to keep up. *I won't leave her.* There was a declaration. But he obviously meant it for right now. Certainly not for tomorrow.

Crown Prince of Cepheus?

'There's immigration…' Ramón said.

'I can sort my papers out,' she said. 'The harbour master's office is just over there. You do what you have to do on the way to wherever you're going. Have your discussion and then come back and tell me what's happening.'

'Jenny…'

But she was starting to add things together in her head and she wasn't liking them. *Crown Prince of Cepheus.*

'I guess the *Marquita* would be *your* boat, then?' she asked flatly, and she saw him flinch.

'Yes, but…'

She felt sick. 'There you go,' she managed, fighting for dignity. 'The owner's needs always come first. I'll stow the sails and make all neat. Then I might go for a nice long walk and let off a little steam. I'll see you later.'

And Ramón cast her a glance where frustration, anger—and maybe even a touch of envy—were combined.

'If you can…'

'Of course I can,' she said, almost cordially. 'We're on land again. I can stand on my own two feet.'

There were complications everywhere, and all he could think of was Jenny. Gianetta. His woman.

The flash of anger he'd seen when he'd confessed that he did indeed own the *Marquita*; the look of betrayal…

She'd think he'd lied to her. She wouldn't understand what else was going on, but the lie would be there, as if in flashing neon.

Yes, he'd lied.

He needed to concentrate on the lawyer.

The throne of Cepheus was his.

Up until now there'd never been a thought of him inheriting. Neither his uncle nor his cousin, Cristián, had ever invited Ramón near the palace. He knew the country had been in dread of Cristián becoming Crown Prince but there was nothing anyone could do about it. Cristián had solidified his inheritance by marrying and having a child. The boy must be what, five?

For him to be proved illegitimate…

'I can't even remember the child's name,' he said across the lawyer's stream of explanations, and the lawyer cast him a reproachful glance.

'Philippe.'

'How old?'

'Five,' he confirmed.

'So what happens to Philippe?'

'Nothing,' the lawyer said. 'He has no rights. With his parents dead, your aunt has organized foster care, and if you wish to make a financial settlement on him I imagine the country will be relieved. There's a certain amount of anger…'

'You mean my cousin didn't make provision for his own son?'

'Your cousin and your uncle spent every drop of their personal incomes on themselves, on gambling, on…on whatever they wished. The Crown itself, however, is very wealthy. You, with the fortune your grandmother left you and the Crown to take care of your every need, will be almost indecently rich. But the child has nothing.'

He felt sick. A five-year-old child. To lose everything…

He'd been not much older than Philippe when he'd lost his own father.

It couldn't matter. It shouldn't be his problem. He didn't even know the little boy…

'I'll take financial care of the child,' Ramón said shortly. 'But I can't drop everything. I have twelve more weeks at sea and then I'm due in Bangladesh.'

'Your team already knows you won't be accompanying them this year,' the lawyer told him flatly, leaving no room for argument. 'And I've found an experienced yachtsman who's prepared to sail the *Marquita* back to Cepheus for you. We can be on a

flight tonight, and even that's not soon enough.'
Then, as the lawyer noticed Ramón's face—and
Ramón was making no effort to disguise his fury—
he added quickly, 'There's mounting hysteria over
the mess your uncle and cousin left, and there's
massive disquiet about Carlos inheriting.'

'As well there might be,' Ramón growled, trying
hard to stay calm. Ramón's distant cousin was an
indolent gamester, rotund, corrupt and inept. He'd
faced the court more than once, but charges had
been dropped, because of bribery? He wasn't close
enough to the throne to know.

'He's making noises that the throne should be
his. Blustering threats against you and your aunt.'

'Threats?' And there it was again, the terror he'd
been raised with. *Don't go near the throne. Ever!'*

'If the people rise against the throne…' the
lawyer was saying.

'Maybe that would be a good thing.'

'Maybe it'd be a disaster,' the man said, and proceeded to tell him why. At every word Ramón felt
his world disintegrate. There was no getting around
it—the country was in desperate need of a leader,
of some sort of stability…of a Crown Prince.

'So you see,' the lawyer said at last, 'you have to
come. Go back to the boat, tell the woman—she's
your only crew?—what's happening, pack your
bags and we'll head straight to the airport.'

And there was nothing left for him but to agree.

To take his place in a palace that had cost his family everything.

'Tomorrow,' he said, feeling ill.

'Tonight.'

'I will spend tonight with Gianetta,' Ramón growled, and the lawyer raised his brows.

'Like that?'

'Like nothing,' Ramón snapped. 'She deserves an explanation.'

'It's not as if you're sacking her,' the lawyer said. 'I've only hired one man to replace you. She'll still be needed. She can help bring the *Marquita* home and then you can pay her off.'

'I've already paid her.'

'Then there's no problem.' The lawyer rose and so did Ramón. 'Tonight.'

'Tomorrow,' Ramón snapped and looked at the man's face and managed a grim smile. 'Consider it my first royal decree. Book the tickets for tomorrow's flights.'

'But…'

'I will not argue,' Ramón said. 'I've a mind to wash my hands of the whole business and take *Marquita* straight back out to sea.' Then, at the wash of undisguised distress on the lawyer's face, he sighed and relented. 'But, of course, I won't,' he said. 'You know I won't. I will return with you to Cepheus. I'll do what I must to resolve this mess, I'll face Carlos down, but you will give me one more night.'

CHAPTER FIVE

SHE walked for four long hours, and then she found an Internet café and did some research. By the time she returned to the boat she was tired and hungry and her anger hadn't abated one bit.

Ramón was the Crown Prince of Cepheus. What sort of dangerous mess had she walked into?

She'd slept with a prince?

Logically, it shouldn't make one whit of difference that he was royal, but it did, and she felt used and stupid and very much like a star-struck teenager. All that was needed was the paparazzi. Images of headlines flashed through her head— *Crown Prince of Cepheus Takes Stupid, Naive Australian Lover*—and as she neared the boat she couldn't help casting a furtive glance over her shoulder to check the thought had no foundation.

It didn't—of course it didn't. There was only Ramón, kneeling on the deck, calmly sealing the ends of new ropes.

He glanced up and saw her coming. He smiled a welcome, but she was too sick at heart to smile back.

For a few wonderful days she'd let herself believe this smile could be for her.

She felt besmirched.

'I've just come back to get my things,' she said flatly before he had a chance to speak.

'You're leaving?' His eyes were calmly appraising.

'Of course I'm leaving.'

'To go where?'

'I'll see if I can get a temporary job here. As soon as I can get back to Australia I'll organize some way of repaying the loan.'

'There's no need for you to repay…'

'There's every need,' she flashed, wanting to stamp her foot; wanting, quite badly, to cry. 'You think I want to be in your debt for one minute more than I must? I've read about you on the Internet now. It doesn't matter whether anyone died or not. You were a prince already.'

'Does that make a difference?' he asked, still watchful, and his very calmness added to her distress.

'Of course it does. I've been going to bed with a *prince*,' she wailed, and the couple on board their cruiser in the next berth choked on their lunch time Martinis.

But Ramón didn't notice. He had eyes only for

her. 'You went to bed with me,' he said softly. 'Not with a prince.'

'You are a prince.'

'I'm just Ramón, Gianetta.'

'Don't Gianetta me,' she snapped. 'That's your bedroom we slept in. Not the owner's. Here I was thinking we were doing something illicit…'

'Weren't we?' he demanded and a glint of humour returned to his dark eyes.

'It was your bed all along,' she wailed and then, finally, she made a grab at composure. The couple on the next boat were likely to lose their eyes; they were out on stalks. Dignity, she told herself desperately. Please.

'So I own the boat,' he said. 'Yes, I'm a prince. What more do you know of me?'

'Apparently very little,' she said bitterly. 'I seem to have told you my whole life story. It appears you've only told me about two minutes of yours. Apparently you're wealthy, fabulously wealthy, and you're royal. The Internet bio was sketchy, but you spend your time either on this boat or fronting some charity organisation.'

'I do more than that.'

But she was past hearing. She was past wanting to hear. She felt humiliated to her socks, and one fact stood out above all the rest. *She'd never really known him.*

'So when you saw me you thought here's a little

more charity,' she threw at him, anger making her almost incoherent. 'I'll take this poverty-stricken, flour-streaked muffin-maker and show her a nice time.'

'A flour-streaked muffin-maker?' he said and, infuriatingly, the laughter was back. 'I guess if you want to describe yourself as that… Okay, fine, I rescued the muffin-maker. And we did have a nice time. No?'

But she wasn't going there. She was not being sucked into that smile ever again. 'I'm leaving,' she said, and she swung herself down onto the deck. She was heading below, but Ramón was before her, blocking her path.

'Jenny, you're still contracted to take my boat to Cepheus.'

'You don't need me…'

'You signed a contract. Yesterday, as I remember—and it was you who wanted it signed before we came into port.' His hands were on her shoulders, forcing her to meet his gaze, and her anger was suddenly matched with his. 'So you've been on the Internet. Do you understand why I have to return?'

And she did understand. Sort of. She'd read and read and read. 'It seems your uncle and cousin are dead,' she said flatly. 'There's a huge scandal because it seems your cousin wasn't married after all, so his little son can't inherit. So you get to be Crown Prince.' Even now, she couldn't believe she was saying it. *Crown Prince.* It was like some appalling twisted fairy tale. Kiss a frog, have him turn into a prince.

She wanted her frog back.

'I don't have a choice in this,' he said harshly. 'You need to believe that.' Before she could stop him, he put the back of his hand against her cheek and ran it down to her lips, a touch so sensuous that it made a shiver run right down to her toes. But there was anger behind the touch—and there was also... Regret? 'Gianetta, for you to go...'

'Of course I'm going,' she managed.

'And I need to let you go,' he said, and there was a depth of sadness behind his words that she couldn't begin to understand. 'But still I want you to take my boat home. Selfish or not, I want to see you again.'

Where was dignity when she needed it? His touch had sucked all the anger out of her. She wanted to hold on to this man and cling.

What was she thinking? No. This man was royalty, and he'd lied to her.

She had to find sense.

'I'm grabbing my things,' she said shortly, fighting for some semblance of calm. 'I'll be in touch about the money. I swear I won't owe you for any longer than absolutely necessary.'

'There's no need to repay...'

'There is,' she snapped. 'I pay my debts, even if they're to princes.'

'Can you stop calling me…'

'A prince? It's what you are and it's not new. It's not like this title's a shock to you. Yes, you seem to have inherited the Crown, and that's surprised you, but you were born a prince and you didn't tell me.'

'You didn't ask.'

'Right,' she said, fury building again. She shoved his hands away and headed below, whether he liked it or not. Ramón followed her and stood watching as she flung her gear into her carry-all.

Dignity was nowhere. The only thing she could cling to was her anger.

'So, Jenny, you think I should have introduced myself as Prince Ramón?' he asked at last, and the anger was still there. He was angry? What did that make her? Nothing, she thought bleakly. How could he be angry at her? She felt like shrivelling into a small ball and sobbing, but she had to get away from here first.

'You know what matters most?' she demanded, trying desperately to sort her thoughts into some sort of sense. 'That you didn't tell me you owned the boat. Maybe you didn't lie outright, but you had plenty of opportunities to tell me and you didn't. That's a lie in my books.'

'Would you have got on my boat if you thought I was the owner?'

There was only one answer to that. If he'd asked her and she'd known he was wealthy enough to afford such a boat—his wealth would have terrified her. 'No,' she admitted.

'So I wanted you to come with me.'

'Bully for you. And I did.' Cling to the anger, she told herself. It was all there was. If he was angry, she should be more so. She headed into the bathroom to grab her toiletries. 'I came on board and we made love and it was all very nice,' she threw over her shoulder. 'Now you've had your fun and you can go back to your life.'

'Being a prince isn't my life.'

'No?'

'Gianetta…'

'Jenny!'

'Jenny, then,' he conceded and the underlying anger in his voice intensified. 'I want you to listen.'

'I'm listening,' she said, shoving toiletries together with venom.

'Jenny, my grandfather was the Crown Prince of Cepheus.'

'I know that.'

'What you don't know,' he snapped, 'is that he was an arrogant, cruel womanizer. Jenny, I need you to understand this. My grandfather's marriage to my grandmother was an arranged one and he treated her dreadfully. When my father was ten my grandmother fell in love with a servant, and who can blame her? But my grandfather banished her and the younger children to a tiny island off the coast of Cepheus. He kept his oldest son, my uncle, at the palace, but my grandmother, my father and my aunt were never allowed back. My grandmother was royal in her own right. She had money of her own and all her life she ached to undo some of the appalling things my grandfather did, but when she tried…well, that's when my father died. And now, to be forced to go back…'

'I'm sorry you don't like it,' she said stiffly. What was he explaining this for? It had nothing to do with her. 'But your country needs you. At least now you'll be doing something useful.'

'Is that what you think?' he demanded, sounding stunned. 'That I spend my life doing nothing?'

'Isn't that the best job in the world?' She could feel the vibrations of his anger and it fed hers. *He'd known he was a prince.* 'The Internet bio says you're aligned to some sort of charity in Bangladesh,' she said shortly. 'I guess you can't be all bad.'

'Thanks.'

'Think nothing of it,' she said, and she thought, where did she go from here?

Away, her head told her, harshly and coldly. She needed to leave right now, and she would, but there were obligations. This man had got her out of a hole. He'd paid her debts. She owed him, deception or not.

'Okay, I'll be the first to admit I know nothing of your life,' she said stiffly. 'I felt like I knew you and now I realize I don't. That hurts. But I do need to thank you for paying my debt; for getting me away from Charlie. But now I'm just…scared. So I'll just get out of your life and let you get on with it.'

'You're scared?'

'What do you think?'

'There's no threat. There'd only be a threat if you were my woman.'

That was enough to take her breath away. *If you were my woman…*

'Which…which I'm not,' she managed.

'No,' he said, and there was bleakness as well as anger there now.

She closed her eyes. So what else had she expected? These two weeks had been a fairy tale. Nothing more.

Move on.

'Jenny, I have to do this,' he said harshly. 'Understand it or not, this is what I'm faced with. If I don't take the throne, then it goes to my father's cousin's son, Carlos. Carlos is as bad as my grandfather. He'd bring the country to ruin. And then there's the child. He's five. God knows…' He raked his hair with quiet despair. 'I will accept this responsibility. I must, even if it means walking away from what I most care about.'

And then there was silence, stretching towards infinity, where only emptiness beckoned.

What he most cared about? His boat? His charity work? What?

She couldn't think of what. She couldn't think what she wanted *what* to be.

'I'm sorry, Ramón,' she whispered at last.

'I'm sorry, too,' he said. He sighed and dug his hands deep into his pockets. Seemingly moving on. 'For what's between us needs to be put aside, for the sanity of both of us. But Gianetta…Jenny… What will you do in New Zealand?'

'Make muffins.' Her fury from his perceived betrayal was oozing away now, but there was nothing in its place except an aching void. Yesterday had seemed so wonderful. Today her sailor had turned into a prince and her bubble of euphoria was gone.

'Make muffins until you can afford to go back to Australia?'

'I don't have a lot of choice.'

'There is. Señor Rodriguez, the lawyer you met this morning, has already found someone prepared to skipper the *Marquita*—to bring her to Cepheus. I've already met him. He's a Scottish Australian, Gordon, ex-merchant navy. He's competent, solid and I know I can trust him with…with my boat. But he will need crew. So I'm asking you to stay on. I'm asking you if you'll sail round the Horn with him and bring the *Marquita* home. If you do that, I'll fly you back to Australia. Debt discharged.'

'It wouldn't be discharged.'

'I believe it would,' he said heavily. 'I'm asking you to sail round the Horn with someone you don't know, and I'm asking you to trust that I'll keep my word. That's enough of a request to make paying out your debt more than reasonable.'

'I don't want to.'

'Do you want to go back to cooking muffins?' He spread his hands and he managed a smile then, his wonderful, sexy, insinuating smile that had the power to warm every last part of her. 'And at least this way you'll get to see Cepheus, even if it's only for a couple of days before you fly home. And you'll have sailed around the Horn. You wanted to see the world. Give yourself a chance to see a little of it.' He hesitated. 'And, Jenny, maybe…we can have tonight?'

That made her gasp. After all that stood between them… What was he suggesting, that she spend one more night as the royal mistress? 'Are you crazy?'

'So not tonight?' His eyes grew bleak. 'No. I'm sorry, Gianetta. You and me… I concede it's impossible. But what is possible is that you remain on board the *Marquita* as crew. You allow me to continue employing you so you'll walk away at the end of three months beholden to nobody.'

No.

The word should have been shouted at him. She should walk away right now.

But to walk away for ever? How could she do that? And if she stayed on board….maybe a sliver of hope remained.

Hope for what? A Cinderella happy ending? What a joke. Ramón himself had said it was impossible.

But to walk away, from this boat as well as from this man… Cinders had fled at midnight. Maybe Cinders had more resolution than she did.

'I'll come back to the boat in the morning,' she whispered. 'If the new skipper wants to employ me and I think he's a man I can be at sea with for three months…'

'He's nothing like me,' Ramón said gently, almost bleakly. 'He's reliable and steady.'

'And not a prince?'

He gave a wintry smile. 'No, Gianetta, he's not a prince.'

'Then it might be possible.'

'I hope it will be possible.'

'No guarantees,' she said.

'You feel betrayed?'

'Of course I do,' she whispered. 'I need to go now.'

The bleakness intensified. He nodded. 'As you say. Go, my Gianetta, before I forget myself. I've learned this day that my life's not my own. But first… '

And, before she could guess what he was about, he made two swift strides across the room, took her shoulders in a grip of iron and kissed her. And such a kiss… It was fierce, it was possessive, it held anger and passion and desire. It was no kiss of farewell. It was a kiss that was all about his need, his desire, his ache to hold her to him for this night, and for longer still.

He was hungry for her, she thought, bewildered. She didn't know how real that hunger was, but when he finally put her away from him, when she finally broke free, she thought he was hurting as much as she was.

But hunger changed nothing, she thought bleakly. There was nothing left to say.

He stood silently by as she grabbed her carry-all and walked away, her eyes shimmering with unshed tears. He didn't try to stop her.

He was her Ramón, she thought bleakly. But he wasn't her prince.

He watched her go, walking along the docks carrying her holdall, her shoulders slumped, her body language that of someone weary beyond belief.

He felt as if he'd betrayed her.

So what to do? Go after her, lift her bodily into his arms?

Take her to Cepheus?

How could he?

There were threats from Carlos. The lawyer was talking of the possibility of armed insurrection against the throne. Had it truly become so bad?

His father had died because he hadn't realized the power of royalty. How could he drag a woman into this mess? It would be hard enough keeping himself afloat, let alone supporting anyone else.

How could he be a part of it himself—a royal family that had destroyed his family?

Jenny's figure was growing smaller in the distance. She wasn't pausing—she wasn't looking back.

He felt ill.

'So can we leave tonight?' He looked back and the lawyer was standing about twenty feet from the boat, calmly watching. 'I asked them to hold seats on tonight's flight as well as tomorrow.'

'You have some nerve.'

'The country's desperate,' the lawyer said simply. 'Nothing's been heard from you. Carlos is starting to act as if he's the new Crown Prince and his actions are provocative. Delay on your part may well mean bloodshed.'

'I don't want to leave her,' he said simply and turned back—but she'd turned a corner and was gone.

'I think the lady has left you,' the lawyer said gently. 'Which leaves you free to begin to govern your country. So, the flight tonight, Your Highness?'

'Fine,' Ramón said heavily and went to pack.

But fine was the last thing he was feeling.

* * *

His flight left that evening. He looked down from the plane and saw the boats in Auckland Harbour. The *Marquita* was down there with her new skipper on board. He couldn't make her out among so many. She was already dwindling to nothing as the plane rose and turned away from land.

Would Jenny join her tomorrow, he thought bleakly. Would she come to Cepheus?

He turned from the window with a silent oath. It shouldn't matter. What was between them was finished. Whether she broke her contract or not—there was nothing he could offer her.

Jenny was on her own, as was he.

His throne was waiting for him.

And two days later the *Marquita* slipped its moorings and sailed out of Auckland Harbour—with Jenny still on board. As she watched the harbour fade into the distance she felt all the doubts reassemble themselves. Gordon, her new skipper, seemed respectful of her silence and he let her be.

She was about to sail around the Horn. Once upon a time that prospect would have filled her with adrenalin-loaded excitement.

Now... She was simply fulfilling a contract, before she went home.

CHAPTER SIX

RAMÓN'S introduction to royal life was overwhelming. He walked into chaos. He walked into a life he knew nothing about. There were problems everywhere, but he'd been back in Cepheus for less than a day before the plight of Philippe caught him and held.

On his first meeting, the lawyer's introduction to the little boy was brief. 'This is Philippe.'

Philippe. His cousin's son. The little boy who should be Crown Prince, but for the trifling matter of a lack of wedding vows. Philippe, who'd had the royal surname until a month ago and was now not entitled to use it.

The little boy looked like the child Ramón remembered being. Philippe's pale face and huge eyes hinted that he was suffering as Ramón had suffered when his own father died, and as he met him for the first time he felt his gut wrench with remembered pain.

He'd come to see for himself what he'd been told—that the little boy was in the best care possible. Señor Rodriguez performed the introductions. Consuela and Ernesto were Philippe's foster parents, farmers who lived fifteen minutes' drive from the palace. The three were clearly nervous of what this meeting meant, but Philippe had been well trained.

'I am pleased to meet you,' the little boy said in a stilted little voice that spoke of rote learning and little else. He held out a thin little arm so his hand could be shaken, and Ramón felt him flinch as he took it in his.

Philippe's foster mother, a buxom farmer's wife exuding good-hearted friendliness, didn't seem intimidated by Ramón's title, or maybe she was, but her concern for Philippe came first. 'We've been hearing good things about you,' she told Ramón, scooping her charge into her arms so he could be on eye level with Ramón, ending the formality with this decisive gesture. 'This dumpling's been fearful of meeting you,' she told him. 'But Ernesto and I are telling him he should think of you as his big cousin. A friend. Isn't that right, Your Highness?'

She met Ramón's gaze almost defiantly, and Ramón could see immediately why Sofía had chosen Consuela as Philippe's foster mother. The image of a mother hen, prepared to battle any odds for her chick, was unmistakable. 'Philippe's homesick for the palace,' she said now, almost aggressively. 'And he misses his cat.'

'You have a cat?' Ramón asked.

'Yes,' Philippe whispered.

'There are many cats at the palace,' Señor Rodriguez said repressively from beside them, and Ramón sighed. What was it with adults? Hang on, he was an adult. Surely he could do something about this.

He must.

But he wasn't taking him back to the palace.

Memories were flooding back as he watched Philippe, memories of himself as a child. He vaguely remembered someone explaining that his grandmother wanted to return to the palace and his father would organize it—or maybe that explanation had come later. What he did remember was his father leading him into the vast grand entrance of the palace, Ramón clutching his father's hand as the splendour threatened to overwhelm him. 'There's nothing to be afraid of. It's time you met your grandfather and your uncle,' his father had told him.

His mother had said later that the decision to take him had been made, 'Because surely the Prince can't refuse his grandchild, a little boy who looks just like him.' But his mother had been wrong.

Not only had he been refused, some time in the night while Ramón lay in scared solitude, in a room far too grand for a child, somehow, some time, his father had died. He remembered not sleeping all night, and the next morning he remembered his grandfather, his icy voice laced with indifference to both his son's death and his grandson's solitary grief, snarling at the servants. 'Pack him up and get him out of here,' he'd ordered.

Pack him up and get him out of here... It was a dreadful decree, but how much worse would it have been if the Crown Prince had ordered him to stay? As he was being ordered to stay now.

Not Philippe, though. Philippe was free, if he could just be made happy with that freedom.

'Tell me about your cat,' he asked, trying a smile, and Philippe swallowed and swallowed again and made a manful effort to respond.

'He's little,' he whispered. 'The other cats fight him and he's not very strong. Something bit his ear. Papà doesn't permit me to take him inside, so he lives in the stables, but he comes when I call him. He's orange with a white nose.'

'Are there many orange cats with white noses at the palace?' Ramón asked, and for some reason the image of Jenny was with him strongly, urging him on. The little boy shook his head.

'Bebe's the only one. He's my friend.' He tilted his chin, obviously searching for courage for a confession. 'Sometimes I take a little fish from the kitchen when no one's looking. Bebe likes fish.'

'So he shouldn't be hard to find.' Ramón glanced at Consuela and Ernesto, questioningly. This place was a farm. Surely one cat...

'We like cats,' Consuela said, guessing where he was going. 'But Señor Rodriguez tells us the palace cats are wild. They're used to keep the vermin down and he says no one can catch one, much less tame one.'

'I'm sure we could tame him.' Ernesto, a wiry, weathered farmer, spoke almost as defiantly as his wife. 'If you, sir, or your staff, could try to catch him for us…'

'I'll try,' Ramón said. 'He's called Bebe, you say? My aunt has her cat at the palace now. She understands them. Let's see what we can do.'

Jenny would approve, he thought, as he returned to the palace, but he pushed the idea away. This was *his* challenge, as was every challenge in this place. It was nothing to do with Jenny.

As soon as he returned to the palace he raided the kitchens. Then he set off to the stables with a platter of smoked salmon. He set down the saucer and waited for a little ginger cat with a torn ear to appear. It took a whole three minutes.

Bebe wasn't wild at all. He stroked his ears and Bebe purred. He then shed ginger fur everywhere while he wrapped himself around Ramón's legs and the chair legs in the palace entrance and the legs of the footman on duty. Jenny would laugh, Ramón thought, but he shoved that thought away as well. Just do what comes next. *Do not think of Jenny.*

Bebe objected—loudly—to the ride in a crate on

the passenger seat of Ramón's Boxster, but he settled into life with Philippe—'as if Philippe's been sneaking him into his bed for the last couple of years,' Consuela told him, and maybe he had.

After that, Philippe regained a little colour, but he still looked haunted. He missed the palace, he confided, as Ramón tried to draw him out. In a world of adults who hadn't cared, the palace itself had become his stability.

Pack him up and get him out of here…

It made sense, Ramón thought. If the servants' reaction to Philippe was anything to go by, he'd be treated like illegitimate dirt in the palace. And then there was his main worry, or maybe it wasn't so much a worry but a cold, hard certainty.

There was so much to be done in this country that his role as Crown Prince overwhelmed him. He had to take it on; he had no choice, but in order to do it he must be clear-headed, disciplined, focused.

There was no link between love and duty in this job. He'd seen that spelled out with bleak cruelty. His grandmother had entered the palace through love, and had left it with her dreams and her family destroyed. His father had tried again to enter the palace, for the love of his mother, and he'd lost his life because of it. There were threats around him now, veiled threats, and who knew what else besides?

And the knowledge settled on his heart like grey

fog. To stay focused on what he must do, he could put no other person at risk. Sofia was staying until after the coronation. After that she'd leave and no one would be at risk but him. He'd have no distractions and without them maybe, just maybe, he could bring this country back to the prosperity it deserved.

But Philippe… And Jenny?

They'd get over it, he told himself roughly. Or Philippe would get over his grief and move on. Jenny must never be allowed to know that grief.

And once again he told himself harshly, this was nothing to do with Jenny. There'd never been a suggestion that they take things further. Nor could there be. This was his life and his life only, even if it was stifling.

This place was stifling. Nothing seemed to have changed since his grandfather's reign, or maybe since long before.

Lack of change didn't mean the palace had been allowed to fall into disrepair, though. Even though his grandfather and uncle had overspent their personal fortunes, the Crown itself was still wealthy, so pomp and splendour had been maintained. Furnishings were still opulent, rich paintings still covered the walls, the woodwork gleamed and the paintwork shone. The staff looked magnificent, even if their uniforms had been designed in the nineteenth century.

But the magnificence couldn't disguise the fact

that every one of the people working in this palace went about their duties with impassive faces. Any attempt by Ramón to penetrate their rigid facades was met with stony silence and, as the weeks turned into a month and then two, he couldn't make inroads into that rigidity.

The servants—and the country—seemed to accept him with passive indifference. He might be better than what had gone before, the newspapers declared, but he was still royal. Soon, the press implied, he'd become just like the others.

When he officially took his place as Crown Prince, he could make things better for the people of this county. He knew that, so he'd bear the opulence of the palace, the lack of freedom. He'd bear the formality and the media attention. He'd cope also with the blustering threats of a still furious Carlos; along with the insidious sense that threats like this had killed his father. He'd face them down.

Alone.

Once Philippe had recovered from his first grief, surely he'd be happy on the farm with Consuela and Ernesto.

And also… Jenny would be happy as a muffin-maker?

Why did he even think of her? Why had he ever insisted that she come here? It would have been easier for both of them if he'd simply let her go.

For she was Jenny, he reminded himself harshly, a dozen times a day. She was not Gianetta. She was free to go wherever she willed. She was Jenny, with the world at her feet.

Yet he watched the *Marquita*'s progress with an anxiety that bordered on obsession, and he knew that when Jenny arrived he would see her one last time. He must.

Was that wise?

He knew it wasn't. There was no place for Jenny here, as there was no place for Philippe.

He'd been alone for much of his adult life. He could go on being alone.

But he'd see Jenny once again first. Sensible or not. Please…

Eleven weeks and two days after setting sail from Auckland, the *Marquita* sailed into Cepheus harbour and found a party. As they approached land, every boat they passed, from tiny pleasure craft to workmanlike fishing vessels, was adorned in red, gold and deep, deep blue. The flag of Cepheus hung from every mast. The harbour was ringed with flags. There were people crowded onto the docks, spilling out of harbourside restaurants. Every restaurant looked crammed to bursting. It looked like Sydney Harbour on a sunny Sunday, multiplied by about a hundred, Jenny thought, dazed, as she made the lines ready to dock.

'You reckon they're here to welcome us?' Gordon called to her, and she smiled.

She'd become very fond of Gordon. When she'd first met him, the morning after Ramón had left, she'd been ready to walk away. Only his shy smile, his assumption that she was coming with him and his pleasure that she was, had kept her on board. He reminded her of her father. Which helped.

She'd been sailing with him now for almost three months. He'd kept his own counsel and she'd kept hers, and it had taken almost all those months for her emotions to settle.

Now…approaching the dock she was so tense she could hardly speak. Normally she welcomed Gordon's reserve but his silence was only adding to her tension.

There was no need for her to be tense, she told herself. She'd had a couple of surreal weeks with royalty. In true princely fashion he'd rescued her from a life of making muffins, and now she could get on with her life.

With this experience of sailing round the Horn behind her, and with Gordon's references, maybe she could get another job on board a boat. She could keep right on sailing. While Ramón…

See, that was what she couldn't let herself think. The future and Ramón.

It had been a two-week affair. Nothing more.

'What's the occasion?' Gordon was behind the

wheel, calling to people on the boat passing them. But they didn't understand English, or Gordon's broad mixed accent.

'Why the flags and decorations?' she called in Spanish and was rewarded by comprehension.

'Are you from another planet?' they called, incredulous. 'Everyone knows what's happening today.'

Their language was the mix of Spanish and French Ramón had used with the lawyer. She felt almost at home.

No. This was Ramón's home. Not hers.

'We're from Australia,' she called. 'We know nothing.'

'Well, welcome.' The people raised glasses in salutation. 'You're here just in time.'

'For what?'

'For the coronation,' they called. 'It's a public holiday. Crown Prince Ramón Cavellero of Cepheus accepts his Crown today.'

Right. She stood in the bow and let her hands automatically organize lines. Or not. She didn't know what her hands were doing.

First thought? Stupidly, it was that Ramón wouldn't be meeting her.

Had she ever believed he would? Ramón was a Prince of the Blood. He'd have moved on.

'Is that our berth?' Gordon called, and she caught herself, glanced at the sheet the harbour master had faxed through and then looked ahead to where their designated berth should be.

And drew in her breath.

Ramón wasn't there. Of course he wasn't. But there was a welcoming committee. There were four officials, three men and a woman, all in some sort of official uniform. The colours of their uniform matched the colours of the flags.

This yacht belonged to royalty, and representatives of royalty were there to meet them.

'Reckon any of them can catch a line?' Gordon called and she tried to smile.

'We're about to find out.'

Not only could they catch a line, they were efficient, courteous and they took smoothly over from the time the *Marquita* touched the dock.

'Welcome,' the senior official said gravely, in English. 'You are exactly on time.'

'You've been waiting for us?'

'His Highness has had you tracked from the moment you left Auckland. He's delighted you could be here today. He asks that you attend the ceremony this afternoon, and the official ball this evening.'

Jenny swung around to stare at Gordon—who was staring back at her. They matched. They both had their mouths wide open.

'Reckon we won't fit in,' Gordon drawled at last, sounding flabbergasted. 'Reckon there won't be a lot of folk wearing salt-crusted oilskins on your guest list.'

'That's why we're here,' the official said smoothly. 'Jorge here will complete the care of the *Marquita*, while Dalila and Rudi are instructed to care for you. If you agree, we'll escort you to the palace, you'll be fitted with clothing suitable for the occasion and you'll be His Highness's honoured guests at the ceremonies this afternoon and this evening.'

Jenny gasped. Her head was starting to explode. To see Ramón as a prince…

'We can't,' Gordon muttered.

But Jenny looked at the elderly seaman and saw her mixture of emotions reflected on his face. They'd been at sea for three months now, and she knew enough of Gordon to realize he stacked up life's events and used them to fill the long stretches at sea that he lived for.

He was staring at the officials with a mixture of awe and dread. And desire.

If she didn't go, Gordon wouldn't go.

And, a little voice inside her breathed, she'd get to see Ramón one last time.

Once upon a time Ramón had been her skipper. Once upon a time he'd been her lover. He'd moved on now. He was a Crown Prince.

She'd see him today and then she'd leave.

* * *

For the *Marquita* to berth on the same day as his coronation was a coincidence he couldn't ignore, making his resolution waver.

He'd made the decision to send his apologies when the boat berthed, for Jenny to be treated with all honour, paid handsomely and then escorted to the airport and given a first-class ticket back to Australia. That was the sensible decision. He couldn't allow himself to be diverted from his chosen path. But when he'd learned the *Marquita*'s date of arrival was today he'd given orders before he thought it through. Sensible or not, he would see Jenny this one last time.

Maybe he should see it as an omen, he decided as he dressed. Maybe he was meant to have her nearby, giving him strength to take this final step.

Servants were fussing over his uniform, making sure he looked every inch the Ruler of Cepheus, and outside there was sufficient security to defend him against a small army. Carlos's blustering threats of support from the military seemed to have no foundation. On his own he had nothing to fear, and on his own he must rule.

The last three months had cemented his determination to change this country. If he must accept the Crown then he'd do it as it was meant to be done. He could change this country for the better. He could make life easier for the population. The Crown, this ultimate position of authority, had been abused for generations. If anyone was to change it, it must be him.

Duty and desire had no place together. He knew that, and the last months' assessment of the state of the country told him that his duty was here. He had to stay focused. *He didn't need Jenny.*

But, need her or not, he wanted Jenny at the ceremony. To have her come all this way and not see her—on this of all days—*that* was more unthinkable than anything.

He would dance with her this night, he thought. Just this once, he'd touch her and then he'd move forward. Alone.

The doors were swinging open. The Master of State was waiting. Cepheus was waiting.

He'd set steps in place to bring this country into the twenty-first century, he thought with grim satisfaction. His coronation would cement those steps. Fulfilling the plans he'd set in place over the last few weeks would mean this country would thrive.

But maybe the population would never forget the family he came from, he thought as he was led in stately grandeur to the royal carriage. There were no cheers, no personal applause. Today the country was celebrating a public holiday and a continuum of history, but the populace wasn't impressed by what he personally represented. His grandfather's reputation came before him, smirching everything. Royalty was something to be endured.

The country had celebrated the birth of a new Crown Prince five years ago. That deception still rankled, souring all.

Philippe should be here, he thought. The little boy should play some part in this ceremony.

But, out at the farm, Philippe was finally starting to relax with him, learning again to be a little boy. He still missed the palace, but to bring him back seemed just as impossible as it had been three months ago.

Philippe was now an outsider. As he was himself, he thought grimly, glancing down at his uniform that made him seem almost ludicrously regal. And the threats were there, real or not.

He could protect Philippe. He *would* protect Philippe, but from a distance. Jenny was here for this day only. Sofía would be gone. He could rule as he needed to rule.

'It's time, Your Highness,' the Head of State said in stentorian tones, and Ramón knew that it was.

It was time to accept that he was a Prince of the Blood, with all the responsibility—and loss—that the title implied.

The great chorus of trumpets sounded, heralding the beginning of ceremonies and Jenny was sitting in a pew in the vast cathedral of Cepheus feeling bewildered. Feeling transformed. Feeling like Cinderella must have felt after the fairy godmother waved her wand.

For she wasn't at the back with the hired help. She and Gordon were being treated like royalty themselves.

The palace itself had been enough to take her breath away, all spirals and turrets and battlements, a medieval fantasy clinging to white stone cliffs above a sea so blue it seemed to almost merge with the sky.

The apartment she'd been taken to within the palace had taken even more of her breath away. It was as big as a small house, and Gordon had been shown into a similar one on the other side of the corridor. Corridor? It was more like a great hall. You could play a football match in the vast areas—decorated in gold, all carvings, columns and ancestral paintings—that joined the rooms. Dalila had ushered her in, put her holdall on a side table and instructed a maid to unpack.

'I'm not staying here,' Jenny had gasped.

'For tonight at least,' Dalila had said, formally polite in stilted English. 'The ball will be late. The Prince requires you to stay.'

How to fight a decree like that? How indeed to fight, when clothes were being produced that made her gasp all over again.

'I can't wear these.'

'You can,' the woman decreed. 'If you'll just stay still. Dolores is a dressmaker. It will take her only moments to adjust these for size.'

And Jenny had simply been too overwhelmed to refuse. So here she was, in a pew ten seats from the front, right on the aisle, dressed in a crimson silk ball-gown that looked as if it had been made for her. It was cut low across her breasts, with tiny capped sleeves, the bodice clinging like a second skin, curving to her hips and then flaring out to an almost full circle skirt. The fabric was so beautiful it made her feel as if she was floating.

There was a pendant round her neck that she hoped was paste but she suspected was a diamond so big she couldn't comprehend it. Her hair was pinned up in a deceptively simple knot and her make-up had been applied with a skill so great that when she looked in the mirror she saw someone she didn't recognize.

She felt like…Gianetta. For the first time in her life, her father's name seemed right for her.

'I'm just glad they can't see me back at the Sailor's Arms in Auckland,' Gordon muttered, and she glanced at the weathered seaman who looked as classy as she did, in a deep black suit that fitted him like a glove. He, too, had been transformed, like it or not. She almost chuckled, but then the music rose to a crescendo and she stopped thinking about chuckling. She stopped thinking about anything at all—anything but Ramón.

Crown Prince Ramón Cavellero of Cepheus.

For so he was.

The great doors of the cathedral had swung open. The Archbishop of Cepheus led the way in stately procession down the aisle, and Ramón trod behind, intent, his face set in lines that said this was an occasion of such great moment that lives would change because of it.

He truly was a prince, she thought, dazed beyond belief. If she'd walked past him in the street—no, if she'd seen his picture on the cover of a magazine, for this wasn't a man one passed in the street, she would never have recognized him. His uniform was black as night, skilfully cut to mould to his tall, lean frame. The leggings, the boots, the slashes of gold, the tassels, the fierce sword at his side, they only accentuated his aura of power and strength and purpose.

Or then again…maybe she would have recognized him. His eyes seemed to have lost their colour—they were dark as night. His mouth was set and grim, and it was the expression she'd seen when he'd known she was leaving.

He looked like…an eagle, she thought, a fierce bird of prey, ready to take on the world. But he was still Ramón.

He was so near her now. If she put out her hand…

He was passing her row. He was right here. And as he passed… His gaze shifted just a little from looking steadily ahead. Somehow it met hers and held, for a nano-second, for a fraction that might well be imagined. And then he was gone, swept past in the procession and the world crowded back in.

He hadn't smiled, but had his grimness lifted, just a little?

'He was looking for you,' Gordon muttered, awed. 'The guy who helped me dress said he told the aides where we were to sit. It's like we're important. Are you important to him then, lass?'

'Not in a million years,' she breathed.

She'd come.

It was the only thing holding him steady.

Gianetta. Jenny.

Her name was in his mind, like a mantra, said over and over.

'By the power vested in me…'

He was kneeling before the archbishop and the crown was being placed on his head. The weight was enormous.

She was here.

He could take this nowhere. He knew that. But still, for now, she was here on this day when he needed her most.

She was here, and his crown was the lighter for it.

The night seemed to be organized for her. As the throng emerged from the great cathedral, an aide appeared and took her arm.

'You're to come this way, miss. And you, too, sir,'

he said to Gordon. 'You're official guests at the Coronation Dinner.'

'I reckon I'll slope back down to the boat,' Gordon muttered, shrinking, but Jenny clutched him as if she were drowning.

'We went round the Horn together,' she muttered. 'We face risk together.'

'This is worse than the Horn.'

'You're telling me,' Jenny said, and the aide was ushering them forward and it was too late to escape.

They sat, midway down a vast banquet table, where it seemed half the world's dignitaries were assembled. Gordon, a seaman capable of facing down the world's worst storms, was practically shrinking under the table. Jenny was a bit braver, but not much. She was recognizing faces and names and her eyes grew rounder and rounder as she realized just who was here. There were speeches— of course—and she translated for Gordon and was glad of the task. It took her mind off what was happening.

It never took her mind off Ramón.

He was seated at the great formal table at the head of the room, gravely surveying all. He looked born to the role, she thought. He listened with gravitas and with courtesy. He paid attention to the two women on either side of him—grand dames, both of them, queens of their own countries.

'I have friends back in Australia who are never

going to believe what I've done tonight,' she whispered to Gordon and her skipper nodded agreement.

Then once more the aide was beside them, bending to whisper to Jenny.

'Ma'am, I've been instructed to ask if you can waltz.'

'If I can...?'

'His Royal Highness wishes to dance with you. He doesn't wish to embarrass you, however, so if there's a problem...'

No. She wanted to scream, *no*.

But she glanced up at the head table and Ramón was watching her. Those eagle eyes were steady. 'I dare you,' his gaze was saying, and more.

'I can waltz,' she heard herself say, her eyes not leaving Ramón's.

'Excellent,' the aide said. 'I'll come to fetch you when we're ready.'

'You do that,' she said faintly.

What have I done?

The entrance to the grand ballroom was made in state. Ramón led the procession, and it was done in order of rank, which meant Jenny came in somewhere near the rear. Even that was intimidating— all the guests who hadn't been at the dinner were assembled in line to usher the dining party in.

If the ground opened up and swallowed her she'd

be truly grateful. Too many people were looking at her.

Why had she agreed to dance?

Ramón was so far ahead she couldn't see him. Ramón. Prince Ramón.

She wasn't into fairy tales. Bring on midnight.

And Gordon had deserted her. As she took the aide's arm, as she joined the procession, he suddenly wasn't there. She looked wildly around and he was smiling apologetically but backing firmly away. But she was being ushered forward and there was no way she could run without causing a spectacle.

Cinderella ran, she thought wildly. At midnight. But midnight was still a long time away.

Courage. If Cinders could face them all down, so could she. She took a deep breath and allowed herself to be led forward. The aide was ushering her into the ballroom, then into an alcove near the entrance. Before them, Ramón was making a grand sweep of the room, greeting everyone. The heads of the royal houses of Europe were his entourage, nodding, smiling, doing what royalty did best.

And suddenly she realized what was happening. Why she'd been directed to stand here. She was close to the door, where Ramón must end his circuit.

She felt frozen to the spot.

Ramón. Prince Ramón.

Ramón.

The wait was interminable. She tried to focus on anything but what was happening. A spot on the wax of the polished floor. The hem of her gown. Anything.

But finally, inevitably, the aide was beside her, ushering her forward and Ramón was right in front of her. Every eye in the room was on him. Every eye in the room was on her.

She was Jenny. She made muffins. She wanted to have hysterics, or faint.

Ramón was before her, his eyes grave and questioning.

'Gianetta,' he said softly, and every ear in the room was straining to hear. 'You've arrived for my coronation, and I thank you. You've brought my boat home and thus you've linked my old life with my new. Can I therefore ask for the honour of this dance?'

There was an audible gasp throughout the room. It wasn't said out loud but she could hear the thought regardless. *Who?*

But Ramón was holding out his hand, waiting for her to put hers in his. Smiling. It was the smile she loved with all her heart.

Was this how Cinders felt?

And then Cinders was forgotten. Everything was forgotten. She put her hand in his, she tried hard to smile back and she allowed the Crown Prince of Cepheus to lead her onto the ballroom floor.

* * *

Where had she learned to dance?

Ramón had been coached almost before he could walk. His grandmother had thought dancing at least as important as any other form of movement. He could thus waltz without thinking. He'd expected to slow his steps to Jenny's, to take care she wasn't embarrassed, but he'd been on the dance floor less than ten seconds before he realized such precautions weren't necessary. He took her into his arms in the waltz hold, and she melted into him as if she belonged.

The music swelled in an age-old, well-loved waltz and she was one with the music, one with him.

He'd almost forgotten how wonderful she felt.

He had to be formal, he told himself harshly. He needed to hold her at arm's length—which was difficult when he was not holding her at arm's length at all. He needed to be courteously friendly and he needed to thank her and say goodbye.

Only not yet. Not goodbye yet.

'Where did you learn to dance?' he managed, and it was a dumb thing to say to a woman after a three-month separation, but the tension eased a little and she almost smiled.

'Dancing's not reserved for royalty. My Papà was the best.'

This was better. There was small talk in this. 'He should have met my grandmother.'

'Yes,' she said, and seemed to decide to let herself enjoy the music, the dance, the sensation of being held for a couple more circuits of the floor while the world watched. And then… 'Ramón, why are you doing this?'

'I'm sorry?'

'Why did you ask me to dance…first?'

'I wanted to thank you.'

'You paid me, remember? It's me who should be thanking. And the world is watching. For you to ask me for the first dance…'

'I believe it's the last dance,' he said, and the leaden feeling settled back around his heart as the truth flooded back. Holding her was an illusion, a fleeting taste of what could have been, and all at once the pain was unbearable. 'I've wanted to hold you for three months,' he said simply, and it was as if the words were there and had to be said, whether he willed them or not. 'Jenny, maybe even saying it is unwise but, wise or not, I've missed you every single night.' He hesitated, then somehow struggled back to lightness, forcing the leaden ache to stay clear of his voice. He couldn't pass his regret onto her. He had to say goodbye—as friends. 'Do you realize how much work there is in being a Crown Prince?'

'I have no idea,' she said faintly. 'I guess…there's speeches to make. Ribbons to cut. That sort of thing.'

'Not so much of that sort of thing.' His hand tightened on her waist, tugging her closer. Wanting her closer. Sense decreed he had to let her go, but still not yet. 'I haven't even been official Crown Prince until today,' he said, fighting to make his voice sound normal. 'I've not even been qualified as a ribbon-cutter until now. I've been a prince in training. Nothing more. Nothing less. But I have been practising my waltzing. My Aunt Sofía's seen to that. So let's see if we can make the ghosts of your Papà and my Grand-mère proud.'

She smiled. He whirled her around in his arms and she felt like thistledown, he thought. She felt like Jenny.

He had to let her go.

He didn't feel like a prince, she thought as he held her close and their bodies moved as one. If she closed her eyes he felt like Ramón. Just Ramón, pure and simple. The man who'd stolen her heart.

It was impossible, he'd said. Of course it was. She'd known it for three months and nothing had changed.

The world was watching. She had to keep it light.

'So it's been practising speeches and waltzing,' she ventured at last. 'While we've been braving the Horn.'

'That and getting leggings to fit,' he murmured into her ear. 'Bloody things, leggings. I'd almost prefer the Horn.'

'But leggings are so sexy.'

'Sexy isn't leggings,' he said. His eyes were on her and she could see exactly what he was thinking.

'Don't,' she whispered, feeling her colour rising. Every eye in the room was on them.

'I've missed you for three long months,' he said, lightness disappearing. He sounded goaded almost past breaking point.

'Ramón, we had two weeks,' she managed. 'It didn't mean anything.'

He stopped dancing. Others had taken to the floor now, but they were on the edge of the dance floor. Ramón and Jenny had central position and they were still being watched.

'Are you saying what we had didn't mean anything to you?' he asked, his voice sounding suddenly calm, almost distant.

'Of course it did,' she said, blushing furiously. 'At the time. Ramón, please, can we keep dancing? I don't belong here.'

'Neither do I,' he said grimly, and he took her in his arms again and slipped back into the waltz. 'I should be leaving for Bangladesh right now. My team's left without me for the first time in years.'

'Speeches are important,' she said cautiously.

'They are.' The laughter and passion had completely disappeared now, leaving his voice sounding flat and defeated. 'Believe it or not, this country needs me. It's been bled dry by my grandfather and my uncle. If I walk away it'll continue to be bled dry by a government that's as corrupt as it is inept. It's not all ribbon-cutting.'

'It's your life,' she said simply. 'You're bred to it and you shouldn't be dancing with me.'

'I shouldn't be doing lots of things, and I'll not be told who I should be dancing with tonight. I know. This can only be for now *but I will dance with you tonight.*'

The music was coming to an end. The outside edge of the dance floor was crowded, but the dancers were keeping clear of the Crown Prince and his partner. A space was left so that, as soon as the dance ended, Ramón could return to his royal table.

Waiting for him were the crowned heads of Europe. Men and women who were watching Jenny as if they knew instinctively she had no place among them.

'You have danced with me,' Jenny said softly, disengaging her hands before he realized what she intended. 'I thank you for the honour.'

'There's no need to thank me.'

'Oh, but there is,' she said, breathless. 'The clothes, this moment, you. I'll remember it all my life.'

She looked up into his eyes and felt an almost overwhelming urge to reach up and kiss him, just a kiss, just a moment, to take a tiny taste of him to keep for ever. But the eyes of the world were on her. Ramón was a prince and his world was waiting.

'I believe there are women waiting to dance with the Crown Prince of Cepheus,' she murmured. 'We both need to move on, so thank you, Ramón. Thank you for the fantasy.'

'Thank you, Gianetta,' he murmured, and he raised his hand and touched her cheek, a feather touch that seemed a gesture of regret and loss and farewell. 'It's been my honour. I will see you before you leave.'

'Do you think…?'

'It's unwise? Of course it's unwise,' he finished for her. 'But it's tonight only. Tomorrow I need to be wise for the rest of my life.'

'Then maybe tomorrow needs to start now,' she said unsteadily and she managed a smile, her very best peasant to royalty smile, and turned and walked away. Leaving the Crown Prince of Cepheus looking after her.

What had he said? *'We can't take it further…'*

Of course they couldn't. What was she thinking of? But still she felt like sobbing. What was she doing here? Why had she ever come? She'd slip away like Gordon, she thought, just as soon as the next dance started, just as soon as everyone stopped watching her.

But someone was stepping into her path. Another prince? The man was dark and bold and so good-looking that if she hadn't met Ramón first she would have been stunned. As it was, she hardly saw him.

'May I request the honour of this dance?' he said,

and it wasn't a question. His hand took hers before she could argue, autocratic as Ramón. Where did they learn this? Autocracy school?

It seemed no wasn't a word in these men's vocabularies. She was being led back onto the dance floor, like it or not.

'What's needed is a bit of spine,' she told herself and somehow she tilted her chin, fixed her smile and accepted partner after partner.

Most of these men were seriously good dancers. Many of these men were seriously good-looking men. She thought briefly of Cathy back in Seaport—*'Jenny, get a life!'* If Cathy could see her now…

The thought was almost enough to make her smile real. If only she wasn't so aware of the eyes watching her. If only she wasn't so aware of Ramón's presence. He was dancing with beautiful woman after beautiful woman, and a couple of truly impressive royal matriarchs as well.

He was smiling into each of his partner's eyes, and each one of them was responding exactly the same.

They melted.

Why would they not? Anyone would melt in Ramón's arms.

And suddenly, inexplicably, she was thinking of Matty, of her little son, and she wondered what she was doing here. This strange creature in fancy clothes had nothing to do with who she really was, and all at once what she was doing seemed a betrayal.

'It's okay,' she told herself, feeling suddenly desperate. 'This is simply an unbelievable moment out of my life. After tonight I'll return to being who I truly am. This is for one night only,' she promised Matty. 'One night and then I'm back where I belong.'

Her partner was holding her closer than was appropriate. Sadly for him, she was so caught up in her thoughts she hardly noticed.

Ramón was dancing so close that she could almost reach out and touch him. He whirled his partner round, his gaze caught hers and he smiled, and her partner had no chance at all.

That smile was so dangerous. That smile sucked you in.

'So who are your parents?' her partner asked, and she had to blink a few times to try and get her world moving again.

'My parents are dead,' she managed. 'And yours?'

'I beg your pardon?'

'Who are your parents?'

'My father is the King of Morotatia,' her partner said in stilted English. 'My mother was a princess in her own right before she married. And I am Prince Marcelo Pietros Cornelieus Maximus, heir to the throne of Morotatia.'

'That's wonderful,' she murmured. 'I guess you don't need to work for a living then?'

'Work?'

'I didn't think so,' she said sadly. 'But you guys must need muffins. I wonder if there's an opening around here for a kitchen maid.'

But, even as she said it, she knew even that wasn't possible. She had no place here. This was the fairy tale and she had to go home.

CHAPTER SEVEN

THE night was becoming oppressive. She was passed on to her next partner, who gently grilled her again, and then another who grilled her not so gently until she almost snapped at him. Finally supper was announced. She could escape now, she thought, but then a dumpy little lady with a truly magnificent tiara made a beeline for her, grasped her hands and introduced herself.

'I'm Ramón's Aunt Sofía. I'm so pleased to meet you.' She tucked her arm into Jenny's as if she was laying claim to her—as indeed she was, as there were those around them who were clearly waiting to start the inquisitions again.

'Aunt…'

Sofía turned to see Ramón approaching. He had one of the formidable matrons on his arm. Queen of somewhere? But Sofía was not impressed.

'Go away, Ramón,' Sofía commanded. 'I'm taking Jenny into supper. You look after Her Highness.'

'Sofía was always bossy,' the Queen of some-where said, but she smiled, and Ramón gave his aunt a smile and gave Jenny a quick, fierce glance—one that was enough to make her toes curl—and led his queen away.

Sofía must rank pretty highly, Jenny thought, so dazed she simply allowed herself to be led. The crowd parted before them. Sofía led them to a small alcove set with a table and truly impressive table-ware. She smiled at a passing servant and in two minutes there were so many delicacies before them Jenny could only gasp.

Sofía ate two bite-sized cream éclairs, then paused to demand why Jenny wasn't doing likewise.

'I'm rather in shock,' Jenny confessed.

'Me too,' Sofía confessed. 'And Ramón too, though we're making the best of it.'

'But Ramón's the Crown Prince,' Jenny managed. 'How can he be intimidated?' She could see him through the crowd. He drew every eye in the room. He looked truly magnificent—Crown Prince to the manor born.

'Because he wasn't meant to be royal,' Sofía said darkly, but then her darkness disappeared and she smiled encouragingly at Jenny. 'Just like you're not. I'm not sure what Ramón's told you so I thought maybe there's things you ought to know.'

'I know the succession was a shock,' Jenny

ventured, and Sofía nodded vigorously and ate another éclair.

'Yes,' she said definitely. 'We were never expected to inherit. Ramón's grandfather—my father—sent my mother, my younger brother and I out of the palace when my brother and I were tiny. We were exiled, and kept virtual prisoners on an island just off the coast. My mother was never permitted to step back onto the mainland.'

Jenny frowned. Why was she being told this? But she could do nothing but listen as Sofía examined a meringue from all angles and decided not.

'That sounds dreadful,' Sofía continued, moving on to a delicate chocolate praline, popping it in and choosing another. 'But, in truth, the island is beautiful. It was only my mother's pain at what was happening to her country, and at losing her elder son that hurt. As we grew older my younger brother married an islander—a lovely girl. Ramón is their son. So Ramón's technically a prince, but until three months ago the only time he was at the palace was the night his father died.'

There were places here she didn't want to go. There were places she had no right to go to. 'He…he spends his life on his yacht,' she ventured.

'No, dear, only part of it, and that's only since his mother and sister died. He trained as a builder. I think he started building things almost as soon as he could put one wooden block on top of another. He spends every dry season in Bangladesh, building houses with floating floors. Apparently they're brilliant—villagers can adjust their floor levels as flood water rises. He's passionate about it, but now, here he is, stuck as Crown Prince for ever.'

'I imagine he was trained for it,' Jenny said stiffly, still not sure where this was going.

'Only in that my mother insisted on teaching us court manners,' Sofía retorted. 'It was as if she knew that one day we'd be propelled back here. We humoured her, though none of us ever expected that we would. Finally, my brother tried to reinstate my mother's rights, to allow her to leave the island, and that's when the real tragedy started.'

'That was when Ramón's father was killed?'

'Yes, dear. By my father's thugs,' Sofía said, her plump face creasing into distress. The noise and bustle of the ballroom was nothing, ignored in her apparent need to tell Jenny this story. 'My mother ached to leave, and we couldn't believe my father's vindictiveness could last for years. But last it did, and when my brother was old enough he mounted a legal challenge. It was met with violence and with death. My father invited my brother here, to reason with him, so he came and brought Ramón with him because he thought he'd introduce his little son to his grandfather. So Ramón was here when it happened, a child, sleeping alone in this dreadful place while his father was killed. Just…alone.'

She stared down at her chocolate, but she wasn't seeing it. She was obviously still stunned at the enormity of what had happened. 'That's what royalty does,' she whispered. 'What is it they say? Absolute power corrupts absolutely. So my father had his own son killed, simply because he dared to defy him. We assume…we want to believe that it was simply his thugs going too far, meant to frighten but taking their orders past the point of reason. But still, my father must have employed them, and he must have known the consequences. This place…the whole of royalty is tainted by that murder. And now Carlos…the man who would have been Crown Prince if Ramón hadn't agreed to come home…is in the wings, threatening. He's here tonight.'

She gestured towards the supper table where a big man with more medals than Ramón was shovelling food into his mouth.

'He makes threats but so quietly we can't prove anything. He's here always, with his unfortunate wife towed in his wake, and he's just waiting for something to happen to Ramón. I can walk away— Ramón insists that I will walk away—but Ramón can't.'

Jenny was struggling to take everything in. She couldn't focus on shadows of death. She couldn't even begin to think of Carlos and his threats. She was still, in fact, struggling with genealogy. And Ramón as a little boy, alone as his father died…

'So…so the Crown Prince who's just been killed was your older brother?' she managed.

'Yes,' Sofía told her, becoming calm once more. 'Not that I ever saw him after we left the palace. And he had a son, who also had a son.' She shrugged. 'A little boy called Philippe. There's another tragedy. But it's not your tragedy, dear,' she said as she saw Jenny's face. 'Nor Ramón's. Ramón worries, but then Ramón worries about everything.' She hesitated, and then forged ahead as if this was something she'd rehearsed.

'But, my dear, Ramón's been talking about you,' she confessed. 'He says…he says you're special. Well, I can see that. I watched Ramón's face as he danced with you and it's exactly the same expression I saw on his father's face when he danced with his mother. If Ramón's found that with you…'

'He can't possibly…' Jenny started, startled, but Sofía was allowing no interruptions.

'You can't say it's impossible if it's already happened. All I'm saying is that you don't have to be royal to be with Ramón. What I'm saying is give love a chance.'

'How could I…?' She stopped, bewildered.

'By not staying in this palace,' Sofía said, suddenly deadly serious. 'By not even thinking about it. Ramón's right when he tells me such a union is impossible, dangerous, unsuitable, and he can't be distracted from what he must do. You don't fit in and neither should you. Our real home, our lovely island, is less than fifteen minutes' helicopter ride from here. If Ramón could settle you there as his mistress, he'd have an escape.'

'An escape?' she whispered, stunned.

'From royalty,' Sofía said bluntly. 'Ramón needs to do his duty but if he could have you on the side…' She laid a hand over Jenny's. 'It could make all the difference. And he'd look after you so well. I know he would. You'd want for nothing. So, my dear, will you listen to Ramón?'

'If he asks…to have me as his some-time mistress?' she managed.

'I'm just letting you know his family would think it was a good thing,' Sofía said, refusing to be deterred by Jenny's obvious shock. 'You're not to take offence, but it's nothing less than my duty to tell you that you're totally unsuitable for this place, even if he'd have you here, which he won't. You're not who Ramón needs as a wife. He needs someone who knows what royalty is and how to handle it. That's what royal pedigree is—there's a reason for it. But, as for a partner he loves… that's a different thing. If Ramón could have you now and then…'

She paused, finally beginning to flounder. The expression on Jenny's face wasn't exactly encouraging. She was finding it impossible to contain her anger, and her humiliation.

'So you'd have him marry someone else and have me on the side,' she said dangerously.

'It's been done for generation upon generation,' Sofía said with asperity. Then she glanced up with some relief as a stranger approached, a youngish man wearing more medals than Ramón. 'But here's Lord Anthony, wanting an introduction. He's frightfully British, my dear, but he's a wonderful dancer. Ramón won't have any more time for you tonight. He'll have so little time... But I'm sure he could fit you in every now and then, if you'll agree to the island. So you go and dance with Lord Anthony, and remember what I said when you need to remember it.'

Jenny danced almost on automatic pilot. She desperately wanted to leave, but slipping away when the world was watching was impossible. As Sofía had warned her, she barely saw Ramón again. He was doing his duty, dancing with one society dame after another.

She'd been lucky to be squeezed in at all, she thought dully. What *was* she doing here?

It wasn't made better with her second 'girls' talk' of the night. Another woman grabbed her attention almost straight after Sofía. This lady was of a similar age to Sofía, but she was small and thin, she had fewer jewels and she had the air of a frightened rabbit. But she was a determined frightened rabbit. She intercepted Jenny between partners. When the next man approached she hissed, 'Go away,' and stood her ground until they were left alone.

'I'm Perpetua,' she said, and then, as Jenny looked blank, she explained. 'I'm Carlos's wife.'

Carlos. The threat.

'He's not dangerous,' Perpetua said, obviously reading her expression, and she steered her into the shadows with an air of quiet but desperate determination. 'My husband's all talk. All stupidity. It's this place. It's being royal. I just wanted to say…to say…'

She took a deep breath and out it came, as if it had been welled up for years. 'They say you're common,' she said. 'I mean…ordinary. Not royal. Like me. I was a schoolteacher, and I loved my work and then I met Carlos. For a while we were happy, but then the old Prince decided he liked my husband. He used to take him gambling. Carlos got sucked into the lifestyle, and that's where he stays. In some sort of fantasy world, where he's more royal than Ramón. He's done some really stupid things, most of them at the Prince's goading. In these last months when he thought he would inherit the throne, he's been…a little bit crazy. There's nothing I can do, but it's so painful to see the way he is, the way he's acting. And then I watched you tonight. The way you looked at Ramón when you were dancing.'

'I don't understand,' Jenny managed.

'Just get away from it,' she whispered. 'Whatever Ramón says, don't believe it. Just run. Oh, I shouldn't say anything. I'm a royal wife and a royal wife just shuts up. Do you want that? To be an appendage who just shuts up? My dear, don't do it. Just run.' And then, as yet another potential partner came to claim Jenny's hand, she gave a gasping sob, shot Jenny one last despairing glance and disappeared into the crowd.

Just run. That was truly excellent advice, Jenny thought, as she danced on, on autopilot. It was the best advice she'd had all night. If she knew where she was, if she knew how to get back to the boat in the dark in the middle of a strange city, that was just what she'd do.

She'd never felt so alone. She was Cinderella without her coach and it wasn't even midnight.

But finally the clock struck twelve. Right on cue, a cluster of officials gathered round Ramón as a formal guard of honour. Trumpets blared with a final farewell salute, and the Crown Prince Ramón of Cepheus was escorted away.

He'd be led to his harem of nubile young virgins, Jenny decided, fighting back an almost hysterical desire to laugh. Or cry. Or both. She was so weary she wanted to sink and, as if the thought had been said aloud, a footman was at her side, courteously solicitous.

'Ma'am, I'm to ask if you'd like to stay on to continue dancing, or would you like to be escorted back to your chambers?'

'I'd like to be escorted back to the yacht.'

'That's not possible, ma'am,' he said. 'The Prince's orders are that you stay in the palace.' And then, as she opened her mouth to argue, he added flatly, 'There's no transport to the docks tonight. I'm sorry, ma'am, but you'll have to stay.'

So that, it seemed, was that. She was escorted back to the palace. She lay in her ridiculously ostentatious bedchamber, in her ridiculously ostentatious bed, and she tried for sleep.

How was a girl to sleep after a night like this?

She couldn't. Her crimson ball-gown was draped on a hanger in the massive walk-in wardrobe. The diamond necklet still lay on her dresser. Her Cinderella slippers were on the floor beside her bed.

At least she'd kept both of them on, she thought ruefully. It hadn't quite been a fairy tale.

Only it had been a fairy tale. Gianetta Bertin—Jenny to her friends—had attended a royal ball. She'd been led out onto the dance floor with a prince so handsome he made her knees turn to jelly. For those few wonderful moments she'd let herself be swept away into a magic future where practicalities disappeared and there was only Ramón; only her love.

And then his aunt had told her that she was totally unsuitable to be a royal wife but she could possibly be his mistress. Only not here. How romantic.

And then someone called Perpetua had warned her against royalty, like the voice of doom in some Gothic novel. *Do not trust him, gentle maiden.*

How ridiculous.

And, as if in response to her unanswerable question, someone knocked on the door.

Who'd knock on her bedroom door at three in the morning?

'Who is it?' she quavered, and her heart seemed to stop until there was a response.

'I can't get my boots off,' a beloved voice complained from the other side of the door. 'I was hoping someone might hang on while I pull.'

'I… I believe my contract was all about muffins and sails,' she managed, trying to make her voice not squeak, trying to kick-start her heart again while warnings and sensible decisions went right out of the window. *Ramón.*

'I know I have no right to ask.' There was suddenly seriousness behind Ramón's words. 'I know this isn't sensible, I know I shouldn't be here, but Jenny, if tonight is all there is then I'm sure, if we read the contract carefully, there might be something about boots. Something that'd give us an excuse for…well, something about helping me for this night only.'

'Don't you have a valet?' she whispered and then wondered how he'd hear her through the door. But it was as if he was already in the room with her.

'Valets scare the daylights out of me,' he said. 'They're better dressed than I am. Please, Jenny love, will you help me off with my boots?'

'I don't think I'm brave enough.'

'You helped a trapped whale. Surely you can help a trapped prince. For this night only.'

'Ramón…'

'Open the door, Gianetta,' he said in a different voice, a voice that had her flinging back her bed-covers and flying to the door and tugging it open. Despite what Sofía had said, despite Perpetua's grim warnings, this was Ramón. Her Ramón.

And there he was. He wasn't smiling. He was just…him.

He opened his arms and she walked right in.

For a long moment she simply stood, held against him, feeling the strength of his heartbeat, feeling his arms around her. He was still in his princely uniform. There were medals digging into her cheek but she wasn't complaining. His heart was beating right under those medals, and who cared about a bit of metal anyway?

Who cared what two royal women had said to her? Who cared that this was impossible?

They had this night.

He kissed the top of her head and he held her

tight and she felt protected and loved—and desperate to haul him into the room right there and then.

But there was a footman at the top of the stairs. Just standing, staring woodenly ahead. He was wigged, powdered, almost a dummy. But he was real.

It was hard to seize a prince and haul him into her lair when a footman was on guard.

'Um…we have an audience,' she whispered at last.

He kissed her hair again and said gravely, 'Do you care?'

'If we walk into my room and shut the door we won't have an audience,' she tried.

'Ah, but the story will out,' he said gravely.

'So it should if you go creeping into strange women's bedrooms in the small hours. I should yell the house down.'

She was trying to sound indignant. She was trying to pull back so she could be at arm's length, so she could see his face. She wasn't trying hard enough. She sounded happy—and there was no way she was pulling back from this man.

'You could if you wanted and you'd have help,' he said gravely. 'The footman's on guard duty. In case the Huns invade—or strange women don't want strange men doing this creeping thing you describe. But if the woman was to welcome this strange man, then we don't need an audience. Gianetta, are you hungry?'

Hungry. The thought was so out of left field that she blinked.

'Hungry?'

'I'm starving. I was hoping you might come down to the kitchen with me.'

'After I've pulled your boots off?'

'Yup.'

'You want me to be your servant?'

'No,' he said, lightness giving way instantly to a gravity she found disconcerting. 'For this night, I want you to be my friend.'

Her friend, the prince?

Her friend, her lover?

Ramón.

Part-time mistress?

Forget Sofía, she told herself fiercely. Forget Perpetua. Tonight she'd hold on to the fairy tale.

'So…so there's no royal cook?' she managed.

'There are three, but they scare me more than my valet. They wear white hats and speak with Italian accents and say béchamel a lot.'

'Oh, Ramón…'

'And there's no security camera in the smaller kitchen,' he told her, and she looked up into his face and it was all she could do not to burst into spontaneous combustion.

'So will you come?' His eyes dared her.

'I'm coming.' Mistress or not, dangerous or not, right now she'd take whatever he wanted to give.

Stupid? Who knew? She only knew that there was no way she could walk away from this man this night.

'Slippers and robe first,' he suggested and she blinked.

'Pardon?'

'Let's keep it nice past the footman.' He grinned. 'And do your belt up really tight. I like a challenge.'

'Ramón…'

'Second kitchen, no security camera,' he said and gave her a gentle push back into her bedroom. 'Slippers and gown. Respectability's the thing, my love. All the way down the stairs.'

They were respectable all the way down the stairs. The footman watched them go, his face impassive. When they reached the second kitchen another footman appeared and opened the door for them. He ushered them inside.

'Would you like the door closed?' he said deferentially and Ramón nodded.

'Absolutely. And make sure the Huns stay on that side.'

'The Huns?' the man said blankly.

'You never know what they're planning,' Ramón said darkly. 'If I were you, I'd take a walk around the perimeter of the palace. Warn the troops.'

'Your Highness…'

'Just give us a bit of privacy,' Ramón said, relenting at the look of confusion on the man's face. 'Fifty paces from the kitchen door, agreed?'

Finally there was a smile—sort of—pulled back instantly with a gasp as if the man had realized what he was doing and maybe smiling was a hanging offence. Impassive again, he snapped his heels and moved away and Ramón closed the door and leaned on it.

'This servant thing's got knobs on it. Three months and they still treat me like a prince.'

'You are a prince.'

'Not here,' he said. 'Not now. I'm me and you're you and the kitchen door is closed. And so…'

And so he took her into his arms and he held her so tight the breath was crushed from her body. He held her like a man drowning holding on to a lifeline. He held her and held her and held her, as if there was no way he could ever let her go.

He didn't kiss her. His head rested on her hair. He held her until her heart beat in synchronisation with his. Until she felt as if her body was merging with his, becoming one. Until she felt as if she was truly loved—that she'd come home.

How long they stayed there she could never afterwards tell—time disappeared. This was their moment. The world was somewhere outside that kitchen door, the servants, Sofía's words, Perpetua's warnings, tomorrow, but for now all that mattered was this, her Ramón. Her love.

The kitchen was warm. An old fire-stove sent out a gentle heat. A small grey cat slept in a basket by the hearth. All Jenny had seen of this palace was grandeur, but here in this second kitchen the palace almost seemed a home.

It did feel like home. Ramón was holding her against his heart and she was where she truly belonged.

She knew it was an illusion, and so must he. Maybe that was why he held her for so long, allowing nothing, no words, no movement, to intrude. As if, by holding her, the world could be kept at bay. As if she was something that he must lose, but he'd hold on while he still could.

Finally he kissed her as she needed to be kissed, as she ached to be kissed, and she kissed him back as if he was truly her Ramón and the royal title was nothing but a crazy fantasy locked securely on the other side of the door.

With the Huns, she thought, somewhat deliriously. Reality and the Huns were being kept at bay by powdered, wigged footmen, giving her this time of peace and love and bliss.

She loved this man with all her heart. Maybe what Sofía had said was wrong. Maybe the Perpetua thing was crazy.

The cat stirred, coiling out of her basket, stretching, then stepping daintily out to inspect her food dish. The tiny movement was enough to make them stir, to let a sliver of reality in. But only a sliver.

'She's only interested in her food,' Jenny whispered. 'Not us.'

'I don't blame her. I'm hungry, too.' Ramón's voice was husky with passion, but his words were so prosaic that she chuckled. It made it real. Her Prince of the Blood, dressed in medals and tassels and boots that shone like mirrors, was smiling down at her with a smile that spoke of devilry and pure latent sex—and he was hungry.

'For…for what?' she managed, and the devilry in his eyes darkened, gleamed, sprang into laughter.

'I'd take you on the kitchen table, my love,' he said simply. 'But I just don't trust the servants that much.'

'And we'd shock the cat,' she whispered and he chuckled.

'Absolutely.'

He was trying to make his voice normal, Jenny thought. He was trying to make their world somehow normal. In truth, if Ramón carried out his earlier threat to untie the cord of her dressing gown, if he took that to its inevitable conclusion, there was no way she'd deny him. Only sense was prevailing. Sort of.

Where he led, she'd follow, but if he was trying to be prosaic…maybe she could be, too.

'I could cook in this kitchen,' she said, eyeing the old range appraisingly, the rows of pots and pans hanging from overhead rails, the massive wooden table, worn and pitted from years of scrubbing.

'The pantry adjoins both kitchens,' Ramón said hopefully. 'I'm sure there's eggs and bacon in there.'

'Are you really hungry?'

'At dinner I had two queens, one duke and three prime ministers within talking range,' he said. 'They took turns to address me. It's very rude for a Crown Prince to eat while being addressed by a Head of State. My Aunt Sofía was watching. If I'd eaten I would have had my knuckles rapped.'

'She's a terrifying lady,' Jenny said and he grinned.

'I love her to bits,' he said simply. 'Like I love you.'

'Ramón…'

'Gianetta.'

'This is…'

'Just for tonight,' he said softly and his voice grew bleak. 'I know this is impossible. After tonight I'll ask nothing of you, but Gianetta…just for tonight can we be…us?'

His face was grim. There were vast problems here, she knew, and she saw those problems reflected in his eyes. Sofía had said the ghost of his father made this palace hateful, yet Ramón was stuck here.

Can we be us?

Maybe they could go back to where they' started.

'Do you want bacon and eggs, or do you want muffins?' she asked and tried to make her voice prosaic.

'You could cook muffins here?' Astonishment lessened the grimness.

'You have an oven warmed for a cat,' she said. 'It seems silly to waste it. It'll mean you need to wait twenty minutes instead of five minutes for eggs and bacon.'

'And the smell will go all through the palace,' he said in satisfaction. 'There's an alibi if ever I heard one. We could give a couple to Manuel and Luis.'

'Manuel and Luis?'

'Our Hun protectors. They think I'm taunting them if I use their real names, but surely a muffin couldn't be seen as a taunt.' His eyes were not leaving hers. He wanted her. He ached for her. His eyes said it all, but he was keeping himself rigidly under control.

'You think we might find the ingredients?' he asked, but she was already opening the panty door, doing a visual sweep of the shelves, then checking out the first of three massive refrigerators. As anxious as he to find some way of keeping the sizzle between them under control, and to keep the tension on his face at bay.

'There's more ingredients than you can shake a stick at.'

'Pardon?'

'Lots of ingredients,' she said in satisfaction. 'It seems a shame to abandon bacon entirely. You want bacon and cheese muffins, or double chocolate chip?'

'Both,' he said promptly. 'Especially if I get to lick the chocolate chip bowl.'

'Done,' she said and smiled at him and his smile met hers and she thought, whoa I am in such trouble. And then she thought, whatever Sofía said, or Perpetua said, no matter how impossible this is, I'm so deeply in love, there's no way I'll ever be able to climb out.

CHAPTER EIGHT

THEY made muffins. Not just half a dozen muffins because: 'If I'm helping, it's not such a huge ask to make heaps,' Ramón declared. 'We can put them on for breakfast and show the world what my Gianetta can do.'

'You'll upset the chefs,' Jenny warned.

'If there's a turf war, you win hands down.'

'A turf war…' She was pouring choc chips into her mixture but she hesitated at that. 'I'm not interested in any turf war. Frankly, this set-up leaves me terrified.'

'It leaves me terrified.'

'Yes, but…'

'But I have no choice,' he said flatly, finishing the sentence for her. 'I know that. In the good old days, as Crown Prince I could have simply had my soldiers go out with clubs and drag you to my lair.'

'And now you give me choices,' she retorted, trying desperately to keep things light, whisking her muffin mix more briskly than she needed. 'Just as well. I believe clubbing might create an International Incident.'

'I miss the good old days,' he said morosely. He was sitting on the edge of the table, swinging his gorgeous boots, taking taste tests of her mixture. So sexy the kitchen seemed to sizzle. 'What use is being a prince if I can't get my woman?'

My woman. She was dreaming, Jenny thought dreamily. She was cooking muffins for her prince.

My woman?

She started spooning her mixture into the pans and Ramón reached over and took the trays and the bowl from her. 'I can do this,' he said. 'If you do something for me.'

'What?'

'Pull my boots off. I asked you ages ago.'

'I thought you were kidding.'

'They're killing me,' he confessed. 'I've spent my life in either boat shoes, bare feet or steel-toed construction boots. These make me feel like my feet are in corsets and I can't get them off. Please, dear, kind Jenny, will you pull my boots off?'

He was sitting on the table. He was spooning muffin mixture into pans. He was holding his boots out for her to pull.

This was so ridiculous she couldn't help giggling.

She wiped her hands—it'd be a pity to get chocolate on leather like this—took position, took a boot in both hands—and pulled.

The boot didn't budge. It was like a second skin.

'See what I mean,' Ramón said morosely. 'And I really don't want to wake a valet. You think I should cut them off?'

'You can't cut them,' Jenny said, shocked, and tried again. The boot budged, just a little.

'Hey,' Ramón said, continuing to spoon. 'It's coming.'

'I'll pull you off the table if I tug any harder,' Jenny warned.

'I'm strong,' he said, too smugly, keeping on spooning. 'My balance is assured.'

'Right,' she said and glowered, reacting to his smugness. She wiped both her hands on her dressing gown, took the boot in both hands, took a deep breath—and pulled like she'd never pulled.

The boot held, gripped for a nano-second and then gave. Jenny lurched backward, boot in hand, lost her balance and fell backwards.

Ramón slid off the table, staggered—and ended up on the floor.

The half-full bowl slid off after him, tipped sideways and mixture oozed out over the floor.

Jenny stared across at him in shock. Ramón stared back at her—her lovely prince, half bootless, sprawled on the floor, surrounded by choc chip muffin mixture.

Her Ramón.

She couldn't help it. She laughed out loud, and it was a magical release of tension, a declaration of love and happiness if ever there was one, and she couldn't help what happened next either. It was as if restraint had been thrown to the wind and she could do what she liked—and there was no doubting what she'd like. She slid over the floor, she took Ramón's face in both her hands—and she kissed him.

And Ramón kissed her back—a thoroughly befuddled, laughing, wonderful kiss. He tasted of choc chip muffin. He tasted of love.

He tugged her close, hauling her backward with him so she was in his arms, and they were so close she thought she must…they must…

And then the door burst open and Sofía was standing in the doorway staring at them both as if they'd lost their minds.

Maybe they had.

The little cat was delicately licking muffin mixture from the floor. Sofía darted across and retrieved the cat as if she were saving her from poison.

'Hi, Sofía,' Ramón said innocently from somewhere underneath his woman. Jenny would have pulled away but he was having none of it. He tugged her close and held, so they were lying on the floor like two children caught out in mischief. Or more.

Sofía stared down at them as if she couldn't believe her eyes. 'What do you think you're doing?' she hissed.

'Making muffins, Ramón said, and he would have pulled Jenny closer but the mixture of confusion and distress on Sofía's face was enough to have her pulling away. The timer was buzzing. Somehow she struggled to her feet. She opened the oven and retrieved her now cooked bacon muffins. Then she thought what the heck, she might as well finish what she'd started, so she put the almost full tray of choc chip muffins in to replace them.

'Gianetta's a professional,' Ramón said proudly to his aunt, struggling up as well. 'I told you she was fabulous.'

'Are you out of your minds?'

'No, I…'

'You're just like the rest,' she hissed at him. 'They're all womanisers, all the men who've ever held power here. You have her trapped. Ramón, what on earth is it that you're planning?'

'I'm not planning anything.'

'If it's marriage… You can't. I know Philippe needs a mother but this is…'

'It's nothing to do with Philippe,' Ramón snapped. 'Why are you here?'

'Why do you think?' Sofía's anger was becoming almost apoplectic. 'Did you think the two of you were invisible? Everyone knows where you are.

Ramón, think about what you're doing. You're no longer just responsible for yourself. You represent a country now! She's a nice girl, I won't let you ruin her, or trap her into this life.'

'I won't do either,' Ramón said, coldly furious. 'We're not talking marriage. We're not talking anything past this night. Jenny will be leaving…'

'Ramón, if she goes to the island now… There'll be such talk. To take her in the palace kitchen…'

'He didn't *take* me…' It was Jenny's turn to be angry now. 'My dressing gown cord's still done up.'

'No one can tell that from outside,' Sofía snapped and walked across and tugged the door wide. 'See? The harm's done,' she said, as two footmen stepped smartly away from the door.

'You can't be happy here,' she whispered. 'No one knows anyone. No one trusts.'

'I know that,' Ramón told her. 'Sofía, stop this.'

'I told her you should take her to the island. I told her. You should have waited.'

'Excuse me?' Jenny said. 'Can you include me in this?'

'It's nothing to do with you,' Sofía said and then seemed to think about it. Her anger faded and she suddenly sounded weary and defeated. 'No. I mean…even if you were suitable as a royal bride— which you aren't—you aren't tough enough. To do it with no training…'

'Sofía, don't do this,' Ramón said. Sofía's distress was clear and real. 'We aren't talking about marriage.'

'Then you're ruining her for nothing. And here's your valet, come to see what all the fuss is about.'

'I don't want my valet,' Ramón snapped. 'I don't want any valet.'

'You don't have a choice,' Sofía said with exasperation. 'None of us do. Ramón, go away. I'll stay here with Jenny until these…whatever you're making…muffins?…are cooked. We'll make the best of a bad situation but there's no way we can keep this quiet. This, with your stupid insistence on dancing with her first tonight… She'll have paparazzi in her face tomorrow, whether she leaves or not.'

'Paparazzi…' Jenny said faintly.

'Leave now, Ramón, and don't go near her again. She needs space to see what a mess this situation is.'

'She doesn't want space.'

'Yes, I do,' Jenny said. Philippe? Paparazzi? There were so many unknowns. What was she getting into?

She felt dizzy.

She felt bereft.

'Jenny,' Ramón said urgently but Sofía was before him, pushing herself between them.

'Leave it,' she told them both harshly. 'Like it or not, Ramón is Crown Prince. He needs to fit his new role. He might think he wants you but he doesn't have a choice. *You* don't belong in our world and you both know it.' She glanced along the corridor where there were now four servants waiting. 'So… There's to be no seduction tonight. We're all calmly eating muffins and going to bed. Yes?'

'Yes,' Jenny said before Ramón could reply. She didn't want to look at him. She couldn't. Because the laughter in his eyes had gone.

The servants were waiting to take over. The palace was waiting to take over.

She lay in her opulent bed and her head spun so much she felt dizzy.

She was lying on silk sheets. When she moved, she felt as if she was being caressed.

She wasn't being caressed. She was lying in a royal bed, in a royal boudoir. Alone. Because why?

Because Ramón was a Crown Prince.

Even when she'd lain with him in his wonderful yacht, believing he was simply the skipper and not the owner, she'd felt a sense of inequality, as if this couldn't be happening to her.

But it had happened, and now it was over.

What else had she expected?

Since she'd met Ramón her ache of grief had lifted. Life had become…unreal. But here it was again, reality, hard and cold as ice, slamming her back to earth. Grief was real. Loss was real. Emptiness and heartache had been her world for years, and here they were again.

Her time with Ramón, her time tonight, had been some sort of crazy soap bubble. Even before Sofía had spelled it out, she'd known it was impossible.

Sofía said she was totally unsuitable. Of course she was.

But…but…

As the night wore on something strange was happening. Her grief for Matty had been in abeyance during the two weeks with Ramón, and again tonight. It was back with her now, but things had changed. Things were changing.

Ever since Matty was born, things had happened to Jenny. Just happened. It was as if his birth, his medical problems, his desperate need, had put her on a roller coaster of emotions that she couldn't get off. Her life was simply doing what came next.

But the chain of events today had somehow changed things. What Sofía and then Perpetua had said had stirred something deep within. Or maybe it was how Ramón had made her feel tonight that was making her feel different.

She'd seen the defeat on Ramón's face and she recognized that defeat. It was a defeat born of bleak acceptance.

Once upon a time she'd shared it. Maybe she still should. But…but…

'Why should I run?' she whispered and she wondered if she'd really said it.

It didn't make any sense. Sofía and Perpetua

were right. So was Ramón. What was between them was clearly impossible, and there'd be a million more complications she hadn't thought of yet.

Philippe? The child Sofía had talked of?

She didn't go near children. Not after Matty.

And royalty? She had no concept of what Ramón was facing. Threats? The unknown Carlos?

There were questions everywhere, unspoken shadows looming from all sides, but overriding everything was the fact that she wanted Ramón so much she could almost cry out loud for him. What she wanted right now was to pad out into the palace corridor, yell at the top of her lungs for Ramón and then sit down and demand answers.

She'd had her chance. She'd used it making muffins. And kissing her prince.

He'd kissed her back.

The memory made her smile. Ramón made her smile.

Maybe the shadows weren't so long, she thought, but she knew they were.

'I'd be happy as his lover,' she whispered to the night. 'For as long as he wanted me. Just as his lover. Just in private. Back on his boat, sailing round the world, Ramón and me.'

It wasn't going to happen. And would she be happy on his island, being paid occasional visits as Sofía had suggested?

No!

She lay back on her mound of feather pillows and she stared up at the ceiling some more.

She stared at nothing.

Jenny and Ramón, the Crown Prince of Cepheus? No and no and no.

But still there was this niggle. It wasn't anger, exactly. Not exactly.

It was more that she'd found her centre again.

She'd found something worth fighting for.

Gianetta and the Crown Prince of Cepheus? No and no and no.

The thing was, though, sense had gone out of the window.

The car crash that had killed his mother and his sister had left him with an aching void where family used to be. For years he'd carried the grief as a burden, thinking he could bear no more, and the way to avoid that was to not let people close.

He loved his work in Bangladesh—it changed people's lives—yet individual lives were not permitted to touch him.

But there was something about Jenny… Gianetta…that broke the barriers he'd built. She'd touched a chord, and the resonance was so deep and so real that to walk away from her seemed unthinkable.

For the last three months he'd tried to tell himself what he'd felt was an illusion, but the moment he'd seen her again he'd known it was real. She was his woman. He knew it with a certainty so deep it felt primeval.

But to drag her into the royal limelight, into a place where the servants greeted you with blank faces…into a place where his father had died and barely a ripple had been created…where Carlos threatened and he didn't know which servants might be loyal and which might be in Carlos's pay… here his duty lay to his people and to have his worry centred on one slip of a girl…

On Jenny.

No.

Could he love her enough to let her go?

He must.

He had a deputation from neighbouring countries meeting him first thing in the morning to discuss border issues. Refugees. The thought did his head in.

Royalty seemed simple on the outside—what had Jenny said?—cutting ribbons and making speeches. But Cepheus was governed by royalty. He'd set moves afoot to turn it into a democracy but it would take years, and meanwhile what he did would change people's lives.

Could he do it alone? He must.

He had no right to ask Jenny to share a load he found insupportable. To put her into the royal limelight… To ask her to share the risks that had killed his father… To distract himself from a task that had to be faced alone…

There was no choice at all.

CHAPTER NINE

JENNY didn't see Ramón all the next day. She couldn't. 'Affairs of State,' Sofía told her darkly, deeply disapproving when Jenny told her she had no intention of leaving until she'd spoken to Ramón. 'There's so much business that's been waiting for Ramón to officially take charge. Señor Rodriguez tells me he's booked for weeks. Poor baby.'

Poor baby? Jenny thought of the man whose boot she'd pulled off, she thought of the power of his touch, and she thought 'poor baby' was a description just a wee bit wide of the mark.

So what was she to do? By nine she'd breakfasted, inspected the palace gardens—breathtakingly beautiful but *so* empty—got lost twice in the palace corridors, and she was starting to feel as if she was climbing walls.

She headed out to the gardens again and found Gordon, pacing by one of the lagoon-sized swimming pools. It seemed the darkness and the strange city last night had defeated even him.

'All this opulence gives me the creeps,' he said, greeting her with relief. 'I've been waiting for you. How about if we slope off down to the docks? It's not so far. A mile or so as the crow flies. We could get out the back way, avoid the paparazzi.'

'I do need to come back,' she whispered, looking at the cluster of cameramen around the main gate with dismay, and Gordon surveyed her with care.

'Are you sure? There's talk, lass, about last night.'

And there it was again, that surge of anger.

'Then maybe I need to give them something to talk about,' she snapped.

The meetings were interminable—men and women in serious suits, with serious briefcases filled with papers covered with serious concerns, not one of which he could walk away from.

This country had been in trouble for decades—was still in trouble. It would take skill and commitment to bring it back from the brink, to stop the exodus of youth leaving the country, to take advantage of the country's natural resources to bring prosperity for citizens who'd been ignored for far too long.

The last three months he'd spent researching, researching, researching. He had the knowledge now to make a difference, but so much work was before him it felt overwhelming.

He should be gearing up right now to spend the next six months supervising the construction of houses in Bangladesh, simple work but deeply satisfying. He'd had to abandon that to commit to this, a more direct and personal need.

And this morning he'd had to abandon Jenny.

Gianetta.

The two words kept interplaying in his head. Jenny. Gianetta.

Jenny was the woman who made muffins, the woman who saved whales, the woman who made him laugh.

Gianetta was the woman he took to his bed. Gianetta was the woman he would make his Princess—*if* he didn't care so much, for her and for his country.

Where was she now?

He'd been wrong last night. Sofía had spelled out their situation clearly and he could do nothing but agree.

He should be with her now, explaining why he couldn't take things further. She'd be confused and distressed. But there was simply no option for him to spend time with her today.

So… He'd left orders for her to be left to enjoy a day of leisure. The *Marquita* was a big boat; it was hard work to crew her and she'd been sailing for three months. Last night had been…stressful. She deserved to rest.

He had meetings all day and a formal dinner tonight. Tomorrow, though, he'd make time early to say goodbye. If she stayed that long.

And tomorrow he'd promised to visit Philippe.

He glanced at his watch. Tomorrow. It was twenty-two hours and thirty minutes before a scheduled visit with his woman. Wedging it in between affairs of state and his concern for a child he didn't know what to do with.

Jenny. How could he ever make sense of what he felt for her?

He knew, in his heart, that he couldn't.

The *Marquita* meant work, and in work there was respite.

The day was windless so they could unfurl the sails and let them dry. The boat was clean, but by common consensus they decided it wasn't clean enough. They scrubbed the decks, they polished brass, they gave the interior such a clean that Martha Gardener would be proud of them.

Jenny remade the bed in the great stateroom, plumped the mass of pillows, looked down at the sumptuous quilts and wondered again, what had she been thinking?

She'd slept in this bed with the man she loved. She loved him still, with all her heart, but in the distance she could see the spires of the palace, glistening white in the Mediterranean sunshine.

The Crown Prince of Cepheus. For a tiny time their two disparate worlds had collided, and they'd seemed almost equal. Now, all that was left was to find the courage to walk away.

Perhaps.

Eighteen hours and twenty-two minutes. How many suits could he talk to in that time? How many documents must he read?

He had to sign them all and there was no way he could sign without reading.

His eyes were starting to cross.

Eighteen hours and seven minutes.

Would she still be here?

Surely she wouldn't leave without a farewell.

He deserved it, he thought, but please…no.

They worked solidly until mid-afternoon. Gordon was checking the storerooms, taking inventory, making lists of what needed to be replaced. Jenny was still obsessively cleaning.

Taking away every trace of her.

But, as the afternoon wore on, even she ran out of things to do. 'Time to get back to the palace,' Gordon decreed.

'We could stay on board.'

'She's being pulled out of the water tonight so engineers can check her hull in the morning. We hardly have a choice tonight.'

'Will you stay on as Ramón's skipper?'

'I love this boat,' he said simply. 'For as long as I'm asked, I'll stay. If that means staying at the palace from time to time, I'll find the courage.'

'I don't have very much courage,' she whispered.

'Or maybe you have sense instead,' Gordon said stoutly. He stood back for her to precede him up to the deck. She stepped up—and suddenly the world was waiting for her.

Paparazzi were everywhere. Flashlights went off in her face, practically blinding her. She put her hand over her eyes in an instinctive gesture of defence, and retreated straight back down again.

Gordon slammed the hatch after her.

'Tell us about yourself,' someone called from the dock. 'You speak Spanish, right?'

'We're happy to pay for your story,' someone else called.

'You and Prince Ramón were on the boat together for two weeks, alone, right?' That was bad enough. But then…

'Is it true you had a baby out of wedlock?' someone else called while Jenny froze. 'And the baby died?'

They knew about her Matty? They knew.…

She wanted to go home right now. She wanted to creep into a bunk and stay hidden while Gordon sailed her out of the harbour and away.

Serenity. Peace. That was what she'd been

striving for since Matty died. Where was serenity and peace now?

How could she find it in this?

'I'll talk to them,' Gordon said, looking stunned and sick, and she looked at this big shy man and she thought why should he fight her battles? Why should anyone fight her battles?

Maybe she had to fight to achieve this so-called serenity, she thought. Maybe that was what her problem had been all along. She'd been waiting for serenity to find her, when all along it was something she needed to fight for.

Or maybe it wasn't even serenity that she wanted.

Then, before she had time to decide she'd lost her mind entirely—for maybe she had; she certainly wasn't making sense to herself and Gordon was looking really worried—she flung open the hatch again and stepped out onto the deck.

His cellphone was on mute in his pocket. He felt it vibrate, checked it and saw it was Gordon calling. Gordon wouldn't call him except in an emergency.

The documents had just been signed and the Heads of State were lining up for a photo call. These men had come for the coronation and had stayed on.

Cepheus was a small nation. These men represented far more powerful nations than his, and Cepheus had need of powerful allies. Nevertheless, he excused himself and answered.

'Paparazzi know about Jenny's baby,' Gordon barked, so loud he almost burst Ramón's eardrum. 'They're on the jetty. We're surrounded. You need to get her out of here.'

He felt sick. 'I'll have a security contingent there in two minutes,' he said, motioning to Señor Rodriguez, who, no doubt, had heard every word. 'I need to get to the docks,' he told him. 'How long?'

'It would take us fifteen minutes, Your Highness, but we can't leave here,' Rodriguez said. The man was seriously good. He already had security on his second phone. 'Security will have dealt with it before we get there. There's no need…'

There was a need, but as he glanced back at the Heads of State he knew his lawyer was right. To leave for such a reason could cause insupportable offence. It could cause powerful allies to turn to indifference.

His sense of helplessness was increasing almost to breaking point. *He couldn't protect his woman.*

'You can see, though,' Señor Rodriguez said, obviously realising just how he was torn. He turned back to the men and women behind him. 'If you'll excuse us for a moment,' he said smoothly. 'An urgent matter of security has come up. We'll be five minutes, no more.'

'I will go,' Ramón said through gritted teeth.

'It will be dealt with before you arrive,' Señor Rodriguez said again. 'But we have security monitors on the royal berth. I can switch our cameras there to reassure you until you see our security people take over. If you'll come aside…'

So Ramón followed the lawyer into an anteroom. He stared at the monitor in the corner, and he watched in grim desperation as his woman faced the press.

They'd pull her apart, he thought grimly—and there was nothing he could do to help her.

The cameras went wild. Questions were being shouted at her from all directions.

Courage, she told herself grimly. Come on, girl, you've hidden for long enough. Now's the time to stand and fight.

She ignored the shouts. She stood still and silent, knowing she looked appalling, knowing the shots would be of her at her worst. She'd just scrubbed out a boat. She didn't look like anyone famous. She was simply Jenny the deckhand, standing waiting for the shouting to stop.

And finally it did. The journalists fell silent at last, thinking she didn't intend to respond.

'Finished?' she asked, quirking an eyebrow in what she hoped looked like sardonic amusement, and the shouting started again.

Serenity, she told herself. She tapped a bare toe on the deck and waited again for silence.

'I've called His Highness,' Gordon called up from below. 'Security's on its way. Ramón'll send them.'

It didn't matter. This wasn't Ramón's fight, she

thought. Finally, silence fell again; baffled silence. The cameras were still in use but the journalists were clearly wondering what they had here. She waited and they watched. Impasse.

'You do speak English?' one asked at last, a lone question, and she nodded. A lone question, not shouted, could be attended to.

And why not all the others, in serene order? Starting now.

'Yes,' she said, speaking softly so they had to stay silent or they couldn't hear her. 'I speak English as well as Spanish and French. My parents have Spanish blood. And I did indeed act as crew for His Highness, Prince Ramón, as we sailed between Sydney and Auckland.' She thought back through the questions that had been hurled at her, mentally ticking them off. 'Yes, I'm a cook. I'm… I *was* also a single mother. My son died of a heart condition two years ago, but I don't wish to answer any more questions about Matty. His death broke my heart. As for the rest… Thank you, I enjoyed last night, and yes, rumours that I cooked for His Highness early this morning are true. I'm employed as his cook and crew. That's what I've been doing for the last three months and no, I'm not sure if I'll continue. It depends if he needs me. What else? Oh, the personal questions. I'm twenty-nine years old. I had my appendix out when I was nine, my second toes are longer than my big toes and I don't eat cabbage. I think your country is lovely and the *Marquita* is the prettiest boat in the world. However, scrubbing the *Marquita* is what I'm paid to do and that's what I'm doing. If you have any more questions, can you direct them to my secretary?'

She grinned then, a wide, cheeky grin which only she knew how much effort it cost to produce. 'Oh, whoops, I forgot I don't have a secretary. Can one of you volunteer? I'll pay you in muffins. If one of you is willing, then the rest can siphon your questions through him. That's so much more dignified than shouting, don't you think?'

Then she gave them all a breezy wave, observed their shocked silence and then slipped below, leaving them dumfounded.

She stood against the closed hatch, feeling winded. Gordon was staring at her in amazement. As well he might.

What was she doing?

Short answer? She didn't know.

Long answer? She didn't know either. Retiring from this situation with dignity was her best guess, though suddenly Jenny had no intention of retiring.

Not just yet.

This was a state-of-the-art security system, and sound was included. Not only did Ramón see everything, he heard every word Jenny spoke.

'It seems the lady doesn't need protecting,' Señor Rodriguez said, smiling his relief as Jenny disappeared below deck and Ramón's security guards appeared on the docks.

Ramón shook his head. 'I should have been there for her.'

'She's protected herself. She's done very well.'

'She shouldn't have been put in that position.'

'I believe the lady could have stayed below,' the lawyer said dryly. 'The lady chose to take them on. She has some courage.'

'She shouldn't…'

'She did,' the lawyer said, and then hesitated.

Señor Rodriguez had been watching on the sidelines for many years now. His father had been legal advisor to Ramón's grandmother, and Sofía had kept him on after Ramón's father died, simply to stay aware of what royalty was doing. Now he was doing the job of three men and he was thoroughly enjoying himself. 'Your Highness, if I may make so bold…'

'You've never asked permission before,' Ramón growled, and the lawyer permitted himself another small smile.

'It's just…the role you're taking on…to do it alone could well break you. You're allowing me to assist but no one else. This woman has courage and honour. If you were to…'

'I won't,' Ramón snapped harshly, guessing

where the lawyer was going and cutting him off before he went any further. He flicked the screen off. There was nothing to see but the press, now being dispersed by his security guards. 'I do this alone or not at all.'

'Is that wise?'

'I don't know what's wise or not,' Ramón said and tried to sort his thoughts into some sort of sense. What was happening here? The lawyer was suggesting sharing the throne? With Jenny?

Jenny as his woman? Yes. But Jenny in the castle?

The thought left him cold. The night of his father's death was still with him, still haunting him.

Enough. 'We have work to do,' he growled and headed back to the room where the Heads of State were waiting.

'But…' the lawyer started, but Ramón was already gone.

CHAPTER TEN

HE MANAGED a few short words with her that night as he passed the supper room. It was all he had, as he moved from the evening's meetings to his briefing for tomorrow. To his surprise, Jenny seemed relaxed, even happy.

'I'm sorry about today,' he said. 'It seemed you handled things very well.'

'I talked too much,' she said, smiling. 'I need to work on my serenity.'

'Your serenity?'

'I'm not very good at it.' Her smile widened. 'But I showed promise today. Dr Matheson would be proud of me. By the way, I hope it's okay that Gordon and I are staying here tonight. The boat's up on the hard, and who wants to sleep on a boat in dry dock? Besides, staying in a palace is kind of fun.'

Kind of fun... He gazed into the opulent supper

room, at the impassive staff, and he thought…*kind of fun*?

'So I can stay tonight?' she prompted.

He raked his hair. 'I should have had Señor Rodriguez organise airline tickets.'

'Señor Rodriguez has better things to do than organise my airline tickets. I'll organise them when I'm ready. Meanwhile, can I stay tonight?'

'Of course, but Jenny, I don't have time…'

'I know you don't,' she said sympathetically. 'Señor Rodriguez says these first days are crazy. It'll get better, he says, but I'll not add to your burdens tonight. I hope I never will.'

Then, before he could figure how to respond, a servant appeared to remind him he was late for his next briefing. He was forced to leave Jenny, who didn't seem the least put out. She'd started chatting cheerfully to the maid who was clearing supper.

To his surprise, the maid was responding with friendliness and animation. Well, why wouldn't she, he told himself as he immersed himself again into royal business. Jenny had no baggage of centuries of oppression. She wasn't royal.

She never could be royal. He could never ask that of her, he thought grimly. But, as the interminable briefing wore on, he thought of Jenny—not being royal. He thought of her thinking of the palace as fun, and he almost told the suits he was talking to where to go.

But he didn't. He was sensible. He had a country

to run, and when he was finally free Jenny had long gone to bed.

And there was no way he was knocking on her door tonight.

He missed her at breakfast, maybe because he ate before six before commencing the first of three meetings scheduled before ten. He moved through each meeting with efficiency and speed, desperate to find time to see her, but the meetings went overtime. He had no time left. His ten o'clock diary entry was immovable.

This appointment he'd made three months ago. Four hours every Wednesday. Even Jenny would have to wait on this.

Swiftly he changed out of his formal wear into jeans, grabbed his swimmers and made his way to the palace garages. He strode round the rows of espaliered fruit trees marking the end of the palace gardens—and Jenny was sitting patiently on a garden bench.

She was wearing smart new jeans, a casual cord jacket in a pale washed apricot over a creamy lace camisole and creamy leather ballet flats. Her curls were brushed until they shone. She looked rested and refreshed and cheerful.

She looked beautiful.

She rose and stretched and smiled a welcome. Gianetta.

Jenny, he told himself fiercely. This was Jenny, his guest before she left for ever.

A very lovely Jenny. Smiling and smiling.

'Do you like it?' she demanded and spun so she could be admired from all angles. 'This is the new smart me.'

'Where on earth…?'

'I went shopping,' she said proudly. 'Yesterday, when we finally escaped from that mob. Your security guys kindly escorted me to some great shops and then stood guard while I tried stuff on. Neat, yes?'

'Neat,' he said faintly and her face fell and he amended his statement fast. 'Gorgeous.'

'No, that won't do either,' she said reprovingly. 'My borrowed ball-gown was gorgeous. But this feels good. I thought yesterday I haven't had new clothes for years and the owner of the boutique gave me a huge discount.'

'I'll bet she did,' he said faintly.

She grinned. 'I know, it was cheeky, but I thought if I'm to be photographed by every cameraman in the known universe there has to be some way I can take advantage. She was practically begging me to take clothes.'

'Gordon said you were upset.'

'Gordon was upset.'

'I should have been there.'

'Then the cameramen would have been even more persistent,' she said gently. 'But I have clothes to face them now, and they're not so scary. So…I pinned Señor Rodriguez down this morning and he says you're going to see Philippe. So I was wondering…' Her tone became more diffident. 'Would it upset you if I came along? Would it upset Philippe?'

'No, but I can't ask you…'

'You're not asking,' she said and came forward to slip her hands into his. 'You're looking trapped. I don't want you to feel that way. Not by me.'

'You'd never make me feel trapped,' he said. 'But Jenny, I can't expect…'

'Then don't expect,' she said. 'Señor Rodriguez told me all about Philippe. No, don't look like that. The poor man never had a chance; I practically sat on him to make him explain things in detail. Philippe's your cousin's son. Everyone thought he stood to inherit, only when his parents died it turned out they weren't actually married. According to royal rules, he's illegitimate. Now he has nothing.'

'He's well cared for. He has lovely foster parents.'

'Sofía says you've been visiting him every week since you got here.'

'It's the least I can do when he's lost his home as well as his parents.'

'He can't stay here?'

'No,' he said bleakly. 'If he's here he'll be in the middle of servants who'll either treat him like royalty—and this country hates royalty—or they'll treat him as an illegitimate nothing.'

'Yet you still think he should be here,' Jenny said softly.

'No.'

'Because this is where you were when your father died?'

'What the…?'

'Sofía,' she said simply. 'I asked, she told me. Ramón, I'm so sorry. It must have been dreadful. But that was then. Now is now. Can I meet him?'

'I can't ask that of you,' he said, feeling totally winded. 'And he's the same age your little boy would have been…'

'Ramón, can we take this one step at a time?' she asked. 'Let's just go visit this little boy—who's not Matty. Let's just leave it at that.'

So they went and for the first five miles or so they didn't speak. Ramón didn't know where to take this.

There were so many things in this country that needed his attention but over and over his thoughts kept turning to one little boy. Consuela and Ernesto were lovely but they were in their sixties. To expect them to take Philippe long-term…

He glanced across at Jenny and found she was watching him. He had the top down on his Boxster coupe. The warm breeze was blowing Jenny's curls around her face. She looked young and beautiful and free. He remembered the trapped woman he'd met over three months ago and the change seemed extraordinary.

How could he trap her again? He couldn't. Of course he couldn't. He didn't intend to.

Yet—she'd asked to come. Was she really opening herself up to be hurt again?

'I can't believe this country,' she said, smiling, and he knew she was making an attempt to keep the conversation neutral. Steering away from undertones that were everywhere. 'It's like something on a calendar.'

'There's a deep description.'

'It's true. There's a calendar in the bathroom of Seaport Coffee 'n' Cakes and it has a fairy tale palace on it. All white turrets and battlements and moats, surrounded by little stone houses with ancient tiled roofs, and mountains in the background, and just a hint of snow.'

'There's no snow here,' he said, forced to smile back. 'We're on the Mediterranean.'

'Please,' she said reprovingly. 'You're messing with my calendar. So, as I was saying…'

But then, as he turned the car onto a dirt track leading to a farmhouse, she stopped with the imagery and simply stared. 'Where are we?'

'This is where Philippe lives.'

'But it's lovely,' she whispered, gazing out over grassy meadows where a flock of alpacas grazed placidly in the morning sun. 'It's the perfect place for a child to live.'

'He's not happy.'

'I imagine that might well be because his parents are dead,' she said, suddenly sharp. 'It'll take him for ever to adjust to their loss. If ever.'

'I don't think his parents were exactly hands-on,' Ramón told her. 'My uncle and my cousin liked to gamble, and so did Maria Therese. They spent three-quarters of their lives in Monaco and they never took Philippe. They were on their way there when their plane crashed.'

'So who took care of Philippe?'

'He's had a series of nannies. The palace hasn't exactly been a happy place to work. Neither my uncle nor my cousin thought paying servants was a priority, and I gather as a mother Maria Therese was…difficult. Nannies have come and gone.'

'So Philippe's only security has been the palace itself,' Jenny ventured.

'He's getting used to these foster parents,' Ramón said, but he wasn't convincing himself. 'They're great.'

'I'm looking forward to meeting them.'

'I'll be interested to hear your judgement.' Then he paused.

'Gianetta, are you sure you want to do this? Philippe's distressed and there's little I can do about it. It won't help to make you distressed as well. Would you like to turn back?'

'Well, that'd be stupid,' Jenny said. 'Philippe will already know you're on your way. To turn back now would be cruel.' 'But what about you?'

'This isn't about me,' she said, gently but inexorably. 'Let's go meet Philippe.'

He was the quietest little boy Jenny had ever met. He looked just like Ramón.

The family resemblance was amazing, she thought. Same dark hair. Same amazing eyes. Same sense of trouble, kept under wraps.

His foster parents, Consuela and Ernesto, were voluble and friendly. They seemed honoured to have Ramón visit, but not so overawed that it kept them silent. That was just as well, as their happy small talk covered up the deathly silence emanating from Philippe.

They sat at the farmhouse table eating Consuela's amazing strawberry cake. Consuela and Ernesto chatted, Ramón answered as best he could, and Jenny watched Philippe.

He was clutching a little ginger cat as if his life depended on it. He was too thin. His eyes were too big for his face.

He was watching his big cousin as if he was hungry.

I feel like that, she thought, and recognized what she'd thought and intensified her scrutiny. She had the time and the space to do it. Consuela and Ernesto were friendly but they were totally focused on Ramón. Philippe had greeted Jenny with courtesy but now he, too, was totally focused on Ramón.

Of course. Ramón was the Crown Prince.

Only Ramón's title didn't explain things completely, Jenny decided. Ramón was here in his casual clothes. He didn't look spectacular—or any more spectacular than he usually did—and a child wouldn't respond to an adult this way unless there was a fair bit of hero worship going on.

'Does Prince Ramón really come every week?' she asked Consuela as she helped clear the table.

'Every week since he's been back in the country,' the woman said. 'We're so grateful. Ernesto and I have had many foster children—some from very troubled homes—but Philippe's so quiet we don't seem to get through to him. He never says a thing unless he must. He hardly eats unless he's forced, and he certainly doesn't know how to enjoy himself. But once a week Ramón…I mean Crown Prince Ramón…comes and takes him out in his car and it's as if he lights up. He comes home happy, he eats, he tells us what he's done and he goes to bed and sleeps all night. Then he wakes and Ramón's not here, and his parents aren't here, and it all starts again. His Highness brought him his cat from the palace and that's made things better but now…we're starting to wonder if it's His Highness himself the child pines for.'

'He can't have become attached to Ramón so fast,' Jenny said, startled, and Consuela looked at her with eyes that had seen a lot in her lifetime, and she smiled.

'*Caro*, are you telling me that's impossible?'

Oh, help, was she so obvious? She glanced back to where Ernesto and Ramón were engaged in a deep conversation about some obscure football match, with Philippe listening to every word as if it was the meaning of life—and she found herself blushing from the toes up.

'We're hearing rumours,' Consuela said, seemingly satisfied with Jenny's reaction. 'How lovely.'

'I…there's nothing.' *How fast did rumours spread?*

'There's everything,' Consuela said. 'All our prince needs is a woman to love him.'

'I'm not his class.'

'Class? Pah!' Consuela waved an airy hand at invisible class barriers. 'Three months ago Philippe was Prince Royal. Now he's the illegitimate son of the dead Prince's mistress. If you worry about class then you worry about nothing. You make him happy. That's all anyone can ask.' Her shrewd gaze grew intent. 'You know that Prince Ramón is kind, intelligent, honourable. Our country needs him so much. But for a man to take on such a role…there must be someone filling his heart as well.'

'I can't…'

'I can see a brave young woman before me, and I'm very sure you can.'

All of this was thoroughly disconcerting. She should just shut up, she thought. She should stick with her new found serenity. But, as she wiped as Consuela washed, she pushed just a little more. 'Can I ask you something?'

'Of course.'

'You and Ernesto… You obviously love Philippe and you're doing the best you can for him. But if Philippe wants to be at the palace… Why doesn't Ramón…why doesn't His Highness simply employ you to be there for him?'

The woman turned and looked at Jenny as if she were crazy. 'Us? Go to the palace?'

'Why not?'

'We're just farmers.'

'Um…excuse me. Didn't you just say…?'

'That's for you,' Consuela said, and then she sighed and dried her hands and turned to Jenny. 'I think that for you, you're young enough and strong enough to fight it, but for us…and for Philippe…the lines of class at the palace are immovable.'

'Would you try it, though?' she asked. 'Would you stay in the palace if Ramón asked it of you?'

'Maybe, but he won't. He won't risk it, and why should he?' She sighed, as if the worries of the world were too much for her, but then she pinned on cheerfulness, smiled determinedly at Jenny and turned back to the men. Moving on. 'Philippe. His Highness, Prince Ramón, asked if you could have your swimming costume prepared. He tells me he wishes to take you to the beach.'

Football was abandoned in an instant. 'In your car?' Philippe demanded of Ramón, round-eyed.

'In my car,' Ramón said. 'With Señorina Bertin. If it's okay with you.'

The little boy turned his attention to Jenny and surveyed her with grave attention. Whatever he saw there, it seemed to be enough.

'That will be nice,' he said stiffly.

'Get your costume, poppet,' Consuela said, but Philippe was already gone.

So they headed to the beach, about five minutes' drive from the farmhouse. Philippe sat between Jenny and Ramón, absolutely silent, his eyes straight ahead. But Jenny watched his body language. He could have sat ramrod still and not touched either of them, but instead he slid slightly to Ramón's side so his small body was just touching his big cousin.

Ramón was forging something huge here, Jenny thought. Did he know?

Maybe he did. Maybe he couldn't help but know. As he drove he kept up a stream of light-hearted banter, speaking to Jenny, but most of what he said was aimed at Philippe.

Did Gianetta know this little car was the most wonderful car in the world? Did she know he thought this was the only one of its kind that had ever been fitted with bench seats—designed so two people could have a picnic in the car if it was raining? Why, only two weeks ago he and Philippe had eaten a picnic while watching a storm over the sea, and they'd seen dolphins. And now the bench seat meant there was room for the three of them. How about that for perfect? And it was red. Didn't Jenny think red was great?

'I like pink,' Jenny said, and Ramón looked as if she'd just committed blasphemy.

'You'd have me buy a pink car?'

'No, that'd be a waste. You could spray paint this one,' she retorted, and chuckled at their combined manly horror.

Philippe didn't contribute a word but she saw him gradually relax, responding to their banter, realizing that nothing was expected of him but that he relax and enjoy himself.

And he did enjoy himself. They arrived at the beach and Ramón had him in the water in minutes.

Jenny was slower. Señor Rodriguez had told her they often went swimming so she'd worn her bikini under her jeans, but for now she was content to paddle and watch.

The beach was glorious, a tiny cove with sun-bleached sand, gentle waves and shallow turquoise water. There were no buildings, no people and the mountains rose straight from the sea like sentinels guarding their privacy.

There'd be bodyguards. She'd been vaguely aware of cars ahead and behind them all day and shadowy figures at the farmhouse, but as they'd arrived at the beach the security presence was nowhere to be seen. The guards must be under orders to give the illusion of total privacy, she thought, and that was what they had.

Ramón had set this time up for Philippe. For a little cousin he was not beholden to in any way. A little boy who'd be miserable at the palace?

She paddled on, casually kicking water out in front of her, pretending she wasn't watching.

She was definitely watching.

Ramón was teaching Philippe to float. The little boy was listening with all the seriousness in the world. He was aching to do what his big cousin was asking of him. His body language said he'd almost die for his big cousin.

'If you float with your face in the water and count to ten, then I'll lift you out of the water,' Ramón was saying. 'My hand will be under your tummy until we reach ten and I'll count aloud. Then I'll lift you high. Do you trust me to do that?'

He received a solemn nod.

'Right,' Ramón said and Philippe leaned forward, leaned further so he was floating on Ramón's hand. And put his face in the water.

'One, two three…ten!' and the little boy was lifted high and hugged.

'Did you feel my hand fall away before I lifted you up? You floated? Hey, Gianetta, Philippe floated!' Ramón was spinning Philippe around and around until he squealed. His squeal was almost the first natural sound she'd heard from him. It was a squeal of delight, of joy, of life.

Philippe was just a little bit older than Matty would be right now. Ramón had worried about it. She'd dismissed his worry but now, suddenly, the knowledge hit her so hard that she flinched. She was watching a little boy learn to swim, and her Matty never would. Everything inside her seemed to shrink. Pain surged back, as it had surged over and over since she'd lost her little son.

But something about this time made it different. Something told her it must be different. So for once, somehow, she let the pain envelop her, not trying to deflect it, simply riding it out, letting it take her where it would. Trying to see, if she allowed it to take its course, whether it would destroy her or whether finally she could come out on the other side.

She was looking at a man holding a little boy who wasn't Matty—a little boy who against all the odds, she was starting to care about.

The heart swells to fit all comers.

It was a cliché. She'd never believed it. Back at the hospital, watching Matty fade, she'd looked at other children who'd come in ill, recovered then

gone out again to face the world and she'd felt…
nothing. It had been as if other children were on
some parallel universe to the one she inhabited.
There was no point of contact.

But suddenly, unbidden, those universes seemed
to have collided. For a moment she thought the
pain could make her head explode—and then she
knew it wouldn't.

Matty. Philippe. Two little boys. Did loving
Matty stop her feeling Philippe's pain?

Did loss preclude loving?

How could it?

She gazed out over the water, at this big man
with the responsibilities of the world on his shoulders, and at this little boy whose world had been
taken away from him.

She knew how many cares were pressing in on
Ramón right now. He'd taken this day out, not for
himself, but because he'd made a promise to
Philippe. Every week, he'd come. Affairs of State
were vital, but this, he'd decreed, was more so.

She thought fleetingly of the man who'd fathered
Matty, who'd sailed away and missed his whole
short life.

Philippe wasn't Ramón's son. He was the illegitimate child of a cousin he'd barely known and
yet…and yet…

She was blinking back tears, struggling to take
in the surge of emotions flooding through her, but

slowly the knot of pain within was easing its grip, letting her see what lay past its vicious hold.

Ramón had lost his family and he'd been a loner ever since, but now he was being asked to take on the cares of this country and the care of this little boy. This country depended on him. Philippe depended on him. But for him to do it alone…

Class barriers were just that, she thought. Grief was another barrier—and barriers could be smashed.

Could she face them all down?

Would Ramón want her to?

And if she did face them down for Ramón's sake, and for hers, she thought, for her thoughts were flowing in all sorts of tangents that hardly made sense, could she love Philippe as well? Could the knot of pain she'd held within since Matty's death be untied, maybe used to embrace instead of to exclude?

Her vision was blurred with tears and it was growing more blurred by the second. Ramón looked across at her and waved, as if to say, *what's keeping you; come in and join us*. She waved back and turned her back on them, supposedly to walk up the beach and strip off her outer clothes. In reality it was to get her face in order—and to figure if she had the courage to put it to the test.

Maybe they didn't want her. Maybe her instinctive feelings for Philippe were wrong, and maybe what Ramón was feeling for her stemmed from nothing more than a casual affair. Her heart told her it was much more, but then her heart was a fickle thing.

No matter. If she was mistaken she could walk away—but first she could try.

And Matty...

Surely loving again could never be a betrayal.

This was crazy, she told herself as she slipped off her clothes and tried to get her thoughts in order. She was thinking way ahead of what was really happening. She was imagining things that could never be.

Should she back off?

But then she glanced back at the two males in the shallows and she felt so proprietorial that it threatened to overwhelm her. My two men, she thought mistily, or they could be. Maybe they could be.

The country can have what it needs from Ramón but I'm lining up for my share, she told herself fiercely. If I have the courage. And maybe the shadows of Matty can be settled, warmed, even honoured by another love.

She sniffed and sniffed again, found a tissue in her bag, blew her nose and decided her face was in order as much as she could make it. She wriggled her bare toes in the sand and wriggled them again. If she dived straight into the waves and swam a bit to start with, she might even look respectable before she reached them.

And if she didn't…

Warts and all, she thought. That was what she was offering.

For they all had baggage, she decided, as she headed for the water. Her grief for Matty was still raw and real. This must inevitably still hurt.

And Ramón? He was an unknown, he was Crown Prince of Cepheus to her Jenny.

She was risking rejection, and everything that went with it.

Consuela said she had courage. Maybe Consuela was wrong.

'Maybe I'm just pig-headed stubborn,' she muttered to herself, heading into the shallows. 'Maybe I'm reading this all wrong and he doesn't want me and Philippe doesn't need me and today is all I have left of the pair of them.'

'So get in the water and get on with it,' she told herself.

'And if I'm right?'

'Then maybe serenity's not the way to go,' she muttered. 'Maybe the opposite's what's needed. Oh, but to fight for a prince…'

Maybe she would. For a prince's happiness.

And for the happiness of one small boy who wasn't Matty.

They swam, they ate a palace-prepared picnic on the sand and then they took a sleepy Philippe back to the farmhouse. Once again they drove in silence. What was between them seemed too complicated for words.

Dared she?

By the time they reached the farm, Philippe was asleep but, as Ramón lifted him from the car, he jerked awake, then sobbed and clung. Shaken, Ramón carried him into the house, while Jenny stared straight ahead and wondered whether she could be brave enough.

It was like staring into the night sky, overwhelmed by what she couldn't see as much as what she could see. The concept of serenity seemed ridiculous now. This was facing her demons, fighting for what she believed in, fighting for what she knew was right.

Dared she?

Two minutes later Ramón was back. He slid behind the wheel, still without a word, and sat, grim-faced and silent.

Now or never. Jenny took a deep breath, reached over and put her hand over his.

'He loves you,' she whispered.

He stared down at their linked hands and his mouth tightened into a grim line of denial. 'He can't. If it's going to upset him then I should stop coming.'

'Do you want to stop?'

'No.'

'Then why not take him back to the palace? Why not take him home?'

There was a moment's silence. Then, 'What, take

him back to the palace and wedge him into a few moments a day between my appointments? And the rest of the time?'

'Leave him with people who love him.'

'Like…'.

'Like Consuela and Ernesto.' Then, at the look on his face, she pressed his hand tighter. 'Ramón, you're taking all of this on as it is. Why not take it as it could be?'

'I don't know what you mean.'

'Just try,' she said, figuring it out as she went. 'Try for change. You say the palace is a dreadful place to live. So it is, but the servants are terrified of your title. They won't let you close because they're afraid. The place isn't a home, it's a mausoleum. Oh, it's a gorgeous mausoleum but it's a mausoleum for all that. But it could change. People like Consuela and Ernesto could change it.'

'Or be swallowed by it.'

'There's no need to be melodramatic. You could just invite them to stay for a couple of days to start with. Tell Philippe that his home is here—make that clear so he won't get distraught if…*when* he has to return. You can see how it goes. You won't be throwing him back anywhere.'

'I won't make him sleep in those rooms.'

And there it was, out in the open, raw and dreadful as it had been all those years ago. And, even worse, Jenny was looking at him as if she understood.

And maybe she did.

'You were alone,' she whispered. ' Your father brought you to the palace and he was killed and you were alone.'

'It's nothing.'

'It's everything. Of course it is. But this is now, Ramón. This is Philippe. As it's not Matty, it's also not you. Philippe won't be alone.'

'This is nonsense,' he said roughly, trying to recover some sort of footing. 'It's impossible. Sofía saw that even before I arrived. Philippe's illegitimate. The country would shun him.'

'They'd love him, given half a chance.'

'How do you know?' he snapped. 'He was there for over four years and no one cared.'

'Maybe no one had a chance. The maid I talked to this morning said no one was permitted near except the nursery staff, and Philippe's mother was constantly changing the people who worked with him. He's better off here if no one loves him at the palace, of course he is. But you could change that.' She hesitated. 'Ramón, I'm thinking you already have.'

He shook his head, shaking off demons. 'This is nonsense. I won't risk *this*.'

'This?'

'You know what I mean.' His face grew even more strained. 'Gianetta…'

'Yes?'

'I hate it,' he said explosively. 'The paparazzi almost mobbed you yesterday. The threat from Carlos… How can anyone live in that sort of environment? How could you?'

Her world stilled. Her heart seemed to forget to beat. *How could you?* They were no longer talking about Philippe, then. 'Am I…am I being invited?' she managed.

'No!' There was a long silence, loaded with so many undercurrents she couldn't begin to figure them out. Through the silence Ramón held the steering wheel, his knuckles clenched white. Fighting demons she could hardly fathom.

'We need to get back,' he said at last.

'Of course we do,' she said softly, but she knew this man now. Maybe two weeks of living together was too soon to judge someone—or maybe not. Maybe she'd judged him the first time she'd seen him. Okay, she hardly understood his demons, but demons there were and, prince or not, maybe the leap had to be hers.

'You know that I love you,' she said gently into the warm breeze, but his expression became even more grim.

'Don't.'

'Don't say what I feel?'

'You don't want this life.'

'I like tiaras,' she ventured, trying desperately

for lightness. 'And caviar and French champagne. At least,' she added honestly, 'I haven't tasted caviar yet, but I'm sure I'll like it. And if I don't, I'm very good at faking.'

'Jenny, don't make this any harder than it has to be,' he snapped, refusing to be deflected by humour. 'I was a fool to bring you to Cepheus. I will not drag you into this royal life.'

'You don't have to drag me anywhere. I choose where to go. All you need to do is ask.'

'Just leave it. You don't know… The paparazzi yesterday was just a taste. Right now you're seeing the romance, the fairy tale. You'll wake in a year's time and find nothing but a cage.'

'You don't think you might be overreacting?' she ventured. 'Not everyone at the Coronation ball looked like they've been locked up all their lives. Surely caviar can't be that bad.'

But he wasn't listening. 'You're my beautiful Jenny,' he said. 'You're wild and free, and I won't mess with who you are. You'll always be my Jenny, and I'll hold you in my heart for ever. From a distance.'

'From how big a distance? From a photo in a frame?' she demanded, indignant. 'That sounds appalling. Or, better still, do you mean as your mistress on your island?'

He stared at her as if she'd grown two heads. 'What the…?'

'That's what Sofía said we should do.'

'I do not want you as my mistress,' he said through gritted teeth.

'So you don't want me?' His anger was building, and she thought *good*. An angry Ramón might just lose control, and control had gone on long enough. She wanted him to take her into his arms. In truth she wanted him to take her any way he wanted, but he was fighting his anger, hauling himself back from the brink.

'I want you more than life itself, but I will not take you.' He took a deep ragged breath. 'I could never keep you safe.'

'Well, that's nonsense. I know karate,' she retorted. 'I can duck and I can run and I can even punch and scratch and yell if I need to. Not that I'll need to. Perpetua says Carlos is all bluster.'

'Perpetua…'

'Is a very nice lady with an oaf for a husband and with very old-fashioned ideas about royal wives shutting up. Ideas that I don't believe for one minute. You'll never see me shutting up.'

'It doesn't matter,' he said, exasperated. 'I want you free.'

'Free?' She was fighting on all fronts now, knowing only that she was fully exposed and she had no defence. All she had was her love for this man. 'Like our whale?' she demanded. 'That's just perspective. Our whale's free now to swim to

Antarctica, but she has to stop there and turn around. A minnow can feel free in an aquarium if it's a beautiful aquarium.'

She hesitated then, seeing the tension on his face stretched almost to breaking point. She'd gone far enough. 'Ramón, let's not take this further,' she said gently. 'What's between us…let's leave it for now. Let's just think of Philippe. Is his room still as it was at the palace?'

'No one's touched the nursery.'

'So you could go in right now and say, *Philippe, what about coming back to the palace for a night or two?* Tell him maybe if it works out he could come for two nights every week. See how it goes.'

'Jenny…'

'Okay, maybe it is impossible,' she said. 'This is not my life and it's not my little cousin. But you know him now, Ramón, and maybe things have changed. All I know is that Philippe's breaking his heart in there, and if he returned to the palace there's no way he'd be alone. Consuela is looking out the window and I wouldn't mind betting she knows exactly what we're talking about. She's bursting to visit the palace, even if she's scared, and if you raise one finger to beckon she'll have bags packed and Bebe in his cat crate and you can still reach your three o'clock appointment. And, before you start raising quibbles like who'll look after their alpacas, you're the prince, surely you can employ half this district to look after this farm. So decide,' she said bluntly. 'You've been making life and death decisions about this country. Now it's time to make one about your family.'

'Philippe's not my family.'

'Is he not? It might have started with sympathy, Ramón Cavellero, but it's not sympathy that's tugging him to you now. Is it?'

'I don't do…love.'

'You already have. Just take the next step. All it needs is courage.' She hesitated. 'Ramón, I know how it hurts to love and to lose. You've loved and you've lost, but Philippe is going right on loving.'

'He can't,' he said but he was looking at the window where Consuela was indeed peeping through a chink in the curtains.

And then he was looking at Jenny—Gianetta— who knew which?—and she was looking back at him with faith. Faith that he could take this new step.

'*You* can,' she said.

'Gianetta,' he said and would have taken her into his arms right then, part in exasperation, part in anger—and there were a whole lot more parts in there besides, but she held up her hands in a gesture of defence.

'Not me. Not now. This is you and Philippe. Do you want him or not?'

He looked at her for a long moment. He glanced

back at the farmhouse, and Philippe was at the window now, as well as Consuela.

And there was only one answer to give.

So, half an hour later—Ramón would be late for his meeting but not much—his little red Boxster finally left the farmhouse, with Philippe once again snuggled between Ramón and Jenny. There was a cat crate at Jenny's feet. The Boxster was definitely crowded.

Behind them, Consuela and Ernesto drove their farm truck, packed with enough luggage to last them for two days.

Or more, Jenny thought with satisfaction. There were four big suitcases on the back. For all she talked of class differences, Consuela seemed more than prepared to take a leap into the unknown.

If only Ramón could join her.

CHAPTER ELEVEN

THE moment he swung back into the palace grounds affairs of State took over again. Ramón couldn't stay to watch Philippe's reaction to being back at the palace. He couldn't stay to see that Consuela and Ernesto were treated right.

He couldn't stay with Jenny.

'We can do this. Go,' Jenny told him and he had no choice. He went, to meeting upon interminable meeting. Once again he was forced to work until the small hours.

Finally, exhausted beyond belief, he made his way through the palace corridors towards his personal chambers. Once again he passed Jenny's door—and he didn't knock.

But then he reached the nursery. To his surprise, Manuel was standing outside the door, at attention. The footmen were posted at the top of the stairs. Had a change been ordered? But Manuel spoke before he could ask.

'I'm not permitted to move,' the man said, and it was as if a statue had come to life. 'But the little boy and Señorina Bertin… I thought you wouldn't wish them harm so I took it upon myself to stay here.'

'Good idea.' He hesitated, taking in the full context of what the man had said. Reaching the crux. 'Señorina Bertin's in there?'

'Yes, sir,' Manuel said and he opened the nursery door before Ramón could say he hadn't meant to go in; he was only passing.

Only of course he had meant to go in. Just to check.

Manuel closed the door after him. The room was in darkness but the moon was full, the curtains weren't drawn and he could see the outline of the bed against the windows. It was a truly vast bed for a small child. A ridiculous bed.

He moved silently across the room and looked down—and there were two mounds in the bed. A child-sized one, with a cat-shaped bump over his feet, and a Jenny-shaped one, and the Jenny-shaped one spoke.

'You're not a Hun?' she whispered, and he blinked.

'Pardon?'

'Manuel's saving us from the Huns. I thought you might have overpowered him and be about to…plunder and pillage. I'm very glad you're not.'

'I'm glad I'm not a Hun either,' he said and smiled

down at her, and he could feel her smile back, even if he couldn't quite see it. 'What are you doing here?'

'Shh. He's only just gone back to sleep.'

He tugged a chair forward and sat, then leaned forward so he was inches away from Jenny's face. Philippe was separated from them by Jenny's body but he could see that her arm was around him. The sight made him feel…made him feel…

No. There were no words to describe it.

'This is Consuela's job,' he managed.

'She was here until midnight. The staff put Consuela and Ernesto into one of the state apartments, and it's so grand it's made Ernesto quiver. Ernesto seems more frightened than Philippe so I said I'd stay.'

She said she'd stay. With a little boy who was the same age as her Matty. In this room that he'd once slept in. He looked at her, at the way Philippe's body was curved against hers, at the way she was holding him, and he felt things slither and change within him. Knots that had been around his heart for ever slipped away, undone, free.

'Gianetta…' he whispered and placed his fingers on her lips, wondering. If she'd found the courage to do this…

'Shh,' she said again. 'He woke and he was a little upset. I don't want him to wake again.'

'But you soothed him.'

'I told him the story of the whale. He loved it. I

told him about his cousin, the hero, saviour of whales. Saviour of this country. We both thought it was pretty cool.'

'Gianetta…'

'Jenny. Your employee. And Manuel is out there.'

'Manuel can go…'

'Manuel can't go,' she said seriously. 'Neither of us is sure where to take this. You need to sleep, Ramón.'

'I want…'

'I know,' she said softly and she placed a finger on his lips in turn. 'We both want. I can feel it, and it's wonderful. But there's things to think about for both of us. For now… Give me my self-respect and go to your own bedroom tonight.' She smiled at him then and he was close enough to see a lovely loving smile that made his heart turn over. 'Besides,' she said. 'Tonight I'm sleeping with Philippe. One man a night, my love. I have my reputation to think of.'

'He's not Matty,' he said before he could stop himself.

'Philippe's not Matty, no.'

'But… Jenny, doesn't that tear you in two?'

'I thought it would,' she said on a note of wonder. 'But now… He fits exactly under my arm. He's not Matty but it's as if Matty has made a place for him. It feels right.'

'Jenny…'

'Go to bed, Ramón,' she said simply. 'We all have a lot of thinking to do this night.'

He left and she was alone in the dark with a sleeping child. She'd given her heart, she thought. She'd given it to both of them, just like that.

What if they didn't want it?

It was theirs, she thought, like it or not.

Bebe stirred and wriggled and padded his way up the bed to check she was still breathing, that she'd still react if he kneaded his paws on the bedcover.

'Okay, I can learn to love you, too,' she told the little cat. 'As long as your claws don't get all the way through the quilt.' Satisfied, Bebe slumped down on the coverlet across her breast and went back to sleep, leaving her with her thoughts.

'They have to want me,' she whispered in the dark. 'Oh, they have to want me or I'm in such big trouble.'

And in the royal bedchamber, the apartment of the Crown Prince of Cepheus, there was no sleep at all.

Once upon a time a child had slept alone in this palace and known terror. Now the man lay alone in his palace and knew peace.

He woke and he knew, but he couldn't do a thing about it.

It'd take him a week, Señor Rodriguez told him,

this signing, signing and more signing. He had to formally accept the role of Crown Prince before he could begin to delegate, so from dawn his time was not his own.

'I need two hours this afternoon,' he growled to his lawyer as he saw his packed diary. 'You've scheduled me an hour for lunch. Take fifteen minutes from each delegation; that gives me another hour, so between one and three is mine.'

'I've already started organising it,' his lawyer told him. 'We all want you to have time with the child.'

'All?'

'I believe the staff have been missing him,' the lawyer said primly. 'It seems there are undercurrents neither the Princess Sofía nor I guessed.'

He didn't say more, but they agreed a message would be sent to Jenny and to Philippe that he'd spend the early afternoon with them. Then Ramón put his head down and worked.

He finished just before one. He'd have finished earlier only someone dared ask a question. Was he aware there were up to fifty students in each class in the local schools, and didn't he agree this was so urgent it had to be remedied right now?

He did agree. How could he put his own desire to be with Jenny and Philippe before the welfare of so many other children? Señor Rodriguez disappeared, leaving Ramón to listen and think and agree to meet about the issue again tomorrow. Finally he was free to walk out, to find the whereabouts of Philippe…and of Jenny.

'They're by the pool, Your Highness.' It was the maid who normally brought in his coffee and, to his astonishment, she smiled as she bobbed her normal curtsy. 'It's so good to have him back sir. There's refreshments being served now. If you'd like to have your lunch with them…'

Bemused, he strolled out the vast palace doors into the gardens overlooking the sea.

There was a party happening by the pool, and the perfection of the scene before him was marred. Or not marred, he corrected himself. Just changed.

The landscape to the sea had been moulded to create a series of rock pools and waterfalls tumbling down towards the sea. Shade umbrellas and luxurious cream beach loungers were discreetly placed among semi-tropical foliage, blending unobtrusively into the magical garden setting.

Now, however… At the biggest rock pool chairs and tables had been hauled forward to make a circle. There were balloons attached around every umbrella. This wasn't tasteful at all, he thought with wry amusement. The balloons were all colours and sizes, as though some had been blown up by men with good lungs, and some had been blown up by a five-year-old. They were attached to the umbrellas by red ribbons, with vast crimson bows under each bunch.

And there were sea dragons floating in the rock pool. Huge plastic sea dragons, red, green and pink, with sparkly tiaras. Sea dragons with tiaras? What on earth…?

Jenny was in the water, and so was Philippe and so was…Sofía? They were on a sea dragon apiece, kicking their way across the water, seemingly racing. Sofía was wearing neck to knee swimmers and she was winning, whooping her elderly lungs out with excitement.

There was more, he thought, stunned. Señor Rodriguez was sitting by the edge of the pool, wearing shorts, his skinny frame a testament to a life spent at his desk. He was cheering Sofía at full roar. As were Consuela and Ernesto, yelling their lungs out for their foster son. 'Go, Philippe, go!'

There were also servants, all in their ridiculous uniforms, but each of them was yelling as loudly as everyone else. And another woman was cheering too, a woman who looked vaguely familiar. And then he recognised her. Perpetua. Carlos's wife! What the…?

He didn't have time to take it all in. Sofía reached the wall by a full length of sea dragon. Philippe came second and Jenny fell off her dragon from laughing.

It felt crazy. It was a palace transformed into something else entirely. He watched as Philippe turned anxiously to find Jenny. She surfaced, still laughing, she hugged him and his heart twisted and he forgot about everything, everyone else.

She saw him. She waved and then staggered—holding Philippe with one arm was a skill yet to be mastered. 'Welcome to our pool party, Your Highness,' she called. 'Have you come to try our sausage rolls?'

'Sausage rolls,' he said faintly, and looked at the table where there was enough food for a small army.

'Your chefs have never heard of sausage rolls,' she said, clambering up the pool steps with Philippe in her arms and grinning as Sofía staggered out as well, still clutching her sea dragon. 'Philippe and I had to teach them. And we have fairy bread and lamingtons, and tacos and tortillas and strawberries and éclairs—and I love this place. Philippe does too, don't you Philippe? We've decided it's the best place to visit in the world.'

Visit. He stood and watched as woman and child disappeared under vast towels and he thought… *visit*.

'Oh, and we invited Perpetua,' Jenny said from under her towel, motioning in the general direction of the pallid little lady standing uncertainly under the nearest umbrella. Perpetua gave him a shy, scared smile. 'You know Carlos's wife? And Carlos, too.'

'And Carlos, too?' he demanded. Perpetua's smile slipped.

'I told him to come,' she whispered. 'When Gianetta invited us. He said he would. He just has to…he's been making silly threats that he doesn't mean. He wants to apologise.' Her voice was almost pleading. 'He'd never hurt…'

And maybe he wouldn't, Ramón thought. For Carlos was approaching them now, escorted by palace footmen. The footmen were walking really close. Really close.

'He's not going to hurt anyone,' Perpetua whispered. 'He's just been silly. I was so pleased when Gianetta rang. He needs a chance to explain.'

'Explain what?' Ramón said and Perpetua fell silent, waiting for Carlos himself to answer.

Ramón's gaze flew to Jenny. She met his gaze full on. She'd set this up, he thought.

One of the maids had taken over rubbing Philippe dry. The maid was laughing and scolding, making Philippe smile back. She was a servant he'd thought lacked emotion.

Had the servants turned to ice through mistreatment and fear?

What else had fear done?

He looked again at Carlos, a big, stupid man who for a few short weeks, while Ramón couldn't be found, had thought the throne was his. For the dream to be snatched away must have shattered his world.

Maybe stupid threats could be treated as they deserved, Ramón thought, feeling suddenly extraordinarily light-headed. And if threats weren't there…

'We invited both Carlos and Perpetua,' Jenny was

saying. 'Because of Philippe. Philippe says Perpetua's always been nice to him.'

'He's a sweetheart,' Perpetua said stoutly, becoming braver. 'I worried about him whenever I stayed here.'

'You used to stay in the palace?' Ramón asked, surprised again. What had Señor Rodriguez told him? Perpetua was a nice enough woman, intelligent, trained as a grade school teacher, but always made to feel inferior to Carlos's royal relatives.

'A lot,' Perpetua said, becoming braver. 'Carlos liked being here. Philippe and I became friends, didn't we, sweetheart. But then Carlos said some silly things.' Her gaze met her husband's. 'I used to believe…well, I'm a royal wife and a royal wife stays silent. But Gianetta says that's ridiculous. So I'm not staying silent any longer. You're sorry, aren't you, dear?'

Was he? Ramón watched Carlos, sweating slightly in a suit that was a bit too tight, struggling to come to terms with this new order, and he even felt a bit sorry for him.

'I shouldn't have said it,' Carlos managed.

'You said you'd kill…'

'You know how it is.' Carlos was almost pleading. 'I mean…heat of the moment. I was only saying…you know, wild stuff. What I'd do if you didn't look after the country…that sort of thing. It got blown up. You didn't take it seriously. Please tell me you didn't take it seriously.'

Was that it? Ramón thought, relief running through him in waves. History had created fear—not fear for himself but fear for family. His family.

A family he could now build. In time…

And with that thought came another. He wasn't alone.

Delegation. Why not start now?

'Perpetua, you used to be a grade teacher,' he said, speaking slowly but thinking fast, thinking back to the meeting he'd just attended. 'Do you know the conditions in our schools?'

'Of course I do,' Perpetua said, confused. 'I mean, I haven't taught for twenty years—Carlos doesn't like me to—but I have friends who are still teachers. They have such a hard time…'

'Tomorrow morning I'm meeting with a deputation to see what can be done about the overcrowding in our classrooms,' he said. 'Would you like to join us?'

'Me?' she gasped.

'I need help,' he said simply. 'And Carlos… How can you help?'

There was stunned silence. Even Philippe, who was wrapped in a towel and was now wrapping himself around a sausage roll stopped mid-bite and stared. This man who'd made blustering threats to kill…

How can you help?

Jenny moved then, inconspicuously slipping to his side. She stood close and she took his hand, as if she realized just how big it was. Just how important this request was.

Defusing threats to create a future.

Refusing to stand alone for one moment longer.

'I can't…' Carlos managed at last. 'There's nothing.'

'Yes, dear, there is.' Perpetua had found her voice, and she, too, slipped to stand beside her man. 'Sports. Carlos loves them, loves watching them, but there's never been enough money to train our teenagers. And the football stadium's falling down.'

'You like football?' Ramón asked.

'Football,' Philippe said, lighting up.

'I…'

'You could give me reports on sports facilities,' Ramón said, thinking fast, trying to figure out something meaningful that the man could do. 'Tell me what needs to be done. Put in your recommendations. I don't know this country. You do. I need help on the ground. So what do we have here? Assistant to the Crown for Education. Assistant to the Crown for Sport.'

'And I'll be Assistant to the Crown for New Uniforms for The Staff,' Sofía said happily. 'I'd like to help with that.'

'I can help with floating,' Philippe said gamely. 'But can I help with football, too?'

'And Gianetta?' Perpetua said, looking anxious. 'What about Jenny?'

'I need to figure that out,' Ramón said softly, holding his love close, his world suddenly settling in a way that was leaving him stunned. 'In private.'

Philippe had finished his sausage roll now, and he carried the loaded tray over to his big cousin.

'Would you like to eat one?' he asked. 'And then will you teach me to float some more?'

'Of course I will,' he said. 'On one condition.'

Philippe looked confused, as well he might.

No matter. Sometimes a prince simply had to allocate priorities, and this was definitely that time. He tugged Jenny tighter, then, audience or not, he pulled her into his arms and gave her a swift possessive kiss. It was a kiss that said he was pushed for time. He knew he couldn't take this further, not here, not now, but there was more where that came from.

'My condition to you all,' he said softly, kissing her once more, a long lingering kiss that said, pushed for time or not, this was what he wanted most in the world, 'is that Señor Rodriguez changes my diary. This night is mine.'

The car came to collect her just before sunset. She was dressed again as Gianetta, in a long diaphanous dress made of the finest layers of silk and chiffon with the diamonds at her throat. Two maids and Sofía and Consuela and Perpetua had clucked over her to distraction. Sofía had added a diamond bracelet of her own, and had wept a little.

'Oh, my dear, you're so beautiful,' she'd said mistily. 'Do you think he'll propose?'

Jenny hadn't answered. She couldn't. She was torn between laughter and tears.

Ramón's kisses had promised everything, but nothing had been said. Mistress to a Crown Prince? Wife?

Dared she think wife?

How could she think anything? After a fast floating lesson Ramón had been swept away yet again on his interminable business and she'd been left only with his demand.

'A car will come for you at seven. Be ready.'

She was ready, but she was daring to think nothing.

Finally, at seven the car came and Señor Rodriguez handed her into the limousine with care and with pride. The reverberations from this afternoon were being felt all around the country, and the lawyer couldn't stop smiling.

'Where's Ramón?' she managed.

'Waiting for you,' the lawyer said, sounding inscrutable until he added, 'How could any man not?'

So she was driven in state, alone, with only a chauffeur for company. The great white limousine was driven slowly through the city, out along the coast road, up onto a distant headland where it drew to a halt.

Two uniformed footmen met her, Manuel and Luis, trying desperately to be straight-faced. There was a footpath leading from where the car pulled in to park, winding through a narrow section of overgrown cliff. Manuel and Luis led her silently along the path, emerged into a clearing, then slipped silently back into the shadows. Leaving her to face what was before her.

And what was before her made her gasp. A headland looking out all over the moonlit Mediterranean. A table for two. Crisp white linen. Two cushioned chairs with high, high backs, draped all in white velvet, each leg fastened with crimson ties.

Silverware, crystal, a candelabrum magnificent enough to take her breath away.

Soft music coming from behind a slight rise. Real music. *There were real musicians somewhere behind the trees.*

Champagne on ice.

And then Ramón stepped from the shadows, Ramón in full ceremonial, Ramón looking more handsome than any man she'd met.

The sound of frogs came from beneath the music behind him. Her frog prince?

'If I kiss you, will you join your friends, the frogs?' she whispered before she could help herself and he laughed and came towards her and took her hands in his.

'No kissing,' he said tenderly. 'Not yet.'

'What…?' She could barely speak. 'What are we waiting for?'

'This,' he said and went down on bended knee.

She closed her eyes. This couldn't be happening. This was happening.

'This should wait until after dinner,' he said softly, 'but it's been burning a hole in my pocket for three hours now.' And, without more words, he lifted a crimson velvet box and held it open. A diamond ring lay in solitary splendour, a diamond so wonderful…so amazing…

'Is it real?' she gasped and he chuckled.

'That's Jenny speaking. I think we need Gianetta to give us the right sense of decorum.'

Gianetta. She took a deep breath and fought for composure. She could do this.

'Sire, you do me honour.'

'That's more like it,' he said and his dark eyes gleamed with love and with laughter. 'So, Gianetta, Jenny, my love, my sailor, my cook extraordinaire, my heart…I give you my love. The past has made us solitary, but it's up to both of us to move forward. To leave solitude and pain behind. You've shown me courage, and I trust that I can match it. So

Gianetta, my dearest love, if I promise to love you, cherish you, honour you, for as long as we both shall live, will you do me the honour of taking my hand in marriage?'

She looked down into his loving eyes. Then she paused for a moment, taking time to gaze around her, at the night, at the stars, the accoutrements of royalty, at the lights of Cepheus glowing around them. Knowing also there was a little boy waiting as well.

Her family. Her love, starting now.

'I believe I will,' she said gently and, before he could respond, she dropped to her own knees and she took his hands in hers.

'Yes, my love and my prince, I believe I will.'

THE SHEIKH'S
DESTINY

BY

MELISSA JAMES

All the characters in this book have no existence outside the imagination
of the author, and have no relation whatsoever to anyone bearing the
same name or names. They are not even distantly inspired by any
individual known or unknown to the author, and all the incidents are
pure invention.

First published in Great Britain 2010
Harlequin Mills & Boon Limited,
Eton House, 18-24 Paradise Road, Richmond, Surrey TW9 1SR

© Lisa Chaplin 2010

ISBN: 978 0 263 87679 6

Harlequin Mills & Boon policy is to use papers that are natural,
renewable and recyclable products and made from wood grown in
sustainable forests. The logging and manufacturing process conform
to the legal environmental regulations of the country of origin.

Printed and bound in Spain
by Litografia Rosés, S.A., Barcelona

Melissa James is a born-and-bred Sydneysider, who swapped the beaches of the New South Wales Central Coast for the Alps of Switzerland a few years ago. Wife and mother of three, a former nurse, she fell into writing when her husband brought home an article about romance writers and suggested she should try it—and she became hooked. Switching from romantic espionage to the family stories of Mills & Boon® Romance was the best move she ever made. Melissa loves to hear from readers—you can e-mail her at: authormelissajames@yahoo.com

PROLOGUE

The road to Shellah-Akbar, Northern Africa

THEY were closing in on him. Time to open throttle.

Alim El-Kanar shifted down into low-gear sports mode, in the truck he'd modified specially for this purpose. He wasn't letting the men of the warlord Sh'ellah—after whose family this region had been named—take the medical supplies and food meant for those the man made suffer, so he could keep control and live in luxury. Alim wasn't going to be caught, either—that would be disaster, but for the people of this region, not him. As soon as Sh'ellah saw the face of the man he'd taken hostage, he'd hold Alim for a fabulous ransom that would keep them in funds for new weapons for years.

When he had the ransom, *then* he'd kill him—if he could get away with it.

But Sh'ellah hadn't yet discovered who Alim was, and he gambled his life on the hope the warlord never would. Even the director of Doctors for Africa didn't know the true identity of the near-silent truck driver who pulled off what he called miracles on a regular basis, reaching remote villages held by warlords with medicine, food and water-purifying tablets.

With a top-class fake ID and always wearing the male headscarf he could twist over his famous features whenever he chose, he was invisible to the world. Just the way he liked it.

Who he was—or what he'd been once—mattered far less than what he did.

He always gave enough medicine to each village to last six to eight hours. Then, when Sh'ellah's men came for their 'share', most of it was gone; they took a few needles, some out-of-date antibiotics, and strutted out again.

The villagers never told Alim where they hid the supplies, and he didn't want to know. They kept just enough bread, rice and grain out for Sh'ellah's men to feel smug about their theft. To Sh'ellah, such petty control made him feel like a man, a lion among mice.

Even Alim, flawed as he was, would be a better leader—

Don't go there. Grimly he shifted down gear, following the indented tracks in the scrubby grass on what was loosely called a road to the village of Shellah-Akbar. He'd had tyres put on this truck like the ones used in outback and desert rallies so he could fly over rocks and sudden holes the wind made in the dusty ground. He also had a padded protective cage put inside the cab, much like the one he'd had in his cars when he was still The Racing Sheikh.

He'd once been so ridiculously proud of the nickname—now he wanted to hit something every time he thought of it. His fame and life in the fast lane had died the same day as his brother. The only racing he did now was with trucks with much needed supplies to war-torn villages. And if the term 'sheikh' was technically correct, it was a privilege he'd forfeited after Fadi's death. It was an honour he'd never deserve. His younger brother Harun had taken on the honour in his absence, marrying the princess Fadi had been contracted to marry. Harun had been ruling the people of his principality, Abbas al-Din—*the lion of the faith*—for three years, and was doing a brilliant job.

Thinking of home set off the familiar ache. He used to love coming home. *Habib Abbas*, the people would chant. *Beloved lion*. They'd been so proud of his achievements.

If the people wanted him to come home, to take his place among his people, he knew an accident of birth, finding some oil or minerals, or the ability to race a car around a track didn't make a true leader. Strength, good sense and courage did—and Alim had lost the best of those qualities with Fadi's death, along with his heart and a lot of his skin. He had just enough strength and courage left to risk his neck for a few villagers in Africa. The fanfare for what he did was silent, and that was the way he liked it.

He growled as his usual stress-trigger, the puckered scars that covered more than half his torso, began the painful itching that scratching only made worse. He'd have to use the last of his silica-based cream on the pain as soon as he had a minute, as soon as he lost these jokers—and he would. He wasn't Habib Abbas, or The Racing Sheikh, any more—but he still had the skills.

Stop it! Thinking only made the itch worse—and the heart-pain that was his night-and-day companion. *Fadi, I'm so sorry!*

Grimly he turned his mind to the job at hand, or he'd crash in seconds. The protective roll cage inside his truck might be heavily padded with lamb's wool so if the truck rolled, he could use his modified low centre of gravity shift and oddly placed air bags to flip back right way up—but it wouldn't help if he was too busted up to keep going.

He checked the mirror. They were still the same distance behind him, forty men packing weaponry suitable for taking far more than a truck. They were too far away from him to shoot accurately, but still too close to shake. He couldn't do anything clever on this rugged, roadless terrain, like spilling oil to make them slide: it would sink straight into the dirt before the enemy reached the slick, and he'd risk his engine for nothing.

But he had to do something, or they'd follow him right to Shellah-Akbar and take the supplies. He had to find a way to beat the odds currently stacked against him like the Spartans at Thermopylae thousands of years ago.

If he could rig something with the emergency flare…could he make it work?

Alim's mind raced. Yes, if he added the tar-based chemical powder he kept to help the tyres move over the sand without sliding to the volatile formula inside the flare, and tossed it back, it might work—

He was used to driving one-handed, or steering the wheel with both feet. He shoved a stone on the accelerator, angling it so it kept going steady, and drove with his feet while pulling the flare apart with as much care as he could, given his situation.

He was nearing the four-way junction ten miles from the village, where he must turn one way or another. He had to stop them now or, no matter what clever methods he employed to evade them, they'd know where he was going. They'd use their satellite phones, and another hundred thugs would be at the village before sunset, demanding their 'rightful' share of the supplies proven by their assault rifles.

He poured the powder in with shaking hands. He had to be careful or he'd kill them; and, murderers though most of the men undoubtedly were, it wasn't his place to judge who had done what or why. He'd had a childhood of extreme privilege, the best education in the world. Most of the men behind him had been born in horrendous poverty, abducted when they were small children and taught to play with AK-47s instead of bats and balls.

He'd leave enough food and supplies behind so their warlord didn't kill them for their failure. Part of the solution or perpetuating the problem, he didn't know; but in this continent where human life was cheaper than clean water, everyone only had one shot at living, and he refused to carry any more regrets in his personal backpack.

He grabbed the wheel as he neared the far-leaning sign showing the way to the villages, and slanted the truck extreme left, away from all of them. Good, the wind was shifting again: it was time for a good old-fashioned wild goose chase.

He put the flare together, closing it tight with electrical tape, shook it and opened the sunroof. He lit the flare, counted one-hundred-and-one to one-hundred-and-seven, shoved his foot hard over the stone covering the accelerator as he tossed the lit flare up and backward, and pulled the sunroof shut.

The truck shot forward and left, when the *boom* and flash came. The air behind him turned a dazzling bluish-white, then thick and black, filled with choking, temporarily blinding chemicals.

Screams came to his ears, the screeches of tyres as their Jeeps came to simultaneous halts. He'd done it… Alim arced the truck hard right, back to the crossroads. He didn't wind down the window to check. He'd either blinded them all, or he'd be dead inside a minute.

Half a kilometre before the junction, he threw out the half-dozen boxes of second-rate supplies he'd been keeping for the warlord's pleasure. They'd find them when the chemical reaction from their tears would neutralise the blindness. There was no permanent damage to their retinas, only to their pride and their ability to follow him for about half an hour. Factoring in the wind shift, all traces of his tyre tracks should have vanished by then, covered with red earth and falling leaves and branches from the low, thin trees. They'd have to split up to find him, and by the time they reached the village he'd be long gone.

Then a whining sound came; air whooshed, a loud *bang* filled the cab, and the truck leaped forward as if propelled before it teetered and fell to the left.

Alim's head struck the side window with stunning force. Blood filled his eye; he felt his mind reeling. One of his specially made, ultra-wide and thick desert tyres had blown. One of the warlord's men was either not blinded in the explosion, or he'd made the luckiest shot in the world, and blown his back tyre. The only drawback to his special, extra-tough tyres was their need for perfect balance. If one tyre went, so did the truck.

He couldn't black out now, or he'd die—and so would the people of Shellah-Akbar. He fought passing out with everything in him. He stopped the truck and pulled on the air-bag lever. As the truck tipped, the four-foot-thick pillows that flew to position outside the doors bounced it back up. As the truck righted itself he took his rifle and blew the tyres, the two on the passenger side quickly, but he had to wait until the truck was up and keeling back over to the right before he could balance it by blowing the driver's side.

The truck landed hard down on the ground as the blackness took over. Alim shoved the truck in first and took off. The rocks and sand would destroy the thick rubber coating with which he'd covered his rims in case of emergency, but he could make far more than the remaining six miles, and there were spare tyres in the back. The tyres weren't modified, and it'd be a miracle if he made it back to the Human Compassion Refugee camp two hundred and sixty kilometres south-west, but it would get him to where the food-aid pilots could pick him up.

He had to reach the village; he was going to pass out any moment. Blood gushed from his temple wound, and his blood pressure was falling by the second. If he could put the truck in the right direction, and set the cruise control…the compass and

GPS system both said he only needed a straight line now to make it.

He pressed the emergency direction finder on his satellite phone; his only hope now was that the nurse he knew lived in Shellah-Akbar had her receiver switched on.

Holding the wheel like grim death, he put the truck in second, made sure the stone was still in place over the accelerator, and fell forward.

The truck came into the village of Shellah-Akbar seventeen minutes later.

A woman was at the wheel. She'd run from her bunk in the medical tent as soon as the emergency signal reached the village. The only one with full medical experience, she'd ridden an old bike as fast as she could while Abdel, the village Olympic marathon hopeful, followed, to ride the pushbike back to the village. While the truck was still moving she'd stopped just in front of the driver's door, tossed the bike down for Abdel to find, yanked open the door and jumped inside. Sprawled beside her, his head in her lap, was one unconscious driver, who had risked his life so that others may live.

'*In-sh'allah*,' she whispered, and recited the words of a prayer taught her from infancy: a prayer that hadn't kept her own life intact, but might help God smile upon this courageous man.

He wasn't going to die. Not today. Not if she could help it.

CHAPTER ONE

'GET the driver into my hut, and get rid of the truck,' Hana al-Sud yelled to two villagers in Swahili when she pulled the truck up outside the medical tent. 'Don't cook the food. Feed plain bread to those who need it most. Bury the rest in Saliya's grave.'

'The fruit will lose its vitamins, Hana,' her assistant protested.

'One seed or core can be found in seconds,' she replied calmly enough, given the urgency of their situation and the rapid pounding of her heart. She ran around the truck to the driver. 'We can get it back out tonight to feed the children, without losing nutritional value. Just do it, please, Malika! And sweep away any traces of tyre marks!'

An older man ran to the passenger side to take the driver as the fittest young man in the village jumped into Hana's place in the driver's seat. The other villagers opened the back of the truck to unload it. Two women ran over with the vital tarpaulins, snatched medical kits and ampoules of antibiotics and insulin to bury it. The future of the entire village depended on everyone working together, and working fast. They'd be here in minutes. The warlord's satellite phones were the best money could buy. Any sniff of betrayal meant unbearable consequences for them all.

'Take the driver to my hut. He's Arabic,' Hana said tensely in Swahili. 'I'll patch him up. When they ask I'll say my husband came for me.'

The men took the unconscious man to Hana's small hut beside the medical tent.

Within fifteen minutes it was as if the truck had never been there. Abdel would leave it somewhere in the desert, take the exact coordinates and return on foot. He was the only one with the perfect cover. As he was a long-distance runner aiming for the Olympics, no one thought it strange if he wasn't in the village at all times.

In the hut, Hana had the injured man laid on an old sheet. 'Wound and suture kit—an old resteril-ised set.' This brave man deserved better, but if she used the new kits he'd brought today and didn't dispose of them in time, the warlord's men would know the truth. They had to get every detail right.

There was blood on his face and shirt. 'Haytham, I need a clean shirt!' Haytham was her friend Malika's husband, and approximately the same size as this man. She stripped off the bloodied shirt and tossed it in her cooking fire, noting the angry, inflamed mass of burns scars criss-crossing his chest, shoulder and stomach on the left side. She'd treat them later. Right now she had to save his life.

She checked her watch. From experience, she knew she had five minutes to get it all done. She cleaned his face of the blood, and prepared to suture the wound. She'd wash his hair after, to remove the last traces of his identity as the driver.

She stitched his wound as fast as she could, grateful it was close to his hair; she'd cover it with his fringe, and would have to risk infection by using cover-stick around the reddened skin. There was no way she could risk a bandage, but she'd use one vital ampoule of antibiotic, needle and syringe; the wound could turn septic with hair and make-up on it.

She injected him between his toes, as if he were a junkie with collapsed veins. It was a place Sh'ellah's men wouldn't think to look for signs of injury and medical attention. 'Bury these fast,' she ordered Malika, who took the precious supplies and ran.

Hana washed the worst of the dirt and blood from his hair with a damp washer, coated with some of her precious essential oils, and covered the wound with the cleaned hair and make-up. Then she rolled the man off the sheet, bundled it up and tossed it in the roaring fire. She put the clean shirt on him— he'd been through several operations for those burns, by the patches of grafted skin over the worst of it—buttoned up the shirt, and checked her watch. Four minutes thirty-eight. Not bad, really. She checked over the hut for any signs of wound treatment.

Nothing, thank God. Hana dragged in a deep sigh of relief, and finally allowed herself a moment to look at her patient's face.

'*No, no,*' she whispered, horrified.

She'd known as she ran to save this man's life that he'd pulled off the impossible today—but the feat suddenly didn't seem quite so impossible, if he was who she thought he was.

Please, God, just make it a freak physical resemblance…because if it was him, then by his mere presence he'd brought far more danger to the village than by any supplies he'd brought.

Even Sh'ellah's followers would know him. Most men loved fast sports and money, and this man combined both. Just put a helmet on him and it was the former face of the world's most expensive racing-car team. He'd won the World Championship twice—and brought both riches and research to a once-struggling nation. He'd found oil and natural gas reserves in a place few had thought to look, with his chemical background and analytical racing driver's mind.

'*La!*' he muttered, in either fever or concussed confusion. '*La, la, akh! Fadi, la!*'

No, no, brother! Fadi, no!

In dread, Hana heard the words in the Arabic native to her childhood home country, begging his beloved brother Fadi to live. It broke her heart—she knew how it felt to lose those she loved—and then she listened in horror as he relived the drive to the village in graphic detail, including the complex mixture of chemicals he'd used to blind Sh'ellah's men.

The fine-chiselled, handsome face—the faint scars of burns on his cheek, the horrific wounds on his body…even his miraculous escape today made perfect sense. He'd obviously had extensive training in the creation of compounds, and how much of each to add to make something new—such as a flare that could blind the men chasing him.

'This is all I need,' she muttered in frustration to the delirious face of Alim El-Kanar, the missing sheikh of Abbas al-Din. 'Why couldn't you be anywhere but here?'

The former racing-car champion kept muttering, describing the flare-bomb he'd made.

At the worst possible moment, the sound of a dozen all-terrain vehicles bumping hard and fast over the non-existent road reached her. Sh'ellah's men all spoke Arabic similar to that of the man lying in front of her. They'd identify him in moments, take him for enormous ransom…and destroy any evidence of their abduction. Within ten minutes she and all her friends would be blown to bits: another statistic to a world so inured to violence that they'd be lucky to make it to page twenty of a newspaper, or on the TV behind some Hollywood star's latest drunken tantrum.

'Fadi—Fadi, please, stay with me, brother! Stay!'

She had to do it. With a silent apology to the hero of her village, she heated a wet cloth over the fire and shoved it over his famous features to accelerate the fever already beginning to burn under his skin; she rubbed him down with a dry towel to make the temperature of his arms and legs rise. Her only chance lay with scaring the men into staying away from him…

And by shutting him up. She put her fingers to his throat and pushed down on his carotid artery, counting a slow, agonising one to twenty, until he collapsed into unconsciousness.

He had to be dreaming, but it was the sweetest dream of angel eyes.

Alim felt the fever creating needle-pricks of pain beneath his skin, the throbbing pain at his temple…but as he opened his eyes the confusion grew. Surely he was in Africa still? The hut looked African enough with its unglazed windows, and the cooking fire in the centre of the single room; the heat and dust, red dirt not sand, told him he was still in the Dark Continent.

'Where am I?' he asked the veiled woman bending over the cooking fire.

When she turned and limped towards him, he recognised the vortex of his centrifugal confusion: his angel-eyed goddess wasn't African. The face bending to his was half covered with a veil, but the green-brown eyes that weren't quite looking in his, gently slanted and surrounded by glowing olive skin, were definitely Arabic. They were so beautiful, and reminded him so much of home, he ached in places she hadn't disinfected or stitched up.

Perhaps it was the limp—anyone who climbed into a moving truck would have to hurt themselves; or maybe it was her voice he'd heard in fevered sleep, begging him to be quiet—but he was certain she'd been the one to save his life.

'You're in the village of Shellah-Akbar. How are you feeling?' she asked in Maghreb Arabic, a North African dialect related to his native tongue—haunting him with the familiarity. She was from his region—though she had the strangest accent, an unusual twang. He couldn't place it.

Intrigued, he said, 'I'm well, thank you,' in Gulf Arabic. His voice was rough against the symphony of hers, like a tiger sitting at the feet of a nightingale.

Her lashes fluttered down, but not in a flirtatious way; she acted like the shyest virgin in his home city. But she was veiled as a married woman, and working here as the nurse. He remembered her rapping out orders to others in several languages, including Swahili.

His saviour with the angel eyes was a modern woman, too confident in her orders and sure of her place to be single. Yet she chose to remain veiled, and she wouldn't meet his eyes.

She must be married to a doctor here. That had to be it.

It had been so long since he'd seen a woman behave in this manner he'd almost forgotten its tender reassurance: faithful women did exist. It had been a rare commodity in the racing world, and he'd seen few women that intrigued him in any manner since the accident.

'Now could you please tell me the truth?'

The semi-stringent demand made his dreams of gentle, angel-eyed maidens drop and quietly shatter. He looked up, saw her frowning as she inspected his wound. 'It's infected,' she muttered, probing with butterfly fingers. He breathed in the scent of woman and lavender, a combination that somehow touched him deep inside. 'I'm sorry. I had to cover the sutures with make-up and your hair, and increase your fever so Sh'ellah's men would believe you had the flu.'

'I've had far worse.' He saw the self-recrimination in those lovely eyes, heard it in the soft music of her voice. Wanting to see her shine again, he murmured, 'You were the one who came to the truck. That's why you're limping.'

Slowly she nodded, but the shadows remained.

'Did you stitch me up?'

Another nod, curt and filled with self-anger. Strange, but he could almost hear her thoughts, the emotions she tried to hide. It was as if something inside her were singing to him in silence, crying out to be understood.

Perhaps she was as isolated, as lonely for her people as he was. Why was she here?

'May I know my saviour's name?' he asked, his tone neutral, holding none of the strange tenderness she evoked in him.

The hesitation was palpable, the indecision. He took pity on her. 'If your husband…'

'I have no husband.' Her words had lost their music; they were curt and cold. She turned from him; moments later he heard the tearing sound of a medical pack opening.

He closed his eyes, cursing himself for not understanding in the first place. It had been so long since he'd dealt with a woman of his faith he'd almost forgotten: only a widow would come here, and one without a family to protect her. So young for such a loss. 'I'm sorry.'

With a little half-shrug, she leaned down to his wound. 'Please lie still. If your wound is to heal—and it has to do that, fast, before Sh'ellah's men return—I have to clean it again.'

He should have known she wouldn't be working on a man in this manner if she was married, unless she'd been married to a Westerner, and then she wouldn't be veiled.

The veil suited her, though. The seductive sweep of the sand-hued material over her face and body covered her form in comfort but protected her skin from the stinging dirt and winds without binding her. And the soft swish of the hand-stitched material as she walked—how she moved so beautifully with a limp was unfathomable, but he knew his angel was also his saviour.

She walks in beauty like the night. Or like a star of the sunrise...

'Thank you for saving my worthless life, Sahar Thurayya,' he said, with a bowing motion of his hands, since he couldn't move his head without ruining her work.

A brow lifted at the title he'd given her, *dawn star*, a courtesy name since she refused to give him her true name, but she continued her work without speaking.

'My name is Alim.'

To give her that much truth was safe. There were many men named Alim in his country, and courtesy demanded she introduce herself in return.

'Though dawn star is prettier,' she said quietly, 'my name is Hana.'

Hana meant *happiness*. 'I think *dawn star* is more suited to the woman you've become.'

She didn't look up from the intricate task of cleaning hair and packed-on make-up from his

wound. 'You've known me all of ten minutes, yet
you feel qualified to make such a judgement?'

She was right. Just because she was here, cut off
from her own people, and was radiant with all forms
of beauty *but* happiness—she seemed haunted
somehow—gave him no right to judge her. 'I beg
your pardon,' he said gravely in the dialect of his
homeland.

'Please stop talking,' she whispered.

It was only then that he noticed the fine tremors
in her hand. So his mere presence, their shared
language, hurt her heart as much as hers did him.
He closed his eyes and let her work in peace,
breathing in the clean warm air and scent of
lavender, a natural disinfectant.

She still wasn't risking using the medicines he'd
brought, then.

When she seemed to be almost done with his
wound, he murmured, 'Where's my truck?'

'Abdel drove it out to a remote part of the area.
The villagers wiped all traces of the tyre tracks
from the way in and out of the village. Don't worry,
he'll hide it well, and will give you exact coordinates so you can get to it when you're feeling
better.'

'Who am I?' When she frowned at him, obviously wondering if concussion had given him temporary amnesia, he added, 'To Sh'ellah's men,
when they came? Who did you say I was?'

The fingers placing Steri-Strips over his wound trembled for a moment; again her agony of indecision felt like shimmering heat rising in waves from her skin.

He waited in silence. It seemed the last thing she needed was his voice, his language and accent reminding her of what she no longer had—though he wondered why she wasn't home with their people. Why his presence hurt her so.

She put the last Steri-Strip over his wound, and stepped back. 'When they came, I wore a full burq'a so they'd assume I was married. If they can't see, there's less for them to be tempted. You know how life is here.'

Intrigued again by this woman and the most prosaic acceptance of the ugly side of life, he nodded.

'When they came in here, they assumed you were my husband. Even unconscious, your presence as my man inspired respect for me, and protected me from abduction and rape—for now at least,' she finished bluntly. 'Sh'ellah still wants us to believe he's our saviour, and we're not giving him any reason to think otherwise.'

Alim saw the bubbling mass of emotion inside her pull apart into distinct, jagged pieces. Memory began returning to him like little shards of glass. She'd risked her life to come to him in the truck; she'd done so again by treating him in her hut, and claiming him as her man. He owed this woman his life at least twice over.

Slowly, as delicately as if he were creating an explosive cocktail of chemicals, he said, 'I'm privileged to be your husband in name, Sahar Thurayya. I'd be more honoured still if you would trust me while I'm here. It won't be long.'

She returned to his bedside with a cup of water. She took a sip first, then handed it to him and he drank in turn, his eyes on hers. The cup of agreement and peace: a traditional sign of mutual respect. A tradition he'd once given and accepted with so little thought—but now, looking in those brave, sad eyes, he felt the full honour of her offer.

It told him far more about this woman than anything that had come from her mouth. She was from Abbas al-Din, no matter what language she spoke.

Her eyes smiled, but her hand didn't touch his as she gave him the cup. 'Thank you.'

He noted she didn't use his name; she still kept her distance. In Hana's eyes, obviously trust was something earned, not given. He wondered how high the cost had been for misplaced trust in the past. Why did a woman with such pain beneath her smile risk her life and virtue in a place where nobody would live, if they had a choice?

'I'm afraid you can't leave yet. They know the supplies went somewhere, and you're the only stranger in the district,' she said as he filled his parched throat with cool water. 'Sh'ellah will have placed a dozen men on every way out of the village. They've been here several times in past months, collecting more than half our millet and corn harvest to feed his soldiers,' she said, bitterness threading through her voice. 'With a stranger in the village, they'll be watching all of us for weeks to come.' She sounded strained as she added, 'So I'm glad of your promise, since we will have to share my hut as husband and wife. There's only one bed here.'

He choked on the final gulp of liquid. Coughing, he turned his gaze to her. Strange that, with a throbbing headache and eyes stinging, he knew where she was at all times. His ears strained for the swish of her burq'a. She made a sound he'd heard all his life so alluring, so incredibly feminine. She seemed to infuse her every movement with life, light and beauty.

She made a sound of distress as she went on, 'I'm sorry, but we can't afford to bring in a spare bed in case Sh'ellah's men raid during the night, or lead a sneak attack. We have to sleep in one bed or risk suspicion—and out here suspicion is explained with an assault rifle.'

Alim stared at her back, so unyielding, refusing to face him. He thought of every day of his adult life spent avoiding this kind of intimacy, using the death of his young wife ten years before—the wife he'd liked but had never loved—as his excuse not to fulfil his duty and remarry. He thought of his adopted career of car racing, travelling from place to place, never settling down—holding himself off from living. Even now, wasn't he in hiding?

And he smiled; he grinned, and then burst out laughing.

'What's so funny?' Hana turned on him at the first sound of the chuckle bursting from his lips. Her veil fell from her lower face, showing lush dusky lips pursed with indignation. Her eyes flashed; even in the midst of angry demand, her voice was like the music of a waterfall. Her face, now revealed for a moment in all its glory, was harmony to its symphony.

And he was a complete idiot to think of her that way.

But it was the first time he'd truly laughed in three years, and he found that once he started again, he couldn't stop. 'It's—it's so absurd,' he gasped between fresh gusts of mirth.

Hana straightened her shoulders and looked him right in the eyes for the first time—and hers were contemptuous. Every feature of that lovely face showed disdain. 'Maybe it's ridiculous to you, but if it saves the lives of a hundred people—and I presume you care about their lives, since you risked your life to come here with food and medicines for them—I'll put up with the absurdity. The question is, will you?'

CHAPTER TWO

'WHAT'S the unusual note in your accent?' the sheikh asked her, his tone abrupt at the subject change, but his dark green eyes were curious. Assessing her beyond the questions his simple words spoke. 'You haven't lived in the emirates all your life.'

Hana felt as if he were dissecting her without a scalpel. So he hadn't been fooled by her use of Maghreb, nor put off by her unaccustomed abruptness.

Not in the six months she'd been here in the village had simple conversation been fraught with such danger. If he knew the truth about his so-called saviour, he could take her freedom away with a snap of his fingers.

Her heart beat faster at the thought of saying anything—but thousands of Arabic girls grew up in Australia. Not so many people from Abbas al-Din had lived in Perth, of course, but enough that she wouldn't be easily traced.

Then she laughed at herself. What a ridiculous thought—as if Alim El-Kanar would care enough to trace her past! This wasn't the kind of information she needed to hide; it wasn't the reason she'd been shunned by her people. 'I was born in the emirates, but raised in Australia from the age of seven,' she answered, realising that a few minutes had passed while she'd been lost in thought—and that he'd allowed her to think without interruption.

'Ah.' He relaxed back on his pillows; she'd barely noticed his tension until then. 'I couldn't place the twang. Are you fluent in English?' he asked, changing languages without a break in speaking.

She nodded, answering in English. 'I lived there from the ages of seven to twenty-one, and went to state-run English schools.'

He grinned. 'You sound totally Aussie now you're speaking English.'

She laughed. 'I guess that's how I consider myself, mostly. My dad—' she'd practised so long, she could say 'dad' without choking up any more '—was offered an opportunity in the mining industry. He was a miner, but saved enough to go to university, and became an engineer. So he was rather unique in that he knew both sides…' *And that was way too much information!* She clamped her lips shut.

'I can see why any big mining corporation would want him,' he said, sounding thoughtful.

She'd started this, she had to finish or the sheikh would remember the conversation long after he was gone. She forced a smile through the lump in her throat, 'Yes, the money he was offered was so large he felt it would be irresponsible to the family to not take it. When we'd been there a little while, he and Mum felt it would be best for us if we retained our culture, but understood and respected the one we lived in. We lived not far from other Arabic families—but while we attended Islamic lessons, we also attended local schools.' And she'd just said more words together about herself than she had in years. She closed her mouth.

After a slow, thoughtful pause, the sheikh—she couldn't help but think of him as that—said, 'So if your father was in the mining industry, you lived in the outback? Kalgoorlie or Tom Price, or maybe the Kimberley Ranges?'

Her pulse pounded in her throat until her breath laboured. 'No, we didn't, but he did. We—my mother, my sisters and brother and I—lived in a suburb of Perth, and Dad lived in Kalgoorlie and came home Fridays. He wanted us to live close to…amenities.'

The sheikh nodded. She saw it in his eyes: he'd noticed the omission of the word *mosque*.

Even thinking the word was painful. She couldn't enter a mosque without people wanting to know who she was and where she was from; and she couldn't lie. Not in a holy place.

So she didn't go any more.

'Did you always wear the burq'a?' he asked, with a gentle politeness that told her he respected her secrets, her right to not answer.

'No. I'm from a moderate Sunni family. I wear it for protection.' She shrugged. 'Sh'ellah's very sweet to us—most of the time. But he could turn without warning.'

He's already sent men to ask if I have a man, or whether they can see whether I am young and pretty enough for his tastes.

She kept the shudder inside. Sh'ellah might be sixty-two, but he was a man of strong passions. Though he kept two wives, he had concubines in droves—and those were the women who pleased him. The others he discarded…and none of them ever came home.

Since she'd had the first warning of Sh'ellah's tastes, she'd kept the burq'a on as a knight's armour, wore her fake wedding ring like a talisman. She'd claimed her husband was travelling, and he'd soon be on his way here.

Her time here was over. Now she'd claimed the sheikh as her husband, Sh'ellah would expect her to leave with the sheikh when he went. Otherwise she'd become fair game. She had two backpacks packed and ready, hidden in the dirt beneath her hut, ready to disappear at a moment's notice, to head by foot to the nearest refugee camp if need be. It was two hundred and sixty kilometres away, but she knew how to find edible plants filled with juice, and collect dew from upturned leaves. With two or three canteens of water, some purification tablets, three dozen long-hidden energy bars and a compass, she could travel at night and make it in fourteen days.

She'd been used for a man's purposes once. She'd rather die than be used that way again.

The sheikh nodded, as if he understood what she'd left unsaid. Maybe he did, if he'd been in the Sahel long enough.

'Were you brought up in the emirates?' She turned to the pit fire as she asked, making an infusion of her precious stores of willow bark for his fever in a tiny hanging pot. If people were seen to be carrying things into this hut, Sh'ellah's men would be searching here in minutes. She'd give them no excuse to pay attention to her.

She didn't have to wonder if he noticed she'd lapsed into their native language; she saw the flickering of those dark eyes, and knew he was sizing her up like one of his chemical equations. He took long moments to answer. 'Yes.'

That was it. Flat and unemotional-sounding, a mirror-world of unhealed pain behind the thin wall of glass, ready to shatter at a touch. She spooned some of her infusion into a cracked plastic mug. 'I'm sorry I have no honey to sweeten this, but it will lessen your pain.'

She saw the surprise come and go in his face. He wasn't going to ask, and she wasn't going to volunteer why she minded her own business; but she knew he'd think about it. Why she asked nothing more, demanded no answers in return for hers. 'Drink it all.'

He nodded, and took the cup from her. His fingers brushed hers, and she felt a tiny shiver run through her. 'You don't call me by my name.'

She drew a breath to conquer the tiny tremors in her hands. What was wrong with her? 'You're a stranger, older than me, and risked a lot to help our village. I was taught respect.'

'I'm barely ten years your senior. I gave you my name,' he said, and drained the cup. He held it back out to her with a face devoid of expression, but she sensed the challenge within. The dominant male used to winning with open weapons…and beneath lurked a hint of irritation. He didn't like her calling him older. She hid the smile.

'You gave your name, but it's my choice to use it or not.' She took the cup back, neither seeking nor avoiding the touch. Just as she neither sought nor avoided his eyes. It was a trick her mother had taught her. *Everything you give to a man he can refuse to return, Hana. So give as little as possible, even a glance, until you are certain what kind of man you face.*

It had been good advice—until she'd met Mukhtar.

'You don't like my name, Sahar Thurayya?'

She washed the cup and returned it to its hook on the wall. Since she had no bench or cupboard, all things were either stacked on a box or hung on walls. 'I'm waiting to see if you live up to it.' She didn't comment on his poetic name for her, but a faint thrill ran through her every time she heard it. Just as she caught her breath when he smiled with his eyes, or laughed. And when he touched her… She closed her eyes and uttered a silent prayer. Four hours in this man's company, three of them when he'd been unconscious, and she was already in danger.

'So I must live up to my name?' Again she heard that rich chuckle in his voice. Without even turning around, she could see his face in her mind's eye, beautiful even in its damaged state, alight with the mirth that made him look as he had four years ago, and she knew she was standing in emotional quicksand. 'My brother always said I was misnamed.'

Alim: wise, learned.

She didn't ask in what ways he was unwise. He'd risked his life over and over for the thrill of racing and winning…

'It seems we were both misnamed,' he added, the laughter in his tone asking her to see the joke, as he had.

Hana: happiness.

I used to live up to my name, she thought wistfully. *When I was engaged to Latif, about to become his wife, then I was a happy woman.*

Then Latif's younger brother Mukhtar came into her life—and Latif showed her what her dreams of love and happiness were worth.

'I need to check on my other patients,' she said quietly. Checking to be certain her veil fully covered her, she walked with an unhurried step towards the medical tent—it hurt to rush since she had twisted her knee climbing into his truck—feeling his gaze follow her for as long as she was in sight.

Alim watched the doorway with views to the medical hut long after he could no longer see her. He still watched while the setting sun flooded the open door, long after his eyes hurt with the brightness and his head began knocking with the pain that would soon upgrade as the foul stuff she'd given him wore off.

She didn't draw attention to herself in any way—quite the opposite, including the burq'a the colour of sand, obviously handmade. She moved as little as possible, said nothing of consequence. She certainly wasn't trying to seem mysterious. Yet he sensed the emotion beneath each carefully chosen word; he saw the pain he'd caused her by saying her name didn't suit her.

She'd been a happy woman once—that much

was obvious. Something had happened to turn her into a woman who no longer saw happiness in her life or future.

There was a vivid *life* inside her, yet she lived in dangerous isolation in an arid war zone, in a hut with no amenities, far from family and friends. She was like a sparkling fountain stoppered without reason, a dawn star sucked down into a black hole.

He wanted to know why.

What would she look like if she truly smiled or laughed? To see her hair loose, wearing whatever she had on beneath the soft-swishing burq'a…

The last rays of the setting sun painted the ochre sand a violent scarlet. He blinked—and then it was blocked as her silhouetted form filled the doorway. She took on its hues, softened and irradiated them until she looked ethereal, celestial, a timeless beauty from a thousand Arabian nights, trapped in a labyrinth, needing a prince to save her.

'Do you need more pain relief yet?' A prosaic enough question, but in her voice, gentle and musical, it turned their native language into harps and waterfalls.

Alim blinked again. Stupid, stupid! He'd obviously knocked the part of his brain that created poetry or something. He'd never thought of any woman this way before, and he knew next to nothing about this one. Perhaps that was the fascination: she didn't rush into telling him about herself, didn't try to impress or please him. He was no Aladdin. If she needed a prince, he wasn't one any more, and never would be again. Then he would become a thief: of his brother's rightful position, stolen by a death he'd caused.

And if he kept thinking about it, he'd explode. Time to do what she was doing: make his thoughts as well as their conversation ordinary. 'Yes, please, Hana.'

The shock of sudden pain hit his eyes when she left the doorway and the west-facing door took back the mystical shades of sunset, vicious to his head. It felt like a punishment for turning his saviour into an angel.

He'd obviously been alone too long—but after three years he still wasn't ready to show any woman his body. If he couldn't even look at himself without revulsion, he couldn't expect anyone else to manage it, let alone find him remotely attractive. Yet there was something about Hana that pulled at him, tugging at his soul—her beautiful eyes, the haunted, hunted look in them…

Hana's unveiled face suddenly filled his vision, and he blinked a third time, feeling blinded, not by the sun, but by her. Catching his breath seemed too hard; speech, impossible.

She didn't seem affected in any way by his closeness. 'Let this swill under your tongue a few moments; it'll work faster that way. You'll feel better soon, and tonight we can sneak in some paracetamol. I'm sorry we have no codeine, it's better for concussion, but stores are limited, as you know.'

Though her words were plain, it felt as if she was doing that thing again, saying too much and not enough. Talking about codeine to hide what she was really feeling.

Had he given himself away, shown that, despite his best attempt at will power, he couldn't stop thinking of her? The internal war raging in him, desire, fascination and self-hate, was so strong it was no wonder she saw it.

Then he realised something. He wasn't itching. He hadn't had the stress-trigger since he'd woken. And the scent of lavender and something else rose gently from his body. She'd rubbed something into his skin while he slept. She'd not only seen the patchwork mess that was his scars, but treated them.

The permanent reminder that he'd killed his brother, his best friend…

Grimly he swallowed the foul brew she handed him, wishing he could ask for something to knock him out again. He handed it back with no attempt to touch her. She didn't want him, and touching her threatened to turn swirling winds of attraction into gale-force winds of unleashed desire that could make him start wanting things he didn't deserve.

'Thanks,' he said briefly, keeping his words and thoughts in prosaic English. Arabic had too many musical cadences, too much poetry for him to hear her speak it, see her lovely form and not be moved to his soul. But she couldn't possibly feel the same after seeing him. He revolted himself, and for more reasons than the physical.

'I'm fine if you need to see to your other patients. I'll sleep now.' He turned from her.

'You should eat first. You don't want to wake up hungry at midnight.'

Irritated beyond measure by her good sense, by her care for what he'd most wanted to hide, he rolled over and snapped, 'If I want food I'll ask for it, *Hana.*' He used cold, deliberate English, to remind her of the danger if she kept distancing herself from him.

In return she made a mocking bow, a liquid movement like the night gathering around her. 'Of course, my lord. I'll bring your food at midnight after caring for you and my patients all day, if such is your wish.' She wasn't smiling, but there was a lurking imp in her eyes…and she still hadn't said his name.

She'd left the hut before he recovered from the surprise that she was making fun of him. Putting him in his place with a few words… He watched her walk away, her body shimmering beneath her shifting burq'a like a fluid dance. 'Hana!' he yelled before he could hold it back.

She turned only her head, but he felt the smile she held inside. 'Yes, my lord?'

Though the term could be a continuation of her

teasing, it made him frown. What did she know about him? 'I'm sorry,' he growled. 'I'll eat whenever you think is best.'

She inclined her head. 'Concussion makes the best of us irritable.' Then she was gone.

It was forgiveness, he supposed, or understanding. He didn't particularly like either—or himself at this moment. He'd lost his inborn arrogance the day Fadi died, or so he'd thought.

Never had he acted with such arrogance with the lowest pit worker, and he'd *never* lost it over a woman's disinterest before. Yet within two hours of meeting Hana he'd become a cliché—a guy in lust with his nurse, cheated because she wasn't entertaining him with flirtation, or distracting him from his pain and lack of control over his body by touching him.

Cheated because she'd touched his body as a nurse, not a woman…by seeing him as a patient—a scarred, angry patient she needed to heal—and not a man.

Growling again, he rolled over and punched the thin pillow, folding it to make it thicker. But rest was impossible while he knew she'd be back.

It was deep in the night when he came awake with a smothered exclamation—smothered because a hand covered his mouth. 'Not a word,' an urgent voice whispered. The bed dipped and sagged as a soft, rounded backside snuggled into the cradle of his hips. Strange back-and-forth motions made the rusted bed squeak.

The hut was a gentle combination of silvery light and shadow. The tender lavender she wore ignited his senses; the feel of her against his body instantly aroused him. Did she taste as sweet and silky as she smelled and felt on his skin? And her hair was loose, reaching her waist in thick waves, falling over his bare arm in butterfly kisses. Like a paradox, the hand reaching backward, covering his mouth, held him silent in ruthless suppression.

'What are you doing?' It came out as muffled grunts.

'Sweeping my body indents from the ground,' she replied in a fierce whisper. 'I told you to be quiet. Now they'll know we're awake, and will want to know why. Take off your shirt.' She stood, and as he stripped off his shirt her burq'a fluttered to the ground, leaving her only in cami-knickers and a thin cotton vest top. 'Lie on me, and pretend to enjoy it,' she mouthed.

Pretend? The moment he was on her she'd know just how far from a game this was. He thanked Allah that though she'd seen and treated his scars, she couldn't see them in the dark.

Moments later she gasped softly and closed her eyes. Lying stiff and cold beneath him, she managed to whisper, 'Make sounds of pleasure.'

He groaned. Moving against her softness, his body realised how long it had been since he'd loved a woman. It was screaming to him to take this pretence to a perfect conclusion. Yet there'd been an odd note of intensity in her whisper. It went beyond what he would have expected in this situation, and from a widow.

Frowning, he looked down at her, moved by the incandescent beauty of her uncovered face, by the glossy waves of hair shimmering across his pillow and over her shoulders in the moonlight. 'It's all right, Hana, I've done this before.'

'What, you've faked it for killers before? What an adventurous life you've led,' she murmured mockingly in his ear; yet her teeth were gritted, her body so taut with rejection of his touch he thought if he moved at all, he might bounce right off her.

Lifting his face to see her more clearly in the glowing half-light, he saw her eyes were still closed, and there was a sheen of sweat on her brow. She was terrified and trying her best to hide it, but of what was she more frightened: the danger all around them, or the fact that the scarred, ugly stranger lying on her body was obviously ready for action?

Working on the instincts that had saved his life several times, he murmured in a croon he kept for intimate situations, but in English so the men outside wouldn't understand, 'Hana, this goes only as far as it needs to for Sh'ellah's men. You saved my life—you're saving my life again right now. I'd never hurt you or impose my will on you.'

She made a moaning sound that wouldn't fool Sh'ellah's men if they were in the radius of hearing. Her eyes remained squeezed tight shut. 'Thank you.' She arched her body up to his and made a more convincing noise of passion.

Feeling her sweet-scented, fluid body against him, he almost forgot his good resolutions.

Then she stiffened and made a muffled noise, as if finding release. 'Alim,' she cried, using his name for the first time. 'Alim, my love, I've missed you so much!'

Moments later a face appeared at the window; its shadow blocked the moonlight. 'Who is there?' Alim demanded harshly in Maghreb. 'Leave us to our privacy!'

The light reappeared as the head disappeared. He heard a whisper in a mixture of English and another language, but was unable to make it out. He spoke all forms of Arabic, French, German and English, but the African cadences were beyond him.

'Swahili,' she whispered, as tense as her body, though her voice had returned to the voice of a stranger, keeping him at a distance. 'They're saying that Sh'ellah—the local warlord—won't be pleased at this. He had plans for me.'

'I know who Sh'ellah is.' Anyone who'd worked

more than a year in the Sahel knew the names of local warlords and what boundaries were where. A wise man also made certain he knew when and where the borders shifted, or he ended up carrion feed. 'He wants you?' he almost groaned in despair. 'That complicates matters.'

'He wants me because I'm young and different to most women in the region. He knows nothing of me. I've always been heavily veiled when his men come. All they or he ever see is my eyes.' She shrugged, in a fatalistic gesture. 'I'm packed and ready to leave. I can go tonight—but you won't make it. We have to wait another day.'

'No.' He knew what she hadn't said: Sh'ellah would think nothing of killing him to have Hana once or twice, before dumping her body in the shifting sands. 'I've worked through injury before. We should get out of here tonight.'

Worried eyes searched his. 'We have to be several kilometres away before they find we're missing, and you were unconscious only hours ago. Fever and concussion aren't conditions to play with.'

Touched by her concern, he whispered, 'I'll be all right.'

She made an impatient gesture. 'No, you won't—but there's no choice. We need to head to the refugee camp. A plane arrives on Wednesdays. It's Thursday now—it will take almost two weeks by foot. With your injuries, we'll need an extra day,

travelling by night. We'll take pain-relief tablets
with us, a suture kit and extra water.'

'If we head for the truck we don't need to take
more than four days. We can drive the rest of the way.'

She frowned. 'That's sixty kilometres away.'

Teeth gritted now, he muttered, 'I'll make it.'

'All right, if you say so.' Those lovely, slanted
eyes stared in open doubt. 'I think you can roll off
me now. It's customary.'

He wanted so badly to laugh, he did, but made it
low and rippling, like a lover's laugh.

He was stunned by her quick thinking and
thorough planning. His respect for her grew by the
minute. Yet Alim was acutely aware of her near-
nude body beneath him, her braless state, the sweet-
ness of her skin and her gentle scent. It was almost
a relief to move away, to gain distance—but she
snuggled into his arms, making sure the sheet
covered the clothes they still wore.

'My love,' she murmured in Maghreb. 'We'll
have to take an old suture kit, and bring only the
willow-bark infusion,' she whispered, making it
seem intimate. 'I'm sorry, but we buried all the
new medications. We can't afford to dig them up
now.'

'It's okay.' He gathered her against him, kissing
her hair—and the lavender filled his head. 'I love
your scent.'

Her mouth tightened. She stiffened in his arms,

and the budding trust vanished. 'It's not meant to entice. It's to keep off fleas, mosquitoes and bed bugs. Scorpions don't like it, either.'

She sounded frozen. Given the stiff revulsion she'd exhibited only moments before, Alim wanted to kick himself for being so stupid as to think she could want him. Right now, he could think of no re-assurance that she'd believe, so he drawled, 'Bed bugs and scorpions…oh, baby, nobody does pillow talk the way you do.'

After a stunned few seconds, she burst out laughing.

Relief washed through him, and he grinned— but the way her face came alive with the smile, the harplike sound of her laughter, made him ache. Now he could see how well her name suited her— or it had once.

Then she whispered, 'I have an aloe and lavender cream for your scars, as well. It looks as though you need pain relief for it. You never finished the plastic surgery you needed, did you?'

She'd ruined their connection by the question, by mentioning his deformity and all its reminders. He moved away from her, trying not to show how hard it was not to fling her away. It was all he could do to ground out a single word. 'No.'

As if she heard his thoughts, she backed off. 'We need to be gone in an hour. There's only one way from the village they won't be covering—where the wild dogs are. It'll be dangerous, but they usually sleep until dawn. We have to be past their territory by then. There's a small track, an old dried stream we can take, which has some shade for sleeping by day.'

'Right,' he replied, wondering if the feel of his skin against her had done anything but revolt her, having seen him unclothed…having treated his burns as no one had done since he left the private facility in Bern three years ago.

He closed his eyes, squeezing them tight. No wonder she'd been so stiff and cold with him. No wonder she'd turned aside when he'd called her his dawn star. He was a poet from the slag heaps, a monster daring to look upon beauty and hunger for what he couldn't have.

Hana wasn't the kind of woman who'd welcome his touch for his wealth, and he was fiercely glad of that—of course he was. He wasn't that desperate.

'I'll ask one of the men here to pack you a change of clothes. We can only take one each; we need the room for water and medicine. I have dried fruits and energy bars stored in my backpack. We'll fill one canteen with willow-bark infusion for your pain. You'll have to be sparing with it.'

He kept his voice brisk and practical, hiding his turmoil of desire and sickening acceptance of her rejection. 'Travelling at night should help. I have some ibuprofen in my pack I can use. Only a dozen tablets, but—'

She rolled up and sat at the edge of the bed. 'Excellent.' She actually smiled at him. His heart flipped over at the look in her eyes, holding no pity, just approval; and even if she only smiled in relief that he wouldn't be moaning and groaning all the way to the refugee camp, he'd take it. He'd take any piece of happiness she doled out to him, because it felt as if she hoarded it like miser's gold. And it might just mean she wasn't totally revolted by him.

What had happened to her to change her from the happy woman she'd been once, he didn't know— but he had at least a week to find out.

CHAPTER THREE

IT WAS close to three a.m. before they left the hut. Flickering lights a short distance away showed Alim how closely the village was being watched.

'We'll need to commando crawl,' he whispered as they watched another cigarette being lit, another flashlight sweep a slow arc. 'These packs are bulky.'

She nodded. 'And we have to move in silence. They have to believe the villagers know nothing except my husband showed up without warning yesterday, and we disappeared at night.' She handed him a bundle of clothes. 'Put these on. You need to blend into the environment.'

He looked at the clothes, some kind of dun colour, smeared with mud and dirt, and felt intense admiration for her yet again. She thought of everything. 'Can you turn your back?' he asked gruffly, unable to stand that she'd be revolted by his body again.

She nodded and turned away. He felt pity radiating from her, but her practical words made him wonder if the compassion he'd sensed had been the workings of his paranoid imagination. 'You won't be able to wear your clothes until we're out of Sh'ellah's reach.'

As he turned to answer she slipped out of her burq'a with a swift movement, and his breath caught in his throat, remembering her lovely curved body in the knickers and camisole…

He swallowed the ridiculous disappointment. Of course she wore jeans and a long-sleeved shirt with running shoes beneath! What colour he couldn't make out in the murky darkness, but probably brown, like his; her hair looked plaited. She rolled the garment up and stored it in her backpack, and shoved her plait beneath a brown cap.

She shouldered her pack and dropped to the ground, and began belly-crawling. 'Let's go.'

Ignoring the severe pounding inside his head, the light fever that still hadn't abated, he lay down flat and followed her.

It took a gruelling half-hour to make it past the village boundaries to the territory of the wild dogs. Now the moon had set past the village, the delicate filigree beauty around him had faded to a grim, dusty night as thick as the dirt coating them further with every movement.

Alim followed Hana around the hut to the fields,

heading towards the only path out, his concentration on two things—being quiet, and trying with all his might not to cough or sneeze. The neckerchief she'd given him to cover his nose and throat was so thickly coated in dirt it was hard to breathe. His scarred skin began to pull and itch in moments.

At the head of the path, she thrust a canteen in his hands. 'Wet the bandanna using as little water as possible, and wring it out,' she whispered in his ear. 'We have to stay flat until we reach the stream bed. Our last opportunity to fill the canteens for fifty kilometres will be there. Move slowly, and try not to let your sweat touch ground. We can't afford to make a sound, or give off any scent. The dogs don't have assault rifles, but they can tear you apart in seconds.'

So that was why she'd only brought dried, wrapped food, and double-wrapped everything in tight-tied bags. Fighting the unwanted arousal her lips against his ear had given him—*damn* his body for all the stupid ideas it had—he nodded and kept following her. Elbows thrust forward and sideways, then a knee, one side then the other, measuring every movement in case it was too big or would dislodge a pebble and make a noise to alert the dogs.

The next hour was excruciating. *Breathing through a wet bandanna, don't move too fast, don't cough or sneeze, don't itch, don't break into a sweat, don't make a noise or you'll become dog meat.* He was forced to follow her, his head pounding with concussion and the stress of aching to go forward, to take the lead and somehow protect her, but this was her turf. She alone knew the way out of danger.

For the first time in his life he had to trust a woman in a life and death situation—but from everything she'd already done, all without flinching or complaint, he knew if there was one woman on earth he could hand control to without fear, it was Hana.

Finally, as he knew he had to breathe clean air or pass out, the flat ground gave way, and they slithered slow and quiet down a little slope; the dust became hard, crusty earth, the cracked mud of a dead stream, and when he heard Hana give a soft sigh he sensed they'd passed at least the first of the current menace facing them.

He slipped the bandanna from his nose and mouth, and dragged in a breath of fresh air without a word. Never had breathing felt so luxurious.

'No water here.' She sighed. 'Our task just got harder, and you're still concussed. Are you sure you're up to this? Once they know we're gone there's no turning back.'

'I can do it,' he reiterated through a clenched jaw. Did she think he couldn't take a little hardship just because of a bump on the head, a touch of fever?

'We have to turn north as soon as we can.' The words breathed in his ear, softer than a whisper, slow and clear, making him shiver in sensuous reaction. 'We still have fifty kilometres to the truck.' The second zephyr of sound stirred his hair and left a small trail of goose bumps.

'Maybe we should leave it where it is and travel south toward the refugee camp by night,' he whispered, as soft as he could. 'If they've found the truck they'll expect us to come for it.'

'You'll never make it to the camp by foot with concussion—it will only worsen without rest. And the boundaries for the warlords change almost daily. If we cross one unseen line, you're dead, and I soon will be, once Sh'ellah finishes with me.'

He shuddered with the force of the flat whisper. 'It'll take three more days to reach the truck, and then we have to backtrack. A hundred and sixty kilometres through enemy lines in a truck so noticeable it practically screams *foreigners*.'

She looked at him, her eyes cool, calm—and how she made him ache with her beauty when she was coated in dust and clumps of mud, wearing a baseball cap and a shirt that looked like charity would reject it, he had no clue. 'Let's go.'

The utter relief to be upright, enjoying the luxury of walking again, flooded him until the headache grew to severe proportions. He said nothing to her until she called for another halt.

After he'd taken some tablets with water, she said, 'We've gone almost as far as we can before sunrise.' She saw him rubbing at his underarm with his arm, trying to scratch unobtrusively. 'How's your skin? Is it itching with all the dirt?'

His jaw tightened and he stopped moving. Yet another reminder: Beauty was letting the Beast know just who he was to her, reminding him what he was to himself. 'I'm fine.'

'I don't want to embarrass you. You won't be able to travel at night if the grafted skin or the burns rip, bleed or itch. We just crawled more than five kilometres. There has to be damage.'

'I said I'm fine.' He sounded curt with rejection she didn't deserve, but he couldn't help it. 'Give me the cream and I'll do it when I need it.'

Hana sighed. 'There are ways to rub the cream in that optimise stretching and physical comfort for you while we're travelling. It will also give you better sleep. I can see you're uncomfortable with my doing it, but we have four days of hard walking to go, sleeping in dirt and mud that could irritate your skin, and—'

Alim heard his teeth grind before he spoke. 'You're not going to stop arguing until you get your way, are you?'

'Probably not,' she conceded with a gentle laugh.

His head felt like a light and sound show, brilliant stabs of pain shooting from his neck to his eyes. He couldn't manage rubbing the entire length of his scars now if he tried. 'Do it, then.'

The words had been clipped, order from master to servant, but she didn't argue. 'Stay still, and close your eyes.' Her voice was gentle, soothing, stealing into his battleground mind with tender healing.

He felt her undoing the buttons of his shirt…oh, God help him for the male reaction to her touch she'd be bound to see. The sun was beginning to rise.

'Your tension won't help, you know. Breathe deeply, relax and let me make it better.'

She might have been speaking to a child, but her warm, wet hands against his itching, burning scars, filled with beautiful, scented oils, took away any power to speak. He breathed, and felt the irritable tension leaving him, leaving him only aroused.

'That's it, much better. I'm sorry I can't use any water to wash away the dirt, but the olive oil is helping.' Her hands were tender magic, kneading softly, moving in slow, deep circles. Her fingers rotated over his skin, deep then soft; her palms pushed up and around, spreading more oil. 'This solution is fifty per cent cold-pressed olive oil, forty per cent pure aloe juice and ten per cent essential oils of lavender, rosemary and neroli. I make ten litres a month for burns victims or scarring from rifle wounds. A village about forty kilometres from the refugee camp is a Free Trade village, and orders everything I need.'

'Hmm.' She could be reciting the alphabet or the

phone book for all he cared. Her voice was a siren's call, an angel's song; her touch was sweet relief, *bliss*, releasing him from the burning ropes of limited movement, giving him freedom to lift his arm as she moved it to massage where the scar tissue was worst. Though she said and did nothing a nurse wouldn't do for any patient, she made him feel like a man again, because she'd treated him like a man.

'It's feeling better?' she asked softly. She sounded—odd.

'Oh, yeah,' he mumbled. Feeling as if he were floating, he opened his eyes to a slit—and if he weren't so utterly relaxed he'd have started. Hana was looking at his body as she massaged, and it held no revulsion, no clinical detachment. Her eyes in the soft rose light of the sunrise looked deeper, softer…her breathing had quickened…she wet her lips…

Then she looked at his face, her cheeks flushed and her lips parted in innocent, lush surprise, and in her expression was something he'd *never* seen from any nurse.

It was something he'd never seen from any *woman*. Those lovely, slanted almond eyes held something like innocent languor…beautiful, breathtaking, aching *desire*. Good, old-fashioned, honest wanting, woman to man.

Then she saw his eyes open, and the look

vanished as if it had never been there. 'Good. I'm glad it helped,' she said, her tone aiming for crisp, but it wobbled a touch. 'Get dressed. If I remember rightly, there's a good overhang a few kilometres away, where we can sleep.'

Was he possibly grinning as widely as he wanted to? 'Why don't we sleep here? You look so tired, and it's been a long, hard day for us both.'

'It isn't far enough from the village.' She was the one now speaking through gritted teeth. 'When we reach the truck, you call the shots. Right now, this is my territory. If you want to live, you're doing things my way.'

Unable to muster up an argument when she'd saved his life again tonight, he shrugged; but he hated that she was right and he couldn't argue, couldn't take charge and protect her somehow. 'Three days,' he said softly. 'Then you'd better believe I'm calling the shots. I'll get you to the refugee camp safely, Hana, that I swear—but you'll obey me, no questions asked.' *And we're going to explore that look you gave me just now,* the man in him vowed, exultant.

She nodded; far from pushing back, there was a suspicious twinkle in her eyes. 'I will obey you joyfully, my lord, for I am a weak woman in need of your strength.' She mock-genuflected before him, touching her forehead to the ground as she spoke. 'It must be the reason why I never left the village before. I was waiting for you to guide and direct me.'

He had to choke down laughter at her unexpected sense of humour. 'Can it, Hana,' he said, using a phrase from one of his former pit crew, 'and let's get going.'

She grinned and bowed again; then, with a grin that held more than a touch of the imp—pretty, so damned *pretty*—she said, 'We should crawl again for a while. It's getting light.'

The prospect made him forget temptation for the present. Alim groaned and dropped to his stomach, but Hana was ahead of him, already wriggling down the hill.

He'd been too busy trying to breathe before to notice how enticing that wriggle was. No—he'd ignored it, thinking it was useless. But after that *look*…

If they'd been anywhere else, had she been another woman…but they were crawling through mud in wild dogs' territory with a warlord's men with assault rifles in every other direction; and this was Hana, who'd frozen beneath him. She deserved his respect, not the burden of unwanted fascination from a man who looked like a damned monster—and he had no magical spell she could reverse with her kiss. The way he looked now was how he'd look for life.

The look had to have been a mistake. He was a

nowhere man with no home, no position. He had nothing to offer any woman but ugliness, emotional baggage and a cartload of regrets—and he suspected she had more than enough of her own without taking his on board. Whatever that look had been, she didn't, couldn't want him. He could take that. Just keep commando crawling *and don't look.*

'The creek bed's lined with stones for the next few kilometres. Take these,' she murmured tersely a few minutes later, flipping some leather gloves back at him. 'You'll sweat, but it's better than leaving a blood trail behind for jackals and dogs to find.'

'Thanks,' he muttered back, pulling them on. The skin of his hands had begun to rip, and his clothes were well on their way to becoming shreds, but his hands were the worst. He pulled out a plastic bag from his pack, and shoved it between his T-shirt and the dying jacket to keep his scars from bleeding. If nothing else, it would stop the blood from touching the ground for a few more minutes.

'Come on,' she whispered in clear impatience as she crawled on.

That was the only conversation they had in two hours.

The sun had risen above the eastern rim of the creek wall before she called a halt. 'We're only seven or eight kilometres from the village, but this overhang's the best shelter we'll find for hours. Let's eat and get some sleep.' She leaned against the overhang wall and stretched her back and shoulder muscles with a decadent sigh before rummaging in her backpack.

Refusing to watch—she was killing him with every shimmering movement of her sweetly curved body, her pretty face—Alim sat beside her and stretched too, over and over to work out the kinks— and he was surprised to find the concussion hadn't left him revolted by the thought of food as it always had before when he had concussion, after hitting his head in a race. Despite that his brain was banging against his skull and his eyes ached and burned, his stomach welcomed the thought with rumbling growls.

So he stared when all she handed him was a raisin-nut energy bar.

'Eat it slowly. It's all we can afford to use. I'd only saved enough for me to escape with, so half-rations are all we have.' She surveyed his face, his eyes. 'You're in pain. Take a few sips of the willow bark before you sleep.'

Irritated by her constantly ordering him around, by seeing him as a *patient* after their gruelling trek, he flipped his hand in a dismissive gesture. 'I'll sleep it off.'

'Don't be stubborn. You'll be no use tonight if the pain gets worse. You're less than twenty-four hours from concussion. Take the willow bark, and some ibuprofen with it.'

She was really beginning to annoy him with her imperious, *'don't be stupid'* tone. No woman apart from his mother had ever spoken to him this way. But she was right, so he obeyed the directive, drinking a long swig of the foul medicine with one precious tablet.

'Go ahead and say it.' She sounded amused.

He turned to her, saw the lurking twinkle in her eyes. There were smile-creases in her face through the caked-on dirt. And no poetry came to his mind. No woman had ever laughed at him, either, unless he'd made a joke. 'What?'

She waved a hand as scratched and cut as his. 'You know, the whole "don't boss me around, I'm the man and in control" routine. You're the big, strong man, and dying to put me in my place. Go on, I can handle it.' Her teeth flashed in a cracked-mud smile.

With her words, his ire withered and died. 'Did it show that much?' he asked ruefully.

She nodded, laughing softly, and he was fascinated anew with the rippling sound. If he closed his eyes, he didn't see the maiden from the bowels of the worst pig-pits, torn and bleeding and coated in mud. She stank; they both did—but he'd rather be here smelling vile beside Hana than in a palace with a princess, because Hana was real, her emotions honest, not hidden because of his station in life. She laughed at him and teased him for his commanding personality, and once the initial annoyance wore off he rather liked it.

'I have no right to assert my authority over you.' Stiff words from a man unused to apologising for anything—but it felt surprisingly good when it was out there.

Flakes of dried mud fell from her forehead as her brows lifted. 'Did that hurt?'

He sighed. 'You really are Australian in your outlook, aren't you? You bow to no man. Your father must have had a really hard time if he was the traditional kind—'

He closed his mouth when he saw the look in her eyes. Devastated. Betrayed. A world of pain unhealed. And hidden deep beneath the pain was defiance. She was fighting against odds he couldn't see, and he sensed she'd refuse to show him if he asked.

If she'd pushed his buttons, she hadn't once pried into his life. He'd done both without even thinking about it. 'Hana…'

She slipped down to lie on the uneven ground. 'I'm going to sleep. I suggest you do, too. We have to go faster tonight.' Her body flipped over as she turned her back on him.

It was another unwanted first in his life—yet it didn't rouse his fierce competitive instincts, but filled him with remorse. She didn't want his apology, because he'd hurt her, a woman who'd risked her life and given up her home for him, a man she'd met less than a day ago.

Aching to reach out and touch her, he contented himself by touching her with words…and this time it wasn't hard. 'Hana, it was a silly joke, but I hurt you. I'm sorry. I won't pry again.'

After a moment, she nodded. 'I'm going to sleep now.' Her voice was thick.

'Goodnight,' he said quietly, feeling an emotion once totally foreign to him, but now all too familiar. Shame.

He didn't sleep for a long time, and he suspected she didn't either.

Hana awoke to the heavy warmth of Alim's arm around her.

It was comforting. It was arousing and it was beautiful. For the first time in years, she didn't wake up feeling so utterly alone…

It was a prison trapping her beneath the will of the man, choking her. Giving in to a man's wants and desires had subjugated her until she'd had no life left.

'Get off me.' She fought to make the words calm. This was Alim, not Mukhtar, whose criminal acts, blind obsession and selfish needs had ruined her life; but she could feel the rising panic, the memories of the night he'd tried to make his lies come true.

'Hmm?' He moved in closer, holding her. He was aroused, moving against her bottom as though he had the right.

'I said get *off*.' It wasn't a half-request any more. She was almost yelling in her fury and panic to get away.

She felt him stir, this time in wakefulness. 'Huh, what? Oh.' Too slowly, still half asleep, he lifted his arm and moved away. 'Sorry, I wasn't awake,' he mumbled in Gulf Arabic.

Hana struggled for a semblance of serenity, breathing deep, closing her eyes. *I am in control of my life, my decisions. I am—*

I am alone. No man controls me.

There. She'd done it. She opened her eyes and said gently, 'It's all right. I know you didn't mean anything by it.' Her nose wrinkled, and she forced a smile. 'Especially with the way I smell at the moment.' She spoke in English, with a marked Australian accent.

'It's not just you, Sahar Thurayya,' he replied in a strange mixture of English and Arabic. 'I currently offend myself. Alim from the Pigpen.' He chuckled, wrinkling his nose in turn.

Hana had to wrench her gaze from him. His laughter highlighted his scars, taking the handsome face a level higher, to a dark, dangerous male beauty. Combined with his poetic turn of conversation, it was no wonder women fell at his feet. It was a wonder she hadn't already—

Fallen for him. Two days and she was already in way over her head, lost in stormy seas without a life preserver, and he hadn't even touched her. But, oh, she'd touched him and she knew... Did he have any idea how it had felt for her, having her hands on his body? Had she given away the aching throb low in her belly, singing in her blood?

Sahar Thurayya. How many women had he named so exquisitely in the past?

'I think a more appropriate name for me at present would be Dawn Stink,' she said lightly, turning to her backpack. 'Or Evening Stinker, since it's after sunset. Are you hungry, Pigpen, or do you need ibuprofen? We have to eat quickly and go. Sh'ellah's men will be looking for us. I just hope they haven't worked out that you were the truck driver, since we ran.'

'I'd like both food and painkillers, please,' he said, warm laughter still in his voice. 'So you can call me Pigpen, but never use my name. It's a telling omission,' he added softly—and she knew he'd seen her reaction to his body yesterday, was testing her...

She handed him an energy bar, ibuprofen tablets and a canteen without looking at him. 'I told you before. I'm waiting to see if you live up to it.'

'Well, I certainly live up to Pigpen.' He took the medicine before eating, and she sensed a question coming before he spoke. 'Do you keep all men at a distance, or is it only me?'

The light tone in no way hid the serious intent of the question, but it wasn't aimed at her. The look in his eyes—haunted by bleak self-disgust—told its tale to a trained nurse. She'd seen it many times with burns patients—the horror-filled self-loathing inspired by seeing how they'd look for the rest of their lives. The soul-deep belief that nobody would ever look at them without revulsion, or, worse, they'd always have to endure the awkward, averted eyes and half mumbles of people who didn't know what to say to the poor freak…

What could she say? Nothing, except the truth—that when she'd touched his body, she'd felt he was anything but a freak. That something had awakened in her, beautiful as sunlight on water or the first shooting of a new flower, and now merely looking at him made that budding desire blossom through her veins as fast as grapes on a vine.

She felt herself flushing deeper than the heat of early night allowed. 'Only the ones who put my village at risk and force me to run from my home,' she replied, the quipping note in it a thin sheet covering her pain: both for him and herself. For the first time since leaving Perth, she'd finally felt safe in Shellah-Akbar, as if she belonged somewhere.

Was that why she felt such a kinship to him… because he was a lost soul, just as she was?

A long silence followed; it pulsed with questions

he didn't ask. 'I'm sorry, Hana. I came to help but did more damage than good. How unusual for me.'

She turned her face at the self-mocking bitterness, but he'd stood, looking around. For a second time, she opened her mouth and closed it. Despite seeing his near-naked body, sharing a bed with him, faking sex and massaging his body, saving his life and waking in his arms, she didn't know him well enough to attempt comfort.

And yet every time she looked in his eyes, she saw the mirror held up to her face...

When will you learn to love yourself, my Hana? Her mother had first asked that when she was about eleven, and its echoes still rang unanswered in her heart. *Always trying to prove something—that you're the fastest, the smartest, the strongest, most independent, that you don't need anyone—and you never see how vulnerable it makes you.*

Looking at Alim now, she felt the echo of her mother's sadness in the heart of a man she'd only known a short time, a man born to wealth and privilege, raised to rule a nation as the spare, thrust into the position after—

Hana closed her eyes. They *were* two of a kind, seeing themselves through a warped reflection of what they'd done...or should have done. Or what they'd left undone. Nothing was good enough.

She ached to comfort him, but didn't even know how to comfort herself after five years. The only thing he could do to forgive himself was to go back to the world that needed him as much as he needed to be there, to find restoration in his family and his people.

But how could she tell him that when she couldn't make herself go home, couldn't face her own family?

'How bad will it be for the village?' he asked as he turned to look at the north.

She glanced at him, saw the readiness to blame himself for anything that happened at Shellah-Akbar, and deliberately softened her tone. 'They'll tear it apart to find the supplies—but they've done that before, and found nothing.' She chewed her energy bar, choosing to hide the worst from him, and acknowledging that she felt some need to protect him. He was carrying enough guilt on those broad shoulders. 'I told Malika and Haytham to hold to the story that you're my husband, and we ran because we overheard the men speaking about Sh'ellah's plans for me.'

'Will they believe it?'

If they told Sh'ellah that, he'd go on a rampage to find me and kill you. She kept her tone gentle. 'They might believe it. If they can't find the food, they'll have nothing else to go on.'

'Where do you hide the food?' he asked, his voice thick, and she knew she hadn't fooled him a bit.

She carefully didn't look at him as she said, 'We trade on the old custom of fear of the dead, and bury everything in graves, usually beneath the coffins of the children.'

'Your people will do that?' he asked, sounding startled.

Understanding what he was asking, relieved to take the topic from anything that hurt him so deeply, she nodded. 'At first they resisted, so I did it myself. Then, when Sh'ellah's men wouldn't disturb the dead, and the spirits didn't destroy me for what I'd done, they helped me. I've found many people will put aside the most frightening of their customs and beliefs in their need to survive,' she said quietly, 'to save their children.' Her parents would have done the same. It was always family first...which was why they'd had to choose: marry Hana off quickly to a bad man, or ruin Fatima's chances of ever finding a good man. Fatima had only been seventeen.

It was said that to understand was to forgive...but though she'd always understood the dilemma her parents had faced, choosing to bow to community pressure, and sacrifice one sister for the sake of the other, she'd never found forgiveness in her heart. *I was innocent, too! Did you ever for a moment think I hadn't done what he said?*

Alim turned towards the south, squinting in concentration. 'What will you do now?'

'Go to the refugee camp.' But she couldn't stay there for long; it was too public, too exposed. Her father might have sent someone to look for her there, ask for her by name, or for a woman with her description, including the Australian accent—which was why the burq'a came everywhere with her, and she spoke Maghreb whenever possible. 'Then they'll reassign me to another village that needs a nurse.'

'There's a dust cloud about four kilometres away, heading towards us,' he said, frowning to the south.

'Pick up anything that tells them we were here, use your jacket to cover footprints and body imprints and let's go,' she said tensely. She pulled a ripped cotton sheet from her backpack in four pieces, and tied two to his ankles, and to hers. 'It's far from perfect, but the ground is so dry our footprints will be difficult for their trackers anyway.'

'Do we run, or try to jump from rock to rock as long as we can?'

Caught by the innate wisdom—he'd assumed they'd keep hiding in the creek bed, and he was right—she smiled at him, and found her foolish lungs trapping air inside her when he smiled back. 'Tonight you've earned your name, Alim. The rocks, as fast as safety allows.'

'I have my moments—as do you, happy woman.' He winked at her. She could tell he was pleased— her foolish heart certainly leaped at the smile, at the unexpected emotional intimacy—and the inexplicable sense of oneness she'd felt with him from the first moment she'd seen him torn and bleeding in the truck came back in double force. She couldn't tear her gaze from him—and the worst part was it was as emotional as it was physical. She felt *bound* to him somehow.

'We have to go,' he said softly, his eyes warm, dark as he smiled, and his mouth—*oh*…

'Yes,' she whispered, her eyes locked on his half-smile, lips parted, breathing fast. A thrill so strong it almost hurt ran through her, breasts to fingertips. Her body swayed towards him.

He bent until his breath whispered along her lips like a tender kiss. 'We must go now, Sahar Thurayya. I won't let him take you, not while there's breath in my body. Let me go first this time, my star. I'm actually useful at jumping rocks and finding the most stable ones.'

She couldn't speak, aching for the almost-touch…but she managed a nod.

He bent to pick up the packet from his energy bar and made a mess of the soil where they'd slept, and the moment passed—no, it didn't pass; it slipped into his pocket, into her heart, awaiting its chance. And she knew it would come.

She followed him from rock to rock, leaping like mountain goats, her mind in turmoil, her heart and body fighting for—what? There could be nothing between them. She'd only known him two days, yet she ached and hurt with desire for him as she never had for any man.

Taking the lead yet asking her first was just another way he'd shown her the man he was. Alim was a complex blend of traditional and modern, Arabic and man of the world—but even with his humour and his kindness, and a smile that melted her inside, he was still a man; and she wasn't free to feel attracted to him, or to dream of a future.

She was trapped…if not by this life on the run, then by tradition, her father's pride—and by Mukhtar. She might not have made the vows herself, but her father had done so for her, and he'd signed the marriage certificate in her name. She hated the man her father had given her to in marriage, but she had no choice. Mukhtar had made sure of that.

CHAPTER FOUR

THEY'D been leaping and running alternately for a couple of hours when Alim's brain began crash-banging against his skull and his feet no longer felt certain on the ground.

He came to an abrupt halt. Hana would have bar-relled into him if she hadn't had superb self-control—or if she hadn't been watching him for signs of collapse. She stopped right behind him and said, softly, 'Ibuprofen and water?'

Yes, she'd been watching, waiting for him to fall. She was thoughtful and high-principled, imperious queen and caring Florence Nightingale rolled into one. She might be the daughter of a miner, but a woman with Hana's integrity and inner strength was destined for some high place.

His mouth and throat, even his lungs felt scorched, parched as the earth beneath their feet. 'Yes.' It took all *his* control not to groan aloud. 'Please,' he ground out.

In moments she'd handed them to him, and he drank gratefully.

'Drink it all, Alim. You're dehydrated. We still have four canteens left, and we'll hopefully reach a small well by nightfall tomorrow.'

She knew her way through this arid wasteland. She'd worked out her escape route well in advance. It told him far more than she intended...and she'd called him by name again. Even if it was because she currently felt superior to him, he felt a grin form. From the moment she'd touched him, her guard had been falling. As unbelievable as it was, she did desire him.

He left a few mouthfuls of water for her. 'You need to drink too, or you'll end up with a dehydration headache, and then where will we be?' he teased, even through the pain.

She mock-bowed again, bending right over and peering up at him from about the level of his hip. 'Yes, O my master,' she rasped, and he chuckled as she took the canteen. She'd had the cringing tone of Gollum down pat. 'Please take this and rub it on your forehead—it will help until the tablets take effect.' She held out a small dark bottle to him.

He took the tiny dropper bottle from her, and sniffed its contents. 'Peppermint and lavender oils?'

She grinned. 'Yes, it is, and no, we are *not* going to use it to kill the stink of sweat and mud. We need it for headaches when we run out of ibuprofen. So use it sparingly, here—' she pointed to his forehead '—and here.' She touched his pulse-point in his throat, a brief, sweet flutter of a muddy finger, too soon over.

She waited until he'd rubbed some of the fragrant oils on his forehead before lifting the canteen to her lips, drinking so fast he knew she'd been as thirsty as he.

She must be closer to dehydration than him. She'd been giving him more water all along, citing his concussion as the reason.

'You love caring for people,' he remarked as she packed away the oil bottle and the empty canteen. 'And being in control,' he added, teasing her to lessen her suspicions that he was digging again— which he was.

'Yes, I guess I do.' She flashed him a rueful smile, her white teeth startling in the darkness and her dirty face. 'It's why I became a nurse—that, and my father wouldn't have allowed me any other profession without being married first.' A shadow crossed her face, her smile vanished. She said no more.

'It must be killing you, not seeing your family,' he said, taking a stab in the dark. Until now he'd thought her alone in the world. Now he sensed the truth lay deeper.

Her eyes sparked in the night with dangerous fire. 'Is it killing you?'

He stared at her unblinking for a moment, and

decided to meet the challenge. 'You know who I am, why I'm in Africa.' *Because it's as far from my privileged, fast-lane life as I could find on short notice…where they wouldn't think to look for the missing sheikh.*

And he'd stayed because—well, because he had to. For the first time in his life, he wasn't the second heir, Fadi's replacement, or The Racing Sheikh. The people here, from the aid agencies to the villagers, needed his skills, not for entertainment, but to save their lives.

Hana bowed again, but without the impish fun, the softness in her eyes vanished. 'It wasn't hard, my lord. Your face is famous. Your disappearance became a worldwide interest story.'

'Especially among our people,' he agreed through gritted teeth. She knew too much about him and his secrets, and he had to piece hers together by all she didn't say.

Even in the black of night, he saw her face pale. 'Stop there.'

'So you are from Abbas al-Din? Are you on the run from your father, or the husband you claim you don't have?' he pressed, wanting something, any part of her, the vulnerability and loneliness he felt beneath layers as strong and as fragile as the burq'a she'd worn the first day.

'Stop.'

She wasn't looking at him, but her tension was

so palpable she looked like a string pulled as far as it would go without snapping. 'All right.' After a few moments he asked, 'Did you know who I was from the start? Was that why you saved me?'

She sighed. 'Not in the truck, or when I stitched you—but I knew by the time Sh'ellah's men arrived. Be grateful for that—if I hadn't known I wouldn't have hidden your face, and they'd have taken you. As for coming with you now, I had no choice—but I would have saved anyone who needed my help.'

He could feel the truth in every word. He should be grateful that she'd been honest with him, but it hurt far more than it should have.

Two days was all that had passed since they'd first met, yet she meant more to him than she should. Possibly because she'd saved him so many times; possibly because she was one of his own, and he hadn't been aware how deep his hunger ran to be with his own people again—

And most probably because she was Hana, his dawn star who shone in a dark world: an honest woman who refused to lie even when it could save her.

'So you're saying I'm just anyone? One of hundreds you've probably saved?' His voice was rough with the weird mix of anger and gratitude simmering in him.

She turned her face to him, frowning. Flecks of dirt fell from her cheeks with the movement.

'Would you *rather* I saved you because of who you are?'

'No,' he muttered. She was right; he wouldn't want that. So what *did* he want from her?

That was the trouble; his emotions felt as confused as his concussed brain. But from the start, Hana had humbled him, amazed him, fascinated him—and the combination was deadly for a man who had as many secrets as he did. But she'd known who he was all along, and said nothing until he'd asked, until he'd prodded her pain and she'd responded without thought.

She'd treated him like any other man. She'd laughed at him, ordered him around—desired him with honest heat…

Or had she? Had everything she'd said and done been a lie, centred on fascinating the deformed, lonely sheikh until he was her emotional slave?

'So what's your plan when we return to the world?' he drawled to hide his sudden, blinding fury. 'There's probably quite a reward for my safe return to Abbas al-Din. Or are you hoping for an even better reward than money—my mistress, perhaps? Or even my wife, if you think wealth and position can make up for having to tolerate me in your bed?'

He didn't know what he expected her to do— slap him, toss half the energy bars and water at him and demand they go their separate ways…cry and protest her innocence…furiously remind him she'd saved his life before she'd known his identity—

Shame scorched him as he remembered that. He opened his mouth—

But then she finally responded: wild, almost jackal-like laughter. 'You have got to be kidding me,' she gasped, her face alight with hard mirth. She doubled over, her gusts of laughter growing stronger by the moment. 'I'm seducing you!'

Alim stared at her, shocked into silence. 'What's so funny?' he asked at last, when she seemed to be sliding into full-on hysteria.

She straightened, still chuckling, but the eyes that met his were diamond-hard, glittering with an emotion he couldn't stand to see in her. 'Until you resume your true identity and position in Abbas al-Din, my lord, you have no right to demand answers of me. Until then, I can safely promise I will *not* be calling the media to collect any reward, and I certainly won't be seducing you at any time in the near future. So *ironic*…' She shook her head and slid down to the ground, laughing with that cold cynicism he'd never thought to see in his deep-principled, caring saviour.

The irony was lost on him, but he saw one thing clearly: something had made Hana run from her world, and he'd tapped into it with his anger—and his believing the worst of her after she'd saved him so many times. That was what it came down to.

What had he *done*?

Through a painful stone lodged in his chest, he forced out, 'Hana, I—'

'Don't waste time with an apology you won't mean and I won't believe.'

Her cool words broke into the apology budding in his heart, stopping it dead. She was back on her feet, shouldering her backpack. 'Silence would be best at this point. Let's go.'

Her face was remote, cool as ice water splashed in his face—and again, she'd treated him like she would any man who deserved her withdrawal. Despite recognising him, he wasn't a figurehead to her. He was Alim, and she was showing him the consequences of his unleashing his foolish mouth on her.

Since meeting her he'd butted in on her private world, hurt her and forced her to flee her village, destroying her fragile illusion of safety in Shellah-Akbar. And now he'd added humiliation to the list, treating her as a mercenary predator willing to sleep with him for what she'd get from it.

The worst of it was he had a feeling that, no matter how ashamed he felt, Hana was shouldering a far greater burden from his unthinking accusations.

It was almost sunrise again. They'd been walking ten hours, and Hana had felt Alim's remorse walking between them like a shadow-creature the whole time. She'd felt it hovering there, aching for release, for the past twenty-four hours.

She'd felt his shame through the last of their night-walk last night, his anxiety to make it better through his care that she rest her head on his jacket as she slept today. She'd heard his worry in his insistence she drink first, and the bigger share of the energy bar he'd given her, saying with an uneven laugh that it held no appeal after the fourth or fifth bar. But though he didn't push her or talk about it, she knew what he craved.

Forgiveness. A simple word, but so hard to practise when people she cared for, people she trusted believed the worst of her, over and over; and now, with a weary acceptance, she knew Alim had been added to that list. People she'd trusted who'd betrayed her. *People that she cared for, who believed she was…*

Oh, God help her, she cared for him, and that he'd been able to accuse her of those things at all meant he'd believed it. Whether he'd believed for a moment or an hour or a lifetime didn't matter; whether it was based on his lack of self-belief didn't change it. It was done, he'd said it, and her heart felt like a lump of ice in her chest. The only way she could survive the next few days and save him, and herself, was to close down until she said goodbye to him for ever.

She couldn't go through it again, couldn't care, couldn't *trust* and have it betrayed, leaving her—like *this*. All she could do was slam the shutters down on her heart, show nothing and hope to heaven she could survive this bleak emptiness a second time.

As they prepared for breakfast the silence seemed so loud it screamed over the sounds of the creatures waking for the day in the scrubby hills to the west. The hope and the need for her forgiveness crouching beneath his compliant quiet filled her stomach with sick churning until she couldn't swallow a single mouthful of her food.

She couldn't give him the absolution he wished for—but she had to say something, so she blurted the first thing that came to mind. 'You haven't used the oil on your skin for a while. It must be itching.' She rummaged in the backpack, and thrust the oil for his scars at him.

After a moment, he took the bottle. 'Thank you. It is uncomfortable.' With an unreadable look he stripped off his shirt, and slapped some of the oil onto his skin, rubbing briefly and moving to the next spot, slap and rub, as if he were taking a shower.

Typical male! With an impatient sigh, she snapped, 'Stop that, it won't do a thing to help.' She rubbed her hands together for warm friction, and took over. Spreading her fingers wide, she moved her hands over his skin, slow and deep, and gritted her teeth against the pressure building in her throat, the moan of pleasure at touching him bursting to be free. 'This is how you do it,' she said as coldly as she could manage, to hide her reaction. 'You have to let the oils penetrate the muscle as well as skin, and soften the scar tissue or it won't stretch.'

'Ah…I—I see.' The words were a low growl, a masculine equivalent of purring desire whispering in her head, symphony to harmony. Was it because her hands were on his body again, or the physical release from the pulling pain the oils gave? 'I think this skill took a long time to learn,' he grated out.

'It, um, did take a while.' Striving to master the craving, she gulped again. Fighting hot-honey temptation…but there were no scars on his neck, or up into his hair. She had no excuse to touch there…and the anger and betrayal that had held her captive for over a day was flying faster than a skier on a downhill run. 'I took a course on massage therapy for burns patients after I worked—at a burns unit,' she said, remembering in time not to give away more information than necessary. 'When I graduated, that's what I wanted to do, work in a burns unit.'

'You don't find the sight of the mangled flesh—repulsive?'

That crazy skier had just flown straight off a cliff, and the ice surrounding her heart cracked, letting out steam. 'I hate the endless agony of burns. I wish there were some new way invented to heal the scars, stop the pulling of the flesh, limiting movement. I *hate* that almost everyone who has suffered extensive burns no longer feels human.' She continued the movements of her hands over his skin, slow and steady, deep and soothing…healing his body as she looked in his eyes. She saw the seething mass of self-revulsion inside, and her heart lurched and sloughed that ice right off, leaving only honesty. 'But, no, I don't find anything about you repulsive—except the ugliness that comes from your mouth.'

The shimmer of his eyes, before they closed, told her how much he felt as he said, 'You have no idea how I regret what I said.'

'What hurt most was that you meant it,' she said quietly—and she was amazed how good it felt to say it, to say to him what she hadn't been able to say to her father.

'Only because of this,' he replied, his hands moving to hers, stilling them, and she caught her breath at the intimacy, at the look in his eyes, so stark and unashamedly vulnerable. 'It isn't you, Hana. If I could take the words back—'

She shook her head, shivering in a breath. 'But you can't, and I can't forget.' She moved her hands until he took his away. 'I can't give you the absolution you want.'

'But you give me what I need—and right now,

what I deserve,' he said softly, lifting one oil-soaked hand in his, and kissing her palm—not in sexual intent, but in reverence, and tears rushed into her eyes as her foolish heart leaped of its own accord, whispering the words her mind refused to accept. 'You're honest with me, Hana. You don't defer to me, to what I am.'

She pulled her hand away, and lifted her chin. 'What you were. You're what I am now, a runaway helping others to try to forget what we left behind.'

'No matter what position we hold in life when we're born, we all spend our lives trying to prove we're worth something, or better than others believe we are.'

The dark heart of all she'd tried to achieve since she'd fled to Africa lay before her, exposed and bleeding. She couldn't answer but turned from him, wrapping her arms around herself in a pitiful attempt at comfort. Her wet, oily hands soaked into her shirt, and the restful lavender drifted up. She wondered why it made her feel so sad.

'Sweet Hana.' The soft murmur came close to her, and she shivered in uncontrollable yearning. 'Strong Hana, who's always giving to others, always saving them…but who comes to Hana when she needs a saviour? When was the last time anyone held you, or saw how alone you are in your strength?'

She couldn't breathe. The jagged lump of tears filling her throat stung her eyes.

'Muddy angel,' he whispered, so close his warmth touched inside her shuddering soul. 'You're more beautiful in your honesty than any woman I've seen in diamonds and silk.'

Tears splashed down her cheeks. 'Stop. I want to hate you.'

Closer, inch by inch, until his arms covered hers, crossing over from behind, and at last she felt strong, no longer alone, if only for a moment. 'But you can't, can you?'

Slowly, she shook her head—and that hurt most of all, that she couldn't hate him. 'I—I don't know you well enough to hate you.'

'Was it Omar Khayyam who wrote that when souls entwine, they're never strangers, though they know each other only moments—and when souls repel, they'll never know each other in a lifetime?' he whispered behind her ear.

She dragged in a breath. 'I don't know the poets. I'm only a miner's daughter.'

'You're a queen in a nurse's skin.' He drew her stiff form back, caressing only her hand, until her body relaxed. 'You're my Sahar Thurayya, my brave, beautiful dawn star. I'm so glad you can't hate me—but can you forgive me for my self-absorbed stupidity?'

Millimetre by millimetre, she moved until she leaned into his warm strength, rested her head against his shoulder.

'Give me one final chance, Sahar Thurayya—a chance for you to trust me again. I want that one chance more than I've ever wanted anything.'

She turned to look up at him in wonder. How did he know? How could he guess the words she'd heard in her head a thousand times, with her father's voice? Could he know what *healing* it brought her, hearing them while she rested in his arms?

'I want a second chance with you more than anything but one thing. You know what that is,' he added, low, and the endless anguish made the mirror of their self-hate melt like a final barrier. He was speaking of his grief, of his brother.

'Yes, I know.' Her voice cracked. She couldn't give him stumbling words that wouldn't comfort, or platitudes that wouldn't help. Only he could come to terms with Fadi's death and find peace…but there was one thing she could give him, and she found it wasn't as hard as she'd thought it would be. Her forehead rested on his shoulder. 'Alim…'

The darkness in his voice lifted like the sun rising behind them. 'Thank you.'

Neither moved to leave each other's arms.

After a long time, Hana twisted in his arms to touch the scarred flesh on his shoulder and chest. 'Some time you're going to need more surgery,' she murmured, not massaging but caressing him. Strangers' souls entwining with the touch. *Trust*.

'Yes,' was all he said in reply, his hand lifting to cover hers, and he smiled. *Healing*.

Hana woke with a start in a shallowed-out rut in the creek bed. Once more she felt the heat and weight of Alim's arm around her waist; but the warmth of his body against hers, and the sweat running down her skin from the late afternoon heat and his close-ness, wasn't what disturbed her the most. Some-thing was wrong.

Then she heard the voices, two men speaking in Swahili coming closer—

By the tension in Alim's body, she knew he was awake. Slowly, he parallel-lifted his legs, keeping them tense and straight. He pushed her legs up with the movement of his, until their legs rested at a ninety-degree angle to his hips. It was intimate, shocking in its sensuality, and necessary to keep them alive. Their bodies were out of the revealing sunlight, backpacks pushed against the curve of her belly.

He rolled them both until she sat on his bunched-up knees. 'Get up and flatten your body against the wall,' he whispered in her ear as he rubbed his back against the damp sides of the creek bed. 'Get in as far as possible, take the backpacks with you and don't breathe out loud.'

She nodded, and, looking down at the ground first for any rocks that could move under her feet and give them away, she moved with agonising slowness until she stood beneath the small overhang of the creek wall, holding the backpacks in shaking hands. She pushed into it until she moulded the mud, turning her face so she could breathe.

The top of her head was against the overhang. Alim was too tall to hide.

Anxiety for him overwhelmed her. She rolled her head to the other side, until she could see him— and wanted to laugh. He lay flat against the thick mud, in the worst patch of mud, stinking with rotting plants and animal droppings, his face turned into the wall. His rolling had turned his hair, and the few remaining clean patches of his clothes, the hue between sand and mud.

He was nothing but a few lumps of mud—as was she.

The warlord's men moved like snails along the creek. Her heart pounded so hard she wondered that the men seeking them couldn't hear her uneven breaths. The men talked almost right above them; one flicked a still-smoking cigarette into the creek bed behind them. Hana, who could never stand the smell, had to fight against choking or coughing. But finally the men moved off, searching further down.

Alim nudged her with his foot, pushing her closer in, and she knew what he wanted. *Stay still a bit longer.* Back aching with the unaccustomed inward curvature of her spine, breathing in more mud and nicotine smoke than air, she held to the wall a few more minutes.

They waited until the sound of an engine gunning up and roaring off told them they were alone. 'I thought I'd choke if I had to breathe in any more of that.' Alim rolled over and flicked the cigarette away, then drew in a deep breath. 'Ah, the delight of fresh—well, muddy-fresh air.' He grinned, his teeth a bright dazzle between the ruthless sunshine and the mud coating him.

She wanted to giggle at his comical appearance, but the fear still walked too close; she was close to shivering in forty-degree heat. 'We can't afford to wash until we reach that waterhole, but would you like to smear some lavender and peppermint oil on, to ease the stink?'

He smiled. 'I think I was lying in warthog droppings, so, yes, I'd love that, thanks.'

Hana stared at him. His smile—it was different. Something inside it—the look in his eyes—made her catch her breath, almost forgetting their recent danger.

She'd *never* forgotten the danger she'd been in since arriving in Africa. But though the threat was more real now than at any other time, her pounding heart was not in fear, but in the strangest, pulsing excitement…

She could barely look at him as she handed him the bottle; but when, in handing the bottle back for her turn, his fingers brushed hers, she wanted to see his face, to know if he meant that look, that slow-burning desire. If he—

'We should move on,' she said when she was done. She cursed the breathlessness in her tone—it must give away the aching in her eyes. What was it about this man that turned her into this aching mass of *need*, living for the next time he looked at her, touched her? Was it because he was out of reach? Or that he was right here within her reach?

After a moment, he shook his head. 'No, this isn't the time.' The laughter had vanished from his eyes; they'd turned dark, sombre. 'We should wait here until dark.' As he'd done from the hour they met, he was reading more into her simplest words than she wanted him to.

Seeing inside her soul…

'Whatever you say, boss,' she quipped, handing him a canteen of semi-clean water. 'What I wouldn't give for a camera now.'

He frowned, asking without words.

She pointed at him, grinning with the teasing that was her best cover against self-betrayal. 'This is how the sheikh of Abbas al-Din hides from the world: he seeks oil in new and foreign territories in his own special way.'

He broke out into soft laughter.

Hana stared at him, riveted by the mud-encrusted, strong, beautiful face. Despite it being her joke, she couldn't share his laughter; she could only watch in strange, burning hunger. He laughed as if he meant it. He laughed as if he hadn't truly laughed in a very long time.

She couldn't drag her gaze away even when he looked up and the laughing words he'd been about to utter dried on his tongue. He looked at her and she wasn't fast enough, couldn't hide what she was feeling. His eyes widened for a moment, then turned soft with languorous intent. 'Hana, don't look at me like that unless you mean it.'

She couldn't answer, couldn't turn away, just kept looking at him, aching, wishing, hoping. She forgot all the reasons why she could never give herself to any man, let alone this one. All she saw was that look in his eyes…

Ah, he was on his feet…one step, two—and his hand lifted, reaching out to her. Asking, not demanding—but, oh, the look in his night-pool eyes compelled her. Of its own volition her arm lifted, her hand rested in his.

A smile curved his fine, sensitive mouth, those fathomless eyes. 'Lovely Hana, always giving to others,' he murmured, his fingers moving over hers, and she was lost. 'You brought me from death and darkness, gave me a second chance at life. Isn't it time you learned to live?'

His thumb slipped between their linked palms, and caressed.

Her eyes fluttered closed as her body wandered the maze of the rush, the overwhelming rush of her blood, the soft singing of feminine desire swelling to a chorus in her. 'Alim…' She couldn't breathe. The lightest touch and he'd wrapped her inside the sweetest, most heady chains she'd ever know.

'I love the way you say my name, as if you mean it,' he whispered.

'Ah,' she whispered back, unable to say more. Her hand moved in his, asking, pleading. *Just keep touching me*.

His thumb brushed her palm, a hardly-there touch that sent her hurtling into a magnificent *aliveness* she'd thought she'd never feel, or understand: the exquisite beauty between man and woman. There was nothing but here and now, and Alim…

A butterfly caress over her lower lip, the single touch of his finger, and her knees trembled. She gasped in a shaking breath. She buried her face in his chest. 'Alim, please….'

'What do you want?' he murmured into her hair. 'Ask me, just ask me, and it's yours.' His body brushed hers and she made an incoherent little cry of need.

'I—I don't—more,' she whispered, her body moving in time to his. 'Oh, please, more.'

Ah, those strong arms were around her, those fine-fingered hands on her back, bringing him close to her, so close his body warmth filled her soul, his light chased away the years she'd spent hiding in darkness. 'I was wrong. Your name does suit you,' he murmured.

The scent of mud and his man's heat and the oils he wore intoxicated her. Her breathing turned erratic again as she raised heavy-lidded eyes to his. 'Why?' she whispered, not because he waited for her answer, but because he waited for her. From somewhere deep inside the pounding, the delicious throbbing controlled her.

Could he see it? Did he know how *much* he affected her?

His voice was tender and rough. 'You bring happiness wherever you go. You have pockets filled with sunshine you hand to others even when your life's at risk. You've brought me to life, filled my soul with laughter…and passion.' A current of hunger as hot as the wind blowing above them moved from him to her, and back.

'I have?' Uncertain of all these new feelings in her body, she wet her mouth with her tongue, and saw his eyes turn dark and light at once. A tender, knowing smile curved his lips.

She wanted to touch the smile with her fingers… to touch him, just touch him.

'You do. You're good for me, Sahar Thurayya.' Slow, gentle, his hand reached to her face, curving around her cheek. A tiny moan escaped her lips. His thumb caressed her mouth. Her eyes closed and she drank it in, thirsting and starving for this man, a stranger just days before, a man as far above her reach as the most distant star. But none of that mattered when he could make her feel like a priceless treasure, like a woman wanting a man…

Her head rolled back, taking in the caress as it moved along her jaw to her ear. 'Why am I good for you?' Her voice was breathless, barely above a whisper. *More, please keep touching me.* She moved against him again, delicious, sweet pain and exquisite hunger.

His hands cupped her throat, and she felt another tiny purr leave her lips, felt her body sway with desire. 'You know why, my dawn star.'

'Say it,' she whispered, her fingers trailing over his hand, his arm. Flaking mud fell unnoticed as she found patches of skin, warm, rough, male.

'You make me laugh at myself,' he murmured. 'You give me a new perspective. You've opened my eyes to the world, to problems far greater than my own. I thought I was alone in this desire, but you want me, too. You want me so much you can't even hide it. But you know that.' Butterfly-soft fingers trailed down her throat.

Yes, yes, I know. And he now knew how much she desired him. She'd given herself away, had let him inside her, to see a small piece of her heart and secrets. How long would it be before he knew everything…?

As far as she was concerned, Mukhtar's rights to

her were nil. Her father had severed the engagement to Latif as if it didn't matter—and Latif had walked away so fast she'd wondered if she had a disease. Nobody believed her. *Nobody*.

And with that thought, the moment was gone. Just thinking of Mukhtar, and the flame inside her began burning bright with pain and betrayal.

'Hana?' The look in his eyes hurt her.

Gulping down a huge wave of disappointment, she dropped her chin and moved out of his touch. 'That was rather irresponsible of us.' She tried to inject lightness into her tone.

His hand remained in the air, reaching out to her for a moment, before it fell. 'Yes, it was, given where we are and the danger we're in.' His eyes searched her face...seeking out her secrets as if she'd given him the right.

'We need to go back to sleep.' She heard the choked note in her voice, and cursed it. But desire was too new to her to fight; she didn't have the weapons.

'You sleep, Hana. One of us needs to keep watch in case they come back. Don't argue with me,' he added, his voice hard, when her mouth opened. 'The concussion's barely there now. You don't need to watch over me any more.'

She frowned, her eyes searching his face for fatigue or stress.

He turned away. 'Just do it, Hana.' He added with

a sigh when she shook her head, 'After a man becomes this aroused, it's difficult to roll over and sleep. If you stay awake, I'll take it as a signal that you want me to keep touching you…and you want to keep touching me.'

The blunt words shocked her, fascinated her. She'd aroused him with such a simple touch of her fingers over his hand and arm, a few brushes of her body against his?

I was aroused only by the way he looked at me. I was totally lost in him.

She still was aroused…and an hour later, lying rigidly still, she wondered if it was the same for women as men, because she couldn't stop the heated pounding deep inside, the lilt and throb of her blood, when the cause of her sweet burden sat but three feet away in exactly the same predicament as her own, guarding her rest.

CHAPTER FIVE

FUNNY, but of all the attacks Alim had imagined during their crawling and jumping life on the run, the one he hadn't thought of was the most likely to kill them. He'd thought of lions, rhinos or hippos, even a warthog, but not—

He awoke with a start. He'd finally fallen asleep after hours of watching her. He'd known the whole time that she wasn't asleep; she was restless with the same ache of desire low in her belly that he felt, and knowing that only made it worse.

How could she have seen the mess of congealed flesh and the patches of grafted skin covering his torso, and still want him, be so vividly aroused by his touch? In all his life he'd never known a woman to have such an extreme reaction to anything he did, even his smile. He'd laughed, and she couldn't drag her eyes from him…

And when he'd talked of Fadi, instead of the usual numbness and agony combined, the feeling of being stuck in an unending dark tunnel, he'd felt—relief. Not forgiveness—he doubted that would ever come—but…he'd thought of Fadi that night, and smiled, remembering other parts of that day. The way big brother had done his best to keep up with him around the track; the laughing challenges; the *relaxed* grin on Fadi's face. Alim hadn't seen him let go of his responsibilities since—since he'd had to take over running the small nation at the age of twenty.

He'd forgotten the joy of that day, until Hana reminded him without even asking.

Could the woman who was his saviour also become his miracle? Was it possible?

At last she'd slept as dusk began filling the sky with its violent magenta. Though he'd known it was time to leave, sleep had rushed on him without his knowledge.

How long had he slept? Day had long since given way to the deep velvet of night—

Rustling in Hana's backpack alerted him to why he'd awoken so suddenly. Some small creature had found their stores.

He grabbed the bag and tipped it upside down—and swore when he saw the damage wrought by the two small mouse-like creatures trying to bolt with their booty. The plastic double bags that were supposed to stop any scent escaping were torn to shreds, and the mice had already eaten two bars, by his count, and were into another two. With an inco-

herent sound of frustration, he dived for one of the
bars the creatures were running off with in their
mouths.

The noise alerted Hana. 'What is it?'

'Mice,' he muttered, jumping after the scurrying
mouse, and yelling in triumph as he managed to
snatch the bar back—or what remained of it.

With a cry of distress, Hana dived after the other
creature with one of the bars, but it disappeared
down a hole in the creek bed with its find.

Hana closed her eyes in despair. 'We couldn't
afford to lose a single bite of food. We're only
travelling eight to ten kilometres a night as it is.
Without enough food, we'll never make it to the
refugee camp.'

'We'll make it,' he said, touching her face in re-
assurance.

She jerked away so hard he thought she'd fall.
'Do you think royal commands will magically
protect us from starvation, my lord?' She rubbed her
eyes in tired frustration. 'Have you ever *had* to
worry that you'll starve to death?'

He couldn't answer. Even on the run, he was a
multibillionaire who helped others by choice, but
could and did return after a food and medicine run
to his luxury villa on the beach at Mombasa. If he
was far from home he could stay at a hotel, wash
off the grime, order a five-star meal and sleep on a
cloud-soft mattress.

'Have you?' he asked, low.

'Why do you think I didn't have enough energy bars? I had hundreds of them, boxes full when I came, and vitamins too—I spent all the money I'd earned on them. I fed the villagers to stop them feeding grass to their children. I fed them until the first harvest came through, and then the supply trucks made it past Sh'ellah's lines.' Her gaze didn't waver. 'You think you know about suffering? You have no idea.'

Her words shook him to his core. He'd known the suffering of loss—his parents had died when he was only nine, and Fadi's death three years ago had dev- astated him—but he'd never gone to bed with his belly aching for sustenance; he'd never known des- peration to stay alive another day, or to save his children.

This was the most uncomfortable he'd ever been in a physical way.

He'd thought himself strong for not complaining about living on energy bars and travelling by foot all night—but he'd never been more wrong. Or more shamed with a few graphic words.

To hide the unaccustomed emotion, he broke the remains of the mouse-eaten energy bar in half, handing one piece to her. 'For what we are about to eat, I am truly grateful.'

She lifted hers in silent toasting, and ate.

'Oh, one thing,' he said in a conversational tone

as he helped her pick up the plastic and ruined food. When she looked up, he smiled. 'Don't call me my lord. You know my name.'

The little smile vanished. 'We are what we are. You can run away from your life all you want, and tell people to call you Alim, but you're still the sheikh of Abbas al-Din. And no matter how many times you call me a dawn star, I'm the daughter of a miner.'

Burning fury filled him, but, tempered by long training, he was able to speak with careful restraint. 'Why is my brave saviour making excuses, hiding behind birth and titles?'

She shrugged. 'It's what people do. King or sheikh, policeman or lawyer, rich or poor, imam or priest, father, mother, man and woman; it's who we are. They're roles assigned to us by the titles we bear, what we do with our lives.'

'What we do, yes—and what you do saves lives. So why are you putting yourself in chains, limiting yourself by birth? I don't expect you to be anything but who you are. I hope for the same from you.'

She sighed and kept her face averted, her eyes closed. 'It's not the same.'

'No, you're right, it isn't. You're protecting yourself from getting too close to me,' he said slowly, not knowing what he was going to say until he heard the words. 'We both chose to run from our reality and live this half-life, pretending that by saving others we can justify our past choices. If I am what I am, the same principle applies to you. No matter how far you run, you can't deny whatever it is that made you leave your family behind.' He gathered her hands into his and looked into her eyes. 'And no matter your status in life, to me, you'll always be a queen in my eyes, my Sahar Thurayya who saved my life, and made me a man again.'

For a moment she stared at him, and though he couldn't see it, he felt the blood pounding in her veins and her pupils dilating with the desire too intense and glowing to leave room for doubt. He was only holding her hands, and she wanted him…

So her words shocked him. 'My delusions might be thin, my lord, but they're all I have, and I'm not ready to let go of them. So please leave me to mine, and I'll leave you to yours.'

Simple words, yet they cut to his heart like the sharpest of scimitars, tearing at their desire and leaving it slashed and bloodied on the ground.

She turned back to cleaning the rubbish without a word. The shining, impish dawn star who'd made this hell of a journey the happiest time he'd known in years had withdrawn again, replaced by the quiet, uncommunicative woman of the first day.

Would he never learn to keep his thoughts to himself?

* * *

Coward, coward. The word rang in her head like a shrieking alarm, awakening her from this half-life, as he'd called it. *Pretending what we do justifies our past choices.*

Did he have any idea how much he'd hurt her?

He'd taken her hands so sweetly, arousing her as much as he terrified her; then he'd dissected her life choices like an emotional surgeon. Tearing her soul to shreds without knowing the reason why she'd run in the first place…and realisation hit her with the thought.

She wasn't falling in love with him; she *was* in love with him. God help her for the world's biggest idiot, she'd let her guard down and fallen for a man she could never have. A beautiful stranger whose soul she'd recognised in moments; a smile from her dreams. At the worst time she'd met her soulmate, all her fantasies come to life in one man…

You can never have him. You'll always be alone, she reminded herself in fierce pain, and huddled a little further away from the warm, living temptation just a touch away.

Hana tried her best to keep that distance every night as they travelled, but, oh, he made it so hard by staying only a step from her at all times, kept talking to her as if she were answering…and he kept *smiling*, making her want to step right into his arms…

Three interminable days later, when the thin

crescent moon was high in the night sky, the creek bed that had served as their cover had widened and flattened to half-marshy ground and the worst of the desert had given way to thin, straggling bush, they finally reached the elusive water source.

She moved forward, out of the cover of the trees, but, too close as usual, he pulled her back. 'Wait.'

She frowned, then nodded as she saw the barbed wire stretching around the waterhole. A warlord had control, and someone was bound to be watching.

'We're out of water!' She'd been hoping for one miracle in their quest: an unguarded water source. 'What do we do now?'

Alim's grin was startling in the deep night. 'We rely on the trained ecological engineer to find water.'

She blinked. 'I thought you were a research chemist?'

'I took geology and environmental studies to balance the knowledge.' He moved back into the shadows of the trees. 'Look for the tallest tree here, where the shrubs are bunched closest together.'

With new respect for this ruler of her ancestral home who hadn't once complained on their desperate journey, who'd given help as much as he'd needed it, and who cared about the planet as well as fame and his country, she did as he asked.

'Quick and quiet as you can,' he whispered. 'I

doubt the forest will be left unchecked all night. It's too tempting for enemies to hide in.' He grinned at her with dogged determination.

He was being strong for her; he knew she was falling down into despair. She nodded in shame and turned away, searching the foliage for where it was thickest.

She gasped when she almost tripped over him some minutes later. He was on the ground, digging hard and fast with his fingers beside a thick tree surrounded by bushy scrub. He shook his head when she was about to speak, and tipped his head in a western direction.

There were lights, and movement.

She fell to her knees and dug beside him in silence. The ground was damp, growing wetter by the moment.

'We don't have time for the dirt to settle. It'll be muddy, but drinkable,' he murmured against her ear as he filled a canteen with a cupped hand.

She shivered with the feel of his breath inside her skin. How could the tentative touches they'd shared feel so incredibly intimate? How did she want him so much all the time?

'Any water's good water,' she murmured. All urge to celebrate their find had been smothered by the danger so close. And she kept digging.

'Move,' he whispered into her ear. 'They're coming. The bole of the tree over the other side's been emptied by honey-gatherers, and the bees are long gone.'

'The hole in the ground,' she whispered frantically. 'They'll know—'

'*Go.*'

Obeying the imperative command, she slipped into the tree. She watched as he covered the hole with all the branches and leaves scattered about, used a branch with leaves to clean off what footprints he could. She ached to help, but knew she'd only ruin his handiwork.

The lights and voices came closer. *Go, Alim, run!*

As if he heard her heart's cry he lifted his head, listening for a moment; then he stood on the branch and, with a mighty leap, he landed three feet up the nearest tree.

'What was that?' a voice cried in Swahili from not far away. 'I heard something.'

Alim shinned his way up the trunk of the tree, fast and quiet, his knees gripping the bole as his hands reached for a thick branch, the backpack slung across his shoulders. He moved so fast he was almost a blur in the night. As he jumped for the branch, he hung in the air for a moment; then he swung his legs up like a gymnast, and landed face down. He lay along the branch, making himself as flat as possible. He reached for the backpack and did something with it, what she couldn't see; but now the men wouldn't find him unless they shone a light on that particular branch of that one tree.

But they probably knew about the hole she crouched in. She held her breath, pushed her back hard against the hollowed-out wood, and waited.

The light seemed shockingly bright as half a dozen torches filled the small copse at once. 'It came from somewhere around here.'

Then a laugh came, followed by others, and she almost gasped in relief. She let the air out, taking in fresh and held it again before one of the men spoke. 'A branch fell, that's all.'

The others made fun of the man who'd called the noise, and after a quick sweep of the area they all moved off.

Soon, Hana heard the sound of a Jeep revving up and driving away—but as they'd done the day before, she stayed still, her thighs and calves cramping and shooting pains darting from her hips to shoulders. For long minutes she heard only the sound of a locust as it whirred from place to place in search of food.

'Hana, I've got the water. We need to leave.'

The whisper was startling in the silence. Hana jumped, and groaned with the pain it induced. Everything felt frozen.

'Hana,' he said again, and even in the hushed voice, she could hear his impatience.

'I can't move,' she whispered back in misery she couldn't hide. She was so *tired*.

She heard him mutter something, and then his head and shoulders appeared before her. 'You're cramped?'

She nodded, feeling ridiculous, a burden at the time she had to be strongest. 'I'm sorry.'

'Don't blame yourself. It was inevitable given the restricted diet we've been on, all the walking and running and where we've been sleeping.' His hands reached for her feet. 'Let me help.' He removed her shoes and socks, and, from their awkward positions, he used his fingers to massage her soles, her heels, her ankles.

And up…up, calves and knees and—*oh*…slowly he pulled her legs straight as he released her muscles from their bondage.

It was bliss. It was an angel's touch, soothing, freeing…arousing. It was symmetry and beauty beyond his poetic words, magic beyond anything the *Arabian Nights* could conjure, and not because he was a prince, a leader, but because he was *Alim*…because it was Alim's touch. Because it was Alim, who enjoyed both her teasing and her imperiousness, her laughter and her silence…Alim, who wanted her only to be herself in his presence.

The ache replacing her pain was languorous, and again she felt more feminine, more *alive* than she'd ever been. How ironic that a sheikh was the only man who'd ever made her feel glad to be a woman…

He'd half pulled her out of the hole before her back spasmed and she cried out in pain.

'Hush, Sahar Thurayya, I have you.' And his hands pulled her the rest of the way out of the hole. He turned her around so tenderly the pain was bearable, and his fingers worked their enchantment on her hip joints, her spine…

She leaned back, falling until her head rested against his chest. She wept in joy with the exquisite relief. 'Alim…ah, it's *wonderful*…' She heard herself moaning his name over and over. The uncoiling of her muscles was almost as incredible as the more sensual awakening. She felt as if she could fly, yet she was chained, chained to him, and it wasn't frightening, it was perfect.

It was Alim, and she'd never felt so alive as when she was with him.

'Yes, my dawn star, it is…wonderful,' he murmured huskily in her ear. He was moving to her shoulders, his thumbs rubbing the rock-hard muscles beneath her shoulder blades. 'Lean on me. Trust me. I'll never hurt you.'

Something in the words made her heart stutter—but then those marvellous fingers moved to her neck, soothing, relaxing, arousing her anew. 'I love the way you talk to me,' she whispered as her head rolled around, luxurious freedom once more.

'I've never spoken to any woman this way before,' he murmured roughly, sounding surprised by the words. 'You inspire me.'

She turned her face, smiling at him, half drunk

on the physical release of her singing muscles; intoxicated by his touch, by the way he made her feel. 'What a beautiful thing to say…especially to a woman who smells so bad she offends herself.' Her eyes twinkled.

He chuckled. 'I think I lost my olfactories with the cigarette-mud infusion.' As if it were the most natural thing in the world to do, he kissed her forehead. 'And I must have lost my taste buds to those energy bars. I can't even taste the mud on your skin, just oats and raisins.'

She was asleep; she had to be. She was on the hot sands dreaming of her perfect man in a strange oasis. Alim couldn't be real, this incredible man who seemed to need her.

She'd always been a late bloomer. She'd waited until she was twenty-five to dream of her teen idol, The Racing Sheikh, and make him hers. Any moment now she'd wake up in Shellah-Akbar, with Malika shaking her awake, and the rounds of the day would face her, caring for the babies and children, cooking the foods their little stomachs could handle, treating the men and women whose hunger made their teeth weak…

Not ready to let go of her dream, she moaned and lifted her face to his. 'Alim…'

The lovely ache sitting low in her belly intensified when he whispered her name and lowered his mouth, hovering just above hers—

'Hana, we have to go now,' he murmured, his breath brushing her mouth like a caress.

Lost in desire and joy and hope, she took a few moments for his words to sink in. 'What?'

Then she noticed the light at the edge of the bush.

'There's a light over there. I think someone's left their Jeep unattended. We have one shot to get it.' He put her shoes on fast, shoving the socks in her pocket; then he helped her to her feet, hands beneath her armpits, holding her up. 'You okay?'

Feeling ashamed by her stupidity—how ridiculous was it to want him to kiss her and he was thinking of their welfare?—she nodded, and in silence bent to shoulder her backpack while he used a branch to eradicate all traces of their presence here.

She set off after him as fast and quiet as possible. He indicated for her to follow his steps. She saw the broken branches, the crackling-dry leaves on the path, and put her feet where his had been every time.

Alim was going faster, circling the edge of the copse away from the waterhole and back to where the light had been. Surrounded by enemies, night bordering on daylight, there was only one chance for them to get out of here: the biggest risk of all.

CHAPTER SIX

ALIM didn't have to tell Hana what to do. She followed him without argument when he took over for the sake of their safety, as she'd jokingly said she would.

A woman who could lead when necessary, yet handed over the reins without question when she knew someone had greater knowledge? Hana was a rare and strong woman...she was everything that his wife Elira had never been, despite Elira's high birth.

Hana was everything he didn't deserve—the happiness, the joy in living he'd taken from Fadi with a stupid dare of a bachelor party...

Don't blame yourself, had been Fadi's last whisper. But how could he not?

He stopped when they came to the thin end of the protecting little maze of bush. Hana, watching his every step, stopped behind him. 'What's the plan?' she whispered in his ear. 'Do we check for keys, or hot-wire it?'

'Both if necessary,' he whispered back, his gaze scanning the area. He scented danger like the changing scent of the wind.

'If it's me you're worried about, don't. I know how to run to the target. I was the naughty child in the family, and learned to bolt to the broken paling in the back fence to escape when my mother came at me with the wooden spoon.'

He turned his face, smiling at her. 'Somehow I can imagine that.'

She grinned, the mercurial imp that lifted his spirits smiling from her eyes, and he rejoiced. 'Which part? That I'm fast?'

'No, that you were the family rebel,' he retorted.

'Why would you think that about me? I've been so obedient to your every command.'

'Right,' he snorted softly. 'Stop making me laugh when we're in danger.'

'Let us joke and laugh, for this morning we could die,' she misquoted, her eyes twinkling like the morning star he called her.

It made him ache to kiss her—but that was his constant companion, had been from the moment he'd first seen her eyes. Whether that craving was friend or enemy he no longer cared. His feelings for Hana grew hour by hour, minute by minute, and he knew she desired him...

What? You find one woman who wants you, and it makes you forget everything you aren't?

She desired him after seeing his deformed body. It was a miracle in itself; he could barely get his mind around it. But when she looked at him like that, every other thought, even the self-hate, flew out of his mind, replaced only with the fast-beating heart, the aching body, the *hope*...

Can it, you fool; you need to save Hana. Having scanned the area as much as possible, he put out his hand. 'Give me your backpack.'

She handed it over, and drew deep breaths. 'Ready.'

There was no way to protect her now. He threw up a prayer for her—Allah's will be done with him, he didn't matter—and muttered, 'Keep as low as you can and zigzag.'

She nodded. 'On your count.'

On three he took off at a dead run for the Jeep, jumping from side to side in case of enemy fire. *Let it be open let it be open...*

He felt Hana beside him all the way as if she were his shadow, running and jumping left, right, left, right. She split from him at the Jeep's front, heading for the passenger side, accepting his driving skills could save their lives.

The driver's door was locked, and he cursed helplessly—but Hana yanked her side open and dived in, unlocking his door. 'No keys, can you hot-wire it?'

'I can try,' he muttered, wishing his training

included less princely duties and more modern-day Aladdin techniques. 'Leave the doors open.'

Within two minutes the wires he was crossing had created no spark. He growled in frustration as he returned each wire to its place. 'I can't do any more. The wires I've taken out might not be in correctly. I can't risk the car not starting or they'll come looking for the cause.'

'Wait.' Hana was feeling inside the glove compartment, and beneath the console. 'Look for a spare key. In these dangerous times they'd need to keep one hidden.'

It was precious moments they didn't have, but there was no alternative. 'You look inside, I'll do the outside.' At least she'd be less exposed in there. He dived back out of the car, crawling beneath the engine, searching frantically.

A few minutes later, he wanted to shout in triumph; from the passenger tyre shield he held aloft a key that had been taped to its inside.

He threw himself back into the driver's seat. 'Get your seat belt on.' He gunned the engine, put it in the lowest gear and took off, avoiding the mine-laden waterhole region and the bushy scrub, and heading for the sand hills.

Mere seconds passed before they heard shots. The third one blew out the rear window, sending shards of glass through the cabin. 'Get down, Hana,' he barked, keeping the gear low and upping the accelerator until the engine whined with the need to gear up. He'd done sand rallies before; this was the only way to manoeuvre the Jeep while going as fast as possible.

This was a chase that only his skill with driving, theirs with bullets, and the depth of the fuel tanks would determine.

He revved the Jeep to breaking point. It screamed in protest, but began the steep climb up the hill. 'Find some ballast if you can,' he shouted, 'any weight to put in the back and keep balance.'

Hana pulled off her belt and crawled over to the back as another shot hit the back door. She didn't scream, but said tersely, 'I can stay back there for a few—'

'*No.*' The single word contained all the authority he'd held in his life. 'Find something that won't blow up if it's shot.' *Or die,* he thought but didn't say.

'There are two twenty litre water containers!' Slowly, groaning with the exertion, she hefted one of them over the back. 'We can keep one back for drinking in case we make it.'

'*In case?* Are you impugning my driving skills, or maligning the water I found?' He tried to sound light, but he was too busy trying to get up the hill, searching for signs of harder terrain.

'Just keep driving,' she muttered. 'These taps aren't so easy to open.' She grabbed their back-packs. 'I'll refill the canteens with fresh water.'

She was right. They needed all the advantages they could get in this race of life and death.

'There are guns in the back,' she cried, sounding exultant.

'Can you shoot?' he shouted as he jerked the wheel left, avoiding more shots from the two Jeeps chasing them, two hundred metres behind, not yet on the hill. Somehow he doubted she could shoot. Saving life was Hana's thing.

'No,' she admitted, 'but I can try. If nothing else it might scare them off.'

'It might also blow a hole in our roof,' he yelled, hating to say it. 'Any change in balance forces me to adjust my driving to that, and we don't have time.'

'Okay.' She crawled back into the front seat, falling back to the middle section with a shocked cry as the jeep jerked with the forced low gear.

'Sorry,' he yelled over the whining engine.

'It's—okay.' The words were strained—too strained to be shock from the fall.

'You're injured.' It wasn't a question.

'Dislocated shoulder,' she said in a breathless voice. 'I can't climb back over.'

He cursed his stupidity. Fool, he'd been relying so much on her intelligence and resourcefulness over the past days he'd forgotten she wouldn't know how to compensate for his sudden driving changes. 'Stay on the floor. Lay with your injured shoulder upward.'

'All right.' A few moments later she said, in a voice laced with pain, 'Tell me when you need to jerk the car again.'

Not even a complaint when she must be in agony—that was his brave, beautiful dawn star. 'Now,' he yelled, and counted to three in his head before shifting the wheel left.

He couldn't hear her over the straining engine, but the adjustments she had to make as the Jeep moved must be making her light-headed. 'You okay?'

'Yup.' She didn't say more, which told him how hard it was for her to speak.

'I can't help you yet, Hana. Can you hang in there until we lose these clowns?'

'Y-yup. I'm good.' She could barely talk now, but she tried—and pride filled him. She was incredible, a woman in a thousand, a queen in a miner's daughter's skin.

More bullets hit the Jeep, but because he was driving up and in a zigzag fashion, he'd made it close to impossible to hit the tyres or fuel tank. He called to her before every adjustment he made, and counted to three each time. She was so quiet she might have passed out with the pain. Concern for her lifted his guilt and urgency to stop to higher levels.

Half a tank of fuel left. Even using precious stores to avoid the enemy and outrun them, he'd have enough fuel to reach his truck, if it was where Abdel had said it was, thirty kilometres northwest of their current position. If the truck was untouched still he had the satellite phone, and could call the pilot who came in three times a week from Nairobi. The four pilots on call had to answer the call to any aid worker in trouble. He could meet them while they were still far from the refugee camp—and he could save Hana.

Up one hill, down another, he shifted gears with the terrain, jerking the Jeep from side to side and over again, finding the strongest terrain for faster driving. This was the race of his life—to save his dawn star.

Hana hadn't let him down once, in all they'd been through. He wouldn't let her down now.

Hana came to with a cry of anguish, as pain more intense than any she'd ever known ripped through her entire body. She struggled to sit up, but something held her down.

'Lie still, Sahar Thurayya. I only have one pull to go—' Alim's hand on her left shoulder pinned her to the ground outside the Jeep, while the other had her injured arm, just below the armpit. By the position of the sun, it was early afternoon. 'Take a deep breath and try to relax. One, two—'

And he pulled her arm before he said *three*, before she could tense up in instinctive response to expected pain. She screamed as the *click* inside her body put tendons, bone and muscle back in their respective places; white cells poured into the injured parts to heal, causing swelling. She fell back to the ground, dragging in jerky breaths until the worst of the agony subsided, and the spinning in her head slowed. 'I'm sorry,' she whispered.

'Nothing to be sorry for,' he said in a neutral tone, wrapping the last of their rags around her body, tying above the shoulder in a makeshift sling. 'I'm sorry my driving put you in this pain, and I couldn't reset your arm before you woke up.'

'How long was I out of it?' she panted, feeling the world shifting beneath her again.

He held out two ibuprofen tablets, and put them in her mouth when she opened it. Then he gently lifted her in his arms and gave her water to swallow them. 'Almost two hours. I wish it had been in a bed.' He touched her face. 'You're the bravest woman I've ever known.'

The gentlest touch, made in compassion, and the earth shifted beneath her again. In her body's pain she was too weak to fight the desire, the longing.

'Alim…' The tiny moan was filled with the longing she couldn't hide, longing so intense it outstripped even her pain.

He bent his face to hers, and she caught her breath. His lips brushed hers, soft, too soft. 'Soon,' he whispered, and she ached with the intimacy of his voice, the desire he didn't bother to hide, combined with the tenderness that broke her defences, already stretched as thin as a balloon. 'When you're safe, my dawn star, we'll have time to see where our hearts lead us. For now, it's my turn to take the lead. Trust me, Hana. I swear I'll save you.'

As he lifted her into his arms and laid her tenderly across the lowered passenger seat, she said softly, 'You've already saved me.'

'They're not far behind,' he replied in grim purpose. 'I had to stop, or your arm could have been permanently injured.' He pulled the seat belt on for her. 'I've rigged my jacket against the roof handle in a loop for you. When I say "now", use your good arm to hold yourself steady.' He roped the torn-and-tied sleeve of the jacket over her good wrist. 'Okay?'

She smiled at him, touched that he'd risked his life for the sake of her arm, when she could have waited longer for treatment…touched beyond measure that a man as important as Alim could put her before his needs. 'I'm good to go.'

His eyes shone—and she swallowed a lump in her throat, seeing the pride there: pride in her. 'Of course you are. That's my Hana.' He closed the passenger door and ran around to jump into the driver's seat. 'If we get lucky there'll be an afternoon wind to cover our tyre tracks; but I'll have to go as fast as possible. I'm going to try for second gear, to reduce engine noise…'

Unable to speak, she nodded. *My Hana*, he'd said…and in his arms, she'd felt so cherished.

In a daze of pain and exhaustion, she closed her eyes and allowed the dreams to come. They were insubstantial things that would wither when the real world returned, but if these sweet phantoms were all she could have, she'd cling to them for as long as she could.

He took off in low gear, building the engine up. The hum and whine of the engine was strangely soothing. She felt him trying to keep the jerks of the engine to a minimum, to save her from pain; and her heart, so long starved of such cherishing, over-flowed in tender gratitude.

She didn't know when she slipped into sleep, but when she opened her eyes, it was past nightfall. Alim was driving with no headlights, bumping over ob-stacles he couldn't see. She didn't have to ask why.

'Are you all right?' She pulled her good arm from the torn jacket to touch his hand.

'I'm fine.' He turned a face filled with strain to smile at her. 'You slept for six hours. Feeling better?'

She nodded. 'What's wrong?'

For answer, he passed a compass to her. 'Are you up to a little navigation? My eyes suffer from night strain—another reason I left the circuit—and my glasses are in the truck. Shifting my focus from the terrain to the compass is giving me a headache.'

'Of course I can navigate—but can't we stop for a minute for the ibuprofen?'

'You took the last of it for your shoulder.'

'I'm so sorry,' she cried. 'You're not yet over the concussion, and eye strain can—'

'Can it, Hana,' he interrupted, his voice warm with laughter. 'I'm the big, strong man in this scenario, in control, and feeling pretty good about it. Me Tarzan, you Jane, remember—so, Jane, I need to know what our current direction is.'

She grinned, and checked the compass. 'We're heading northwest, Lord Greystoke.'

He chuckled. 'What degree?'

She squinted at the compass, and told him.

'Put your arm back in the jacket, Hana. I need to adjust the Jeep. We're ten degrees off course.'

He didn't need to tell her why; he'd been letting her sleep. She threaded her arm through, tugged hard and nodded. 'Go.'

He turned the wheel hard towards the north. Hana gritted her teeth, but the pain was far less savage than she'd expected. The combination of muscles and bone being back in place, and the tight sling he'd fashioned for her, had promoted rapid healing.

Now her first concern was for him. 'You've been awake twenty-four hours, Alim. No wonder you have a headache. You need to rest, and we still have the willow bark.'

'What I need is coffee,' he said in grim humour. 'If you can pull that off for me, I'd be *really* grateful. A few days without it and my body's still in withdrawal.'

'You must be exhausted. Can't we—?'

'Not now. The afternoon winds were too minor to make a difference. We need to keep ahead.' He jerked a thumb back. 'There's a dust cloud five or six kilometres back. If I can see theirs, they can see ours—and they can drive in shifts.'

She sighed. 'I could take my share of driving if I hadn't fallen.'

'If you want to help, talk to me. Keep me awake. Tell me something interesting.'

That took her aback. 'Such as?'

'All the down and dirty details of your life,' he said, but in a warm, teasing voice. 'What made you want to nurse in the Sahel, of all places?'

What would he think if she answered honestly? *It was as far removed from my life in Perth as possible, and too far out of Mukhtar's limited range of imagination in his search for me.* 'The Florence Nightingale effect,' she said, shrugging. 'I saw documentaries on Africa, the ads for Médecins Sans Frontières and CARE Australia. I wanted to help.'

'How long have you been in Africa?'

She stared out of the window, seeing nothing but

blackness, and felt a tug of longing for the pretty, twinkling lights of the city against the Swan River in her beloved Perth. 'Five years.'

'How long did you live in Shellah-Akbar?'

'Six months.' Six short months, yet she'd been there longer than anywhere else. She was always ready to disappear. Her superiors expected it, knew she was on the run from someone. Her stores of food and canteens, the burq'a she used but that she didn't attend the mosque, told everyone what she was, but they didn't ask questions. They reassigned her whenever she showed up at one of the refugee camps—always a different camp, and a village in another direction.

She'd hoped to remain at Shellah-Akbar longer. For the first time in a long time, she'd felt among friends. Despite Sh'ellah's interest in her, she'd felt part of the wider family with the villagers' unquestioning acceptance and friendship. She'd felt— almost safe.

'It's a good place to hide,' he commented in a thoughtful tone as he geared up to drive down a hill. She started, so closely did he mirror her thoughts.

She didn't answer him, couldn't without lies.

'Thank you,' he said gravely. 'I'm glad you couldn't lie to me.'

'I owe you better than that.' She blinked hard against the stinging in her eyes.

He put the pedal to the floor to ride up yet another

hill. 'You owe me nothing, Hana…but you're not going to tell me your story, are you?'

It wasn't a question, so she didn't answer that, either.

'We should only be half an hour from the truck.'

She said awkwardly, 'That's good.' The sooner she got away from him, the sooner she could start her life over without these silly dreams.

'Have you been back to Abbas al-Din since you left as a child?' was his next question.

'Only twice.' Once for three months, during her sister Fatima's meeting with her future husband and during the time of their courtship and marriage; once to meet Latif. She'd still be there now, happily living with Latif in a house beside Fatima, if only—

'Did you like it?' he asked, oddly intense.

Out of nowhere she heard Mukhtar's last words to her, the night she knew she had to get out fast and never come back. *I have to get out of Abbas al-Din. You're my passage to a new life in Australia. Hate me all you want, I don't care. I'm still rich enough to give you a wonderful life, and to take care of your family. Latif won't have you now. Your family has accepted the marriage will happen. You will marry me, Hana!*

She shuddered, wondering if Mukhtar had managed to find a way out of the country without her; if Latif had found another wife—

'Was it so bad?'

She willed calm, even managed to smile at him. 'It has wonderful culture, some amazing beauty.' It certainly wasn't the fault of the country that one of its sons had run drugs through the family import-export business, and that he was good at covering it up. If she hadn't caught him making a deal when she'd come to visit Latif—

'How long has it been since you were there?' she asked, to turn the conversation.

He looked at her, his eyes like a blank wall she'd run into. 'You know, don't you? The world knows what happened.'

He'd left three years ago, and he'd never returned. He'd checked out of the hospital the day after Fadi's funeral, long before his graft surgeries were finished. According to news reports, he'd sent a letter asking his younger brother Harun to take his position.

'You must miss home. I know how much I miss Perth.' Awkward words; she cursed her clumsy mouth. So inadequate for all the pain he'd been through.

'So Australia is home to you?'

She shrugged at the deft turning of the subject. 'I grew up there. Perth is beautiful, isolated from the rest of the country. Like Abbas al-Din it has deserts all around, and spectacular beaches. It has similar seasons, too. Hot and hotter.' She grinned. 'I think we're a tad too far west again.'

He nodded. 'We had to avoid some bad territory—*now*,' he warned her of the Jeep's movement.

She hung onto the loop. When he'd turned the Jeep, he asked, 'You feel Australian?'

Slowly, she said, 'Yes and no. It's an unusual experience, growing up between two diverse cultures.'

'I didn't spend much time in the West until I was a man,' he said thoughtfully. 'How was it for you?'

She bit the inside of her lip and thought about it. 'We spoke Arabic at home, and English everywhere else. We dressed modestly, but in Western clothing,' she said, feeling awkward. 'We were brought up to respect our faith and to live in peace with our neighbours, but we were still…different, you know?'

She shrugged again. 'I never quite knew who or what I was, but I was happy enough.' That was why her dad had encouraged her to return to Abbas al-Din, to meet Latif when she finished her nursing degree. Australia had been good to their family socially and financially, but her parents had wanted their children to know their home country and culture, and marry where they'd feel comfortable.

She'd gone into her engagement with eagerness. Latif was a gentle, kind man in his mid-thirties from a good family, successful and ready to become a husband. He'd listened to her, made her smile, and with Latif she had felt happy. And best of all, when he'd promised to respect her opinions and wishes, she had known she could believe him. She'd *liked* Latif, very much.

He didn't listen to me when I said Mukhtar was

lying, she thought sadly, nostalgic for that happy time rather than for Latif himself.

'Do you know where you belong now?' Alim asked, breaking into her dark reverie.

'Does anyone?' She sighed and shrugged.

'Sometimes we can't be where we belong.'

The curt tone didn't hide the intensity of suffering beneath. Hana glanced at him, saw his jaw tensed, his eyes focused too hard on the way ahead. 'You can't go home until you've forgiven yourself for what happened to your brother.'

He turned to her, and what she saw now took her breath away: turbulent, beautiful male, endless *anguish.* 'You can't go back, and I'm guessing you only let your family down. I took a good, potentially great leader from a nation before his time.'

'And what did you lose?' she asked, seeing the half-truth inside his words.

It was the untold halves that left them both here in Africa, half-people suffering inside everything left unsaid.

He geared down. 'Now.'

She held onto the loop again, knowing he wouldn't say more—unless she pushed him. 'Abbas al-Din lost a good man, a strong leader—but they survived, they moved on. You lost your brother, and you've given up on life.'

'Fadi was more than a good man or strong leader,' he snarled without warning. 'He was a father to Harun and me when our parents died, our guide and mentor. He taught me everything, was my dearest friend and closest confidant.' The next words came out twisted with self-hate, and she ached for him. 'You have no idea. Fadi's with me everywhere I go, a permanent reminder that it was my fault he died.'

And that, she suspected, was the first time he'd said anything so emotional since Fadi's accident. 'Alim…'

'Don't tell me he'd hate to see me like this. I know he'd want me to become the ruler he'd have been.' He spoke right over her before she could say the words forming on her tongue. 'But I don't deserve to take his place—it'd be as if I walked on his grave and took his life from him a second time!'

'I see,' she said, after a long silence.

He frowned at her, but said nothing. Perhaps he feared opening a can of worms.

'I think I'd feel exactly the same.' She pointed ahead. 'Watch where you're going.'

He turned, saw the massive rock looming ahead, and corrected his direction. 'But?' he asked, with a grim awareness in his voice. 'There is a "but" hiding in there somewhere.'

She smiled at him. 'Yes, there is a "but". But—this is about more than your private grief and personal feelings. Abbas al-Din lost a good, strong leader—but it could have a leader who's learned from his mistakes, and learned compassion from suffering.'

'My brother Harun is all that,' he said, through gritted teeth. 'He did everything right, even married the princess Fadi was contracted to wed the week after the accident happened.'

Wondering why Fadi had so recklessly risked his life a week before his wedding, she touched his hand, gripping the wheel with whitened knuckles. 'I can't blame you for refusing. That was asking too much of you.'

He lifted a brow. 'Thanks for the absolution, Sahar Thurayya.'

The blatantly sarcastic words didn't hurt her; his grief was as raw as if it had happened yesterday. 'But—I still haven't finished my "but",' she added, smiling gently, 'did you ever *ask* Harun what he wanted, or did you take it for granted he'd do it all and better than you?'

A long silence followed. 'What is it you're not saying?'

She bit her lip. 'I understand why you don't watch news reports of home, but it's left you with a wrong supposition. Your brother Harun isn't doing as well as you suppose.'

At that he put his foot on the brake and ground the Jeep to a halt, leaving the engine running. He turned to her and said in a near-snarl, 'What's wrong with my brother?'

His pain, his guilt was so intense beneath the façade of anger. She blew out air as she tried to think of a gentle way to say it. 'I'm in contact with a few aid workers from the region. Local gossip has it that Harun is ruling Abbas al-Din well—but the people want you back. And while Harun's doing his best for the country, and helped put the nation back on its feet after Fadi's death, he has no personal happiness of his own.'

'Why not?' he asked, his voice dark and grim. 'Amber's beautiful, a genuinely nice person, too—and don't tell me he doesn't like her. I saw it in his eyes when they met. He was crazy about her.'

She replied with a reluctant sigh. 'Perhaps he was—but how did she feel about having to marry the youngest brother within weeks of Fadi's death? Tradition would have stated that you marry her—isn't that right?'

She almost felt the tightness of Alim's jaw. 'Yes.' He didn't repeat himself. Marrying Amber would have been repulsive to him—as repulsive as marrying Mukhtar was to her, but for different reasons.

'Palace gossip says he and the princess Amber are far from happy. In three years they haven't been seen smiling at each other in the way of lovers, let alone touching. Her ladies swear Harun doesn't visit her bedroom at night—' she lifted a hand as he scowled and opened his mouth '—and it's backed up by facts. In three years she hasn't fallen

pregnant.' She paused to let him absorb the knowledge of his brother's marital unhappiness before she
went on. 'If there isn't an heir soon, you know what
will happen next.'

CHAPTER SEVEN

ALIM stared ahead at the empty-seeming darkness: as filled with pitfalls and boulders as Hana's conversation. He did indeed know what would come next: the sharks would begin circling, from other princely families in the region to neighbouring countries, to powerful Western corporations and nations with greedy eyes fixed on their oil and gas reserves.

And he knew everything Hana wasn't saying. Was Harun drowning beneath the load of responsibility he, Alim, had tossed on him by disappearing? Why wasn't he happy with the beautiful princess he'd—he'd been forced to wed?

For the first time Alim realised how selfish he'd been to leave his younger brother alone and grieving. Drowning in his own grief, he'd been blind to Harun's needs. As Hana had said so eloquently, he'd expected Harun to pick up the pieces of a shattered royal family and a nation on his behalf. He'd known serious, stable Harun would do the right thing, do a better job than he, Alim, ever could—right down to marrying the princess when he couldn't face it.

'Thank you for telling me,' he said, and couldn't help the terse anger in his voice. He only hoped she knew it wasn't directed at her, but a reckless, passionate young man who'd led a charmed life until the fateful day he'd talked Fadi into racing him.

'I hope it helps you make the right decision.' Hana looked out of the window into the empty night. She was leaving the decision to him.

They both knew there wasn't a decision to make. He had to go home, ask Harun what he wanted, to stay on as sheikh or not, to remain married to Amber or not. Maybe if he had a bit of time out, he and Amber could work it out—

Then he glanced in the rear-vision mirror, and gunned the engine again. 'And what happens next might come to us, and sooner than we think if we don't move. I should never have stopped the Jeep.'

Hana turned her face to the back window, and paled. 'They're close.'

'Four kilometres, maybe more,' he corrected gently, cursing himself for scaring her. 'The dust looks closer than it is out here, in the darkness.'

She nodded, and didn't speak again for long minutes. Then she said in a strained voice, 'It wasn't my place to tell you about your brother.'

'Maybe it needed to be said. And maybe I needed to talk about it,' he replied, surprising himself with the realisation that what he'd said was true. She'd made him want to live again, to stop running, merely by telling him of the suffering his little brother endured on his behalf.

She was holding onto the broken jacket as if it were her only lifeline. 'Not to me, Alim. Don't ask me, don't confide in me. I can't even help myself out of my own mess.'

'Maybe you don't have to, Hana,' he said quietly. 'Maybe life, fate or God brought us together for a purpose. Maybe we can help each other.'

'What, we met for the express purpose of solving each other's problems?' she asked, with the same hard sarcasm he'd unleashed on her only minutes before.

He shrugged. 'I don't know. I'm no prophet.'

'And I'm no wise woman,' she retorted. 'I'm just a half-Arabic, half-Australian miner's daughter who doesn't even know where she belongs.'

The self-hate in her voice was like a hand shoved in his face. *Don't go there.* But somebody had to open that door and show her the monster in her personal cupboard wasn't as big or bad as she feared—

But this wasn't the time, and he wasn't the man for the job. He couldn't even frighten off his own monsters. Why would God send a man who was such an obvious failure at his life to teach Hana how to live hers?

He said quietly, 'Science and the Quran teach us that we're all one family, Hana, from common ancestry. So if you see a division between us, it's only wealth. The division of high or low birth exists only in your mind.' To lighten the mood—he could sense her inner struggle to not look back—he added, 'We all need to eat, drink, sleep and use the bathroom, no matter how much some of us pretend we don't.'

'I have to believe that after the past few days.' She grinned at him. 'My poor energy bars really affect you, don't they?'

He mock-frowned at her. 'My bodily functions are a state secret to be kept between us alone; but once we reach safety, I swear I'll never eat another energy bar.'

Her musical laughter came rippling from her throat, and he ached again: ached to touch her hand, to draw her close, look in her eyes and see the restless need in her again when he finally tasted her lips. When they weren't talking, the need grew to unbearable proportions.

Which was why he'd poked his nose into her life, and allowed her to step an inch inside his. It had come to this: anything to stop himself for another minute, another hour, because if he touched her again he'd lose control. He was still in exquisite pain from massaging her; touching her made him want far more than an hour's release. His fingers on her bare skin, hearing her murmur his name in feminine awakening… He almost groaned aloud thinking about it. How *beautiful* it was to caress her—it made him feel…whole. As if he'd come home.

Whatever had happened in Hana's past, he was the first man to truly arouse her. He couldn't doubt it after seeing the glimmering dawn of desire in her eyes when he'd cupped her cheek in his palm. Such a simple movement for such an unforgettable reaction. What he wouldn't give to see her face vivid and alive for him for the rest of his life!

He'd give anything…anything but his brother's happiness. He could do nothing, say nothing until he knew the direction of the rest of his life. If he *had* a life after this.

'Be grateful for my poor energy bars—they saved your life,' she mock-admonished him, willing to play the game, too, to stay away from his hot buttons.

'As grateful as you were for my muddy water?' he retorted, mimicking the motions of tossing water out the window, and she laughed again.

Neither of them looked back, but kept laughing and joking. Neither spoke aloud their belief that they'd be dead in less than an hour.

'We're not far from the truck, if I followed Abdel's instructions well enough.'

She nodded. 'This is a fairly deserted region, and the scrub is high to the right.' She pointed to a thick wall of darkness. 'It'd be easy to hide a truck inside it, so long as you don't mind the duco being scratched to Billy-o.'

He grinned at her. 'Scratched to what?'

She turned her face to his, filled with comical guilt. 'It's an Australian term. I've got no idea what its exact meaning is—think it means pretty bad?'

He chuckled. How often he'd laughed in her company; far more than he had in the three years preceding it…and it no longer felt like a betrayal to Fadi that he could laugh. 'Knowing you has been an education,' he said gravely.

'I live to serve,' she replied, bowing her head with the same gravity. 'I strive not to be completely forgettable.'

I'll never forget you, he thought but didn't say. Even if he never saw her again after this adventure, she'd for ever shine in his memory like the star he'd named her. But he *would* see her again, at least once—he'd make certain of it. 'Maybe you're not completely forgettable—just a little bit,' he conceded in a drawl.

'Oh, thank you so much,' she retorted, trying not to laugh—and he smiled inside at the indignation flashing in her eyes. She gave away her feelings for him with everything she said, and everything she left unsaid.

'Hold on tight and keep your eyes open, Hana. We have to find the truck.' He swerved the wheel, and the Jeep turned hard right. 'Look for some kind of opening. If we hide in time, they might pass our tracks in the night.'

'There,' she cried seconds later, pointing. 'Let me out. There's a track to the left there, covered with branches, exactly as Abdel described it. I'll clear it for you.'

'It'll go faster if we both do it.' It would be useless to command her to stay in the Jeep. After hours of enforced rest, she was determined to pull her weight. 'Try to run where the tyres will make indents. It'll make for less cleaning later.' He stopped the Jeep, and they both ran for the track, clearing branches and rocks in their way. Clever Abdel had done all he could to make certain the truck wasn't found. 'Keep the debris close by. We need to replace it for cover.'

After a few minutes, when they'd cleared all they could, he said, 'Get in the Jeep, Hana. You can't cover our tracks without putting your shoulder out again.'

She made a sound of frustration. 'What can I do to help?'

'Can you drive the Jeep?' he asked tersely. 'Just drive straight inside without turning, keeping it in first gear, and stop when the back of the Jeep is about twenty feet in.' He picked up a branch covered in leaves as he spoke, and headed for the furthest point he dared, given the enemy was only a few kilometres behind now.

Hana jumped into the Jeep, driving it into the opened track while Alim brushed traces of the Jeep's tyres for a hundred feet, then trailed the branch behind him as he ran inside the track.

'Alim,' she called urgently, 'I can see dust rising behind us.'

'Wait.' He threw the debris back across the track, covering their trail as best he could. 'That'll slow them down a bit,' he panted as he jerked open the driver's door. He lifted her up and over the gear stick to the passenger seat, strapping her seat belt on. 'You'll need the loop to hang onto if this gets bumpy.'

She pushed her arm through the torn jacket, holding tight. 'Go.'

He took off as slow and quiet as he could to minimise their dust cloud, praising God she'd thought to keep the engine going; with the enemy so close, starting the Jeep would surely have attracted their attention. Hana thought of things ahead of time, and didn't let her worst fear turn to mind-numbing panic. She was a woman he could rely on to be by his side through the worst of times, not wailing or expecting him to save her.

He flicked a glance at her as he drove through the pitch-black trail. In the reflected light of the dashboard panel, she stared ahead with calm resolution. She looked ghostly, like a phantom of wisdom and strength in the night.

Even now, she didn't panic or make demands for him to hurry every few moments, knowing it would make him more on edge. Her tranquillity in this worst of situations, her good sense was something more than any physical beauty a woman could own. She was a woman in a million; he'd never find another woman like her; and when this was over—

'When this is over and we're safe, I'm going to marry you.'

And in her silence, his jaw dropped a little at the outright gall of the proposal. He'd meant to tell her how he felt—but his words had come out so blunt even he was shocked. He flicked another glance at her, and saw her fists were clenched; her cheeks were white and nostrils flared. He called himself all sorts of names for stupid. If he'd shocked himself, he'd stunned Hana.

Yet he'd never meant any words more. *Idiot*, why couldn't he have said something romantic and poetic, to soften her and win her over first?

Well, why not? She loved it when he called her Sahar Thurayya—if he told her he thought of her as a queen above any born to the title—he scrambled to get his thoughts in order—

'No.'

The single word was neither blunt nor stunned; it was final. Just that one word, yet it encompassed a world of rejection. Now, when it was too late and she'd rejected him, his mind turned calm and focused; he had the fight of his life on his hands, but that was okay. His agenda was out there, and at last he had a reason to make her speak. Or so he hoped. 'Why?'

After a few moments, she said, 'Just no.' But there was a telltale quiver in her voice.

'Would you marry me if I wasn't who I am?' he asked, though he knew the answer.

'N-no. You don't mean it.'

No longer a quiver; she was stammering her words. She *was* considering it.

'Yes, I do. I want to marry you.'

'Well, you can't.' Desperation laced her voice. Though she was sitting right beside him, she was bolting away in her mind and heart.

'Don't you think I deserve a reason, my dawn star?' he asked in Gulf Arabic; he'd noticed before that she became more emotional, more vulnerable in her native tongue, and when he called her by the name he loved.

'I can't give you one,' she said, in Arabic. 'Please, just stop.'

'You like me,' he went on, his mind clear, his aim on target. 'You like me as much as I like you.'

'I—yes.'

He kept the smile inside; the situation they were in was too serious to waste moments chalking up points. 'To like each other is a rare thing, far better and stronger than mere desire, and it lasts a lifetime.

Yet you desire me as well, Sahar Thurayya—you ache for me as much as I ache for you.' He didn't make it a question; they both knew the truth.

'Please stop.' The words sounded raw, hurting. 'This is ridiculous. We have people trying to kill us, and you want to talk about this?'

'I know the danger we're in, Hana. And if they take us, kill us, this hour, this minute is the last we'll ever be alone together. So say it, my honest dawn star.' Gentle, remorseless. Dragging her out of emotional hiding.

'Yes, all right,' she snapped. 'There's no point hiding what you've already seen. When you smile at me, my heart soars. When you touch me, I—I ache, something inside me starts burning and I can't think of anything else but you!'

He struggled against the joyous laughter bubbling up inside. Never had he heard an angrier declaration of a woman's yearning for him…and never had it meant so much. 'So is it my birth, my position that you don't like?'

He kept his gaze focused on the trail ahead, but his mind was completely on her. On doing this last thing for her, bringing her out of a hiding far more complex than his disappearance. On saving her, if he could. His plan to rescue her was done—and if the worst happened, she'd at least know how he felt about her.

After a long silence, she grated out, 'It's not a

matter of what I like or don't like. You know I'm not suitable. The country would be in an uproar if you didn't marry someone who could bring diplomatic or financial advantage to them all. That's how it works.'

He did know—but he also knew how to fight it, to use his power and people's devotion to his advantage. But though he could see that wasn't the real issue, not yet. 'Yes, it seems that Harun and Amber know it, too—to their cost. Is that what you want for me?'

'No!' She sounded so frustrated he decided to take a chance.

'What's the real reason, Hana? What hurts you so much you can't even say it out loud?' he asked, with so much tenderness in his heart he saw her gulp and press her lips together.

'Stop it. Just get us to the truck.'

'There it is, right ahead of us.' He didn't press her further; she was almost at breaking point—and it told him what he meant to her. 'Let's go, and pray constantly there's an exit to this track, and they're not waiting at the end of it.'

Hana opened her door and grabbed her backpack with her undamaged hand, and ran for the truck without looking back. The stiffness of her spine was a clear *back off* species of its own.

Does she know how her body language gives away so many of her thoughts and emotions? He ran after her and threw himself in the truck. He found the keys in his backpack zip pocket and, after ensuring all the other entrances were double-locked, he started the truck. 'It won't be easy with the truck's tyres gone, but—'

And he cursed inside as he saw the fuel levels.

'What is it?'

He turned to her, knowing he couldn't protect her now…but he knew what he had to do. 'We need to refill the fuel tank. I have twenty gallons and a hose in the back, but…'

'But it's time we don't have.' She searched his eyes for a moment, her face white. 'We're going to be taken, aren't we?'

'We're not done yet,' he said with grim purpose. 'We're not giving up.' And from beneath the console he pulled out his ace in the pack: a satellite phone. As he drove down the trail, he speed-dialled the first number on memory, and spoke quickly. 'Brian, it's Alim from the northern run. I need help. I'm with one of the aid nurses from Shellah-Akbar. She's injured and needs medical assistance—' He listened as the pilot interjected with a vital question for the help he needed. 'No, she's not a local; she's Australian. We escaped the village a few days ago and are currently sixty kilometres north-northwest of the village with Sh'ellah's men not far behind. We need to get out, and fast. Is anyone in the region?' He nodded at the answer, and said grimly, 'If it helps, my surname is El-Kanar. Yes, I'm *that*

Alim El-Kanar.' He felt Hana's wondering gaze on
him as he listened again. 'Thanks, Brian, we'll meet
him there.' He disconnected and tossed her the
phone. 'We're meeting the pilot in twenty minutes
at a prearranged spot. We'll only have a minute to
get away.'

'You're going back to your life,' was all she said.

'Yes.' He flicked a glance at her; her face was
pale, and she hadn't touched the phone. 'In case this
doesn't work out, would you like to call anyone,
make your peace?'

It was a tradition in Abbas al-Din, to make peace
as a final thing; it prepared the heart to meet their
maker. Hana looked down at the phone, her face
filled with a hunger so pitiful it wrenched at his gut;
then she pushed it away. 'No.'

She sounded as final as she had in rejecting him,
with the same desperate resolution. His poor dawn
star; how she suffered for whatever happened to her
in the past. How small and lonely she looked,
shutting him out from helping her. How brave and
beautiful, with mud and blood from multiple
scratches encrusting her skin and mouth, her hair
splitting and breaking from its plait, stiff with the
dirt plastered through it, and a cap torn so badly
spikes of hair pushed through. Just Hana…his
woman, his queen, even if she rejected him for the
rest of her life.

He didn't flinch from the tasks ahead of him. To

save her he'd do anything, endure whatever he must. And save her he would—from this current situation, and from what held her in such invisible chains. He'd set her free, no matter what it took.

Here we go, he thought as he saw headlights at the end of the trail. Grimly he shoved the gear down and pressed a series of buttons: his own special modifications for attack and defence. 'Hang onto the roll bar,' was all he said to her, and floored the accelerator.

Hana gasped as they headed straight at the Jeep blocking the path. 'Alim, we can't possibly make it past—'

He laughed, hard and defiant. 'Who's The Racing Sheikh here? You have no idea what I can do with this baby. Just hang on and watch—and trust me.'

She lifted a brow and smiled back, her chin high. 'Bring it on, Your Lordship. I'm ready.'

The truck bumped hard as he kept pedal to the metal, slowly increasing speed, the engine revving hard and high. Shots fired, but only made cracking sounds on the double-reinforced bulletproof glass he'd made at his private lab in the basement of his Kenyan house. Hana shrieked the first time and dived down, but soon re-emerged with the same *come-and-get-me* laugh he'd done a minute ago. And the truck gunned straight for the Jeep blocking the path, more than twice its size and with the

massive spiked bars now protruding from the front
and sides—

The warlord's men dived out the doors seconds
before connection, screaming as they bolted to
safety. More shots cracked the glass but it held.
And the truck lifted high, higher, as the specially
modified rims lifted up and over the Jeep, crushing
it beneath its weight and the rollers he'd lowered
between the front rims.

He heard the men shouting as they took off, and
grinned.

'Is there anywhere they can damage us with their
guns?' Hana asked, sounding awed.

He slashed the grin her way. 'Nope. Only a
bazooka or bomb will break this baby. It must be frus-
trating for them with no tyres to shoot out, the fuel
tank triple-lined with hard-coated plastic over rein-
forced steel and boxed in lead casing, and bulletproof glass. They'll have to surround the truck to
stop us.'

'They obviously don't have bazookas or bombs.
And if they do surround us, we can run them over.'
She sounded excited, gripping his arm instead of
the roll bars.

Good, she hadn't thought about the fuel situation.
He didn't want her to remember, just as he didn't
tell her that the rubber rims on the tyres had only
been made to last a hundred ks at most. By the time
they ran out she'd be safe—that was all he wanted.

He drawled, 'Is this enough excitement for you, my dawn star?'

She laughed. 'My parents would say this was my destiny. I was born to be killed in a shoot-out or car chase. They could never stop me watching those kinds of shows or reading suspense novels.'

It was the first time she'd mentioned her family without pain—but he didn't have time to pursue it. 'Here they come. Four Jeeps, about a hundred metres back. They're probably waiting for reinforcements to arrive before taking on the truck.'

'They won't be able to surround the truck before we reach the plane.' She sounded exultant. 'We've done it, Alim. *You've* done it!'

He fought to keep the sense of inevitability from his voice as he replied, 'No, we did it.' He revved the truck to its limits before changing gear. 'This is going to get rough.'

She held to the roll cage as he took the straightest route, right over rocks and on shifting sand and dirt. She bumped and lifted right off the seat so many times, her shoulder had to be in agony, but she didn't make a sound, except when he asked her to check the GPS built into the console, to be sure they were still heading in the right direction. Nor did she look back.

There was a blinking light to the west, only a hundred feet up and falling when they drew near to the assigned meeting place. The enemy was only five hundred metres behind.

He put the headlights on high beam and flashed the old distress call in Morse code, as prearranged: CQD. Then he geared down and stopped. 'Hurry, Hana. We only have seconds.'

She nodded and grabbed at the backpacks. 'Leave them,' he said as he opened her door for her, rough with the exhaustion hitting him, almost thirty-six hours awake. 'Plane weight has to be kept to a minimum.'

She nodded and took the hand he held to her, stumbling at a dead run for the Cessna.

The small plane hit ground and skidded as it twisted to avoid the truck. The second it was still, the door flew open. 'Get in,' the pilot yelled, but Alim had already scooped Hana into his arms, and was putting her in. 'Go.'

Hana's eyes widened as she saw it was only a two-seater plane; the back was loaded to the ceiling, with no time to unload to make room for him. She struggled against the pilot as he strapped her in. 'No, Alim, you can't do this!'

'Go!' He slammed the door shut, hardening himself against the sight of her anguished face, the hands against the windows, as if she could reach him from behind the invisible barrier.

Swirling dust covered him as the plane began to move. Red dust choked him from behind as the warlord's men arrived.

'Alim, don't do this! *Alim!*' she screamed through

the Perspex, hitting it with her fist. Tears rained down her face, his brave Hana who never cried or complained. *'Alim!'*

'I'm coming back for you, you hear me? I'll find you, Hana,' he yelled to her, with such conviction even he almost believed it.

The plane took off on a short run as the Jeeps screeched past Alim, aiming their rifles high, ready to shoot them down—

'My name is Alim El-Kanar,' he announced in Gulf Arabic, calm, imperious in all his mud and torn clothing. Praying one of them knew enough Gulf Arabic to get the gist before somebody killed him. 'I'm the missing sheikh of Abbas al-Din. I am worth at least fifty million US dollars in ransom to your warlord.'

It seemed they all understood well enough. Twenty assault rifles dropped from the skyward aim, and levelled at his chest.

CHAPTER EIGHT

Compassion For Humanity Refugee Camp,
North-western Kenya
Nine days later

'HANA, you're wanted in Sam's office,' one of the nurses called to her as she passed, bearing a box of ampoules for immunising babies. 'Looks like your transfer's come through.'

'Thanks.' She put down the box, and headed for the director's office, sick with relief. Soon she'd be out of here, in a remote village where there was no radio blaring in the main tent, replaying the ongoing story of The Racing Sheikh and his capture by the warlord Sh'ellah, demanding a hundred million US dollars for Alim's safe release. In the village she wouldn't see newspapers with pictures of him as he was released two days before, so tired, with bruises on his face and arms that showed how brutal his stay with the warlord had been.

Everywhere she went, aid workers talked about him. Who'd have known? Sure, they never saw his face—he always hid it behind the full flowing scarves of an Arab man—but the quiet, withdrawn driver was The Racing Sheikh?

Women lamented missing out on a chance with him. Men wished they'd gone out in that *wicked* truck of his to see his skills firsthand. And Hana moved around the camp like a lonely ghost, waiting, waiting for word from him, for his voice…

I'm coming back for you… I'll find you, Hana.

It obviously wasn't going to happen. He was the sheikh again. He had a life that could never include her.

She walked through the flap—

'You have the burq'a on again.'

The air caught in her lungs as her diaphragm seized up. Slowly she turned towards the main desk, hardly daring to believe—but he was there, he was *there*, standing by the side of the desk, and smiling at her as if it had been only hours since he'd seen her. Smiling as if she was something beautiful and special to him.

'You're out of hiding, I'm back in it,' she said, when she could speak. Pulling the veil from her face, her hair, without even thinking about why she did…knowing they were alone without even checking.

He made a rueful face. 'I'm clean at least.'

'You look different without the mud.' One step, another, and they were only inches apart—which of them was moving? She thought it was her, but she was in front of him too fast, shaking and gulping back more foolish tears. 'You're here.'

His smile was tender; his gaze roamed her face. 'I told you I'd come for you.' He added, 'Sam's gone for ten minutes. Any longer and someone could come in and find us.'

Hana barely heard him; she shook her head, mumbling, moving to him, 'They hurt you…' Her hands were on his face, trembling, drinking in his skin, warm, living skin—he was alive, *alive*. And she was crying again. 'Alim, I was so scared—' She put her hand over his heart, felt it beating. 'You're alive, *alive*.'

'I'm alive,' he agreed, still smiling with all that emotion shimmering in those dark-forest eyes. His fingers reached out, touched her cheek. Beauty ripping through her, stealing her soul with a touch.

Then without warning her bunched fist hit him, attacking without power, as weak as the knees buckling beneath her. 'You frightened me half to death,' she sobbed, collapsing against his chest and his arms enfolded her for the first time. 'I couldn't eat, couldn't sleep for worrying. How could you risk your life like that, Alim? How *could* you?'

'For you, it was for you,' he murmured into her

hair. 'For my beautiful, brave dawn star, I'd sacrifice more than my freedom for a week.'

'Don't risk yourself for me, I'm not worth it,' she whispered, tears raining down her face, aching for him. 'You could have died, Alim! Your country needs you!'

'Not as much as I need you.'

Simple words, stealing her breath. She stared at him, her eyes asking the questions her heart dared not risk.

He glanced at the watch on his wrist. Its understated magnificence stood between them like the fire-wielding angels barring the way to paradise; it must have cost more than she made in all the five years she'd been here. 'The plane's waiting. We have to go, Hana.'

A rock fell on her chest, constricting breath. 'I— I understand.' She wheeled away before he saw the devastation in her eyes.

'I don't think so. A delegation from the UN wants to speak to us about our experience, to know about the new borders and Sh'ellah's weaponry and acts against people in the region. They'll be at my house in Mombasa tomorrow.'

Joy streaked through her at the same moment as panic. She'd be with Alim again, if only for a short while. Where the UN went, so did the media. 'I can't!'

He gathered her hands in his. 'I agreed to it on

the condition that your face and identity were kept out of it. You have my word I'll keep your identity out of any interview. But what we say could help the people of Sh'ellah's region escape from his violent domination.'

'Oh.' She felt small-spirited and petty standing before him, thinking of herself when the people she cared about still suffered far more than she ever had. Hating that she still couldn't face her reality…and that, too soon, she had to tell Alim the truth of why she couldn't marry him, or be his lover. 'Of course,' she said, hiding the shivering inside. 'I'll get my things.'

'Your things are already in the plane,' he said, adding when she stiffened, 'Neither of us has a choice, Hana. Sam's going to tell those who ask that you've been reassigned, so there's no connection between us anyone could take to the media. I've spoken of the nurse that saved my life, of course, but you're still safely obscure.'

Strange, but, though he'd spoken without inflection, when he said 'safely obscure' she felt like the most miserable of cowards. 'Thank you.' She lifted her chin, refusing to apologise for or explain her life choices.

'There's a car right behind the tent. I have to ask you to walk to the front of the camp while I ride there, so if I'm recognised entering the car, we aren't seen together.'

She nodded and, realising too late that she still had her hands on his chest, blushed and dropped them. 'That's fine.'

'We'll talk in the plane, Hana.' His eyes glittered with soft meaning.

'All right.' She all but bolted from the room.

The director, Sam, had done his job well. At least six people wished her well at her new assignment as she headed for the gates, and she felt like a miserable liar. What was the difference? Wasn't that what she'd been the past five years?

I can't make myself lie to Alim. And that terrified her, given the ordeal facing her.

The car wasn't fancy or designed to draw attention, she noted in relief as the back door opened, and she hopped in. The windows were tinted, and Alim sat in the furthest corner from the people milling around in front of the gates. The dark glass between the driver and passengers was pulled up, creating a sense of intimacy.

The car took off, purring with the quiet smoothness that screamed *expensive*. 'Not quite as loud as the truck or the Jeep,' she commented, aiming for lightness, her heart pounding hard at the look in his eyes.

He shook his head, moving closer to her. 'It's twenty minutes' drive to the plane. I never said hello before.' He tipped up her face and, before she could react, pulled aside the veil she'd replaced after leaving the office, and brushed his mouth over hers, soft, lingering, too soon over. 'Hello, Sahar Thurayya. I've missed you…as you can probably tell.'

Her pulse beat so fast in her throat; she couldn't make her tongue move or her mouth open. Their first real kiss…so gentle and chaste—he was treating her with the honour of—

She closed her eyes. Despair washed through her like a river's surge, leaving her entire body feeling unclean in the wake of arousal she had no right to feel. One kiss, and she was so alive, so vivid and aching for him—but she could never have him, not as husband or lover. She gulped down the pain in her throat, but still couldn't speak. All she could do was shake her head.

'No?' he asked softly. 'You didn't miss me? It's hard to believe, given the greeting you gave me.' The fingers at her chin caressed her skin. She shivered with the power of his simplest touch, chains far stronger than any Mukhtar could shackle on her. 'Look at me, Hana.'

Long moments passed, but the pain only grew worse as she hesitated. She lifted her lashes.

'I know you said it doesn't revolt you, but that was in a life-and-death situation. This time, I want you to look carefully.' He pulled his light linen shirt over his head, leaving his chest and stomach bare—revealing the pinkish grafts over twisted scars running across one shoulder, half his chest and down over his stomach. 'More surgery will help but there's only so much anyone can do for such extensive second-degree burns. I'm trusting that the nurse in you will be able to refrain from feeling physically ill at the sight of me,' he said, with a wryness that tore at her heart. 'I have scars on my thighs as well, since some of the graft skin came from there when a couple of the other patches didn't take.'

She didn't have to ask where the rest of his skin came from. *Fadi's with me everywhere I go,* he'd said. Yes, his pride and his pain in one, the eternal reminder of his loss; he did have Fadi with him wherever he went. His brother's dead body had been his donor.

More tears rushed up, useless, bittersweet longing and empathy. Her trembling fingers touched his ruined skin, almost feeling the flame that had destroyed his clean flesh. Her fingers drank in the proof of survival against the odds. Oh, the agony he must have suffered!

His hands covered hers. 'Do you find me revolting—not as a nurse, but as a woman?' he said, guttural. 'If so, it ends here. I'm for ever in your debt, Hana. What happens from here is in your hands. My future rests with you.'

She heard nothing after the word 'revolting'. She pulled her hands out from under his, and the quivering grew as she touched him, yearning and pain intertwined. She didn't realise she'd moved forward, falling into him, until her lips touched the mangled scars on his shoulder, her tears mixing salt to the warmth. And once she'd started, she couldn't stop; it was beautiful, so unutterably exquisite that the thought of not touching him, not kissing him, was agony. She must, she *had* to kiss him again…

'Alim,' she whispered, the ache intensifying, a woman's hollow throbbing of need for her man, unfamiliar and beautiful and addictive. She kissed the skin of his throat, chest and shoulder again and again, her mouth roaming over what he was now, what he'd always been, and both filled her with the deep anguish of feminine need, because his suffering had shaped him into the man she loved. 'Alim, Alim.' Breathless voice filled with the restlessness of desire unleashed, her hands growing fevered in intensity of wanting.

His hands lifted her face. 'No, no,' she mumbled in incoherent protest, palms and fingers still caressing him. 'No, more, I need more…'

Then she saw his eyes, lashes spiky with tears unshed. 'My Hana,' he said, husky. 'My sweet, healing star, you've sealed our destiny.'

With a cry she pulled him to her, falling backward, his aroused body landing on hers as their lips met. Her fingers twined through his hair, caressed his neck, moving against him and moaning in need, wanting more of him, so much more. So many years feeling half dead, living only for others, existing inside the shadows of fear; now she was alive at last. More kisses, deep and tender, growing more passionate by the moment, and, oh, at last she knew how it felt to be filled with love given and returned…

The car pulled up. Loud engine noises came from outside. They were at the airstrip. He was hovering just above her, smiling in such tenderness her heart splintered, and she came back to a sense of herself—who she was; *what* she was.

What she'd done to him…and to herself.

The happiness shining in his face shattered in silence. He helped her to sit up, tossed the shirt over his head before the door opened. She shoved the veil back in place, eyes lowered, mouth— foolish, needing mouth—pushed hard together to stop words tumbling out. Not yet, not yet. On the plane. In Mombasa. Anywhere but here and now.

The plane was a small jet, pure luxury in appointments. She'd never seen anything like it. Strapped into her seat beside him, she looked out of the window, waiting for him to speak, to ask the questions. Praying that, from somewhere deep inside, she'd find the strength to tell him.

They were in the sky before he spoke. 'If I know you, you went straight back to work when you arrived at the camp, right?'

He sounded so ordinary. He was teasing her a

little. It was a gift; he was moving past the awkwardness and embarrassment, allowing her time, letting her tell her story when she was ready. And she felt a smile form at the opening; she couldn't stop it. 'Well, I did shower and change. Not the best thing for open wounds or sick people, all that mud.'

'It wouldn't inspire much confidence in your hand-washing methods.'

She chuckled. It felt surprisingly good, the banter. With Alim, she could be herself, be teasing, silly Hana, and he liked it. 'You should have seen people's faces as I walked in. A friend stopped me from coming in, thinking I was a refugee, so dirty and everything crumpled.'

'You definitely smell better now.' He inhaled close to her. 'No lavender though. What is that?' he asked, sounding nostalgic, as if he missed the lavender—and she resolved to wear it again before she could stop the thought. Foolish woman, wanting to please him.

'Spiced vanilla. A local soap made from goat's milk. You know, Fair Trade and all that. The locals bring carts in and sell to whoever they can.'

'They must be doing well to be able to afford the scent.'

'The director got the original makers in touch with the Fair Trade organisation, and first sales were so good they began branching out into scented soaps. The whole village is part of the industry now.'

'I wonder if we can get Shellah-Akbar interested in some similar kind of project.'

'They have a new nurse,' she said, sadness touching her. She missed her friends, the sense of accomplishment at seeing babies grow; the serenity of having, not somewhere to hide, but somewhere to belong.

'I've had preliminary reports from the region. Sh'ellah's not happy, even with the money from my ransom.'

Her stomach thudded. She knew what that meant: he'd been looking forward to having her, and would take it out on whoever he could. 'Is everyone all right?'

He covered her clenched fist with his hand, opening it and threading his fingers through hers. 'Don't worry, Hana. I told my brother they helped save my life, the risks they took to cover our traces.' He added, 'Harun visited the five villages in the region yesterday. He gave them the choice of ongoing protection or a new home in Abbas al-Din, their own village in a safe, arable area under the sheikh's personal protection. Given Sh'ellah's rampages, many of them have chosen to come. Harun's negotiating with the government to look the other way while our special forces evacuate them.'

In a region where 'negotiating' meant millions changing hands, she wondered how much they were paying to save these people who should mean nothing to them. She held tight to his hand, even knowing she shouldn't. 'Thank you,' she choked.

'My brother is a good man, and a strong ruler.' He bent to kiss her knuckles. 'There are advantages to marrying me, Sahar Thurayya,' he murmured, between husky and teasing. 'You'll find more as we go along.'

The shock of his words ran through her, his agenda out in the open when she wasn't ready for it. She dragged in a breath, pulled her hand from his and then said it, hard and blunt. 'I can't marry you, Alim.'

'Why not?' he asked, calmly enough. 'Don't say you don't love me, Hana, not after the way you kissed me in the car. I won't believe it.'

Her stomach knotted; her diaphragm jerked, and she had to hiccup the words. 'I'm already married.'

CHAPTER NINE

A HOLE opened up beneath him, sucking down all his hopes and dreams. Alim stared at the only woman he'd ever loved, thought of all the sacrifices he'd made for her sake, how she'd risked her life for him. 'You led me to believe you were a widow.' The tradition was for the sheikh to wed a highborn virgin like Amber—but given the choice he intended to present the people, he'd believed they'd accept her, accept his marriage. But now…

'I know.' So tiny, her voice, filled with shame.

'You said you had no husband. You said that!'

She made a frustrated sound. 'I don't.'

'What?' He shook his head, trying to clear it; it felt as if the mud he'd washed off two days before had entered his brain. 'You either have a husband or you don't.'

She wouldn't look at him. 'I was married by proxy. I disappeared before they could force me to marry him, and I never returned. So I'm married, but I don't have a husband.' Her mouth twisted, and she mock-bowed. 'Bet you've never met a five-years-married virgin before.'

His mind raced with the information even as his sense of betrayal grew. 'You danced around the truth. You led me to believe you were free!'

'You asked the first day. You were a stranger. What did you expect, my life story?' Flat words hit him like a slap, locking him out.

'When I proposed to you—'

'Stated your intention, you mean,' she retorted with a hard laugh. 'You never asked me, never proposed...my lord Sheikh.'

He felt his nostrils flare at the goading title. 'Okay, so it wasn't the most romantic proposal, but saving your life was taking up my energy at the time. I thought you'd understand.'

'Oh, I understand. Yet another male knows what he wants, and I'm expected to fall into line, just like Mukhtar! He ruined my engagement to his own brother to cover up what he'd done. He thought marrying me by force would buy my silence. So he told my father and Latif that I'd *seduced him*.' She pressed her lips together, and wheeled away. 'So I'm married, thanks to the El-Kanar family's male-oriented laws that allow them to buy and sell their daughters like dogs or cattle—and I'm a whore for touching you.'

Alim didn't need the dots connected to see the

picture. His anger against her, his sense of betrayal withered and died; he saw her manic laughter the other day in its true light. It truly was *ironic*, as she'd said. He'd accused her of seducing him, just as Mukhtar had, yet she was still a virgin.

When he could recover his voice, he said, 'Your fiancé believed his brother?'

She nodded.

'And your family?' he asked, the diffidence unfeigned.

She shrugged. 'Mukhtar told his family. The scandal devastated my parents, stopped me marrying elsewhere, and ruined my younger sister's chances of finding a good husband. To save Fatima, Dad went along with Mukhtar's plan. A woman can't testify against her husband in Abbas al-Din,' she finished in bitter mockery.

Dear God in heaven, what a mess, Alim thought. In Abbas al-Din society, if Hana didn't marry the man she'd supposedly slept with, she'd be shunned—and the news would reach the community in Australia long before she could return there. So rather than marry a man she despised, she'd chosen to live as an outcast—but she'd lost everything.

No wonder she'd reacted so harshly to his slightest dictum, or mocked him for taking the lead. No wonder she'd turned him down flat for announcing their marriage as a fait accompli…

His mind raced to find a solution for her, his saviour, his love. Aching to reach out, to draw her against him and let her know she wasn't alone, he asked, 'Do you know where they are? Your family, and Mukhtar?'

If anything, her back stiffened more. 'I know you want to help me, but if he finds out where I am…even you can't interfere between husband and wife.'

The thought of her as Mukhtar's wife through lies and treachery sent fury flooding through him, a primal urge to find him and take him apart, piece by piece…but that was the last thing Hana needed right now. Only practical action could help her—and she had no idea of what he could do. 'What is it you hold over him?'

She shook her head. 'He's family now. Exposing him destroys my family.'

Moved by her loyalty in the face of so much loss, he reached out to her, let his hand fall. She didn't need his love, she needed—

She needs a miracle, he thought grimly. It was a tangle past unravelling—but he had enough of the puzzle pieces to try to pull at the threads, and see what fell. She hadn't contacted any of her family in five years; she could only be going by what she knew then, a girl on the run.

He said the only thing he could say without causing her further suffering. 'All right, Hana. I understand. I won't pressure you any further.'

After a long stretch of quiet, she said huskily, 'Thank you.'

She was crying in silence, and, bound by his promise, he couldn't reach out to her. They sat inches but miles apart. He ached to comfort her, his silence the only gift he could give.

He'd had such plans for tonight…but now he had other plans to make.

'This isn't a good idea,' she said as she entered Alim's house in Mombasa as the sun began to set. The wide glass doors to the balcony had a gorgeous beach view onto the Indian Ocean, the warm breeze rustling through the palms lining the sand. The crashing of the waves felt like her heart, constantly pushing its tide against the immovable earth of her situation.

The table was set for two, with candles and soft lighting…

'I've arranged for your accommodation in a bed and breakfast down the road.' Though the words were expressionless, her gaze flew to his face. 'Your reputation is precious to me,' he said quietly. 'As for all this—' his jaw tightened '—I ordered it when I believed we'd be engaged tonight. We might as well eat, and there are two chaperones here. My staff will never tell anyone you were here—and they'll take you to your accommodation when the meal's over.'

What could she say? He was putting her needs above his, and wasn't blaming her for the ruin of his hopes. 'All right.' The words felt choked. 'Alim, I—I am sorry.'

His eyes softened as he seated her at the table, removing her veil with such tender hands she wanted to cry. 'You have nothing to be sorry for.'

He'd stopped calling her *my star*. He hadn't called her anything at all since he'd stopped fighting for what never existed in the first place. He barely touched her, and when he thought she wasn't looking his eyes darkened with pain. He'd accepted it was over, before it had even begun—and, irrationally, she felt like screaming. *Aren't you going to fight for me?*

Even if Mukhtar didn't exist, Alim could never marry the daughter of a miner—and she couldn't become his lover. It would destroy her family, and, no matter what they'd done, she loved them. They were good people, even if they'd put worry about what their world would think above her needs, and tried to hush up what they saw as their daughter's shame.

The meal was delicious, rice and curries of the region, lamb and fish with potatoes and traditional spices, and fried plantain. It was a shame neither of them ate much, only using food as an excuse to be quiet.

Soft music played from the CD, ballads that fitted the sunset, so soft and pretty from this south-eastern beach. After a while, Alim pushed his chair back. 'This is ridiculous,' he said, with a violent touch.

'Yes,' she agreed, relieved to be saying something, anything.

'I can't pretend like this.'

'I should go,' she said, soft, sad.

'No.' He'd pulled back her chair and had her in his arms before she could move away. 'Don't go,' he murmured, his cheek rough against hers. 'I hate being with you knowing I can't have you, but being without you is worse.'

She ached to wrap herself around him, to share the kisses of this afternoon; but the time had gone, the words *I'm married* had made everything real. 'This only makes things harder.'

He held her tighter. 'Things have changed in my country. Proxy marriages have been illegal in Abbas al-Din since Fadi's rule. I don't know if your father knew that—'

She closed her eyes when they burned. 'Even if that's true, I can't repudiate the marriage after all these years. It would humiliate Dad.'

'He ruined you.' The words were filled with fury. 'And don't you think your running away from the marriage he'd organised for you shamed him publicly, embarrassed the entire family? Don't you think clearing this matter will be better for them all?'

'He'll never forgive me,' she whispered. 'That's

why I can never go back. And you—you need a suitable wife, a princess who knows how to help you.' She pulled back to look into his face, his beloved face, one last time. 'Please, just let me go.'

'I won't let you go, not knowing you live in hiding, never planning beyond your next escape—' He held her shoulders, his eyes blazing. 'Come to Abbas al-Din. I'll buy you a house, and we can…'

'I can't be your mistress,' she murmured, broken. 'It would destroy my family's good name. I can't hurt them that way after everything else.'

'You're the one who's suffered because of them,' he snarled. 'After what they did to you, you care so much?'

She shivered and moved closer to him, burrowing into him as if the night were cold. 'I thought I didn't. I want to hate them, but I can't. I can't—I have two sisters and a brother who are innocent of anything against me.'

Alim's mind raced like his cars around the circuits. 'Then we'll marry here in Africa. We can stay here.'

'No!' she cried. 'You can't renounce your position for me. I'd always be the woman who stole the sheikh from his people—and my family would be humiliated again.'

'So they're more important to you than what we have?' he grated out. 'Or are you just making excuses to leave me? Was the way you kissed me in the car just a sham, a nice goodbye to the infatuated freak?'

'*Don't.*' She pushed at his chest. 'I'm doing this for you. You know how much I feel for you—but this can't work. I'm the wrong woman for you!'

'You think any woman of high birth is what's best for me?' Finally he released her. 'You know I married a princess once, right? It was a nightmare. They said she died of a rare form of pneumonia—but the truth is Elira killed herself after the doctors said she couldn't bear the sons the nation needed from her. She was the perfect wife in public—but unstable, highly emotional in private, always screaming and crying, wanting what I couldn't give. In three short years she drove me nearly insane, Hana. I won't marry for reasons of state again.'

The words were so cold, bitter, she shuddered again. 'Not all princesses are like that, surely?' She tried to laugh—but he moved away, his eyes blank. 'We had a semi-affair of a week's standing. A few touches, a few kisses, can't become the love of a lifetime,' she went on, trying to smile, to be brave for his sake.

He interrupted her noble sacrifice with words dripping with ice. 'I'm thirty-seven, not a raw boy. I know what I want. I want you. If you won't marry me because I'm a sheikh, I won't be one. Harun's become an outstanding ruler anyway—the people only want me because I was once famous. If you won't marry me, I'll live alone.'

How could a heart soar and crash at the same time? She didn't know whether to laugh or cry. 'Sooner or later, you'll surely find a suitable woman you can…love—'

'Will *you*?'

The savage words threw her into confusion. 'Of course not, I've told you I can't—'

'If he was dead, would you come to me—or would you find someone else? A suitable man— what is that to you?'

She shivered at his freezing tone. 'I'd go home,' she said quietly.

'And find someone else?' he pushed in a snarl. 'Would you?'

She shrugged helplessly. How could she *stand* another man to touch her after what she'd shared with him? Brief moments, enough to live a lifetime remembering…

'Tell me, Hana. Say the words just once.'

A raw command filled with all the betrayed hurt he wasn't ashamed to show her. She gulped and looked at the floor. 'I shouldn't.'

'Hana, it's all I'm asking of you—well, all I'm asking it seems you *can* give me,' he amended, with such painful honesty her heart melted. 'You made no vows to Mukhtar, so you won't betray your father; but only tell me if it's the truth—if your kisses were real, if your desire for me was true. If it wasn't, just walk out now and you'll never see me again.'

Alim was right: the vows made hadn't been *her* vows; she hadn't made them. Alim's pain melted her wavering resolution. Why not tell him how she felt, just one time?

She couldn't look at him as she said words she'd never said to any man. 'I love you,' she said softly, and joy so poignant it hurt her soul spread through her, shining from within. Then she looked up into his eyes, glowing with bliss stronger, more lovely and heartbreaking for its being only for tonight. 'I love you, Alim, I love you.'

His eyes were full of anguished love. How well he knew her; he knew she was saying goodbye. 'I love you, Hana.' He pulled her into his arms, and all that was cold and dead in her came to beautiful life. 'I love you.' And he kissed her.

Shouldn't, wouldn't, couldn't all went out the window as she threw her arms around him and deepened the kiss to beautiful, pure passion that sent dark memories of Mukhtar's one attempt to arouse her spinning to the mental garbage. This didn't make her feel shamed or dirty, because it was Alim…

She felt him removing the rest of the burq'a to reveal her plain cotton skirt, rose-hued shirt and sandals as she wound a hand into his hair, the other holding him tight at his waist. She loosened his shirt and slid her hand beneath, palms and fingers drinking in the man she loved. 'Ah,' she cried as his mouth trailed over her jaw, her ear, shivering with a primal force growing with each time they touched. 'Alim, say it one more time, call me your star.'

'I love you, Sahar Thurayya,' he whispered in her ear. 'My bright, beautiful dawn star, you lit me up when I was hiding in the darkness, you made me a man again.'

Clinging to him, whispering clumsy words to him of her love, she felt the change begin, her joy fail. Their love was like the dawn star he'd compared her to: seen for a brief, shining moment, lighting her life like the morning sky, but it was impossible to hold within her hands. She was a beggar maid to his king, a gutter snipe to his poet. This wasn't real love; it was gratitude for saving him, she knew that…but that he even *thought* he loved her now was her life's private treasure. It had to be enough, because it was all she could have.

'I have to go,' she muttered as his kisses grew so frantic she knew it was now or never—and for his sake it had to be never.

'Stay with me tonight,' he murmured against her throat, hot, rough, demanding.

She shivered again, fighting temptation with all she had. 'I can't,' she whispered, feeling a jolt of pain rush through her as she took her hands from him. 'Please don't,' she cut in when he began to speak. 'It will only make things worse.'

She had to cut the connection while there was a chance he'd get over it. He had to produce heirs for the sake of his nation—and she wasn't kidding herself that he'd love her for ever. She knew she wasn't unforgettable by the way Latif had left her life at a speed faster than Alim could create in his best Formula One car.

The passion died in his eyes, but the love, the care for her, grew stronger. 'If he finds you, Hana…do you want that to be your first time? Or will he do worse to you to protect himself?'

She wheeled away. If he knew what she believed Mukhtar would do to her, no force on earth would stop him from trying to protect her from him. 'I'll be fine. I promise.'

'You can't promise. In the Russian-roulette life you live, there'll always be another Mukhtar, another Sh'ellah.' His voice was harsh, but not aimed at her. 'Come back with me to Abbas al-Din. I swear you'll be happy—and I couldn't be otherwise if you're near me.'

The lure of happiness pulled at her heart and soul, poor, helpless fish—but the hook he dangled with the lure was a killer. 'I'll be fine. I survived twenty-six years before I met you—' she forced the teasing twinkle into her eyes '—I'm fairly sure I can stumble through the days, aft…' The words dried up, and she closed her eyes. She couldn't say it. *After you're gone*.

'For thirty-seven years I tried everything the world could offer, education, travel, excitement—and my heart wasn't in anything, Hana. Then I met you and it was as if I crammed an entire lifetime into a few days. Strangers' souls entwined for ever, my star. What we feel is for life, whether you believe it now or not.' He turned her back to him, caressing her arms as he looked into her eyes. 'This isn't over. I won't let it be over. I won't let you hide from me.'

She blinked hard, but the tears welled up faster than she could control them. 'It has to be over. Please don't ask me again.' She hiccupped on the last word.

His thumbs brushed her cheeks; his mouth followed, kissing her tears away, and more fell. 'I mean it, Hana. This isn't over. I'll find a way for us. You have my heart, my wise, cheeky star, you bring light and love to my life. I refuse to endure life without you.' He smiled down at her, as strong as he was tender, and another hiccup escaped her, a half-controlled sob of loss. His arms enfolded her. She snuggled in, trying to catch her breath, to stop her throat *hurting* so badly.

'You're tired. I'll call Yandi to take you to your accommodation,' he murmured, after a long time had passed, and the music on the CD player had faltered to silence.

She nodded against his shoulder. Alim helped her back into her burq'a, her old friend and shield that had begun to feel like her enemy, symbolising all she was leaving behind. Again.

When Yandi was waiting outside the house for her, Alim held the door open, and she almost ran through it. At the top stair of the wide balcony leading to the night-flooded beach, she turned for a moment. Taking her last look at him.

'It's not over. I'll find a way for us,' he said, low and intense.

She shook her head. 'Go home. Be the man you were always meant to become. And—and be happy, Alim. I need you to be happy.'

She fled down the stairs before she could do something stupid, like tell him she'd changed her mind, she'd do anything to be with him another day. Another moment.

CHAPTER TEN

The next afternoon

THE female UN delegate looked directly at Hana. Alim could see she wanted to squirm every time one of them paid attention to her. She'd sat through the interview for three hours in silence unless someone asked her something directly. 'Hana, you did a brave thing in saving Sheikh El-Kanar. If you ever need help with anything, please call me.' She handed her a card.

'Thank you,' she said yet again, and rose. The need to get away, to hide once again was so strong on her face, he wondered if they could all see it. 'I'll leave you all now.'

With ten long strides he caught up to her in the doorway. 'Hana.'

She gave a silent, mirthless laugh as she turned at the outside door. 'I don't know if I'd have been more disappointed or relieved if you hadn't followed me.'

'I told you we're not over,' he said, gently pushing her outside the door, closing it behind him. The sun shone brightly on them both; the warm breeze caressed them.

'Please stop,' she whispered with an anguished glance around, to see who watched. 'We can't do this, Alim, you know we can't.'

His eyes blazed, but he spoke gently. 'I made a few calls last night. There are things you need to know.' He pulled a thick roll of paper from his jacket without ceremony.

Her gaze lifted, searched his for a moment. Slowly she took the paper from his hand.

'I hereby find the marriage ceremony between Mukhtar Said and Hana al-Sud, signed by Malik al-Sud on behalf of his daughter Hana al-Sud, to be illegal according to Amendment 1904 of the year 2001 by The Supreme Ruler of beloved Memory, Sheikh Fadi El-Kanar, and therefore declare the marriage to be void. Signed, Mahet Raad, Supreme Justice of the nation of Abbas al-Din.'

She read the document aloud in Gulf Arabic in a dazed voice. Eyes glazed with shock stared into his. 'The marriage is void? But how…Alim, I told you—my family…?'

'I found Mukhtar,' he replied grimly. 'He was persuaded to give me a written confession to his lies, and the deception he practised on your father and the imam. He'd forged your signature on a betrothal agreement, so they'd believe the marriage was legal.' He held out a second piece of paper, Mukhtar's confession. He didn't tell her about Latif's heartfelt apologies. He didn't want any ghosts between them.

When she finished reading the second paper, her hand lifted unsteadily to her forehead. 'Alim…I'm *free*?'

Her other hand reached out to him. He took it in his, again feeling the inexplicable sense of home-coming. 'You're free, Sahar Thurayya. Free to do whatever you wish.'

Her eyes darkened; she shook her head. 'But… my family? Do they know?'

'They know,' he said grimly. 'They're waiting to see you. You're coming to Abbas al-Din with me—' he checked his watch '—in five hours.'

Her hand gripped his, her eyes dazed. 'What? I— I didn't hear you…' She swayed.

Alim cursed himself, and scooped her into his arms. 'Too many shocks in a few minutes.' He opened the door and, without looking to see if the assemblage of people inside his house watched them, he carried her into a spare room, laying her down on the bed. He removed the veil that was her shield, her protection against the world, and caressed her cheek. 'I took your strength for granted, my star. Rest here until it's time to go.'

Eyes huge with uncertainty stared up at him. 'What did you say before?'

She really hadn't heard him. He sat on a chair by the bed, taking her hand in his. 'I got all the information within hours—Mukhtar's escape plan failed when you left, and he ended up in prison. He was persuaded to tell the truth in exchange for a transfer to a lower-security facility.' He didn't mention the hours of haggling negotiation with Mukhtar's lawyer as Mukhtar tried to gain freedom in exchange for his confession. Instead he moved to the point he knew really interested her. 'I talked to your father last night, Hana. They're in Abbas al-Din now, visiting your sister. They know you told them the truth. Any more is their story to tell—but they want to see you. We fly out in five hours.'

A shiver raced through her. She looked anything but happy. Slowly she shook her head. 'No.' The word quivered, but sounded final.

'No to what?' he asked, frowning. His mind was sieving through mud right now after a sleepless night arranging for Hana's freedom.

'No to everything.' She turned her face from him. 'I need to go.'

'No, damn it, you don't. You're not running away again, Hana. I won't let you play the coward,' Alim snarled, losing it without warning—and she stared up at him, her eyes huge, and filled with the strangest mixture of uncertainty, stubbornness…and intrigue.

Exultation shot through him. She *wanted* to say yes, he could feel it—and she was responding to his fury with interest instead of in mockery. Hana would never accept orders—unless she *trusted* him, wanted and loved him enough to hope there could be a future for them…

But one thing was painfully obvious to him: if she was thinking of a life together, she wasn't ready to admit it. He'd known that last night even as she'd said *I love you*. She might want a future with him, but she didn't believe in it. But if she came to Abbas al-Din with him, he was hoping to show her that, again, her deepest fear was over. It existed only now in her mind, like the monster in her childhood cupboard.

'You've faced and passed the hardest tests on earth the past five years—so why are you being such a coward now?' He purposely kept his voice hard. 'You're free of Mukhtar, free of the chains holding you. Your family made the wrong decision, and yes, they hurt you—but you love them. It's time to stop running from them. It's time you forgave them.'

'You don't understand,' she muttered, a frown between her brows.

'You say that to *me*?' He laughed in her face, pushing her away to bring her closer. 'Do you have any idea how hard it was to face Harun, knowing what I've put him through in the past three years? Yet he paid my ransom without thinking twice, and came to meet me the hour I was released.' He lifted her chin. 'At least your family deserved your distrust. I deserved for him to let me die at Sh'ellah's hand.'

Her lashes fluttered down, reminding him of the hour they'd met—it was the only time she'd hidden her real self from him. Secrets, yes, but never had she hidden the person she was. 'I'm not ready for this.'

'You think I was ready to face Harun? Yet I was the one at fault, needing his forgiveness,' he demanded, his caressing finger beneath her chin at odds with his uncompromising tone. 'So tell me, Hana—when will you be ready to forgive them? Would you like to pick a day when you'll finally feel brave enough to do the right thing?'

'When would you have been ready, if the circumstances hadn't forced you into it?' Her cheeks blazed with colour; her lashes lifted to reveal eyes as aroused as they were furious.

She was consumed with desire, because of a simple movement of his finger, and a plan flashed into his mind.

Acting on it, he laughed in her face. 'What circumstances? You mean that I *chose* to save your life and risk my own for you? Or do you mean that I announced my name and offered a ransom so you could get away safely? Are they the *circumstances* that forced me?'

Her mouth set in a stubborn line.

He shrugged. 'I'm calling your bluff, Hana. Come back with me, or I tell your family how you've been risking your life for five years rather than face them—and then I'll send them to you. You know I can,' he growled as she stared up at him in mingled desire, fury and resentment. 'This is going to happen, so accept it and move on.' Before she could argue he bent and kissed her, deep and hard, gathering her close. He wasn't above using any means possible to convince her to come with him. She needed reconciliation with her family as much as he'd needed to face Harun and apologise for the nightmare he'd created of his brother's life by disappearing.

Half expecting a rebuff, or for her to lie stiff and cold beneath him, he felt jubilation soar when she moaned and wound her arms around his neck, meeting his passion with blazing flame. She arched against his body, moving in delicious friction, her hands in his hair, caressing him with ardent eagerness. Oh, how she wanted him! All her slumbering fire belonged to him—and he'd do almost anything to keep it that way for the rest of their lives.

For now, though, he had no promises he could make her; he didn't know yet what his future held, or what place she'd take in it. But there'd be nothing, no future for them if he couldn't even make her come to Abbas al-Din with him.

It felt as if he ripped his heart from his chest as he pulled away. 'We leave in five hours,' he snarled, but his fingers trailed slowly down her throat, across her shoulder, and he saw her quiver again. He wanted to shout in joy for the heady knowledge of how badly she desired him. 'Sleep for an hour or two; you'll need it. When you wake, we'll walk on the beach and talk.'

Heavy-lidded eyes lifted to his, aching with as much painful wanting as anger, and he knew he'd won the battle—she'd come to Abbas al-Din, and face her family—but on the issue of marrying him, the war was far from over.

It was another incredible sunset, softer than the rich, rioting colours in western-facing Perth, but the soft rose tipped the foaming waves, and the palm trees lining the beach caught the rustling-soft breeze. A star winked at them from low in the sky, the first of the night.

'It's so beautiful, isn't it?' Hana murmured, awed, forgetting her fury with him for a moment. 'Africa's a place of such amazing contrasts. There's so much beauty and faith, as well as the war and suffering.'

'It's the same as anywhere else, with the same people, good and bad,' Alim replied. 'Oil in Nigeria, gold and diamonds in South Africa, Mali and Mozambique bring the greed. But the beauty—' He took her hand in his—she revelled in the simple connection to him, had been wondering why he hadn't touched her during the half-hour they'd been walking—and said, softly, 'The unique beauty of Africa is why I keep coming back. It—gives me rest.'

You give me rest.

The thought flew out of nowhere—or maybe it came from everywhere, everything he'd been to her. She'd never had a friend who could laugh with her and let her be herself; a man who listened to her and wasn't too arrogant to learn from a woman; a man whose smallest smile made her day, whose touch, who cared enough to give her a compelling honesty that brought her out of emotional hiding, and face her cowardice. He'd looked inside her turbulent soul and calmed the storms; he brought her from a state of darkest cynicism to trust, tenderness and, unbelievably, forgiveness.

If she'd brought him *back* to life, he'd *given* her life. She could be what she'd always wanted to be: a normal woman, wearing rolled-up trousers and shirt, barefoot and holding hands with the man she—she—

Couldn't resist, couldn't turn from, could barely say no to.

And that was why she was going to Abbas al-Din. He'd literally kissed her into capitulation. Far more than merely desiring him, or liking him, she *needed* him. She loved him, had to be where he was. It was as simple as that—and as impossible.

Impossible was never more obvious than today, with so many reminders all around him, the armed guards keeping a discreet distance. His current location might be secret, but it wouldn't take the media long to find out—and they'd want to know who she was. How long would it take them to find out? A day, a week? *Drug runner's ex-wife is our sheikh's saviour…*

Tonight, here on the beach, in the jet, would be their last hours alone together—and she intended to cherish them, even if they were surrounded by armed minders all the way.

They might as well flash a neon sign; *Go home, low life, you can never have him.*

'I can see why you love Mombasa,' she finally replied, her fatalism and her love tearing her heart in two. *Run. Run as far and fast as you can…don't leave him, now or ever…*

'I'm keeping the house,' he said quietly. 'The family of my housekeeper will look after the house while I'm gone, and I've given them the cottage out back to live in permanently.' He led her around a late surfer who'd just flopped on his towel. 'You've taught me to look outside myself, Hana. I thought being here, helping, was enough to justify my existence, and I could keep my life, my*self*, separate. I know now I can't, and I don't want to.'

Wonderful words, yet they sounded like a farewell, even before they boarded the jet. Yet he was smiling… Her gaze riveted to his mouth, her lips tingling and her body aching, she managed to say, 'I didn't do anything.'

Still with that tender smile curving his mouth he stopped, turned her around. Her heart pounded like the waves against the sand as he bent to her. The kiss was soft, sweet, perfect…and too soon over. 'You're like that,' he murmured, pointing at that low-slung star, 'like the story of those men who were led to the Christian Messiah. I was lost in the darkness of self-hate, and you showed me the way to redemption, to joy in living, without even knowing you did it.'

She couldn't help it, couldn't stop herself from lifting up on her toes, kissing him again—and then again. 'You did the same for me,' she whispered. 'You saved me.'

'We saved each other.' He rested his forehead against hers, and she adored the intimacy of it while still aching for more. 'Face the truth: we're souls entwined, Sahar Thurayya. We need each other.'

Yes, their souls were entwined, and as far as she was concerned they always would be; but how could she believe this was anything but a lovely fantasy, a romantic idyll she'd treasure when she left him? When they reached Abbas al-Din, everything would change. She'd have family responsibilities again, and Alim would discover he *was* a sheikh, his country needed him—and he'd need a woman who could be a helpmate, a queen in every sense. And when that happened she'd let him go with a smile, doing her best not to show her life was over.

But for now he was Alim, the man whose soul was inextricably part of hers, who'd quietly reached inside her and taken her heart before she'd known it was gone. So she smiled back and murmured, 'Yes,' not wanting the dream to end. Not yet.

He moved his cheek against hers. 'One day you'll believe in us, my star,' he murmured in her ear, making her shiver. 'Maybe when we're married ten years and have seven children.'

Uncomfortable with his perception, how finely tuned he was to her emotions, she laughed. 'Hey, you want seven kids, you can give birth to them. I sure won't be going past four.'

He chuckled, and kissed her cheek. 'Four it is, then…so long as at least one of them is a cheeky girl who shows the boys how to not take themselves so seriously.' When she didn't answer—her throat had seized up with longing and useless dreams—he checked his watch, and made a smothered exclamation. 'We need to head to the airstrip.' Turning quickly, still holding her hand, he led her back towards the house.

When they arrived everything was already packed and in the sleek limousine—and the beautifully attired driver winced when Alim opened the door for her. 'I'm too messy,' she protested, reluctant to enter this gorgeous vehicle in rolled-up trousers and vest top, with bare, sandy feet and mussed hair. 'Is there a garden hose here? I can wash it off, and not dirty the car.'

'No need for that.' Alim frowned at the driver, who immediately apologised gravely for any embarrassment he'd caused her, and offered to fetch her a towel, which made her feel worse. She whispered, almost squirming, 'He shouldn't have to clean up after me. It's not right. It isn't as if I'm anyone important.' With a lowered gaze she walked to Alim's front garden and turned on the tap, washing off the sand.

'See what I mean?' Alim's laughing, rueful voice sounded right behind her, and she started, turning to him. 'You teach me by example to not be so arrogant.' He shoved his feet beneath the water, rinsing off and turning the tap off.

'It's your car, you can do as you want,' she mumbled, feeling her blush grow.

'Yes, I can, and I would have, but for you.' He lifted her hand to his cheek, cradling it, and she forgot all about the watching chauffeur, his minders, the state of her hair or anything else. 'You consider everyone. It's something I've never had to do. Our parents trained us to treat all people as equals, and our position means we serve the people, but some lessons need a brush-up.' He kissed her palm.

Even as her eyes grew heavy and her body

swayed towards him everything they'd been through suddenly overwhelmed her, and she needed—needed him. 'Alim,' she whispered.

He saw it, his eyes darkened. 'I'm all yours once we're in the car, Sahar Thurayya.'

Without thinking she turned and bolted for the limousine, and hopped in without waiting for the driver to hand her in. When Alim joined her, she barely waited for the door to close before she threw herself into his arms. 'Hold me,' she whispered.

The limousine took off smoothly, and the passion in his eyes gentled as he drew her closer, up into his lap. He held her close for a long time. 'It's been a hard time for you.'

She nodded into his shoulder. 'I thought you were going to die when they took you—and then you come to me, but covered in bruises. They hurt you for my sake, Abbas al-Din loses millions to save me because you sacrificed yourself for me…and then, then you give me back my family, my freedom…' She hiccupped.

'Give me a chance; I'll be everything you ever want or need, my star,' he murmured into her hair. 'I can even give you a happily ever after—but not with a prince. A simple sheikh will have to do for you.'

Simple? In a top-of-the-line limousine, about to board a first-class jet? She choked back a giggle. 'Just call me Cinderella? I'm more like the little matchstick girl.'

Alim tipped up her face, his eyes full of tenderness at her deliberate roughening of her voice. 'Do you see your ending as tragic as hers was? Need it be?'

All her smart cracks withered under the tender fire of his questions. He saw too much. 'Maybe not tragic,' she conceded, 'I just don't see the whole palace-and-prince/sheikh thing. It was never part of my dreams.'

He stilled, and she felt the question without his asking. 'I dreamed of a man who came home to me at night, played chess or Scrabble or backgammon, and held me as we watched the news, and played with the kids and occasionally brought home dinner when I was tired,' she said quietly. 'All I ever wanted was an average guy who could accept me as I am.'

'You can have all that,' he replied, just as quiet, caressing her shoulder. 'I've never tried to change you, Hana, only circumstances around you, for your sake.' He lifted her chin, and kissed her lips. 'I'd move mountains if it would make you happy.'

'You already have,' she whispered. That was what made it so hard. How could she have all her dreams come true in a man whose life gave her nightmares? 'But average? It's something you can never be.' *In any way,* she thought, sadness piercing her.

'I can. I have been for the past three years, Hana.' He caressed her hair, and love swamped her. 'If

Harun is happy to continue as the sheikh, we can return here and—' He frowned as she shook her head. 'I realise that now the world knows where I've been it'll be harder, but we could find another area that needs our combined skills.'

'It's useless,' she said sadly. 'You know it, Alim. People will know you…and they'll sell your whereabouts for money. I can't blame them for that—but your life would become a circus. Face it, you had one shot at disappearing, and you did it well—but it'll never work again.'

'Then we start our own aid programme, and run it as ourselves. I'm a multimillionaire in my own right, from my racing days. We can live comfortably enough even if I gave ninety per cent of it away.' Then, as she sighed and shook her head again, he said, 'Don't tell me you don't love me, Hana. I know you do.'

Unutterably weary, she climbed off his lap. 'I haven't had one good night's sleep in two weeks, Alim. I'm tired, I feel numb and scared and in about two hours I have to face my family, the family I still don't know how to forgive, and you're asking me to change my life for you.'

Alim stilled. 'Actually, it's me constantly offering to change my life for you,' he said harshly. 'You don't seem willing to give an inch. I guess that shows what I mean to you beyond desire. I guess it shows what those three words last night were worth to you.

Was it anything more than a nice goodbye to you, Hana? Is what you feel just not worth the fight?'

Shame heated her cheeks. 'We're at the airstrip,' she mumbled.

He climbed out of the car, and handed her out with grave courtesy, as if she were a dignitary instead of an aid nurse with bare feet and sand in her trousers. They walked up the red carpet and into the jet, a barefoot sheikh and his Raggedy Ann saviour, in silence.

CHAPTER ELEVEN

ALIM watched in grim empathy as Hana grew paler, her fingers twitching more with every movement of the jet towards Abbas al-Din.

He'd forced her into this, and now he was facing the consequences in her silent misery. As she'd told him, she wasn't ready to face a family pitifully eager to ask forgiveness, to make amends for the five years of unbearable loneliness and pain they'd caused her.

How could they possibly make amends? Even if Hana found forgiveness for them in her heart, how could she ever trust them again?

Then he noticed his own foot was tapping against the ground. He had to wonder if Harun could ever trust him again, either. He'd let his brother down as badly as Hana's family had done to her. He'd even, by his desertion, forced Harun to marry a woman he, Alim, hadn't been able to face as his wife. Harun had found no happiness with Amber, and that was Alim's fault, too.

God help them both, this surely had to be a worse homecoming than the fabled prodigal son ever endured.

When a servant brought their bags with changes of clothing and shoes, Hana thanked the woman gravely and then walked into the gold-fitted bathroom without a word to him. She emerged in a beautiful ankle-length skirt the shade of sunrise, and a creamy long-sleeved shirt embroidered with tiny beads that shimmered as she walked. Plain sandals adorned her feet. Her hair was braided back. She wore no jewellery or make-up. She took his breath away.

She didn't look at him as she sat, put her seat belt back on, and her hands and feet began twitching again. He came back from his change in the gold-and-scarlet attire expected—

Of what? A prodigal brother, a runaway sheikh?

She flicked a glanced at him, and her eyes slid down to her clothes, so simple and modest.

He felt the distance growing between them without a word spoken.

I'm still Alim, he wanted to shout; *look at me, touch me, I still breathe and hurt.* He'd thought her the one person who could look beyond appearances, and see him.

It seemed he'd never been more wrong.

As the jet began its descent Hana struggled not to throw up. The duality of love and betrayal, longing and anger tore her heart into shreds.

A hand touched hers, stilling the tremors. 'It'll be okay, Hana.'

Glad of an excuse to relieve hours of bottled-up anguish, she turned on him. 'Are you telling that to me, or yourself? Look to your own reunion with your brother and the wife that should have been yours, because you know nothing of how I'm feeling right now!'

He turned his face away. 'How can I know what you keep locked away from me? Your heart is like a tap that keeps switching from hot to cold, burning and freezing me.'

Her head, already buzzing, felt as if a swarm of bees inhabited it, but she sat straight and proud in her seat. She had enough to think about without letting the shame in. He'd saved her life, made this reunion possible, had erased Mukhtar from her life, and—

'I'm just trying to make the farewell easier,' she whispered so soft he wouldn't hear, wanting to lay her arms on the flight table, her forehead on her arms; but then he'd know how weak and needing she was, how she longed for his comfort.

And that would wrinkle his silken magnificence.

Too soon, the jet made its descent, landing, and then they walked along another red carpet into another limousine—Alim must have asked for no welcoming party, for which she was grateful—and the whisper-quiet saloon purred towards the palace.

As they drove through the streets Hana shrank further down into the seat. No one seemed to know Alim was back; there was no fanfare, no cheering crowds, yet still she felt like a miserable fraud.

A whisper close to her ear, 'The truck cost twice as much as this car. It was a top-of-the-line Mercedes. You didn't seem uncomfortable in that.'

She turned to him in wonder. 'It looked all beaten up.'

His brows lifted. 'Drawing attention to myself wasn't the point. Staying safe in a strong ride was the sole reason I bought it. I enjoyed taking off all the strips that showed its maker, and making it look so old. Taking a hammer to the panels and scratching the duco to—what was it? Billy-o?—was really fun.'

Her mouth twitched.

'I suppose there are hammers and chisels, and sandpaper, somewhere at home,' he mused. 'I'll have to check out the cellars, or ask the carpenter.'

She frowned, tilting her head in wordless question.

He shrugged. 'If you're only going to be comfortable with who I am if you only see me as a normal man when my ride looks broken down, and I'm covered in mud and bruises, I'll have to make the arrangements.'

The coolness in the words made her flush. 'You make me sound like a snob.'

Another half-shrug. 'It isn't me doing the judging, is it? It isn't me not giving you a chance, or saying you're not good enough.'

She gasped. 'I never said you weren't good enough!'

'No, you said *you* weren't. You judge yourself—but you *have* judged me. You tell me what I need in my life when I don't even know what my future's going to be yet.'

Hana blinked, opened her mouth and closed it. He'd dissected her again—but once more, he was right. Innate honesty demanded she stop arguing, so she turned and looked out again—and saw people pointing at the crest on the doors of the saloon, speculating…waving…

'I've got a present for you.'

Startled, she turned to him. She said, hard and flat, 'I don't want it.'

A tiny smile played around the corners of his mouth. 'Don't judge my gift before you see it.' He handed her a gorgeously wrapped box, tied with a golden ribbon. 'Just open it, Hana, before you judge me or what I've given.'

Shamed by the reminder, she kept her eyes on the box as she untied the ribbon and opened it—and burst into startled laughter. Inside the intricately crafted sandalwood box lay a card saying 'Hana's Emergency Escape Kit.' Beneath that were a few dozen energy bars, four canteens…and two little dropper bottles of lavender.

She looked up at him, still laughing. 'Um, thank you?'

He leaned forward and brushed his mouth over hers. 'I accept that some time soon you're going to want to run, my star. But as the song says, if you leave me, can I come too?'

Huskily, knowing it was a pipe dream, she murmured, 'I'd like that.'

'We're going to be okay, Sahar Thurayya.' He kissed her again. 'Souls entwined bring us greater strength than one alone.'

The shining happiness in his eyes lodged her breath in her throat. She touched his hand. 'Thank you. Thank you for accepting me as I am.'

Then she saw they'd already swept through the two sets of ornate, protective gates, and were at the private rear entrance of the palace.

Suddenly she understood what he'd done for her. He'd taken her mind from her family just when she couldn't stand *thinking* about them any more. He'd planned the gift before she'd even agreed to come, knowing she'd need her mind turned from the turmoil within.

'Thank you for distracting me,' she murmured, her stomach filled with bats without sonar, crashing around inside her; but she turned to him and, before she could chicken out, leaned into him and kissed his mouth. 'You're a truly good man, Alim El-Kanar.'

His eyes, dark with emotion as she kissed him, turned bleak. 'I wish I could believe that.' The moment the car stopped he was out, not waiting for a servant to open it and hand him out as custom demanded. He waved the servant away, and turned to help her. 'Your family's waiting inside, in an antechamber to the left.'

Her legs turned to jelly and she wanted to throw up. She clung to his hand, just trying to breathe. 'Come with me. Please,' she whispered.

He led her up the wide marble stairs and through the gold-lined oak doors. 'I can't stay beyond introductions. Unfortunately, I have my own ghosts to face.' Swiftly his mouth brushed hers. 'We'll survive this, Hana. We can meet for recon after.' He showed her to the wide double doors where her family waited, and led her inside.

Five people on luxurious woven settees jumped to their feet the moment the doors opened. Five people dressed in their best, either for her or to impress Alim, she didn't know. People who'd once meant the world to her—and her heart jerked, as if telling her what she wanted to forget: they still meant so much…too much.

'Hana,' her mother murmured, voice cracking with emotion. Her plump, comfortable frame had lessened; her face was lined, her eyes weary and filled with tears. A hand reached out to Hana, and hovered there, as if asking a question her mouth couldn't ask.

'Hello, Mum,' she greeted her mother in stilted English, bowing her head. The word fell from her lips, rusted with disuse. She kept her hands by her sides: keeping a distance for the sake of safety. The last time she'd seen her mother, she'd been wringing her hands and asking why, *why* hadn't she come to her mother and *said* she wanted Mukhtar instead of Latif…

She couldn't look at her father—then she couldn't *not* look at him. A flicked glance—enough to see the painful guilt and eagerness to make amends—and she looked away. 'Amal and Malik Al-Sud, this is…' Now her uncertain gaze swung to Alim, taking in the utter opulence of the white-and-gold room as she turned. How did she introduce him?

'Alim El-Kanar,' Alim went on so smoothly it was as if he were on the other side of a mirror from her, able to finish her sentences. He moved forward, hand extended to her father. 'I'm very pleased to meet you. You've raised a daughter of amazing strength and courage.'

After the men gripped hands to the elbow, a custom of respect here, and Alim bowed to her mother, there was an awkward moment. 'Hana,' her mother said again, taking a step forward.

Hana closed her eyes, shook her head. She didn't want contact. *Who sees how alone you are in your strength?* She'd given her time, strength and self away, but no one but Alim had held her, comforted her in years; she'd been alone.

A hand rested on her shoulder, warm and strong. Alim. 'Were you given coffee?' he asked, giving her time, space from the emotion.

She wanted to rest back against him, to lay her hand over his and thank him for again coming to her rescue. How well he knew her, even when she'd done her best to lock him out—and she knew then that his accusation in the jet had been a hollow drum, a distraction for her sake: her heart was laid bare for him to see.

'Yes, thank you, my lord.' Her father's voice, the first words of his she'd heard since that fateful night. *You will marry Mukhtar, Hana, for your sister's sake. It's not Fatima's fault you couldn't control your passions!*

'I can't do this. I—I have to—' Hana whirled for the door.

'Hana, don't go. Please. We love you. We've missed you so much.'

Fatima's voice, choked up. Hana stopped as if frozen in place. Slowly, her hands curled into fists. 'At least you all had each other.' Flat words, locking her sister out; she had no alternative unless she wanted to cry like a baby. 'I hope you had a lovely wedding, Fatima. Better than mine was...or so I hear mine was. I missed the party.' She turned, looked at her father for a moment, saw the anguish.

'Perhaps we can have a family celebration of the annulment. I'd really like to be there to celebrate one major event in my life.'

Another stretch of silence that felt like dead calm water after a long storm, and she felt their pain as clearly as her own, and she tried to strengthen herself, to harden her heart. She felt close to breaking...

'You're thinner.' Her mother's voice quivered.

Still she couldn't turn around, or look at them. 'Rather hard to get enough to eat at times,' she said, light and shadow together. 'You either toughen up or fall apart in the Sahel.'

'You served in the Sahel,' Fatima said, her voice faint. 'It's the most dangerous place on earth...'

Hana shrugged. 'As I said, you get tough when just finding enough to eat each day is the greatest challenge facing you. It makes other problems, like being forced into marriage with a drug runner, seem...insignificant.'

'Excuse me, please. I have to meet my brother,' Alim said quietly, and left the massive room, closing the doors behind him.

Hana watched him go, and hated him for leaving her here with these people...her family, half strangers now, just people she'd once known.

'You saved his life,' her brother Khalid muttered, shaking his head. 'My little sister saved our sheikh and brought him back to his people.'

She shrugged, and didn't answer. In this place, talking about Alim seemed too hard.

'You are being touted as a national heroine,' her mother said, shaky, emotional. Again her hand lifted, reached out to her.

Hana stepped back, aching, angry. 'That'll only last until the media finds out about Mukhtar. Then I'll be a national disgrace, won't I? Will you disown me then, too?'

'Hana, please.' Her father spoke, his voice pleading. 'I know what I've done to you. When Mukhtar was arrested, and we knew you spoke the truth, I looked for you—'

'Oh, only then?' she asked lightly. 'You didn't try to find me before, force me back to my lawful master to spare you all any more family embarrassment? How long did it take you to work out that I didn't lie to you, that I couldn't possibly have slept with my fiancé's brother?'

Her oldest sister Tanihah said quietly, 'Hana, it's over now, we know the woman you are. Now you're back with us, where you belong. Can't we move past this?'

'I belong nowhere.' Hana shook her head. *Just don't cry, don't cry...* 'There's nowhere to move to. You can't possibly understand what it's like to live as I have the past five years.' Always running, terrified of being forced into Mukhtar's bed— 'The damage is done, Tanihah.' Saying her sister's name—they'd once been so close—broke her. 'I have to go.'

She ran to the door, yanked it open, and fled through into the main entrance, heading with unerring instinct for the nearest escape.

A burly guard blocked the way. 'Miss al-Sud, my lord Sheikh has asked that you await him in his private chamber when your meeting was over.'

The look on the man's face—calm, implacable—told her there was no way out. Alim had anticipated her escape, and made certain she couldn't outrun her ghosts. She lifted her chin, nodded and followed the man to another room, knowing her family watched her through the open doors. She felt their hunger, their pain—the guilt eating at them.

Yet if it weren't for what had happened, she'd never have met Alim…

With all her heart she yearned to go back in that room, to tell them it was all right, she forgave them, would be part of the family circle again. But the circle had fractured five years before, and, even if she could make peace, the cracks in the join would always show.

The damage is done.

'Welcome home, Alim,' Amber said in her quiet way. Alim felt the repressed emotion beneath. 'It's good to have you back.'

Is it? He smiled and played the game with his beautiful, cold sister-in-law. Truth was vulgar.

Sweep all the dirt under the carpet and believe it never happened. 'Thank you, Amber.'

This room had been Fadi's reception room where he met foreign dignitaries. Alim had thought it would be too hard to be here, to see the reminders, but Hana's painful reunion had somehow changed things for him. He felt warm, comforted by the memories…and if he still hadn't forgiven himself for his part in Fadi's death, and maybe never would, he knew it was time to come back to stay—and Fadi wouldn't want it any other way. Fadi would always have wanted him to do his duty, and care for their people as they'd shared the care for their little brother…

He saw Harun watching his wife, cautious, reserved—his pride hiding the hunger only his big brother would know. Harun noticed Alim watching him, and said—they'd done the emotional thirty seconds when Sh'ellah released him—'I've moved out of your room. It's ready for you, as is your office, as soon as you want to resume your duties.'

Alim felt the savagery repressed inside his brother, a seething cauldron of resentment beneath. 'Let's not pretend. Don't talk as if I've been sick for a few weeks. I was gone for years, and left all the grief and duty to you. Harun…'

His brother shrugged with eloquent understatement. 'It wasn't so bad.'

Wasn't it? He saw the distance between husband and wife, lying there like all the arid wasteland of the

Sahel. 'I wanted to say, the choice is yours now. You've done a magnificent job of running the country, of picking up the pieces after Fadi's death and my disappearance. If you want to remain the sheikh—'

'No.'

The snarl took him by surprise—because it came from both Harun and Amber. He took the easier option, looking at Amber. Sure that her reasons would be easier to hear than Harun's.

She flushed, and glanced at Harun; fiddled with her hands, shuffled a foot, and burst out, 'I won't play sheikh's happy wife for anyone's sake. I'm tired of the pretence that everything's all right. I don't care what my father wants any more. I want a divorce.'

She turned and walked out of the room with regal grace, as if she hadn't just thrown a live bomb between the brothers.

Stunned, Alim could hardly bear to look at Harun, but when he did he saw Harun had been waiting for him to turn; his brother didn't even look surprised. 'And that's why I said no,' he said quietly. 'I'm also tired of pretending everything's all right. I've been standing in your place since long before Fadi died, helping him run the country while you were off playing the glamorous racing star, and again when you took off to play the hero. I've had ten years of living your life for you, Alim, including the wife who wanted you, not me. I've left ev-

erything you need to know in your office. I want my
own life. The country's yours, brother.'

Harun followed in his wife's wake, leaving Alim
to face the consequences of ten years of loving and
respecting his brother without truly seeing him.
'Fadi, where are you?' he muttered, and rubbed his
temples. The welcome home for the prodigal
brother was far from what he'd hoped.

As he entered his office where she waited for him,
one look at Alim's face told Hana his meeting had
been as devastating for him as hers had been for her.
The blank, dark eyes, the lost misery melted her
heart; his need was hers.

She walked into his arms, holding him close.
'That bad?'

He nuzzled her hair with his lips. 'Probably
worse. You?'

'Horrible,' she whispered, and shuddered.

'Harun and Amber are separating. Harun expects
me to begin my duties immediately.'

She hugged him, wordless comfort—what could
she say? 'My family wants me to move past it and
forgive them, and be a family again.'

'They expect us to behave as if all these years
never happened.' There was a curious note in his
voice. 'For me, that's only what I deserve. But you…'

She held him closer. 'I want to forgive them,
Alim. I just can't look at them…'

Softly, he said, 'Then maybe you should close your eyes and say it, really fast—and see how you feel when it's out.'

'I—' Hana blinked and stared up at him, awed. 'That just might work.' She grabbed him by the hand and strode into the room where her family still waited; they knew her, knew she couldn't hold out against them for long, no matter what they'd done.

'Hana, my darling, if you'll just listen—'

She lifted a shaking hand to stop her mother's rush of words, trying to make better what would never be truly mended. She closed her eyes and said, hard and fast while clinging to Alim's hand, 'I forgive you. I want to be part of the family again, but I don't want to be rushed. Don't crowd me and don't expect me to hug you and act like everything's fine.'

A stifled sound from her mother was drowned out by her father's voice. 'We understand, *nuur il-'en*. If you will try to find true forgiveness in your heart one day, we can wait.'

Nuur il-'en: light of my eyes. Her father hadn't called her that since the day Mukhtar—

Suddenly her breaths caught over and over until she was wheezing and hiccupping at once, and she couldn't do anything but gulp while tears flowed unchecked, and broken words poured from her. 'You thought I could cheat on Latif within weeks of the engagement, hurt you all, and risk my little sister's future. You believed a stranger over your own daughter. You sacrificed me for Fatima's sake, when I'd done nothing wrong. Why, *why* did you believe him, *why*?'

After a moment, her father said, simple and sad, 'You have so much inside your heart to give, *nuur il-'en*. We always knew that when you gave your heart, it would be for life—but you didn't give your heart to Latif. You merely liked him. You only agreed to marry him to please everyone. Then Mukhtar came along, and he was ten years younger, handsome and charming. We didn't believe it at first—not until Latif said he'd always known you didn't love him, and you and Mukhtar seemed to get on so well, always laughing and joking.'

Hana stilled at the innate truth she hadn't wanted to hear. *She hadn't loved Latif.* She'd been willing to cheat him of a real, loving wife because she'd wanted to make everyone happy. And, yes, she had found Mukhtar a fun companion at first, until she saw the real person beneath the surface charm. That was why Mukhtar had been so convincing.

Then her father's words slammed inside her soul like iron doors clanging. *When you gave your heart, it would be for life.*

Strong arms around her waist held her up when her knees shook. She turned into Alim's warm, strong body, trying to gain composure, but she couldn't stop crying. Since she'd met him all the emotion she'd stored deep inside her heart had begun flowing, and something deep inside told her she couldn't find that safe place of distance ever again. She'd given her heart to Alim and would never have it back. She'd spend her life yearning for a man she couldn't have…

'My lord, you and our daughter seem very close,' Hana's mother said quietly.

Alim felt Amal al-Sud's gaze on him, searching. In fact all five members of Hana's family were staring at him. Hana moved as if to leave his arms, but he held her there. 'Yes, we are.' He made no apology for it.

'You both must have gone through a life-changing experience,' Hana's brother Khalid said in a thoughtful tone, 'but, my lord, you know…'

'You're aware we're ordinary people,' her father finished the sentence for his son, 'and our daughter's happiness is more precious to us now than ever.'

'I want her happiness, too, because that's what she's brought to me.' He thought of the meaning of her name, and smiled at Malik al-Sud. 'I've already asked her to marry me, sir.'

'Ordered me, you mean,' the cheeky mumble came from the depths of his chest, but loud enough to make the entire family gasp.

He chuckled, and caressed her hair. 'She's right,

I did—and I will marry her.' He smiled down at Hana, knowing the effect it had on her. 'Just as soon as she says yes.'

CHAPTER TWELVE

'You can't marry her,' Malik al-Sud said, his tone deferential yet firm. It reminded Alim of Hana. 'This is impossible—it's a fantasy based on her saving your life, my lord. The country won't accept her as your wife.'

'That's what I've been telling him,' Hana said, for once in sync with her father.

'It's only been a few weeks. You can't know if it's real, what you want, what you're feeling,' her mother added.

Her brother and sisters nodded in agreement. Alim saw the same disbelief in six pairs of eyes…especially in Hana's. Fury filled him at her lack of faith in him, but he controlled it. 'If you won't believe in us, Sahar Thurayya, then I'll have to believe for both of us—because I am going to marry you.' He bent and kissed her, feeling the little catch of breath in reaction, the tiny purr in her throat.

He lifted his head and smiled at Malik al-Sud, seeing the fire in the older man's eyes.

He frowned and shook his head, an infinitesimal movement Hana wouldn't feel. He wasn't going to answer the unasked suspicion, and hurt Hana over again. Even now, her family should know her better.

'You've raised a fine, principled woman, sir,' he said quietly, 'a woman who's a queen in every way but birth…and if she doesn't marry me, the people will have to be content with my brother as my heir, because I won't marry.'

Dead silence met his pronouncement—then Hana moved out of his arms. 'I told you, Alim, this is ridiculous. You think you love me, but you haven't been home a day. And I—I told you what kind of man I wanted…' But the telltale hiccup gave her away.

He shook his head. 'When you gave your heart, it would be for life,' he repeated her father's words in strong deliberation. 'You gave it to me, Hana. You said the words.'

Her eyes were cold, bleak. 'That was before we arrived here.' She waved at all the opulence he took for granted after all these years, because this was home. 'I grew up in a house the size of this room. I caught buses and trains when I wanted to go somewhere. I'm more Australian than Arabic in many ways. It isn't just about the people's reaction, Alim, or the press. I—I do care for you, but this life isn't what I want!'

Looking in her eyes, he saw the absolute sincerity—and something died inside him. 'You mean that.'

He heard the doors closing behind her family.

Hana's eyes were drenched in tears, lovely pools of green-brown finality. 'I've spent five years in huts and camps, working with people who have nothing. This—' She shook her head. 'I can't be what I'm not, Alim. I couldn't live this way, not when friends, people I love…'

Strange, but coming here today, he hadn't thought about how his childhood home would affect a woman who'd lived with death by starvation every day of the past five years. He'd been too busy thinking of their families, of making her see they were meant to be together. Coming here, he'd finally made peace with Fadi's death, come to terms with his future, and the only question that remained in his mind had been when Hana would marry him.

Now, without even looking around, he saw the palace through Hana's eyes—the gold lining the walls, the knick-knacks worth thousands and millions, meant to impress dignitaries who'd been there, done that a hundred times, in every other nation—

He saw in his mind's eye the multimillion-dollar cheques for racing a million-dollar car around a circuit…the oil that had turned his country from a rural backwater barely known outside the emirates to a world player. Riches, power, and the trappings of wealth everywhere…he saw all his life's achievements through her eyes.

Then he saw the people of Shellah-Akbar risking their lives to save him, people lean with hunger and bent with long hours of hard physical labour every day. He saw Hana in her burq'a, her capable hands saving his life, her sacrifices for his sake.

He was trapped here, unless he lumbered everything back on Harun's shoulders—and as Hana had said, he'd had one shot at disappearing. He couldn't do it again. He could offer to give it all away to please her, to save others, and still it wouldn't be enough.

For the first time in his life, Alim was speechless.

'I think it's best if I go to my sister's house,' she said quietly, breaking into his inner darkness, but not lightening it as she'd always done before. She knew.

'You're running again.' He felt his jaw tightening. 'You can go anywhere in the world, you can escape again, do the noble thing and return to the life we lived before. But it will always be running away from the hard option.'

Her gaze turned from him. 'I know,' she mumbled.

He brought her back to face him. 'I might not have a choice any more, but inside I'm still the guy in the truck. This isn't the life you think it is. Yes, I live in luxury, but being the leader of any country is as hard as anything you've done in the Sahel in many ways—and from now on, it'll be harder, Hana. I'll be working for those I now know.'

Her eyes glimmered softly, tears and pride combined. 'I know that, Alim. You're a truly good man.'

It was a farewell he refused to believe. 'My job would be easier if I had someone beside me. A woman who knows and understands the common people—who's lived the life of those who suffer the most. A permanent reminder for me never to forget, or to become arrogant.' He kissed her again. 'You can take the hard option or the easy one, Hana. Save a few with your hands, or save hundreds of thousands with your courage and great heart. You can take on a new job with a real challenge, working night and day for the good of so many more at a time than one village alone.'

He saw the doubt in her heart, the uncertainty in her eyes, and had to be satisfied with that. 'I'll be here, waiting,' he said, a soft growl.

'Don't. Don't wait for me, Alim.' Her voice cracked. 'Thanks for the escape kit. Thank you—for everything.'

And she was gone.

'Thank you,' he said softly to the air she'd left behind. He breathed in lavender—she must have put on some from the bottle he'd given her—and felt aching loss.

* * *

As she'd predicted, the world media didn't take long to dig up her story—and Hana became a celebrity and disgrace at once.

Sheikh's Saviour is a Drug Runner's Ex-wife!

She didn't have to read the papers to know that all she'd done through the years counted for nothing. Even saving Alim's life meant less than the scandal they could create to sell papers. They found Mukhtar and called the prison for his point of view. They found out about Latif, and, though Latif refused to comment, they ran the whole sordid story as they saw it, and speculated on her relationship with Alim.

Sex sells.

She wanted to laugh and cry at once. Such exquisite irony: the virgin who'd slept with two brothers at once, and seduced a sheikh. What would she do next?

Alim had taken up his duties with a vengeance. According to the papers, he'd had the villagers resettled in the countryside west of Sar Abbas, the capital, and gave them land with water and all they needed to restart their lives. He'd given a speech on his life the past three years. The passion in his words as he spoke of life in the Sahel, as relayed on TV, brought such longing to her heart she couldn't speak, couldn't move. Oh, how she loved him…

He was creating a foundation for the forgotten

people, calling for funds to send engineers and geologists to find water, to buy generators and pumps so every village could have a water source. He talked about his time in captivity, and how he hated that his ransom would create a further cycle of misery for the innocent.

Alim was as good as his word. He was using his position to help others. Taking the hard road and making something of it in a way one single nurse in a village never could.

For the first time in years Hana knew how it felt to be trapped physically. She was holed up in her sister's house with hundreds of people outside, and she couldn't hide. She couldn't run to the next place, and put her fears and her misery behind her. She couldn't run from her family when they wanted to talk, to get close, to ask her about Alim.

For the first time in years, she had to deal with her feelings instead of hiding behind others' problems, using them to ignore her own, or to feel good about herself and her sacrifices. *My Hana, always needing to be the strong one, the clever one, the fastest and the best. When will you learn to love yourself, and know that all you need to be loved is just to be yourself?*

Fourteen-year-old words of wisdom had finally caught up with her. Stuck in Tanihah's house there were no excuses any more. She couldn't hide behind her grades or her job or her burq'a, her family's betrayal or her lower position in life. The mirror she'd outrun for so many years was being held right up to her face, and she was the one holding it.

Alim was right: she was a coward, and no matter how dangerous a place she went to next or how many lives she saved, she was still a frightened child trying to prove she was strong. She'd chosen Latif for safety; she'd run from Mukhtar—and she was running from Alim, using birth and a lie to keep herself at a safe distance from him. But this time it hadn't helped; she loved him more every day, ached for him, and struggled against the knowledge that the only thing keeping them apart was her fear.

When you give your heart, it will be for life...

Almost two weeks after the story hit the news she sat in her niece's room, on the bed she shared with Atiya, needing space and quiet. When night fell, and they'd finished prayer—Ramadan had begun, and eating in the hours of sunlight was forbidden unless you were a child—she came to eat with the family, and answered their questions at random, giving them stark honesty but not even knowing she did. The doorbell had stopped ringing at last, but the sharks were surrounding the house still, hoping for some juicy gossip. Hana barely noticed that either. Totally lost in the self-knowledge she'd avoided all her life. Thin delusions, as she'd said to Alim, were stripped away and she saw the person she was.

To her shock, she didn't hate herself as much as she'd feared. She was a coward, but one who'd saved lives. Yes, she ran from emotion when it became too hard, but now she was facing the hardest emotions of her life, she was okay. She hid behind her position, behind Alim's position so she didn't have to say, *Yes, I'll stop running and I'll marry you*—

And to change that one, she'd have to face Alim again.

And do what? she asked herself wearily. There was no getting around the facts as presented by the media—her birth wasn't and never would be good enough, her fake marriage put Alim way out of her reach—unless she could make the changes herself.

If you won't marry me, I'll live alone.

I'm thirty-seven, not a boy. I know what I want. I want you.

I'll be here waiting.

It came to this: she could be a safe, lonely coward for the rest of her life, or she could finally *live*. Live with the man she loved, and make a difference to the world.

She waited for a lull in the family dinner conversation, and threw her bomb. 'I want to tell the media the truth. All of it, about Mukhtar and why I was in the Sahel.'

They all turned to stare at her, even the children at the small table.

She held her father's unfathomable gaze with one of her own. 'I love Alim,' she said, and it felt amazingly good to have it out there. 'I want a future with him.'

'It won't happen while the people believe the worst,' her father agreed, still with that Sphinx-like face.

Her mother said in a muffled voice, 'Many don't believe the worst, Hana. The letters to the editor are overwhelmingly in your favour.'

She hesitated, but decided to say it. 'It will embarrass the family, make you look bad.'

Her dad's eyes swept the table and everyone on it. 'I made choices I believe others will understand—and if they don't, then it's a judgement I deserve.' He pushed back his chair. 'This is my responsibility.'

'Dad…' she mumbled, using the loving title for the first time since returning.

He smiled at her. 'You need to find that man of yours and tell him how you feel. Leave the story to me. Trust me, *nuur il-'en*. I won't let you down this time.'

With tears in her eyes, she too stood, walked around to her father and touched his arm: the closest she'd voluntarily come to him in five years. 'Thank you, Dad.'

There was only one way. She called the number on the card Alim's driver had given her—Alim's private number. 'Hi. It's me. I'm stuck in my sister's house, surrounded by the media. Can you send a car for me, with some men to help me through the crowd?'

'Of course.' Alim's voice was reserved, so tired. 'Do you need anything more?'

'I need to see you. We need to talk.' She gulped and coughed to clear the thickness in her throat. 'Can I come to you?'

'I'll come to you.'

'The house is surrounded, Alim. In the palace they can't get to us, or put cameras through the windows. Tell the guards to come to the back door and knock four times.'

'All right, then. I'll be waiting for you in my private study.' He sounded so neutral…

What more did she deserve? But now, this night, she wasn't giving in to fear again. This wasn't about protecting herself from pain. She'd done that for too many years, and had only emptiness as her reward. She hung up and raced for the shower…

Fifteen minutes later, she was ready when a knock came at the back door. She opened it, and two burly, exquisitely dressed guards ushered her down the stairs and around the front. The press, all avidly listening to her father, made a dash for her as she ran to the saloon car, but the guards yelled,

'Miss al-Sud has no comment,' and elbowed any intrepid reporter out of the way.

The trip to the palace was followed by a dozen cars, and a few racing motorbikes with photographers snapping pictures of her.

The gates opened. The car drove around the back. The guards handed her out and raced her up the stairs, inside and to the left.

They opened the doors for her, and in another exquisite room, quietly appointed in cherrywood and strong masculine pieces, Alim stood by the empty fireplace, his forehead resting on his hand. 'Hi,' she said when the guards closed the door behind her.

He didn't look up, didn't turn to her. 'Hi.'

He sounded so unutterably weary, her heart jerked. 'A rough few days?'

'A rough few weeks,' he agreed. 'I'm exhausted, Hana, so let's get this over with.'

For the first time since their rescue, he wasn't opening his heart to her. He was expecting a kiss-off…or maybe he wanted one.

I will not run. I won't be a coward again! Alim deserved to know how she felt.

But as she drew close to him she chickened out. 'I thought you should know Dad's with the press now, telling the true story, about Mukhtar, Latif and me…and you.' She took a step to him, and another, her heart aching.

'My press secretary told me. It's already on the TV,' Alim said on a sigh. 'That's good of your father. Your name's being cleared. They'll all love you again.'

'But that wasn't why I came,' she blurted out, angry with herself for being so weak. 'I came to say…to say…' She sighed in self-fury, and closed her eyes and said whatever came to her head. 'I can't do this any more, Alim. I can't lie to myself and pretend—'

'Pretend what, Hana?' he asked, his voice hard and ragged at once. 'While you've been hiding out with your family to support you, I've been facing the press, the people, learning the job over again. Harun and Amber left the same day you did. He's gone incommunicado and left me with everything. I'm doing it alone, barely getting three hours' sleep a night, so can we get this over with?'

She blinked at him…but saw in his words the blunt honesty of a man on the edge of falling down. A man who desperately needed her but wouldn't say it. Expecting her to run again and refusing to fight any longer. He accepted her as she was, even now…

At that, Hana forgot her needs and fears, and ran to him. She put down the box she'd brought on the desk beside them, and took him into her arms. 'You're not alone. I'm here,' she whispered, kissing his cheek, holding him—and it felt so good to be giving, this time in honesty. 'I came to give you something.'

'Do I want it?' he muttered into her hair, holding onto her as if she were a lifeline, breathing in deeply, and she was glad she'd put on the lavender again.

She smiled. 'I hope so.' Reaching behind her, she brought the box to him. 'Open it.'

He looked down at the sandalwood box he'd given her in the car weeks before. 'Why…?'

'Just open it,' she insisted softly. She couldn't wait much longer.

He opened the box. On top of the emergency escape kit he'd given her was her burq'a. He stared at the contents, then looked up at her, his eyes hollow with exhaustion. There was a question there.

'Read the note,' she said quietly.

He found it beneath the burq'a. *Hana cannot run without these.* And he looked at her again. Either he wasn't getting it, or he wanted her to say it.

She reached up and kissed those poor, tired eyes, one by one. 'I'm giving them to you. I'm entrusting you with my treasures, Alim. I won't run without them, and I don't want to run without you. You're my peace, my best friend, my love. If you can't disappear when the going gets tough, neither will I.' She held his face in her hands and said, 'I won't be a coward any more. I love you, Alim, and whatever you need me to be—whatever the country will allow me to be for you—I'll be it.'

With a swift movement, he tossed the box in a far corner. 'Hana,' he said hoarsely, turning her face and kissing her mouth like a man parched. 'My star, you'd better mean this, because I'll never give you this box back. I'll never let you go again.'

'Good,' she said, intense with all the emotion she'd kept from him all this time, giving him every-thing but the one thing he'd needed: *herself*. Now she was open to him at last, and she'd never hide from him again. 'I need you so much, Alim. I need to be beside you every day of my life. If the people won't let us marry—'

He pulled back to grin at her. He looked haggard, hollow-eyed, and so happy she knew she'd never be a coward again. The rewards for true courage were perfect and life-changing. 'You haven't been reading the papers, have you? There's been a huge backlash against the stories about you. The people know I'd never have come back but for you. You saved my life and gave me back to them. That's far more important to them than any bloodline.' His eyes darkened. 'But if the whole country was against us I'd still marry you, Sahar Thurayya. They might need me, but I need you.'

'And I need you. I love you so much.' She melted against him. 'I really need you to kiss me,' she murmured, reaching up to bring him down to her.

The long, frantic kiss was everything she'd dreamed of in the longest two weeks of her life without him; being close to him, feeling his love for her—

'I've been going insane without you,' he whispered between kisses. 'I thought you'd never come back, that I had nothing to offer you that would make you stay.'

She kissed him again and again. 'You,' she mumbled back. 'You're all I need—and to be needed, Alim. Seeing you on TV, how strong and brave you are but so alone…'

'You'll take the job?' he asked, moulding her body along his, as if making an imprint of her on him. 'It's not an easy place to be, Sahar Thurayya. But we can change the world from here. We can help make things better.'

'An irresistible offer to a control freak like me,' she laughed, and kissed him again. 'But I warn you, my love, I won't be your common, garden variety queen.' *Me, a queen,* she thought in wonder. Was she in a fairy tale, or dreaming? But Alim felt so wonderfully real against her, the desire filling her so perfect… 'You know I won't bend to the rules all the time, and will break them half the time.'

He chuckled, and another long kiss followed. 'Think I don't know that? I know you, my star— and I happen to think rattling some cages will be good for the stick-in-the-muds. I intend rattling more than a few cages myself.'

The doors burst open after a quick knock. 'My

lord, there's something you need to see—' The man goggled at the sight of his ruler locked in an embrace with the woman who'd saved his life, and began backing out of the room with profuse, mumbled apologies.

Alim said coolly, 'Put everything on hold unless it's national emergency, Ratib. I'm spending quality time with my wife-to-be.'

'Yes, of course, my lord…' The doors closed.

He winked at her. 'Ten, nine, eight…and the whole palace knows.' And from behind him, in a drawer in the desk, he brought out a long, wide, dark-red velvet box and opened it. 'Your engagement present,' he said gently. 'When my mother knew she was dying, she chose these for my future bride, hoping she'd like diamonds. I've kept it with me like a talisman the past few weeks, trying to believe you'd come back to me.'

Hana gasped, staring down at the rose-gold ring with a dazzling diamond solitaire, with bracelets, earrings and a necklace to match. 'Oh…oh, Alim…'

Alim took her left hand from his shoulder, and, with a smile, slid the ring onto her finger—he'd had it resized with the help of Hana's parents, with whom he'd been in daily contact. 'At last,' he growled softly, and leaned to do something he'd fantasised about through the long, lonely weeks without her: nibble on her ear. 'No more doubts. No running away.'

'Never,' she breathed, her face alight and shining with desire and love. He kissed the pulse-point behind her jaw and her head fell back, her face flushed and her chest rose and fell with breaths of growing passion. 'Alim, I love you, I want you so much. Don't make me wait for a massive wedding,' she cried, her voice throbbing with desire.

He'd come a long way from the man who believed no woman could want him—but when he nuzzled her neck, he revelled in the way her body quivered against him. Then he drew back, his face holding the rueful acceptance in his heart. 'We have little choice in the waiting, my star. You're going to be a ruler's wife, the equivalent of a queen. The people will expect to share in the full, traditional courtship. We also have to coordinate a time that the Heads of State who wish to come will be able to attend. We can't offend anyone. It'll take at least four to six months.'

Her eyes closed hard; her lips pressed together. 'I thought you'd say that,' she whispered glumly, 'but, oh, it's going to be so hard, waiting months for you. I want you *now*.' She buried her blushing face in his chest. 'I'm sorry, I know I'm not the traditional view of what I should be, but I can't help it. I love you, I want you so much.'

She spoke of the ancient tradition where a woman must fight her man against his taking her to prove her innocence and chastity, a woman worth keeping…but Alim already knew that and more about his brave, lovely dawn star. She'd healed him heart and soul, made him a man and a ruler again…for the first time in his life, he truly felt whole. He smiled, moved by the depth of her love for him. 'And never was a tradition broken that means more to me,' he replied, kissing her nose, her mouth. 'Nothing about us has followed tradition, my star, but for a little while, now, we have to. It's important that the people see our courtship as pure and honourable.'

He heard her gulp. 'All right…then we shouldn't be alone at any time until we're married, because all you have to do is touch me, and I quiver and ache with need for you.' She held him hard as his mind blanked out with the intensity of his happiness. 'I didn't mean that I don't want to see you. I want to be with you all the time, but when I am, all I want is to touch you. And when I touch you, all I want is to make love with you.'

How could he not love, adore this woman? He lifted her face to his. 'Hana, your parents named you perfectly, because you are my happiness.'

She smiled up at him. 'And your parents were right, too, because you've been so wise in every-thing you've done for me, and in waiting for me.' She went up on her toes to kiss him again and again. 'I want to be by your side every day, every night for the rest of my life.'

'You will be,' he murmured as he turned her around to clasp the diamond necklace around her throat, the bracelet around her wrist: the traditional signs of a bridegroom who cherished his wife-to-be. As he placed the gold and amber veil of the engaged woman on her head, the final part of his first engagement gift to her, he murmured again, 'You will be.'

EPILOGUE

Eight years later

'SHE'S all scrunched and wrinkly,' four-year-old Tariq pronounced. He was looking down at his only sister, born the night before, with a touch of distaste.

'She's supposed to be, silly. Babies are all ugly—but she'll get prettier, and you're still ugly,' their oldest, six-and-a-half-year-old Fadi, said, shoving at his little brother with an open palm. Tariq responded with a shove back, setting off their youngest son Sami, making the two-year-old wail in indignation.

'Boys, boys, Mama's too tired for this—and you'll wake Johara,' Alim reproved his sons, but with an indulgent air as he gathered their youngest son in his arms to comfort him.

Having their children with them every single day, all the time when they weren't immersed in affairs of state, was a tradition Hana had begun with Fadi's birth. She'd refused every argument against breast-feeding her children, and insisted on both parents seeing their children for at least a few hours every day—she called it playtime. The family also ate together on every night there were no visitors of state.

With the boys being natural children who knew how to behave—well, mostly, but their occasional childish outbursts made people laugh more than they censured—almost everyone in the nation was convinced of his wife's wisdom. The initial resistance to their marriage, in the more traditional, old-fashioned sector of the nation, soon faded when they saw how much Hana loved him. The people loved Hana for being one of them, remembering her roots and being proud of them. Alim loved that his children felt free to climb on his lap or come to him for a cuddle instead of their nanny or tutor when they were tired or had hurt themselves. His children were completely themselves, felt free to laugh or play or yell when the family were alone…and they knew they were loved by their parents.

And Alim knew his wife utterly adored him.

Hana had taken months of lessons in royal deportment, but they hadn't lasted long. She'd completely failed at royal reserve in public; she spoke her mind, and the people loved her for being their advocate against highborn self-interest.

They also loved her for not being able to hide that she loved her husband to distraction.

His two oldest sons kept fighting until Alim put up his hand. 'I said Mama's tired. Fadi, you're old enough to control yourself for your mother's sake. She's in pain.'

Fadi sobered, looking anxiously at Hana. 'Did you hurt yourself, Mama?'

Hana gave her boys a tired, loving smile. It had been a quick but painful birth for her, and as usual, she'd refused pain relief. 'It always hurts having a baby, my angel—but Johara's worth the pain. You were all worth the pain.'

Alim quickly took a sleeping Johara from his wife's arms as the boys, hearing the 'Mama needs a cuddle' note in her voice, scrambled over the bed to reach her first. Sami wailed again when he didn't win, and his older brothers staked their claim all over her; but Hana made a place for him at her breast, and he snuggled in with a happy sigh.

An hour later, when he could see Hana was struggling to keep her eyes open, Alim called for Raina, the nanny, who ushered the children out after many lingering hugs and kisses. The boys would be spending the night with Hana's parents, in the magnificent house near the palace Alim had given them as a bride gift. Hana's brother and sisters and their families were joining Malik and Amal, to celebrate Johara's birth. Harun and Amber were coming also, from wherever in the world they were now. Harun, finally free to do as he wished, had first fought for

his marriage, and won Amber back. To his surprise,
he'd discovered the wife he'd barely known shared
his passion for ancient history—so when he'd gone
back to his archaeology studies, she'd studied right
alongside him. Now his little family—they were
due to have their third child in about twelve
weeks—roamed the world as they discovered the
past together.

And Alim couldn't be happier for him.

He put his sleeping daughter in her cradle by the
bed and covered her tenderly. About to leave the
room—there was a mountain of work waiting in his
office—he saw his wife watching him, saw the
'Hana needs a cuddle' look on her face, mentally
tossed the work out the window and lay beside her
on the bed, taking her into his arms. 'You okay?'

She made a small sound of contentment as she
snuggled close, her head in the hollow of his
shoulder. 'I am now.'

The sleepy note in her voice was infectious, and
he found himself yawning too. 'Hmm, maybe I can
grab a quick nap.' Though Hana had cared for the
baby last night, he'd woken most times with her,
changed the nappies, and could never resist holding
his tiny daughter in his arms for a few minutes, just
looking at her, loving her. Much as they loved their
boys and wouldn't change them, they'd wanted a
daughter for so long.

At his words, Hana rolled carefully over to the

phone, and dialled four, to her personal assistant. 'Roula, I want no disturbances for either of us for an hour, please. My husband and I are tired. Yes, thank you.' She moved back into his arms, smiling up at him, her eyes heavy with exhausted love. 'No talking now. Johara will wake up soon enough for a feed.' She snuggled down, rolling over so he held her close.

They both loved to sleep that way. Hana said they were like koalas—they slept spoon-shaped, one holding the other like a koala baby on its mother's back, and when one rolled over, so did the other, and they cuddled that way.

Waking or sleeping, if they were alone, if he wasn't touching her, she was touching him. They loved being together as much now as when they were newlyweds…and he knew that, even in pain now from childbirth, Hana would soon be counting the days until they could make love.

I don't want separate royal bedrooms. When we're married, I'll sleep where my husband sleeps, she'd said firmly within a week of their engagement, creating her first scandal with the unexpected pronouncement. She'd caused her second scandal soon after, when she'd constantly dragged him into cupboards and private antechambers to kiss him during the long months waiting for the wedding, causing staffers no end of headaches as they tried to find him. But they'd shared a room continuously since their wedding night, and she loved and cared for her family in a way few ruling wives had ever done. The children loved that she got down on the floor with them to play, to invent things, even to show them how to behave in political and social situations by using their toys and stuffed animals as heads of state.

As for Alim, he was the happiest man in the nation. His loving, unconventional wife was everything he'd always dreamed of but never thought he'd be blessed enough to find.

He'd finally found a measure of peace for his part in Fadi's death, thanks to Hana. He'd accepted the joy as well as the responsibility in his position, and found a deep, abiding happiness he'd never imagined with his family life. In return, he'd helped her grow closer to her family, to let forgiveness come from the heart. As for Alim, he loved Hana's family, and had long been grateful to them. He was even grateful to Mukhtar. If not for that episode in Hana's life, she'd be Latif's wife, and he would never have met her.

'Alim,' she murmured moments later, obviously half asleep.

Clouded in a tired haze himself, Alim stirred. 'Hmm?'

She made that happy little sound he loved. 'Nothing,' she mumbled, her arm over his, her hand holding him there. 'Just—my Alim. Mine.'

He was sliding towards sleep, a smile curving his

lips. 'Mmm-hmm. Always.' He pulled her even closer, and drifted into dreams.

They were still in the same position when their daughter woke them nearly two hours later.

0710/02

ROMANCE 2-in-1

Coming next month

DOORSTEP TWINS
by Rebecca Winters

Strangers Gabi Turner and powerful Greek Andreas Simonides
are thrown together to care for their baby twin nephews.
Just as they start to feel like a family – the twins'
real father arrives!

THE COWBOY'S ADOPTED DAUGHTER
by Patricia Thayer

Hired to run a quilting course at the A Bar A ranch, Allie is
appalled when brooding cowboy Alex Casali accuses her
of trespassing. Then her little daughter utters her
first words in months – to him...

SOS: CONVENIENT HUSBAND REQUIRED
by Liz Fielding

May Coleridge has one month to find a husband and save her
home. Adam fits the bill, but he's been left holding his sister's
baby! May loves babies...can they make a deal?

WINNING A GROOM IN 10 DATES
by Cara Colter

Geeky Sophie is all grown up when her childhood crush
returns from the army. She still dreams of winning Brandon as
her groom but she's only got ten dates to do it!

On sale 6th August 2010

Available at WHSmith, Tesco, ASDA, Eason and all good bookshops.
For full Mills & Boon range including eBooks visit
www.millsandboon.co.uk

2 FREE BOOKS
AND A SURPRISE GIFT

We would like to take this opportunity to thank you for reading this Mills & Boon® book by offering you the chance to take TWO more specially selected books from the Romance series absolutely FREE! We're also making this offer to introduce you to the benefits of the Mills & Boon® Book Club™—

- **FREE home delivery**
- **FREE gifts and competitions**
- **FREE monthly Newsletter**
- **Exclusive Mills & Boon Book Club offers**
- **Books available before they're in the shops**

Accepting these FREE books and gift places you under no obligation to buy, you may cancel at any time, even after receiving your free shipment. Simply complete your details below and return the entire page to the address below. You don't even need a stamp!

YES Please send me 2 free Romance books and a surprise gift. I understand that unless you hear from me, I will receive 5 superb new stories every month including two 2-in-1 books priced at £4.99 each and a single book priced at £3.19, postage and packing free. I am under no obligation to purchase any books and may cancel my subscription at any time. The free books and gift will be mine to keep in any case.

Ms/Mrs/Miss/Mr _____ Initials _____

Surname _____

Address _____

_____

_____ Postcode _____

E-mail _____

Send this whole page to: Mills & Boon Book Club, Free Book Offer, FREEPOST NAT 10298, Richmond, TW9 1BR